# AT THE HOUR BETWEEN DOG AND WOLF

# *At the Hour Between Dog and Wolf*

*A NOVEL*

Tara Ison

NEW YORK, NY

Ig Publishing
Box 2547
New York, NY 10163
www.igpub.com

ISBN: 978-1632461-45-2

PRINTED IN THE UNITED STATES OF AMERICA

FIRST EDITION | FIRST PRINTING

"*entre chien et loup*"
—French expression: "*between dog and wolf,*"
i.e, twilight or dusk

"To do evil, a human being must first of all believe that what he's doing is good."
—Aleksandr Solzhenitsyn

## *MY LIFE*

*by Marie-Jeanne Chantier*

*10 March, 1941*
*La Perrine, France*

*My name is Marie-Jeanne Chantier, and I am twelve years old. My parents named me for the Blessed Virgin, and also for Saint Jeanne d'Arc, the young girl who had short hair and saved France from hostile foreign invaders a long time ago. I pray one day I will be that heroic and brave. Maman and Papa died last year in a tragic car accident outside Paris, bringing toys to poor orphans at the convent. Now I live here in the country in La Perrine, with tante Berthe, tonton Claude, and cousin Luc, who were very kind to take me in with good Christian charity and give me such a wonderful home.*

*Every morning I love to milk the pretty red cow. I like the warm hay smell of the barn and the cool clay of the root cellar when I help tante Berthe sort potatoes and carrots. We send most of what we grow to the brave German soldiers, of course, who are fighting to save us from the godless Communists.*

*But the happiest part of the week is Sundays when it's holy and I go to church. I always pray first for our dear leader, Marshal Petain, who is saving France for us, and helping us return to honor and good moral order. Then I pray for my dear Maman and Papa, then for the poor children everywhere who aren't so fortunate as me to have warm clothes or enough to eat.*

*I miss my parents, but I'm grateful to our Heavenly Father for all the blessings in my new life. I know Maman and Papa are watching over me with Jesus, the Blessed Virgin, and Saint Jeanne. And one day we will all be together again, in Heaven.*

What a joke.

It's all lies, every word of it. That made-up girl. A stupid assignment I had to write for school here. I added the "poor orphans" part at the last moment, and my teacher just loved that, he doesn't see it's all a made-up story. But that's good, it means I'm doing everything right. Keeping everyone safe. And he's so easy to lie to. Everyone in this place is. It's funny, really. Claire would think it's funny.

Claire? Are you asleep? Are you brushing your hair so it crackles? Laying out your pink skirt for school tomorrow? Maybe you're sitting on the red velvet sofa with your maman and papa, all of you together, listening to music on the radio? I hope so.

Are you worrying where I am? How I am?

Maybe if I think to you hard enough, you'll hear me. Or maybe you'll feel it, inside, and think back about me, I'll feel that, too, and it won't be so empty cold dark all the time.

I miss you so much, Claire. I have no one to talk to, only people I can lie to, and that's not the same. I wish I could write you a real letter, not just think the true things to you, but that man Claude says it's too dangerous, the government opens and reads everyone's letters now, but that's good, it's for our own protection.

I'm sorry I couldn't say goodbye, or write you a note, but my mother made us leave so quickly. I try not to think about her, though, or my father, when I do my throat gets hot and sharp inside like something is burning stuck there I can't swallow away, or maybe I'll start crying and not stop, I'll break and smash in a hundred glinty pieces like a bottle on the sidewalk, and they'll hear me, they'll come with the knives and guns and burning gas, the end of everything and all my fault.

But I won't cry. I just have to keep lying and not make a mistake, and that's not so hard, like being an actress in a movie, maybe. And I'm good at it. And it's just for a little while anyway, my mother promised she will come back for me when the war is over and she's done being Underground, and everything will be just the same as before. Except for my father, but I don't want to think about that. And you and I will go to America and become famous movie actresses together, like Deanna Durbin or Shirley Temple, like we always said.

You remember that, Claire, don't you? You haven't forgotten me, have you?

Because they can't stop me from remembering you. Or from thinking the true things to you and being the real me inside my own head. It's like knowing a secret trick, like the magician at your birthday party when we were little made that lady disappear, *poof*, remember? So I know I can't ever really disappear. I know inside forever I'll always be Danielle.

~

**FEBRUARY, 1941**

"Marie-Jeanne?"

Who?

She turns over in the hard bed, presses the pillow to her ears. There is no one here by that name. No one here is called that,

"Marie-Jeanne, the cow does not milk herself!"

and there is no cow here, no milking or grimy, fly-buzzing barn. She curls herself under the rough blanket, it's so cold, she'll hurry back to sleep, where it's satin warm, and now she is strolling through a gleaming city of polished stone, like diamonds shiny with fire. But the city is on fire, she realizes, *hurry*, she must run, is running, there is blazing air, the river a white boil, houses cracking to splinter and flame, no, that's boots, soldier boots *crack cracking* on pavement, and drums *beat beating* inside her bones. A howling boy, a flash of metal, the boy's hands are sliced off, the boy is reaching for her, reaching with bright dripping stumps, crying for her to help him, save him, and she doesn't know how. *Hurry, hide, flee!* Paintings and marble angels smeared with human filth, glass shattering, lungs seared and bursting into blood, *Maman*, she cries out, *Papa*? Where are they, did they leave her here all alone? And she must hide, be hidden, hurry, her mother said so, *You'll be safe here, Danielle!* But it's still after her, the *march marching* soldiers and hot knives, the choking gas, blistering flesh, the screams, the golden bubbles of blood, and she startles awake, again.

She blinks. It's still dark, still quiet. In this strange room, bed, house. But safe here, yes. Just a bad dream. That *beat beating* is just her heart. She breathes the cold air deep, closes her eyes again, waiting, listening, for any moment now,

*Wake up, lazy girl*, she will hear Maman call, *You'll be late for school*!

And she'll leap from the satin-coverlet bed she shares with her doll Adele, sink her feet in pink carpet, hurry to braid her hair and button her blouse. She'll run downstairs for a bowl of milk, a butter and jam tartine, a pipe-smelling kiss from Papa, Maman chiding for her messy braids or a lost glove. The three of them planning the weekend, maybe dinner at Drouand's? A movie with Papa on Sunday, and hot chocolate, a wafer cookie before their walk home over the bridge?

*Danielle*, she will hear. *Danielle*, they will call, any moment now, calling for—

"Marie-Jeanne!"

Not her mother's voice. She tightens her closed eyes, pushes her face against the coarse pillowslip. That is a strange woman's voice, it's that woman Berthe, calling for *Marie-Jeanne*. It's been this way for six mornings, in the early dark before she opens her eyes and is still home, in Paris, her real home, real bedroom. Still *Danielle*, her grandmother once told her that means *God is my judge* in Hebrew, she remembers. Not anymore. It's Marie-Jeanne, now.

She pulls the scratchy wool blanket over her face, tries to twist herself back and away into sleep, it doesn't matter what frightening thing awaits her there. But she sees her mother, and that woman, Berthe, the first night here, in this house, hunched over a candle in the smoky, cabbage-smelling downstairs, whispering about papers while that strange man Claude paced and cracked his knuckles, all of them busy coming up with the first lie, the biggest, most important lie. The lie of a name.

"Marie-Jeanne!"

A man's shout, that man Claude, and then a boy's mean laugh. That boy, Luc. It used to be his job to milk the cow every morning and now it's hers and he just loves that, loves watching the cow's tail slap-sting her face, loves watching her struggle to lift the full pail, the wire handle a knife blade in her frozen hands, and then step-sliding in chicken droppings and dirty straw. She pushes the blanket aside, opens her eyes. In the growing-blue light she sees the braid shapes of onion and garlic hanging from raw wooden beams overhead. This is her room, now. She knows above her on the wall is a wooden crucifix with Jesus on it from when he died, but at least she doesn't have to see it when she's lying in this bed. She sits up, shivering in her nightgown. She sees the slight trickle-shine of ice on the wall, where the wet comes through a crack in the window frame Claude said he'd fix but has not. Downstairs will be a piece of tough bread that hurts to bite, the merest scrape of butter, no milk, just a cup of water clouded with the smallest tip of cream. Most of the milk gets sent to the Germans, and most of their stored vegetables, too, which means the aches of helping Berthe stuff dirty, winter-cold potatoes into heavy sacks. Once she saw Berthe spit on them and curse.

But no breakfast at all today, Berthe has told her. Not on Sunday. The Christian Sabbath. It is her first Sunday here, first Catholic Sunday, first time going to the village. First time going to church. Berthe has explained it, how the priest will drink wine and put the *blessed host* in her mouth, *Just like the bread and wine at the Last Supper, Marie-Jeanne, but it's now the very body and blood of Jesus Christ, His precious gift to us, isn't that beautiful?* She'd tried to smile and nod, as if that wasn't both horrible and ridiculous to think about. Maman and Papa drink, *used to* drink, special sweet wine on Shabbat, with a tiny sip for her from the silver cup, a bite of rich yellow challah bread, but no one pretended it was anything but wine and bread. Why is that so beautiful to these people, eating pretend flesh and blood?

And why do they have to go to church at all, really? Papa says, *used* to say, God wasn't only in synagogue and church and reciting old prayers, He was in the everyday kindnesses we do, and the shapes of petals and shells, the rhymes of words, the shiver of cello strings and the colors of the twilight sky and everywhere there were beautiful things. Maybe today will just be like going to a museum then, she thinks. Like a school trip to study the art.

But Berthe hasn't allowed her beyond the garden for six days, *Too dangerous,* she'd warned, so why does she have to go now, today, out where the danger is, strange people to be *Marie-Jeanne* for, the whole village watching and judging? It would be so easy to do something wrong. Make a mistake. Get found out, get taken away, *hurry run hide,* the knives and guns, blood in gutters, hot and sticky thick, screams and smoke and--

"Marie-Jeanne!"

She throws the blanket aside and stands, feels the wood burn like ice beneath her bare feet. Yes. That is who you are now. A lie of a girl. She shivers.

This is what is real, now.

"*Our Father who art in Heaven . . .*"

"*Hail, Holy Queen, Mother of mercy . . .*"

"Come, Marie-Jeanne, let's hear them again. *Our Father . . .* ?"

"Why can't I wear my own dress? My blue one?"

"This will be fine on you, just be still."

She is standing by the kitchen stove with Berthe, trying to absorb its meager warmth, while Berthe buttons her into an old wool dress, taken in by handfuls on the sides and up at the knees and still too big. It's an ugly dun yellow, home-sewn, clean but stiff with stale air and dust.

"Shouldn't I dress up for church?" It's practically new, her blue dress. A special dress, velvet, satin sash, tiny roses on the cuffs. Claire was so envious of that dress, but she never let her borrow it. It wasn't Claire's color. And a lady always knows which colors are most becoming, Maman says. *Used* to say. Blue and green are best for a girl with red hair, like Maman, like Danielle.

"We dress as good as you people do," Luc says. He's at the table, rubbing his cracked black shoes with a rag. He's fourteen, with a mottled forehead and chin, always simmering and annoyed and he smells different from how girls smell. He has black hair that juts out everywhere, and black eyes with dark circles around them like a lady's smudged makeup. His ears stick out from his head and his long bones bump out from his shoulders and wrists, although Berthe treats him like her precious baby boy, fussing about his eating enough and buttoning his coat. They're supposed to be cousins now, Berthe tells her, and love each other like brother and sister, but he glares at her when she eats Berthe's food, he kicks at dead birds he finds on the ground, and she tries to stay out of his way.

"You people don't even kneel down to pray." He spits on a shoe.

"Hush," Berthe says to him, then a glance at Danielle's face.

Ignore him, she thinks. Just pretend you're somewhere else. Somewhere pretty. She tries to picture the shop windows on the way to school, where she and Claire always stop to study the clothes, yes, and she will try to talk Claire into the pink dress, which is more becoming for a girl with brown hair. Then they'll study the movie posters at the Odeon. Claire likes Charles Boyer and Clark Gable, and she likes Franchot Tone and Spencer Tracy, and they will argue over which they will marry when they grow up.

"You don't even show that respect to our Lord," Luc is saying.

"Luc," says Claude. "Enough." He wipes his face at the sink, straining his bulk at an awkward angle, trying not to splash his black suit gone gray at the elbows and knees, his carefully ironed shirt.

"She must've packed it," she says, her pretty blue dress, the picture in a magazine, she remembers hurrying with her mother to the Galleries Lafayette, her promises not to get it wrinkled or stained. Just a few months ago, glossy magazines and smart dresses in shop windows. Perfumed department stores, a new winter white coat with a fur collar, the matching hat. She'd worn them on the train when they left Paris, the middle of the night, just a week ago, how can it be only a week? Maman in a stylish traveling suit, hers had a fur collar, too. But no lipstick, no jewelry, her hair in a loose braid. She'd never seen her mother leave the house without a well-placed piece of jewelry, without her red hair curled in a perfect shining crown. And she wore a pair of Danielle's father's boots, *Hurry, Danielle, just do what I'm telling you!* Her mother never wore anything but high heels. And that tone of voice, full of edges. *No, you can't say good-bye to Claire, you can't bring*

*Adele, you're a big girl now!*

"It should be in the suitcase," she insists. The small leather valise, her mother handed it over to Berthe that first night and she hasn't seen it since. She's been wearing the same gray dress, the same green sweater, hating the animal-dung-and-old-vegetable smell of barn gripping her hair and clothes after doing her chores. Maman lets her dab perfume on her wrists, choose from the crystal bottles on her vanity table, *You choose, cherie.* Chanel No. 5 or Jacqueminot.

The scent of roses in the sun . . .

"Really, Berthe, why can't I just wear my own dress?"

"This was my Sunday dress when I was little." Berthe finishes the buttons, turns her around. "Now, again. *Hail, Holy Queen, Mother of Mercy . . .* ?"

"I've practiced all week, Berthe. I've said them a million times."

"*Tante* Berthe."

"When it's just us, here? Why do we have to—"

"Don't argue with your aunt, Marie-Jeanne." Claude dampens his comb and arranges hairs across his freckled scalp, still bent forward. He has a stiff arm he can't raise above his head, a shoulder wound from Verdun, Berthe has told her, proud. He looks crooked when he stands, his jacket pulled out of alignment on one side. *Tante* Berthe and *tonton* Claude, more lies, just her grandparents' old butler and maid, who she doesn't even remember. What a joke. She can't picture this *uncle* ladling soup from a porcelain tureen to her frowning grandfather on Passover or Yom Kippur. She can't see him cracking his knuckles in front of them, taking up so much space. Berthe, too, is a thick person, doughy, as if she and Maman could be sisters! Her brown and gray hair is scraped into a potato-sized bun at the back of her head, pierced with wooden pins. There's a ruddy lace of broken veins across her nose; her fingers are always swollen and red. Danielle has seen her twist the green tops off whole bunches of turnips with those angry-looking hands. She can't imagine those hands folding linen napkins into flowers for her grandmother's table.

"You need to understand this isn't a game." He peers in the small mirror above the sink, smooths his mustache. "How dangerous this is, for all of us."

"I do."

"Claude," Berthe says. "It was our Christian duty."

"Yes, and she needs to appreciate the sacrifices we're all making."

"I *do*. Really." She is tired of hearing about their Christian duty to take her into their home, about all the danger she brings, and Doesn't she know how lucky she is? She wishes they could just let her alone, like her first days here, to lie curled on her oniony bed or sit by the stove and wind mutton-smelling balls of wool, or work by herself in the garden, scattering straw on the frozen ground. She was so tired, those first few days, her feet swollen, legs with hot bone aches, toe blisters that ran a thin fluid then turned to crust, and when she awoke those first mornings her eyes were puffed up so sore and tight she could hardly see. Berthe has said she hears her crying at night sometimes, calling for *Maman* or *Papa*, but she doesn't believe that. How could she cry and not wake up? And she is trying so hard not to cry, ever, no, she will never cry again. She swallows, hard.

"I do understand," she tells them. "I'm not a baby."

"Then say it again. *Our Father . . .* ?"

Fine. She takes a deep breath. "*Our Father who art in Heaven hallowed be thy name . . .*" All in one breath, delivered fast, good.

"We believe in one God, the Father almighty . . . ?" Claude prompts.

"*Maker of Heaven and Earth, of all that is seen and unseen . . .*" she recites. How hard is it, really, memorizing a few sentences? Like in school, La Fontaine, she recited three fables in a row that time. Maman and Papa applauding. She'd won a ribbon. All those ribbons, on the wall at home. An empty home, now. Or maybe not. Maybe there's another family living there, now. A German family. A little blond-bright German girl, sleeping in her covered-with-roses bed, cuddling with Adele. A German woman combing her blond hair at her mother's vanity, a German soldier cracking the spines of her father's precious books,

"*we look for resurrection of the dead, and lifeoftheworldtocome, amen.*"

She swallows again, tries to catch her breath.

"Very good, Marie," Claude says.

Luc shrugs. "I knew them all when I was three."

"Hail Mary . . . ?" Berthe urges. She's crazy about the Virgin Mary, that big picture of Mary over her bed, blue robe and gold-flecked halo. She acts like Mary is a movie star.

Berthe begins braiding her hair. Too tight, too hard. "Marie, go on, Hail Mary, full of grace . . . ?" She's seen Berthe dig those big bare hands into frozen ground for carrots. Fill a bucket with dried manure. Snap a soft brown rabbit's neck.

Deep breath. "*HailMaryfullofgracetheLordiswiththee . . .*"

Berthe is nodding along, mouthing the words, beaming. "Every time you say the Hail Mary, dear, you're handing a beautiful rose to our Blessed Mother."

"Uh huh."

"Her love and mercy are always with us. Our prayers will be such a comfort to you, Marie. When you open your heart that way."

"I know, you said."

"You'll be able to forget about everything, from before. That's what's best." Berthe finishes the braids. "Remember, cross yourself when we do. Bow your head. You cannot make a mistake."

"I *know*, Berthe." And she'll have to kneel and then not kneel, sing and then not sing, pray to saint statues, eat and drink all that pretend body and blood. Maybe you can tell them you don't feel well, she thinks. Maybe tell them you'll go next Sunday, and by then maybe they'll have forgotten anyway.

"*Tante* Berthe. Remember that." Berthe picks up Danielle's coat, her new coat with the white fur collar.

"*Tante* Berthe," she repeats. "*Tonton* Claude. *Cousin* Luc. I know, don't worry. But maybe, maybe I'm not . . . what are you doing?"

Berthe has a knife in her hand, is cutting, digging around the fur collar.

"Oh, don't do that, please!" Like gutting that rabbit, those red hands at the soft white belly skin, the moment of shiny purple insides spilling through. She closes her eyes. Her beautiful coat. She tightens her hands into fists.

"Baby's going to cry now," Luc says.

"I am not!" she snaps.

"You'd stand out in these things, Marie." Berthe tosses the collar in the fire; the white fur catches then leaps up as brief flame. "Don't worry, dear, I have something nice for you." She fusses inside a small oak trunk. "Such pretty red hair you have. Golden red." She lifts out a fistful of fraying yellow ribbons. "And that fair skin. You always looked Irish to me. Or Scottish. Such a beautiful people, the Scots. When you visited with your maman, you'd sit on my lap, I'd brush your hair. Do you remember?" She advances on Danielle's braids.

"I can tie those myself." She reaches. Yellow, not a good color for me, she thinks.

But Berthe is already seizing, twisting a braid with ribbon. "She'd be dressed up fancy to go out with your grandparents. All that beautiful jewelry of hers! The necklaces and earrings and bracelets she wore! Like a queen." Berthe jerks a tight bow. "And you'd come running to the kitchen. 'I get to stay with Berthe!' you'd yell. We'd play games together all evening."

"I don't remember that."

"No?" Berthe looks disappointed. "You don't look much like your parents, really. Certainly not your father."

Her father. She looks, looks for her father's face in her mind, it flickers, blurs, but—

*Our Father, who art in Heaven . . .*

—soon, he'll be back soon, she thinks, confused. Her father. With eggs,

"But you have your mother's beautiful red hair."

and her mother, too, she'll come back for her when the war is over, she promised

*Holy Mother of God, always with us . . .*

they will be together again, and her mother will hold her, like on the train here, dark and rumbling, German soldiers examining people's papers, her mother smiling bright at them, taking off Danielle's fur hat—why?—finger-combing Danielle's hair forward, on display,

"I always wanted a daughter. A little Marie. You know," Berthe turns to her husband, "she hardly looks at all . . ."

the Germans are smiling back, at her mother, at her,

"like a Jew."

smiling at her pretty golden red hair.

"Not *my* Marie, no—"

"Stop it," jerking her head from that woman's hands, "I'm not your Marie! You aren't my family. Mary isn't my blessed mother, there's no father in Heaven, stop pretending this is real, it's all just a big *lie*, a joke, it's not—"

The slap is like missing a bottom step she didn't see, that snaps at your ankle and makes your stomach lurch. It doesn't feel like hurt until the lurch stops and she feels her face burn. No one has ever slapped her. She is stunned silent, without breath. Luc is grinning. Berthe's red fingers are pressed to her mouth. Claude cracks his knuckles in the quiet.

"I'm so sorry, Marie." Berthe crosses herself. "Marie-Jeanne?"

She looks down, away, so they won't see her cry. No, she squeezes her eyes shut, *you're a big girl now*, looks at her clenched hands, sees a thin line of dirt under her nails, a peasant girl, that's what you are now, wearing their old rags, scrubbing their potatoes and floors. *Run, hide, flee*, yes, why can't she? Escape this icy house and dead wet fields, hurry down those black mountains and away from this place. Go home. No, go find her mother Underground, wherever that is. Maman's fingers lacing her hair, the scent of roses, her soft hand on her face.

But no, she's gone. She left you here, with a woman who slaps. There's nowhere to go, no place to run away *to*. So act like it didn't hurt. Go on. Pretend, like you're supposed to. Lie.

"No, *I'm* sorry, tante Berthe," Danielle says, raising her head. "Really, Tonton, Cousin Luc, please forgive me."

She smiles brightly at Berthe, and Berthe smiles back.

"I know this is hard for you, dear. We know you're doing your best. And we're so happy you're here with us."

Claude puts his big square hand on her shoulder. "We are, Marie-Jeanne. All of us." Claude looks at Luc, who shrugs, looks away. "Really."

She nods, smiling, smiling. Go on, thank them for their scraps and rags, she thinks. Their Christian charity. Tell them how grateful you are. But she can't bring herself to that, not yet.

"Well, she's going to make us late," Luc mutters. "And you should make her practice the Creed again. She got it wrong yesterday."

"I know it now, I promise," she says to all of them. "I'll be perfect. Please don't worry."

"Yeah, well if she messes up . . ." Luc heads out of the kitchen, slamming open the heavy wood door. "I'm not getting shot just because of her."

Before the Germans marched into Paris last June, everyone acted like the end of the world was on its way, marching across the map. They'd marched all the way up into Denmark and Norway, across to Belgium and right into France, sneaking in through the unlocked back door, sweeping through the Maginot Line like brushing off strands of spider silk, slaughtering as they went, our brave men butchered, our women and children chopped to bits. Danielle heard the terrible stories everywhere, people babbling in the cafes, the shops, the cinema lines about what horrors were coming next, Get ready for war, they say it's marching toward us, blood and death, marching, the end of our ways, of our pride our honor our France, of everything we know, can't you feel it, the coming end? And she *could* feel it, the *end* of everything coming at her, sneaking inside her room at night to pound her chest and beat blood in her fingertips and ears when she tried to sleep, hoping the lace curtains and satin coverlet would shield her, hide her, keep the dangerous butchering thing out. Maybe she should say a prayer, the way her grandparents always told her to, *Please God,* she mumbled into her pillow, *Please, God, please* . . . but wasn't sure which words came next. Anyway, it wasn't nice to pray only when you wanted to ask for something, that isn't why God is there, her father always said.

People sewed newspapers into curtains for the coming blackouts, dried fresh plums into prunes, dug out old gas masks from the Great War for the looming bombs. Urinate on a handkerchief when the gas comes, hold it to your face, they say it kills the burn! Save up your butter, you'll need it to soothe blistered skin! Everyone said the Germans were barbarians, dirty Huns, *sale boches,* and they would beat everyone up and steal and kill, yes, the Germans are inhuman, no, *super*human, they must be, to have beaten us this way, godlike in their

Herculean strength, striding whole-limbed and golden across our fields, conquering without sweat, and the British troops, our allies—our *friends!*—fleeing Dunkirk while our own French soldiers were left bleeding into the sand and sea. Danielle saw people running away, then, running with stunned, stupefied faces, big suitcases and paintings and boxes of books, mattresses on their backs, dragging children by the hand, *hurry, hide, flee!* Officials dumped files into the Seine and burned papers in huge bonfires that sent black smoke blooming overhead for days and into her nose and throat and made the whole city smell like singe. Oil depots were exploded, to keep them from German hands, and their oily flames streaked the sky in hot oranges and blacks. She saw shopkeepers running with chickens flapping under their arms, women tripping with birdcages, with hatboxes from the rue de la Paix, and two men carrying a big rolled-up rug overhead, making a wild stagger as they went, and shouldn't she and her parents be running away too, she thought, hurrying and hiding from the knives and guns and burning flesh? She worried which of her blouses and shoes she might carry away, which favorite books. Everywhere, people were fleeing, in cars, on bicycles, on foot, and rumors whispering their way back of children lost in the crush at train stations, people abandoning their possession-filled cars on dusty roads for lack of gasoline and walking south, women dying of premature childbirth in ditches, old people dropping dead of exhaustion and being scratch-buried in fields, towns overwhelmed with refugees forced to sleep in churches, looting and pillaging, spates of suicides, mayors offering themselves as hostages to the German army, hoping to spare their villages, their towns. She saw a spotty brown dog roaming their street all day, yelping, and talked her mother into letting her give the dog a plate of scraps. But then there were more dogs, all the dogs people couldn't take away with them in the exodus, yelping in the streets then turning on each other with howls and snapping bloody jaws, and her mother told Danielle to leave them alone, they'd gone wild from hunger, they would just have to fend for themselves.

Most of their neighbors fled, and their maid Sophie went home to Geneva, and her parents' friends who used to come on Shabbat to argue about God and art, who was or was not betraying France, and whether the war was real or just rumor and threat, a *drole de guerre,* a phony war. Her mother sent Danielle to bed early on those Friday nights, when the arguments were less about French politics and God and more about Poland and ghettos and the Nazi man in charge of Germany, Hitler. But Danielle listened at the door,

*You're blind, Paul,* she heard them say, *Jews and the academics, it's who they always come for first. Jews and academics.*

But *This is our home,* her father said. *This is our country! We're not running away.*

And she lay in bed, blood pounding, are they coming, would there be blood in gutters, would the poison gas burn through her curtains to blister her lungs and shred her skin, rolling tanks crushing those wild dogs in the streets, and shouldn't they flee? But no, her father wanted to stay, and surely he would shield her, keep them all safe, of course he would, yes.

Then the soldiers did arrive, marching in their shiny black boots, the streets going muddy green with uniforms and harsh with German accents like constant coughs. They marched right in, with their soup bowl helmets and rumbling tanks, in tidy rows like chess pieces, but no blood or boiling oil, no screaming horses or babies speared on bayonets, and the last of the smoke just thinned away. But they did carry guns, machine guns hanging from shoulders or big pistols in holsters at their sides. Her parents wouldn't let her go to school, and her father stopped going to the University. And she waited, still, for the *end* of everything to come get them, like everyone said, the whispers of neighbors and friends, they say Hitler has invaded

Britain, they say the United States has attacked Germany, the Pope has committed suicide, the Germans are planning to burn Paris to the ground, *they say, they say.* Our leaders have been taken prisoner, they say, have been tortured and killed; no, they've all fled to North Africa, to Bordeaux; no, they're fleeing further east, to Vichy. The invaders are marching thousands of our men back into Germany, guns pointed at their heads, German soldiers are cutting off the hands of French boys so they can't grow up to fight, German soldiers use French citizens as human shields when they march, German soldiers smear their excrement on our precious works of art.

And then the voice on the radio, thin and scratchy, like a frail old woman with bad lungs. An old war veteran brought back from the dead, her father told her, Marshal Philippe Petain, the hero of the Great War, of Verdun. *I am giving myself to France,* the voice said, *to offer myself in her hour of need, to ease her pain.* Her father muttering, *Who does he think he is, Christ?* Petain would not flee, as so many others did; no, he would stay to lead them, to share their sorrows and misfortunes. And, his decree: *The fighting must stop*. We must lay our weapons down, accept an honorable defeat. Her mother crying, *He's giving France to the Germans, just handing us over, that's what he's doing!* But was that so bad, Danielle wondered, if it meant no more fear, no more worrying, with each breath, if you were inhaling that burning, blistering gas, no more poor frightened dogs gone savage and yelping in the streets?

Yes, everything returned to normal again, almost. So what if there's no more President or National Assembly, no more *Republique*, they said in the long lines forming at shops, We're safe now, we have Marshal Petain to lead and protect us, a true hero of France! And Pierre Laval as Deputy Prime Minister, well, he's a thug, with his hooded eyes and bad teeth, none of the Marshal's natural elegance, that's for sure. But a real political operator, that Laval, look how he persuaded our National Assembly to dissolve itself, wipe out the 3rd Republic, to hand full powers over to Marshal Petain! Isn't that just the kind of shady character we need to deal with the Germans? Two million of our men held in German prisoner-of-war camps, but they'll come home soon! Yes, that's what they say! Yes, not since Louis XIV have we had such a strong leader, such a bright future!

And so what if clocks were moved forward an hour, to match German time? So what if there were fewer cars on the streets, no gasoline to fill them, except for Germans in their shiny coupes and sedans? So what if meat and cheese became hard to find, and no more whiff of baking bread or sausage or chestnuts when you walked along the avenues, so what if roasted acorns and saccharine became bitter *ersatz* coffee and *ersatz* sugar? Just laugh about it, everyone laughing it off together. So what if there were no more dinners at Drouand's, no more Sundays at the cinema? She could go back to school. And they could go for walks again in the Tuileries, she and her father, among the people roaming with empty baby carriages and wheelbarrows in hopes of finding something, anything, to eat or hoard or trade. They could watch people trapping pigeons in makeshift cages to take home for a meal, although her father hurried her away when a man grabbed at a bird, seized its tiny bird head and body in tight fists before a loud *crack*. They could still stroll past the Hotel de Ville, although the pretty French flag was gone, the *tricolore,* and the ugly German flag flapped there now, red and white with the thick black scar marching around it forever in a jagged circle, more and more of those flags, flapping on terraces, atop monuments. But she didn't have to look at them, or the tightening outline of her father's face as they went by. Yes, long walks with her father, just like always, no more wafer cookies or chocolate or carousel, but still, the two of them together, Papa not caring about her messy braids or her gloves stuffed in her pockets, walking on slow Sunday afternoons until the sun began its drop and they'd stop on the Pont Neuf, to watch the candles and lamplights twinkle on in the buildings.

*Watch the colors change, Danielle,* he'd say, pointing to the sky, *look how beautiful. Look at all the shadings, always changing, from silvery lemon, over there, to that deep sapphire, look how it's turning to ink. It's like a painting. We're 'entre chien et loup' at this hour. Now look carefully, and you show me the moment when day changes to night, when the light turns to dark. Can you see it?*

And she'd look and look but could never see exactly when the shift happened, when the dog became the wolf. And that didn't change, the twilight sky, just because the Germans were there.

*Occupation,* she thought, well, it isn't so bad. The German soldiers on the street were always well-mannered. Perfectly correct. They smiled, tipped their caps to ladies and showed clean necks and well-trimmed hair. They bought postcards of the Eiffel Tower, took photographs in front of Notre Dame like giddy tourists on holiday. Once she saw a young captain help old Monsieur Lesaire carry a stack of newspapers across the street, and he was a Jew, too, who fought in the Great War, his *Legion d'Honneur* medal always pinned to his chest. And the German saluted him! Clearly, these weren't the bad barbarian Germans. She almost stopped noticing all the guns, the accents, the sound of marching boots.

And one of them offered her mother a seat in the Metro once, like a gentleman, and his French was perfect, too, but her mother refused, haughty, and turned her back. Danielle whispered why was she being so rude? But her mother just jerked her arm, *You ignore them, you walk away! Don't you ever forget who they are, who* you *are!* in a terrible tone of voice, a tone she'd never heard before.

But one time there was the soldier with the chocolate. Her mother had left her in line for tea while she tried to get sugar, she'd heard a rumor there was real sugar to be had, *Dessert we'll have tonight, cherie, I promise!* The German, strolling along, nodding in a friendly way at the long snaky line, although everyone looked away from him, pointedly, their chins stiff, and he'd smiled at Danielle, very polite, white oval teeth and pretty blue eyes, just like the pale bright sky before the sapphire. When he held out the candy, well, she didn't want to be rude, like Maman had been, like all the other people in line. She knew who she was—she was a girl with nice manners! She didn't believe the rumor of real sugar, anyway, and when did she last get to have chocolate? So she took it, thought of saving half for Claire, but it smelled so rich and real, nothing like the metal of saccharine, nothing *ersatz.* She smiled at the German soldier, said *Merci,* added a sort of curtsy-bob, hoping the others would see her polite example, although they looked away from her, then, too. And she tucked the whole entire piece of chocolate in her cheek so it would melt slowly and stay there fat and sweet a long time. And she kept her face turned away from her mother the whole walk home so Maman, her hands empty of sugar (no dessert, of course not) wouldn't smell it and speak with that terrible edged voice.

Papa even went back to his classes. Jews weren't allowed to teach anymore, but Claire's father, Monsieur Beaumont, the Dean, was standing up to the Germans, refusing to let Paul go.

*You see, Rachel?* Papa said, *we have friends, good friends. We'll be fine. This will pass.*

Then in September, the call for a Census. Her father told her the Germans had cut France in two; they took the top half and left the bottom for Marshal Petain to be head of down in Vichy, that tacky spa town, yes, our *Head of State,* her father said, waving the forms, our puppet king! The Census meant the Germans wanted Marshal Petain to count the Jews in the Occupied Zone, he explained. It's nothing important, Danielle, just paperwork. But a few weeks later her father came home and told them he'd lost his job at the

University. Jews were forbidden to teach, by the new Jewish Statute, and forbidden to write for the newspapers, serve in the military, work in the arts, hold any public office or perform any public function or serve in any *professions that influence people,* and there was nothing anybody could do, not even Claire's papa. Danielle had been sent home from school, too, which made no sense to her—she was the best student in the class! They should send the *stupid* students away, she told her father, but he just shook his head, absently, as if at something beyond her.

*It's just the end of school for a while, Danielle, not the end of the world.*

So here was an end of something, yes. But she didn't know if it was the beginning of other ends to other things, perhaps bigger than just the end of chocolate and movies and going to school. But Claire came over after class and sometimes brought sweet treats while they watched strolling German soldiers through the lace curtains of Danielle's window, and tried to choose which of them they'd marry if they had to. And she liked Papa being home to teach her. So yes, everything was fine, just as her father said, and he would never break a promise, would never ever lie to her.

He gave her a lesson one day, in fractions and percents. A chilly October day, too early for such icy air and wind, a day to stay inside with sweaters on and bake cookies with Sophie, but Sophie was gone and there was nothing to bake cookies with. And her father talking about tarts, of all things, "Take a large tart," he explained, drawing a circle in pencil to show her. "Now, it's all there, just out of the oven. The whole tart. One hundred percent of it. Or you can cut it in two pieces," he said, scoring a line across the circle, "and if you eat one half, you have one half left. Fifty percent is gone, and fifty percent is saved." Too easy, for Danielle, she had already studied fractions in school, she was growing bored. And hungry.

"I understand, Papa, it's like France. We're cut in halves now. Fifty percent is Free and fifty percent is Occupied."

Her mother came from the kitchen to watch, leaning, frowning, arms folded inside a too-big sweater of her father's, her braid down and over her shoulder.

"Very good. Or a different example, say," he said, carefully scoring more lines across the tart, "your mother's parents were both Jewish. Your Grandmother Sarah and Grandfather Jacob. And all four of her grandparents. So your mother is . . . ?"

"Four-fourths Jewish. One hundred percent." When did they last even *see* a tart?

Blueberry, apricot, raspberry . . .

Her father smiled. "Correct. But me," clearing his throat, drawing another, separate circle, another scored line, "my mother was Christian. Only my father was Jewish."

"So you're just half," Danielle said. Half a tart, even that would be plenty. Blueberry, definitely. With cream. "You're only fifty percent Jewish."

"Not if you ask the Jews," her mother said. "And not if you ask Petain," she added, a bitter tone, when did she start sounding that way all the time? "Isn't *that* ironic?"

Her father didn't answer. "And so you, Danielle, that means you are . . . ?"

"I'm three-fourths Jewish."

He tugged her braid in approval. "That's right. You are definitely head of your class."

"But there's no 'only' anymore," her mother said. "That's what she needs to learn, Paul. In your little bakery."

Her father looked down, then, studied his pencil-circle-tarts. He drew a squiggly line at one edge for a crust, was silent.

"But . . ." Danielle wasn't sure if the lesson was over, why this silence felt so loud, suddenly wasn't the same thing as quiet. "We're hardly Jewish at all, are we? We hardly ever go to synagogue."

Her father pondered a moment, the way he always did when she asked questions, his face reassuring her she was right to ask, then explained the Germans say you are Jewish if you practice the Jewish *religion*, go to synagogue and keep kosher and say your Hebrew prayers and so on. Or if you have more than two grandparents who did those religious things. But Vichy has now said if you have at least two grandparents who are Jewish, you are fully Jewish, no matter what you do or don't do. It is in your blood. It is your race. It is who and what you are. He showed her his identity card, *Marton, Paul*, stamped *Juif*. And her mother's, *Marton, Rachel, Juive*. Danielle had seen those cards a hundred times, they didn't have those stamps before.

"So, Papa, the Germans and the Jews would say you're *not* completely Jewish, but Marshal Petain says you *are*? That makes no sense."

"No," he said. "It doesn't. But it's true."

"But why did you lose your job, then, if the Germans are in charge here in our Zone?" Her father glanced at her mother, gave a small shake of his head.

"Because your father married me, Danielle," her mother said. "And it's our French government who made that law."

"So, it *isn't* about your blood?" She was even more confused, now. And Jewish, what did that even mean, really? Sips of silver cup wine on Friday nights, your grandparents' boring singsong prayers? But the unquiet silence was there again, too loud to ask another question in.

Her father abruptly pushed the paper and pencil and identity cards away. He opened a book before him, hard, a slam-open on the table that made the empty sugar bowl jump, and a look on his face, a twitch in his jaw, that made her stay very still. Baudelaire. He loved Baudelaire, sometimes read a poem or two to Danielle, although her mother said she was too young for that kind of thing. Her mother shook her head, now, at everything, returned to the kitchen. But she stroked her hand along the back of Danielle's father's neck as she passed, and he reached, touched her hand, held it there a moment.

*Mein oitser,* she whispered, soft. My treasure.

Her mother made carrot soups, pureed orange soups that got thinner and yellower every week, with less and less cream and more and more water. And Danielle's glass of milk got bluer each day with the water her mother added, she tried not to complain, really, but couldn't help sometimes groaning and wrinkling her nose. And her father trading the very last of his pipe tobacco for flour to bake bread, her parents whispering late at night about the black market and so little money left, the coming winter, the already icy mornings and not enough fuel. She heard her mother whisper about fleeing to the Free Zone, Spain, a cousin who lives in England . . .

*This is our home, Rachel. Is that what you want? To run away?*

They had friends, this will all pass, he whispered. There was still his collection of rare books, they're valuable. And Rachel's jewelry to trade or sell, *a small fortune there,* we'll be fine.

Then in December, a happy rumor, *eggs* for sale! Her father rushing out to stand in line, *We'll have an omelet tonight,* her mother said, *I promise!* They waited, and waited more, past the curfew hour when he should have been home, reminding each other about long twisty lines and Papa's absent-mindedness with ration cards, how he was always leaving his somewhere and patting the pockets of his coat, about the time her mother stood in line for five hours to get butter and then it was just rancid margarine, and wasn't that dreadful, certainly not worth all the wait and fear, and how funny this is now, her mother's face stretched in a smile, Papa out in that icy wind, how cold it is tonight! All for a few eggs, when they used to use them so carelessly, Sophie used eight of them for a single soufflé, remember, a dozen for a loaf of challah, her mother forcing laughs, and then a knock at the door, loud and fast. It was Claire's papa, Monsieur Beaumont.

Danielle's father came to the University, he told them, out of breath. To demand his job back. There were Germans there. They wouldn't let him pass, although I tried to convince them. They told him to go home. They were respectful, Monsieur Beaumont said, but he wouldn't go! And he got angry with the soldiers, her papa, yelling about scraps left for dogs and sawdust for bread and children living on water, and they called him a *sale Juif*, a dirty Jew. And then Paul reached out and hit one of the soldiers, I tried to stop him, Monsieur Beaumont babbled, was he crazy? They grabbed him, they dragged him into the street and Monsieur Beaumont ran after, he saw the other soldier shoot Danielle's father—Monsieur Beaumont's voice cracked—right in his belly, one loud shot, and he went down, lying there in the street, bleeding, and Monsieur Beaumont tried to help him—I did, I did, their guns pointed right at me!—he tried to telephone Rachel but the lines were dead, tried to find a doctor, get him to a hospital, but no Jews allowed. But Papa's only fifty percent, Danielle thought, confused, as her mother started to shriek, wailing ugly shrieks that filled the air, made her face finally break open and go ugly, too, hurt Danielle's ears and went burning sharp into the back of her throat, made her run to her room, into her bed, hold onto Adele and tell her Papa would be there in the morning when they woke up, that's all, no reason to cry. He'd give her a kiss, take her for school shoes, for a cup of chocolate and wafer cookies. He wasn't lying on the street, in the gutter, bleeding, dead, it wasn't that kind of an end, no. That kind of end was too endless, too big, it wouldn't fit anywhere in her room, in their apartment, already full with her mother's shrieking and crying anyway, no space left for her to cry, for her own tears, everything suddenly too huge to fit anywhere in the world.

She pictured instead one small thing, the moment he left the apartment that afternoon, waving goodbye, hurrying to get in line, get her an egg . . . but what jacket was he wearing? What tie? She couldn't remember and it isn't fair, that she couldn't know it was the last time when it was the last time and so pay more attention to those things. Which jacket, which tie? Just his face, a glimpse of it, hurried, a flicker of it over his shoulder, saying he'd be back soon.

"He was a hero, Danielle," her mother kept repeating for days, choking, her voice and face still wrong somehow, a different face shape, another mother's voice. "Your papa was a hero. You have to remember that, always. He died for the Jews, and freedom and for France, to save those things. For us, for you."

"Yes, Maman, of course," kissing her mother's swollen damp cheek. But which face of his was it? Was he smiling, happy to think about those eggs for her dinner? Or was he scrunched taut, worried the eggs would be all gone? Or his smooth listening face, nodding to music, pondering her questions? She looked and looked, but even his faces were blurring, she realized, all of them blurring and disappearing away, so

*Please God, please let me see his face again, just one more time, please,* she begged, but no. Maybe God was displeased she was asking, even for that one small thing.

And then a few weeks later, her mother shaking her awake in the middle of the night, *Get dressed, No, I'll explain later,* getting on the train, riding for rattling rumbling hours in the dark as she jerked in and out of chilly sleep, then hurrying from a depot, *Where are we going, Maman, please?,* into the back of a truck, *Be quiet, Danielle,* her fingers and toes going dull hot with cold, finally crying with all the frightening freezing pain, *And don't cry, you have to be a brave girl now, you're twelve years old, hush,* her mother handing an envelope to the driver, a speechless old man with grimy wrinkles, two missing fingers and a cap pulled low over his eyes, and driving at sharp angles, upward, bouncing against the walls of the truck, then walking for more hours up shadow black hills, staggering as her mother pulled her along by the hand, *I know you're tired, just keep walking,* through a mountain's crack into a small valley, across snowy fields and frozen dirt roads to this village she's never even heard of or seen on a map, to here, *Maman, don't leave me,* clutching at her, *I'll be so good, I promise!,* to this place, this Berthe and Claude's doorstep, *You'll be safe here, Danielle,* her mother crying, too, *I'll be thinking about you every moment of every day,* but then turning away, pulling her skirt from Danielle's grip, *cherie, no, please, let go,* disappearing into what dark ink was left of the night, running away as the lemon light began to creep over one mountain's rim.

*I'll come back for you, I promise!*

Yes, forget all that, from before, that's what's best. She's glad there's nothing in this place to remind her, no more roses, no pipe smell, not even a photograph. And no praying to God anymore, too late for that now, too. She just won't think about them, Underground and dead, about faces and voices or any of it anymore, is all. Certainly not every moment of every day.

~

The village is twenty minutes' walk away, along a road edged by a ragged rock wall, past scraggled fields with old corn stalks hanging like bleached rags, past small farms with hay-stuffed barns and squat stone houses with dirty white shutters, mountains thrust up in a hard ring around it all. La Perrine, the middle of nowhere. Other people leaving those houses, too, bundled in their peasant best, everyone hurrying, huffing, their breath puffing out in brief little clouds. She trudges after Berthe, Claude and Luc, wearing her thready collarless coat, its hem now tugged at by Berthe to look correctly well-worn. A deliberate shadow of mud on her shoes. Suddenly they're there, walking past village houses and shops, plain stone and wood and uncurled, unflowered iron trim. Everything looks gray and cracked with cold. The bells hurt her ears. A charcuterie, a bakery, a dry goods shop. The bus stop, for the bus to and from Limoges. Barely a village. No cinema, no museum, no bookstore. A café, no, she sees two, a small café/tabac, and a larger one next to the *mairie*, where the tricolore flag is still flying, that's nice to see, at least. But everything is shuttered, closed. Sunday. Time for church. There, up ahead, stones, arches, ugly wire grate to protect the stained glass, but so tiny, such a tiny church to hold up a huge, high cross like that. There were churches in Paris, of course, everywhere, but they were surrounded by other tall buildings, with lacy curtains, flowery iron work and flourish'd shop signs, and all those crosses just blended in, they didn't rise up and follow and stare at her that way.

They walk across the square's broken paving stones, past the monument to the Great War, the names of La Perrine's sacrificed young men carved in stone. She sees other children, walking with their families. A chubby blond girl, with a mother wearing loud costume jewelry. Another girl about her age, with sharp, curious glances, holding her little sister's hand. A pretty girl walking alone, long dark hair pulled back like Claire's, turns to give her a shy smile. Nicely dressed, that girl, a pink dress, pink satin bow, good colors for her, good shoes, no twice-turned peasant clothing there. Tomorrow is her first day at school here; they will be her schoolmates. What kind of games do they play, here? Do they stand up to recite, or stay seated? She's never been the new girl in school. Certainly never a phony girl, a lie of a girl. At home the new kids had to stand in front of everyone and introduce themselves, tell about their parents and their favorite things to do. Do they do that here? What will she say? Her mind suddenly stumbles, she blinks. Is going to the Odeon her favorite thing, or is milking the cow? Is she a girl who wears blues and greens, or yellow? What's the matter with her, how did who she was become impossible to sort from who she's supposed to be, in just a week?

But these kids are mostly ignoring her now—they're scuttling after their parents or busy with each other. She's still just some visiting stranger, a nobody girl, not worth their questions or handshaking. Still safe, yes. Until tomorrow.

"Marie-Jeanne?"

She is introduced to a Madame and Monsieur Leroux, a Madame Gaillard, les Druots, a Madame Richie. Some lady owns the dry goods shop, she is told; les Leroux own the small café/tabac. Madame Gaillard, with the ugly jewelry, is the grocer. Monsieur Druot, who runs the big café with his wife, also serves as our honorable Monsieur le Mayor. She shakes hands politely, then the adults turn away and jabber. Luc kicks at rocks, glances at the pretty girl with the pink bow, who ducks her head, then bends, kneels to tie her shoe. Danielle hears *My dear sister's child,* hears *Tragic car accident,* hears *All alone in the world, Yes, a home with us, now.* The adults clucking:

"*La pauvre!*"

"*Chère enfante!*"

And they look at her with pity, eyebrows high, charitable smiles and nods. It's begun.

She tries to look like a poor little thing, a dear sweet child, all alone in the world with her tattered coat and dirty shoes. Berthe smiles, motions to her. Time to go inside.

She hesitates. You're just going *into* a church, she tells herself. It's a building you walk into, is all. You aren't going *to* church, that's more a place you go in your heart and soul. God understands the difference. He won't mind.

She steps forward, through the doorway. You can do this, she thinks, No one's getting shot just because of you.

There's the Jesus on the cross. Claire wore a tiny gold one around her neck, and the hanging and dying Jesus on it was a tiny thing, smaller than a beetle. The one above her bed is small too, but this one is huge, an anguished, mostly naked man hanging in a brutal sag from nails punched into his hands and feet, a bleeding gash carved on his belly. It hangs high and looming, it's awful, why do we have to look at it all the time?

Berthe nudges her, glances at a small bowl pinned to the wall. Danielle follows Claude, Berthe and Luc, dips her fingers, is surprised at the chill of the water. Everyone has tiny breath clouds in here, too, it's so cold, high stone walls, the smell of cold damp rock, like her grandparents' chilly wine cellar. She mimics Claude, Berthe and Luc, touches her forehead, heart, shoulder, shoulder, finger to her lips, *Amen.* There, the zigzag, just as she's practiced in Berthe's kitchen, just water, so why does it feel different here? It's holy water in the church, she remembers Berthe telling her, it's been blessed by the priest. Now her fingers smell like stale water, like icy stone. Maybe the water being blessed makes it colder, makes it smell like that.

There's another smell now, incense, Berthe told her. It's sweet, a smoky perfume. Like a pipe, like someone's father's pipe, a long time ago. She hurries to walk after Claude, Berthe, and Luc down the aisle, follows them in kneeling and another zigzag-cross, before filing into a row of rickety wooden chairs. She bows her head, hands clasped before her, sees Berthe watching, a tiny nod. Like Maman at the theatre, watching to make sure she was behaving properly, looked just right, doesn't look at all like a Jew, does she?

No, Scottish. She looks Scottish, yes. She pulls her braids in front, her golden red braids with their unbecoming yellow ribbons. It's good she doesn't look like a Jew. It means she's safe, they all are. It must have something to do with that one-fourth of her blood, the Christian part from her father's mother. But isn't all her blood mixed up inside her, anyway? How can you keep the non-Jewish blood and the all-Jewish blood separate inside one body?

And how different would she look if she were more percent Jewish, she wonders. Like the Jews in the Marais, maybe, where all the kosher shops were, the more different, foreign- looking ones. The men with their beards and hats and Shirley Temple curls at their ears, black suits with long white fringe, the women's heads covered with scarves, but not how her mother wore scarves. They all must have been fully Jewish, four-fourths, eight-eighths, one hundred percent. But the children still looked like her, like Claire, like anyone, school uniforms and knee socks and braids. Maybe that's why the Germans needed the Census, she thinks, to count the kids. Because how else would you know who had what percent kind of blood?

She hears voices singing, pretty uplifted young-boy voices, not the minor-key grovel songs of the rabbi and cantor, *shalom aleychem, ata echad,* she remembers. She looks quickly at the stained glass window up front, that's pretty, too, how it jewels the light. The crucifix catches her eye again, the bleeding, the wounds, no, that's not real, just a pretend dying Jesus, but suddenly there's another bleeding belly, she sees a bullet exploding there, a man bursting open, a man lying on the street, blood running in the gutter hot and thick. She sees his face twisted tight, and she swallows, her empty stomach cramps, *He died for you,* she hears. Died yelling in the street, *Juif,* in a bold stamp, dirty Jew. *Sale Juif.* Other people's fathers didn't die that horrible way. *Marie-Jeanne's* father didn't die that way, no. He died in a tragic car accident. Maybe taking food and clothing to orphans, even, when that happened. He was a hero, yes, Marie-Jeanne can be proud, glad he died like he did. Remember that. She turns away from the dead man.

A creaking of wood as everyone shifts, rises, turns toward the rear of the church. The priest is coming, Father Tournel, Berthe had told her, in a long black dress with a purple vest hanging down. There are boys in white smocks, one swinging a smoking metal basket on a chain. Father Tournel smiles at everyone as he passes to the front, wafting more sweet smoke, *"In nomine Patris, et Fillii, et Spiritus Sancti . . ."*

*"Amen,"* everyone says, and how pleasant his voice is, friendly and soft,

*"Gratia Domini nostri, Jesu Christi, et caritas Dei, et communicatio Sancti Spiritus sit cum omnibus vobis."*

*"Et cum spiritu tuo,"* Danielle responds with everyone. Perfect. What was that movie with Spencer Tracy, where he was a priest? Father Tournel seems nice like that, like a favorite teacher at school. The rabbis are scarier. She can imagine Father Tournel reading La Fontaine to them in his pleasant, soft voice. Although now she can't understand a single word he's saying.

Oh yes, the *Confiteor,* Berthe told her, we think of our sins and how we can become better, do a better job of serving God. *Mea culpa,* she hears everyone mumbling, *Mea culpa, my fault,* and you promise not to do the bad thing again and it all gets just swept away clean, so easy, like magic.

This is all so easy. More standing, kneeling, sitting, everyone's murmured responses like the drone of horseflies. Father Tournel, still speaking his incomprehensible Latin. He *could* be reciting La Fontaine, for all anybody knows. Like the rabbi, speaking Hebrew. Sitting with her mother in the synagogue, *shalom aleychem,* when her grandparents were alive and she and her mother would go visit them in Louveciennes, and *Baruch atah Adonai eloheynu melech ha-olam.* Her grandparents, Sarah and Jacob, their huge chilly house full of silver and crystal and porcelain, hard fragile things locked in glass cabinets. They kept kosher, so two sets of everything, china plates and silverware and different cupboards, even. She'd asked her mother what was wrong with milk and meat touching, and Maman just laughed, said her grandparents were old-fashioned, that's all, but God doesn't mind if we mix meat and milk at home, He doesn't judge for things like that. And if her grandparents ever ask, she should just lie and say they keep their milk and meat separate at home too, it would make them happy and God wouldn't mind that, either, such a kind little lie.

Father Tournel climbs a tiny wood staircase against the wall, and there's an upward ripple and creak as everyone sits straight. Pay attention, she thinks. He smiles down at them, smiling right at her, too, and she hurries to smile back.

"My friends. I welcome you this morning. I welcome you every time we are here, together, celebrating our Blessed Lord. It *is* a joy, is it not?"

Everyone smiles, nods. Danielle nods, too, smiling bright. Good Catholic girl.

"But this day I must make a confession to you. Yes, it is my turn for this, to seek your understanding. My dear friends, I must confess . . ." his smile, wavering, he glances down as if shamed, ". . . I must tell you how I am struggling now, to accept the joy our Lord wishes every one of us to find in His gentle embrace. I am finding this joy is tainted. Tainted by fear. This is a fearful time, a time of war and division, and perhaps there are those among you who are afraid as well. And so, I wish to share with you my fear, in brotherhood, to offer my comfort that you are not alone.

"We gather here to celebrate the Holy Sacrifice together. And we know that Christ is with us, to bless us with His mercy and His love. But Christ is not merely *present*, my friends. He *acts*. Through the giving of His own body and blood, through his sacred passion and death, He grants Salvation to us."

But dying is the end, she thinks, of everything. A dead person can't do anything, can't save anything, for anyone. No, listen, she reminds herself. Look as if you're listening, at least. Heavenly Father, yes, salvation, sacrifice, body and blood . . .

"And if Christ is not passive, neither can we be. Devotion is not merely showing up in body, going through the motions of ritual, reciting the words of ceremony. Christ was of flesh and blood, yes, but it is not the sacrifice of his body for which we owe our devotion. No, it is the sacrifice of *self*. And so, my friends, I must ask, are you giving wholly of yourself when you partake of the blessed host? Are you *truly* present with Christ, here in heart and mind and soul?"

How could she be more present? She nods more vigorously at Father Tournel, raises her clasped hands to her chest.

"Because if not, if we attend Mass and make our devotions as mere *show*, as *display* for our neighbors . . . If we content ourselves with prayers recited by a distracted mind . . . Then, my friends, this is *false* piety. It makes a *mockery* of faith. It is fraud. Deceit. A lying soul is an unclean soul. And that is a true sin before God."

He is looking right at Danielle now, looking through her, his tremulous smiles gone. He must have heard inside her head, somehow. When she was thinking about La Fontaine, Spencer Tracy. Remembering Hebrew. Laughing at *mea culpas*. Marie-Jeanne wouldn't be thinking any of that, no, she wouldn't be making a mockery. She swallows.

"And I fear for those among us who are guilty of that sin. Who sit here in body but are absent in spirit, who are not honest and true. You will be found out. You will be *judged*."

*God is my judge,* Danielle's judge, yes, it's true . . .

"My dear friends, open your heart to the holy feelings contained in the words of prayer, in this precious drop of blood! As St. Paul tells us. 'Whoever eats this Bread or drinks this Cup unworthily,' *unworthily*, my friends, 'He will be guilty of the Body and Blood of the Lord!'"

But she isn't guilty of all that, she can't be! God wants her to do this, He understands she has to lie. Doesn't He? Just little lies, to keep everyone safe. Kind little lies. Her breath is coming hard, fast, her heart beating in her fingertips, along her jaw. She sees Berthe glance over at her, wills herself to stop breathing, clench her teeth, to keep herself more perfectly still.

"Do not be the poor wretch to whom St. John Chrysostom spoke when he said, 'They slaughtered his most holy body, but *you* . . ."

*Her*, yes, Father Tournel is glaring at her,

". . . *you* receive him with a filthy soul!" glaring into her lying, unclean soul.

"Do not be guilty of this sin! Do not condemn yourself to the infernal tortures of Hell! The hell of eternal solitude, eternal banishment from His grace and light and love!"

God won't send her to Hell, will He? He won't banish her, abandon her. He wouldn't. He won't.

"My friends, I beg you, turn your face and open your soul to God. Under His wings, you may trust. And His trust shall compass you with a shield.

*"Agnus Dei, qui tollis peccata mundi . . ."*

It's over, then, the lecture. All over. She lets out a deep grateful breath, feels sweat at the roots of her hair, on her palms, the moist where the fingers clasp tight. Everyone is standing again, filing into the center aisle. Time to take Communion. Time to celebrate the sacrifice of Christ, when wine and bread become His body and blood. Hurry up, follow Luc. She stands, but her legs wobble, and she grabs for the back of Luc's coat. He doesn't notice, he's murmuring in prayer, he's present in heart and mind and soul, his head bowed. Breathe slowly, she tells herself, don't look deceitful. Don't look like a fraud. Like someone who is going to Hell. Like a Jew.

No, trust God. He'll compass me, shield me, of course He will . . .

But which God? She stumbles again, and a sharp glance from Berthe. The Jewish God or the Christian God? It must be the *Jewish* God who wants her to lie, she realizes. But it's the Christian God who is here, in church, seeing her filthy unworthy soul. How can she do this if she and Marie-Jeanne have two different Gods? Which God understands her? Which God's wings is she under? Maybe the Jewish God only expects three-fourths of her to do this, and the Christian God is watching the other one-fourth. But there's only one God, isn't there? And she can't separate her blood, divide herself in parts like a country, like a raspberry tart . . .

*Hear O, Israel, the Lord our God is One . . .*

She stumbles after Luc, up to the front where Father Tournel stands behind a railing. She will be found out. She will be judged. Liar, fraud. *Sale Juif.* They will come after her, marching and beating, her heart is beating in her fingertips now, her temples, the back of her throat, her throat is so dry, her throat has a hot rock in it. And who will come for her when she is found out, God or the Germans? She kneels when they kneel, it hurts her knees. And which Germans? The German soldier with the chocolate and the pretty twilight eyes? No, it must be the other Germans, the bad barbarian Germans. Do both kinds of Germans have the same God? She bows her head but watches sideways as Father Tournel holds up a round white thing, mumbles in Latin to Claude, who closes his eyes, tilts back his head, holds out his thick tongue. Then Berthe, then Luc.

"*Corpus Christi . . .*"

Her turn. Father Tournel is huge, looming, he'll see, he'll judge. He'll tell the Germans, everyone taken away and. . . She closes her eyes, holds out her dry tongue, just as rehearsed. How does the body of a dead person taste? She feels the thing placed on her tongue, closes her mouth around it. It's hard, flat, thin. But it tastes like nothing. Like a piece of matzoh at Passover. The seder dinner, matzoh wrapped in a linen cloth, the *afikomen,* hidden for her to find. She hurriedly crosses herself, stands, follows the family back to their row. It's over, you're safe. The host begins to soften on her tongue, melt. Like a wafer cookie. Not sweet, but how it melts to pulp in your mouth if you don't swallow right away. Like the wafer cookie you get with a cup of chocolate, every Sunday with her father, the music, a carousel. She'd eat hers right away, crunching it fast and loud, he'd smile, laugh in that way like a hug, then offer up his, every time, and this one she eats slowly so it will last, the one that tastes . . . *blessed,* she thinks, yes. Like holy water, maybe. It's melting on her tongue, a sweetish pulp in her mouth, and she smells the smell of incense, of him, smells his walking-away smell of pipe tobacco, smoky-sweet, and fountain pen ink and paper, leather binding and the dust of books. And she sees him, her father, not lying, dying on the street, not bleeding from his belly, not anguished, she sees him alive and for real, before the end of him. Before he died for her. She sees the curly dark hair he keeps short and brushed smooth, sees the fine threads of blue jacket—the blue one!—with the bits of green and gold in the weave, and the forest green tie, sees the small indentation on his third finger, right hand, from always holding a pen his whole life, sees his hand reaching up to show her the shifting twilight colors of the dog-to-wolf sky, *Look, Danielle, can you see, how beautiful?* And she looks, *Yes, Papa!,* and can see his face, smiling, *I'll be back soon,* and yet he's *here,* with her, her Papa, inside her very flesh and body and bones.

She opens her eyes, and she is sitting again, beside Luc and Berthe and Claude in the pew, and the last of the wafer is melting away. The feeling of him gone ghostly, fading, drifting away. She wants another wafer cookie. Another blessed host. She wants to get up, get back in line with the last of the villagers still at the altar with Father Tournel, taking their Holy Communion, and do it again. She tries not to swallow, doesn't want to lose the last of him in her mouth, doesn't want the taste and scent and sound of him to leave. But then it's gone, the very air just blank now, empty and cold. Baked flour. But next

Sunday. She can have this again, have her father, her blessed father, with her, good. With me, always. My Father.

"Dear Father, may the holy reception of Thy sacrament cleanse us from our old life and into the saving mystery through Our Lord, Jesus Christ. Let us pray."

Amen.

The kitchen looks pretty tonight, the fire snapping, the candles lit. All the flickers, the glow. The copper colander on the wall, the big wooden bowls, ceramic pitcher, the heavy sacks of dried corn and beans. A special Sunday supper, fresh bread and potatoes and rissoles with rabbit gravy, enough for everyone. A whole glass of fresh warm milk, she almost couldn't finish it but didn't want to be wasteful.

"We were very proud of you today, dear. You did very well."

"Thank you."

She's helping wash the dishes. She rubs a cracked plate around and around in the cooling oily dishwater. So many dishes, for four people. No, don't complain, she tells herself, even in your head. No electric lamps, yes, but a proper sink, at least, with running water. And a proper bathtub and toilet off the kitchen, be grateful for that. She thinks of Berthe washing her family's dishes, her grandmother, grandfather, Maman, her, then Berthe and Claude's own dishes, and little Luc's, too, that's dishes for seven and multiply that by two, because two sets of everything. She should be thankful Christians don't keep kosher. She should be thankful for so much. No more milk in Paris, and she hated the taste of pigeon. And Berthe says she'll always keep a few vegetables back from what we have to send north, just for our family, they're ours, after all, and no one will ever know. Be thankful for that, in these fearful, trying times, fresh vegetables to eat.

"School tomorrow, Marie." Berthe is busy with the pans of milk she'd put out that morning, fussing with the cream separator, but she's looking at Danielle. She's still worried.

"I know. I'm ready." She wipes her hands dry on a mended towel. She feels dreamy, sleepy, full of a clean and warm light. The wool dress Berthe made her wear this morning, it's softened now, fitting her better, warm. She would have been cold in her velvet dress today. She sees herself in the tiny mirror on the wall, sees the worn yellow ribbons on her braids, probably Berthe's from when she was little. She'd saved them all these years in that oak trunk, hoping she'd have a little girl someday, her own little Marie, and she could tie them on her Sunday braids. And all she got was Luc. No, Luc is a good son, she thinks, he never complains, maybe he doesn't milk the cow anymore, but he helps his father a lot, look at him now, carrying in that big bundle of kindling, stacking it by the oven for Berthe. And Claude, he's just not used to having a girl around, that's all. She watches Claude, by the fire, doing something with a small piece of wood, and her milking pail. Sanding a piece of wood smooth, fitting it against the sharp metal handle. For her, she realizes, Berthe must have told him how it hurts her to carry that pail when it's full, how the handle cuts into her palms. They're making sacrifices, they are, taking her into their home, giving her vegetables and milk, warm clothes. Good Christian charity, it's true. Berthe is sitting now, knitting from a skein of gray wool, the needles swift bright clicks, how does she do that so fast, her fingers swollen and split the way they are? They work so hard. Not mere show or display. And all she's done is act like a spoiled baby. An unworthy girl.

*Mea culpa*, yes.

"Good night, tante Berthe." She leans over to kiss Berthe on her round cheek.

"Good night, Marie-Jeanne." Berthe looks at her, startled, but pleased. "Sleep well, dear." She smooths her dry puffy hand over

Danielle's hair.

"Good night, tonton Claude." She hesitates, then pecks his rough face.

He pats her shoulder, reaching up awkwardly with his stiff arm. "Good night, child."

"Good night, Luc." She can't bring herself to kiss him, not yet, but she gives him a little wave where he stands near the stove, making up his bed on the floor. He twists his mouth in disdain. But he doesn't say anything mean. "And I'll be ready for school tomorrow. I promise."

"I know you will, dear . . . Marie-Jeanne?"

"Yes?"

"You'll say your prayers, won't you, before you go to bed?" Berthe looks hopeful. Her knitting at rest in her lap.

"Yes, tante Berthe." Danielle smiles at her. She will, she'll truly pray, just as her grandparents always told her to, not just ask for things, she'll turn her face to God with an open heart and soul. Trust in His shield.

And she'll learn to knit. Marie-Jeanne would know how. Tante Berthe will like teaching her.

"Good night."

She takes her candle, heads upstairs to her room in the flickery dark. There's a scent of fresh earth when she enters; the crack at the window, where the wet cold blows in, has been stuffed with a layer of clay. Tonton Claude, so kind of him. The room already feels warmer than before. She pulls her flannel nightgown from under the pillow, begins to unbutton her dress. Even Luc, she thinks. She sees him down in the kitchen, readying his pallet bed on the floor. In the corner, by the stove. A cramped space for such a big boy. She sees the crucifix on the wall above the bed, and her fingers stop unbuttoning. This was *his* room, she realizes, his bed. He gave up his room for her. How did she not see that? She should go thank him. Go thank them all, now.

She heads back down the stairs, careful in the shifting, unfamiliar shadows, then pauses at the middle landing, before Berthe and Claude's open bedroom door. What should she say? She hears murmuring voices from the kitchen, sees the wavers of light on the wall. Just tell them thank you for keeping you safe and warm, she decides. Tell them how much you truly appreciate the sacrifices they're all making. How grateful you are.

Inside the entrance to their bedroom is a small alcove, a rough curtain pulled across. She sees a lump near the bottom of the curtain, an angle of brown leather poking out. Her suitcase, there it is. Her father's small valise, the one her mother brought with them on the train. Her other clothes must be there, the nice things her mother must have packed. Maybe Berthe can snip off the bits of ribbon or lace, the dangerous too-fancy parts. She should learn to sew, too, she can be more help to Berthe that way.

She creeps inside, pulls her suitcase from behind the curtain, kneels, struggles to unsnap the latch. Her green dress with the pleats, it's just plain linen, and the suitcase opens. Maybe trim the lace from her blue blouse, and there's a cloth packed inside, stuffed full. She untucks it, and there's a sudden clinking and glimmers of light, flashes of color, the feel of hard and cold. A tangle of silver and gold, diamonds and emeralds and sapphires. Maman, dressing for the theatre, the Opera, to go out to dinner, like a queen. The pearl earrings, bracelets and brooches, the glittering combs. *All that beautiful jewelry of hers.* A small fortune, to trade or sell.

A payment.

The milk in her stomach makes a sour heave, the rabbit rises to acid in her chest, but she swallows it down, feels her throat seal itself up tight. She throws the cloth over the gleams, closes the lid of the suitcase, snaps it shut. Shoves it back to its hiding place in the alcove.

Closes the curtain.

She climbs back up the stairs to the darkening chill of her attic room. She kicks off her shoes, feels her sock catch on a crooked nail in the floor. She feels the thread pulled loose, the small hole made. She gets into the cold bed without bothering to change into her nightgown. She curls into a ball, shuts her eyes, and turns her face to the wall.

## *MY FRIENDS*

*by Marie-Jeanne Chantier*

*10 May, 1941*
*La Perrine, France*

*I am fortunate to have many good friends at school here in La Perrine. Hortense Gaillard has pretty blond hair and always knows all the answers in class. Her mother, Madame Gaillard, runs the grocery and Monsieur Gaillard is still a prisoner-of-war in Germany, but he will come home soon. Simone Leroux has sharp eyes and makes clever jokes—her parents run the café/tabac, and sometimes she brings old magazines for us to look at, and her brother is also a prisoner-of-war.*

*But my best friend is Genevieve Clermont. She is an only child, too, like I used to be before my dear cousin Luc became like a brother to me, so I know how sad and lonely that can be. Big families are happier and are very good for France because during the Republic not enough French women were having babies, and also so many of our brave and honorable young men have fallen in service to our country.*

*Genevieve and I both want to have many children someday, and be very good mothers. We both love to read, and we share all of our secrets. She has pretty long hair, and a pink satin bow to tie it back with, which is very becoming for a girl with dark hair.*

*Genevieve and I sit next to each other in school and walk*

*home together after church, and we promise we will always be like sisters.*

As if she could be best friends with anybody but Claire!

No, it's just for the bread, really. She stops for a moment, to admire her graceful penmanship, her actress-in-a-movie words, to warm her hands at the tiny candle glow. She wishes she had saved a morsel from supper to eat, here in her room before bed, when she can feel her stomach gnaw. They're allowed to keep less of their wheat now and Claude is always grumbling that Genevieve's father could charge less at the mill or keep back more grain than he does. And then Berthe always reminds him Vichy officials are going to weigh the sacks of flour he sends, but Claude grumbles anyway. He still sends his sunflower seeds to the mill to be pressed for oil, and his wheat and dried corn. They can keep some of their own corn without anyone noticing, though - Berthe has been making the family's bread with less and less wheat, and more and more corn, and it's too sweet, it doesn't smell as rich or fill you up the same way. But we aren't really hungry, not most of the time, Danielle chides herself, we're lucky about that here in La Perrine. They say it's so miserable and hard to be in the Occupied Zone these days, but those stories can't all be true, can they? When they show Paris in the newsreels everyone looks so happy and fine, free of all care.

Are you happy and fine, Claire? she thinks. And your maman and papa? Remember how your papa lifted me up on his shoulder at your birthday party that time, to show me how the magician made the illusion with his swirly cape? Your papa was always a little bit like mine and my papa was always a little bit like yours, and so we were almost sisters, and one big family for real. Are you safe, all of you? I worry about you a lot, even though I don't talk to you as much inside my head anymore. But you don't need to worry about me, I'm just so busy these days with chores and school . . .

How worried she'd been, how frightened, that very first day in class! But school was so easy here, and boring, no music or literature, it's all what country invaded what country when and why, and when Monsieur Monzie wrote equations on the board it was always goats from the flock or bushels of grain being carried to market. And the other girls, Simone and Hortense, they were friendly, asking about Paris and ladies' fashions and what did the German soldiers look like were they all blond and handsome, did they want to marry French girls? The questions made her nervous at first, until she realized they were just unsophisticated peasant girls, is all. So she made up stories, how *Marie-Jeanne* lived in an unfashionable neighborhood, her mother made gloves and took in fine sewing, her father was just a regular middle-school teacher. Oh no, *Marie-Jeanne* has never been to the Opera! She's never been to one of those fancy tea shops they see in the old magazines Simone's father lets them read. They talk about mending socks and saving up for hair ribbons and which boys at school are dreamy, and Danielle steals bits to put in her own Marie-Jeanne stories and tell right back to them, *Oh yes, I want lace edging on my Confirmation dress, too!* And they believe it all. But being fake friends that way, where nothing you say is real or true, is like having doubled sentences in her head all the time and having to keep the true sentence trapped inside while the lie of a sentence comes out her mouth. Like when she studied English at her *lycee* in Paris, how she made the real French sentences in her head first then said them aloud in English, and she'd feel so sleepy and a little dizzy afterward. But maybe someday she'll get used to translating the truth into the right lies without doubling up like that.

Sometimes she sees her real mother in her mind, wearing her embroidered gloves she ordered special from St. Junien, and her real father, at a lectern at the University, but then that burning in her throat begins, the clutch in her belly that isn't a hunger for food, so she just wipes those pictures out of her head, she pretends her mind is a chalkboard she can sweep clean. Like *mea culpas* sweep away sins, *pouf*! Easier that way, like Berthe says, it's best to forget everything, from before.

Genevieve was that pretty girl she saw at church the first time, all by herself, who Luc mean-glared at, and who she'd had to sit next to at school the first day, *Chantier* next to *Clermont*. She was still wearing that satin bow and hardly spoke at all to Danielle, sort of snobby, the rich girl of the village showing off, she'd thought. But the first time Danielle went to get Claude's sunflower oil from the mill, Genevieve invited her in. There was a nice fresh-baking smell coming out the door and she figured they could probably have all the wheat they wanted, Genevieve and her papa, and maybe Genevieve would be neighborly about that and share, so she went. They didn't have wallpaper or carpet but there was a kitchen at one end and a proper living room at the other, with a sofa and crocheted doilies. But the best thing, they had books! Shelves and shelves, poetry and novels, even. The only books at Berthe and Claude's were an old bible and religious ones she was supposed to study but were too boring to actually read. And she could smell the books, too, that dusty paper smell, even better than bread, she missed real books so much, wanted to touch them, open them, but then she thought, would *Marie-Jeanne* like to read that much? She was standing there, trying to decide if that was dangerous or not, and Genevieve said, "You can borrow them, my father won't mind."

Then she said, "I'm so sorry about your parents."

Everyone knew the fake story about her, well, Marie-Jeanne's parents, and how they died, but the whole village has someone dead or killed in their family now, from before the Armistice, and no one talks much about it. So she was surprised to hear someone say that, about her parents. And Genevieve was looking at her as if she knew there was something else, a real thing to be sorry about, and Danielle wondered if she was trying to trick her, get her to make a mistake, and how maybe Berthe was right, she should just keep to herself and not get too friendly with anyone because that's safer. So she shrugged and asked for her jar of oil. She said she needed to go help tante Berthe in the garden, she had chores to do. But Genevieve unwrapped a cloth from something, a loaf of bread left to cool, she was slicing the bread, fresh hot nutty-brown wheat bread, Danielle could see the steam, see how good it would taste. And Genevieve offered her a big piece, a warm brown grainy slice with melting butter. So she sat and ate the bread and Genevieve talked about her favorite books and was Marie-Jeanne going to see the new movie when it arrived, and she was wishing the whole time she could send Claire a piece of that good bread. She felt so lonely for her. But then she realized Genevieve might be lonely, too, only her father to talk to. Genevieve's mother had died when she was born so she never had a mother at all, a real or a fake one, and maybe that's why she looked sad that way.

So, "I'm sorry about your mother," Danielle said, and then Genevieve looked surprised—people probably hadn't said that to her in a long time, either. Monsieur Clermont came in from the mill, he was very nice but he looked so old, she could see all the wrinkles on his face under the wheat dust like when a lady wears too much face powder, and he had a strange accent that left letters out of some words and twisted up others. He fetched the jar of sunflower oil for Danielle, and a sack of flour, and Genevieve helped her carry them home, but then Luc met them on the road and yelled at Danielle for being late. He grabbed the flour from Genevieve, gave her a long mean look, and she turned a hot pink, Danielle could see her trembling, like she was scared of him, and Luc told her she better get home, too. She doesn't know why Luc hates Genevieve so much, always bringing her name up just to make mean cracks.

But don't worry, Claire, she thinks. I won't be real friends with her. Just pretend friends.

So I can eat that bread, sometimes.

She brushes a lead-speck from her last crossed *t*. Perfect. Monsieur Monzie will be so happy. She sets her nub of a pencil down, rubs her cold fingers, still so cold here at night, and there's that stomach-gnaw again. She puts her essay away in her satchel, blows out the candle, hurries into her icy bed.

Remember, Claire, she thinks, how I used to cross my eyes as a joke for my father, and he'd laugh and tell me if I blinked they'd be stuck that way, the whole world doubled up and crossing over itself forever? I was always just careful not to blink. But now the Marie-Jeanne me and the Danielle me have to be crossed over and doubled together all the time, and it's such a queasy feeling. I still have to be so careful. I'd hate to get stuck this way forever, just because I blinked.

~

**July, 1941**

*Work, Family, Homeland!*

Claude is affixing a large color poster of Marshal Petain on the kitchen wall, so his eyes will now gaze down at them every minute of the day. But better to have Marshal Petain staring at them all the time than the dying Jesus, Danielle thinks. And they are kind eyes, a pretty ice blue, even the white mustache looks kind, and the hat on his head like a monkey's cap. Claude is crazy about Marshal Petain, the way Berthe is crazy about the Virgin Mary. He served under the Marshal at Verdun, our brave heroic leader, the only one who truly loved his men, who fought with us and wept for us, the foot soldiers, the cavalry, the ones in the trenches, carrying the burden, losing our lives, our arms and legs, our lungs, our sight, he was the only one to truly appreciate our sacrifice! Claude wears his *Legion d'Honneur* pin, is proud of the colored threads in his buttonhole and the old medals he's dug out of Berthe's trunk and polished and wears on Sundays, proud to be a member of the new veteran's club, *La Legion des Combattants,* created by Marshal Petain to honor the forgotten men of the Great War. Most of the older men in the village have joined, some of them blind or with a stiff and crooked limb like Claude, or missing fingers, a hand, or a whole leg like Simone's father, Monsieur Leroux, who wears a jointed wooden one with a wooden foot that creaks. They meet once a week at Monsieur Druot's big café and talk about helping the prisoners-of-war and planning patriotic events, or they listen to the endless radio broadcasts from Vichy. Although Berthe has told Danielle she thinks it's mostly an excuse for the men to sit around and complain about the cost of sulfur or finding tractor parts, to drink pastis and swap old war stories they already all know by heart. Even Father Tournel attends, although he was too young to serve in the Great War, and Berthe is certain he doesn't drink the pastis. Claude is proud to be in service to the Marshal again, to have sworn his oath of eternal loyalty and help *remake a people, restore a soul to France!* Yes, Petain will save us. Shield us, redeem us.

"Petain *is* France," Claude insists, the phrase he inserts now in every conversation he has. "*Work, Family, Homeland*! That's the true spirit of our country! True patriotism!"

"Yes, Tonton," Danielle says, nodding. She is sewing an apron of coarse linen, trying not to prick her fingers. She used to leave tiny blood spots on cloth she was working with, had angered Berthe more than once that way. But she is better at it, now; Berthe has allowed her to make this apron all by herself, only now and then checking the work. Well, not really all by herself—she has sometimes taken the apron to Genevieve for help, not wanting Berthe to see how clumsy she still was. She is glad to focus on making those tiny stitches even, glad Claude is satisfied by her nodding along at his words. She hears enough of these speeches from Monsieur Monzie at school, at church on Sundays, from the newsreels, from Marshal Petain himself on the small wireless Claude has purchased so they might all listen to his broadcasts as a family. It is a litany, it reminds her of learning the prayers when she first got here six months ago, the same words over and over until they're flat and seamless in her mind and she can forget worrying about what they actually mean. Or like how Berthe knits, her fingers automatic, barely ever glancing down at her work. Danielle can't imagine how many ration tickets that radio cost, but at least Claude lets them listen to music in the evenings, too, when there isn't a speech from Our Glorious Leader or news reports about German progress in Bulgaria, in Yugoslavia, in Greece. When Germany and Italy declared war on the Soviet Union, Claude was ecstatic for days, *Finally,* the Communists will know defeat! Better Hitler than Stalin, far far better! She hopes he will not rant too much about the Communists tonight. But it confuses her how sometimes Claude talks so happily about the Germans winning the war, then turns around and calls them *krauts, sales boches*. Wasn't it German shrapnel that destroyed his shoulder in the Great War? So how can he want to walk hand-in-hand with them now? Well, if Stalin is so much worse than Hitler, she reasons, Soviet shrapnel must be far worse than the German kind.

Claude has also bought a present for Berthe, a scarf of real silk, red and blue and white, emblazoned with Marshal Petain's face and a border of double-bladed axes, the symbol she sees everywhere now, on the posters pasted to buildings, at the beginning of newsreels, on the front pages of newspapers at the tabac. It is the symbol of *La Revolution Nationale,* a glorious new era for France. A return to honor, Claude says. And moral order, and discipline, the rule of law. Berthe doesn't like the scarf much, Danielle can tell, although she wears it to church or when she visits with other women in the village. Danielle had seen the scarf in Madame Richie's dry goods shop, knows exactly how many ration tickets it cost and thinks it's sad that Berthe doesn't appreciate the quality of the silk. There are pictures of Philippe Petain on everything now, Petain playing cards, ashtrays, clocks. Hortense's mother, Madame Gaillard, keeps a Petain bust on their fireplace mantel, right next to a photograph of Hortense's killed-in-the-war brother and her prisoner-of-war father. Madame Gaillard likes to tell everyone it's marble, although Danielle knows it's really just plaster of paris—*Like she tells everyone those pearls around her neck are real*, Berthe says, *but they're really just paste*!—and it's Hortense's job to keep it dusted and festooned with fresh flowers. Simone's little sister has a Marshal Petain coloring book that teaches the alphabet by assigning each letter to an important activity the Marshal performs as Head of State, or to various fine qualities of his character: *A* for *amour*, for Petain's love of France; *H* for the *honneur* he brings their country; *T* for *travail*, all his hard work on their behalf. The two new baby boys in the village have been named Philippe. At school Monsieur Monzie stands beneath the huge portrait of Marshal Petain and hands out special vitamin cookies, to be sure they won't have any deficiencies, and it reminds Danielle of eating that Communion wafer below the big bleeding Jesus. They stand at attention every morning, after reciting the Our Father, to sing the new anthem, *Marechal, nous voila*!

*A sacred flame rises from our native soil,*
*And enraptured France*
*Salutes you, Marshal!*
*All your children, who love you,*
*And honor your years,*

*Have answered your supreme call*
*By saying Here!*

And she sings along with the others, loudly, chest puffed out. It's just a song, after all, meaningless as all those stupid prayers.

Once a month everyone at school has to write to the Marshal, telling him what they are doing to help the National Revolution and thanking him for all he does. Danielle and Genevieve make things up in their letters—*This week we knit three pairs of socks for our brave prisoners- of-war! This week we got up early and performed calisthenics, to keep ourselves healthy and strong for France!*—and they laugh together over their lies. When Monsieur Monzie shows the once-a-month movie for everyone at the schoolhouse—some forgettable comedy or melodrama, or the men-in-the-shadows espionage ones Luc loves, only old French or German films now, nothing from America or England since the embargo, but hardly anyone goes when it's a German one—the newsreels show young boys planting oak trees in Marshal Petain's honor, skinny athletes showing off to his proud applause, the Marshal on all his tours of small towns, waving to the cheering crowds, being presented with flowers and gifts, awarding medals to mothers of large, pure-French families—bronze for five children, silver for eight, a gold medal for ten! And, to a fifteenth child, the honor of the Marshal himself standing as godfather! He pats schoolchildren on the head, urges them to sacrifice, to show their patriotism by working hard, to conserve every scrap of paper and metal and rubber and glass and wood. *I am counting on you children to help me rebuild France!* he announces, and she and Genevieve laughed together at the Marshal admiring the stick-figure drawings children scribble for him. And laughing with Genevieve reminds of her, just a little, of being with Claire.

"*Liberte, egalite, fraternite,* where did *that* lead us, I ask you?"

Claude is asking the wall, hammering away at a nail. "Communists, enemies of the Church, fancy university men who never did an honest day's work, who promised us, what?"

*Jews and academics,* she hears, feeling the needle pierce cloth then fingertip skin, almost, and she catches herself, after all, Marie-Jeanne's father wasn't a professor, not weak and soft, just a regular old middle-school teacher, yes . . .

"The *Republic.*" Claude says that word with disgust, like always, as if he'd like to spit. "A republic of *cronies.* No discipline, no respect for duty. Godless schools. Petain's right, it wasn't our brave troops that failed us, it was the politicians. The corruption. He was right to purge our prefectures and government offices of such men. We can hold our heads high now. Take our place again in the world."

"Yes, Tonton, of course." Nodding, nodding. She studies her fingers. No blood, but look at her hands, her nails broken, cuticles split, how horrified her mother would be! And callused, too, from struggling to wield the big pitchfork, roughened from handling raw wool and splintered wood, from scrubbings in icy water and Berthe's harsh homemade soap that smelled of rancid fat. But the soap in Madame Richie's shop cost too many ration tickets. Everything gets counted in tickets now, it's impossible not to always be figuring in her head. So-many mouthfuls of meat (when they can even *get* meat, the charcuterie in the village selling mostly rabbit and some wild fowl now, no more sausage or ham) costs so-many tickets; so-many steps in a new pair of leather shoes (new boots for Luc, that is), so-many cigarettes for Claude to puff, pinches of salt, drops of oil to light the lamps. Everything has its value calculated by those small colored paper squares.

Even her. She knows Claude and Berthe count her every sip of tea, every scrape of butter on her flavorless wheat-and-corn bread. They admonish her not to stay up so late doing her homework, reading all those books, to think of the many candles she burns. She is still too careless with things, is constantly reminded the new ceramic bowl for her milk cost *x* number of tickets and can't she be more careful when she washes it next time, to avoid getting it cracked, to think next time of the cost? The waste and cost of *her*, she knows that's what they mean. She has come to be truly grateful for everything they can make or grow themselves and thus spare some tickets—and herself more chastisement—to use for hoarding or trade. There are murmured rumors of people going hungry in the northern Occupied Zone, Paris and Tours and Reims, boiling their shoes and eating rats, mayors posting notices warning against the eating of cats. More and more of France's good food is being given to the Germans, they say French people are beginning to starve, are begging in the city streets, although the newsreels show people everywhere looking happy and well-fed and busy with all their industrious work. Are you free of all care, Claire, she wonders. Are you getting enough to eat? Are you safe?

And she wonders, sometimes, when she lets that kind of wondering slip in, if her mother is begging on a city street somewhere, rummaging through trashcans and dumpsites. Or in the countryside, wandering from farm to farm, begging for scraps, chewing on rotted, bird-pecked cobs of corn. How is her mother, her elegant mother, who sniffed at day-old bread and poured out unfinished bottles of fine wine and went without coffee rather than sip that bitter ersatz drink, who peeled skins from potatoes in thick wasteful slices, even after the Germans came, how is her mother eating, getting by? She wonders if her mother is boiling her father's boots for a meal. Chasing fat rats down alleys. Killing and stewing a stray cat and becoming ill, lying sick in the streets, feverish and covered with lice . . . She gets the hot burn in her throat when she wonders that, tries not to think about it, tries to sweep that image clean from her mind.

Yes, she has come to be grateful for milking the cow, after the first weeks of her awkward and nervous squeezing, forever, it took, to fill the pail, Luc sniping instructions and the revolting smell of rotting hay and manure in her nose. She is grateful for her daily rich glass of milk, for the cheese Claude can slice without measuring grams. She has come to be grateful for weeding the vegetable garden, for the sudden summer explosion of green-then-red tomatoes they can eat without counting, the abundant cabbages and squashes and leeks, the gritty potatoes and turnips and rutabagas to dig and stack in the root cellar for the coming winter, even the onion and garlic she strings and braids into bumpy ropes to hang from the beams in her attic room, leaving the reek on her hands for hours. She's grateful to the sheep for the sweater she wears, a warm one Berthe miraculously spun and knit for her from a scribble of greasy wool, the pretty green one she brought with her is full of tiny holes now, and practically outgrown anyway. She's grateful for the brown rabbits that produce babies for them to raise and kill and eat, although she still can't bear to look when Berthe or Luc snap their necks or strip their skins from the purple muscle. She's grateful when Berthe sends her to gather wild dandelion leaves or berries, grateful to escape from the dark house and be alone for a few hours to recite fables to herself or remember her favorite movies, imagine the shivery red-velvet moment of the cinema curtains parting to reveal the screen, the singing and dancing and lovely women wearing satins and jewels, although in those quiet alone spaces she must often sweep away the visions of another beautiful woman in satin, a dark-haired man proudly listening to her recite, applauding. She is happy to tug fruit from the scratchy brambles that line the creek, to have to scrub berry stains from her dress, all so they can have their morning spoonful of jam, never mind how that jam gets more and more bitter as the sugar ration gets cut, and then cut again. Berthe walks into the village twice a week to trade those berries with Madame Gaillard at the grocery, for tea; their extra potatoes and onions go to Monsieur

Leroux at the tabac. This is not, strictly, allowed, this kind of trade. But even Claude, to get an extra few cigarettes' worth of tobacco, is willing to bend Marshal Petain's rules. The *gray market*, they call it, *le systeme*, it's just how you make do, and it's in the spirit of France to keep our community, our one large family, healthy and strong. They even send Luc to work at the mill sometimes, to help Genevieve's father, to trade his labor for some extra wheat, and when Luc arrives home he grumbles and scowls even more than usual, and won't speak to anyone for hours. When she'd started school Danielle was mortified to learn Claude and Berthe expected her to trade with her schoolmates; they sent her to class with eggs hidden in her pockets and school satchel and instructions to trade with Simone. But Simone, practical-minded, a merchant's daughter, took this as matter-of-fact, even gave her a lesson in bargaining: *No, Marie-Jeanne, you must offer me eight and tell me no more, I will insist on ten and no less, and in the end you say nine and I'll accept. What do you think "bargaining" means?* Danielle brought back several old magazines from the tabac for those nine eggs; Berthe tears them to strips for the family to use as toilet paper.

Yes, even she is worth *x* number of tickets. Once a month a stuffed envelope arrives, addressed to *Monsieur Claude Morel*, with no return address and never the same postmark. Each envelope contains food and clothing ration tickets; she is not allowed to handle them, but she has seen Claude and Berthe counting the paper squares, and she knows it is a generous and illicit share. Her heart began to pound, that first time with Berthe at the dry goods shop, watching Berthe quietly slip those extra tickets to Madame Richie and waiting for Madame Richie to question them or alert the authorities. But Madame Richie had merely nodded, tucked the tickets in her pocket and hurried to fetch bolts of cloth. She knows these extra tickets are *black market* tickets, worse than the gray market, dangerous and very much against the rules. But again, this seems to be a rule Claude is willing to break. Once a month he smokes cigarettes more luxuriously, one after another, sucking in deep mouthfuls of smoke and the smell of it lingers for days. And Berthe's Petain scarf, too, knotted around her neck just days after that last package arrived.

The first envelope had appeared two weeks after Danielle came to La Perrine. She'd been allowed to open it and her hands were eager, despite herself. Inside, only a crisp *carte d'identité*, issued by Vichy, obligatory for all French citizens, for a *Chantier, Marie-Jeanne,* age twelve; status: orphan; address: c/o Monsieur Claude Morel, uncle, La Perrine, Limousin. A photo of herself Danielle recognized from over a year ago, when her father had taken her to a portrait studio as a gift for her mother, her hair in smooth braids and tied with green ribbons, her cheeks rounder than they seemed now in the tiny mirror on the kitchen wall. There was also a baptismal certificate, appropriately well-worn, dog-eared, the print slightly faded, the official stamp embossed but weathered flat, attesting to Marie-Jeanne Chantier's baptism, at L'eglise St. Pierre in Paris, parents Paul and Rachel Chantier. The printed names on these documents were startlingly official. Her first identity card, but it wasn't her. Official, but a lie. And she must keep this card with her at all times, even here in the Free Zone. No, the *Unoccupied* Zone; the Germans have recently forbidden it to be called *Free*. All French citizens must show their identity card at once to any French official who asks, *Your papers, please, papers?* We are still in charge of ourselves here, Claude always points out, there are no Germans policing us here, no foreigners telling us what to do.

But no letter, no handwritten note in her mother's graceful hand. There has never been any word at all. Every time an envelope arrived she felt the flutter in her chest and her stomach go clutch, could hear a light laugh, see a shiny red crown of a braid, smell the scent of rose, *I'll come back for you!* She would be able to *see* those words, a promise written down, in ink, real and official, not just a fading memory-voice in her head. Berthe saw her face the first few times those envelopes were opened, their illicit tickets spilled out, and quietly told her afterward how dangerous a letter or note would be. But she's better at keeping her face still now, uninterested. She doesn't even bother to open them when Claude offers. Those envelopes have nothing to do with her, she reminds herself. Just a business exchange. A bit of bargaining. Like toilet paper for eggs. Like jewelry for her. But she wonders, sometimes, if her mother has her own fake identity, Undergound. A fake name, fake religion. But that leads to wondering other things. Maybe she has a fake daughter she tells lies about. A perfect daughter, who always wears her gloves and keeps herself tidy, never has messy braids or makes a mistake. Maybe, for her mother, she is not only not Marie-Jeanne, but no longer even Danielle.

Or—this has never occurred to her before, the needle paused in the cloth—what if her mother didn't go Underground at all? What if that was a lie? What if her mother left her here, then strolled back to Limoges under the lightening sky, boarded a train, simply gone home? What if she's back in Paris, in their apartment, sitting at her vanity mirror, putting on lipstick, dabbing on rose perfume, preparing for a night at the theatre, an elegant restaurant? Maybe she's spotted her mother in a newsreel, even, one of the free-of-all-care women walking so cheerfully along the streets of Paris. No more husband or little girl ghosts to worry about, no. Because a handsome sky-eyed German soldier offered her a piece of chocolate, and she was so hungry, maybe, and ill from living on rats and cats and so she took the sweet fat chocolate from him, ate the entire thing herself without a daughter to complain about no dessert and watery milk, and now a well-pressed-uniformed German officer is waiting to take her arm, escort her to the Opera. There have been rumors about this, German officials dining at Maxim's, squiring beautiful French women about like trophies of war, all of them laughing as they open bottle after bottle of expensive champagne and feast on chocolates and the best cuts of beef. Such women, what dishonor, what shame! Danielle has heard such women whispered about among Berthe and her friends in the village, *hussies, tramps,* before Berthe notices her listening, and hushes Madame Richie.

This is even worse than her mother starving, begging for food. A German officer fastening pearls around her mother's fragrant neck, giving her jewels to make up for the ones she traded away . . .

No, sweep that all away. She focuses on the linen in her lap. Takes a fresh stitch.

"And the Freemasons, Papa," Luc is saying. "They were always plotting against us. And the Jews. That's where the corruption really comes from."

"Luc," says Berthe, glancing up from her knitting and over at Danielle. Danielle says nothing. A crooked stitch, better pull it out, start over.

"Maman, everyone knows that. It isn't some big secret." Luc is working polish over his leather boots. He has new boots, now, as a member of the *Chantiers de Jeunesse,* the Vichy-blessed youth group, obligatory for boys in their late teens, although Claude still had to use four full months' of ration tickets to get them. Luc was officially too young to enlist, but had begged and begged, and Claude and Monsieur Druot privately agreed to alter Luc's carte d'identite by a few years, so Luc might leave school and go off with the older boys to learn how to march and drill, pitch tents, make charcoal for fuel, stuff boxes and sacks with La Perrine produce to send north. They are contributing to the regeneration of France, these fine young men. They are receiving a *physical, spiritual, and moral education!* the newsreels announce, showing thin-limbed boys marching out of sync while singing patriotic songs of duty and sacrifice. Danielle thinks they look ridiculous, strutting around in their boots. Her own shoes are wearing down at the heels. Starting to pinch.

"They infiltrated our government and drove us into war, so they could profit. They try to look normal and make people think they're like everyone else, but"—she stabs her needle into the cloth and tugs, splitting the threads—"they're not. They're physically and morally unclean. And now they're laughing at us, the rich ones are, anyway, they're off having a good time in Nice and Monte Carlo, with our money. We can't ever let that happen again."

"Such foolishness." Berthe knitting, waves at his words without missing a stitch.

"Vallat said so himself, Maman. At the *CGQJ*."

"What is that?"

Luc sighs, takes on the air of a know-it-all student, the look that reminds her of Hortense, always showing off in school. "The General Commission on Jewish Affairs. In Vichy. Xavier Vallat's in charge now. He's a real patriot, too, he doesn't want the krauts running everything, telling us what to do."

"No one's telling our leaders what to do, Luc. We're still a sovereign nation."

"Of course, Papa. That's why the Marshal brought in Vallat. He believes in French independence. He wants us to handle the problem in our own way."

"What problem?" Berthe asks.

"The *problem*. They're doing studies in Paris all about it. The racial differences between us and them."

"Racial differences, what is that? As if we're people and goats. People and cows. God made us all in His image. We all get cold in winter and warm in summer, that's all there is to it."

"I'm talking about *science*, Maman. They can measure things in people now, like in cells with microscopes. They can test blood. It's all being proved. The Jews aren't like regular people, they carry their own special diseases that can infect us and—"

"All right, that's enough, Luc." Berthe thrusts her knitting aside. "You're just wasting polish on those boots now. You go bring some wood in for me." She gets up, turns her back on him to fill the teakettle. "Marie, dear," she says in a softer voice, "would you see if we have any tea left, please?"

"Yes, Berthe," she says. Tea, yes, *the Jews*, Luc going on again, she fumbles with the tea tin, hoping there's enough, maybe she should go take some turnips to Madame Gaillard to trade . . . No, there's some left. She hands the tea to Berthe, picks up her sewing again, picks at the crooked stitch, the needle slipping in her sweaty fingers, she could leave, take the apron to Genevieve's, they could sew together at her house, so quiet there, that would be nice . . .

"We're all His children, it's that simple, and I want you to remember that," she hears Berthe saying. "Your fancy science doesn't tell me anything different."

"Maman, you don't *see* the danger. That's what's so perilous. How they can infiltrate everywhere. Someone just walking down the street, they look like everyone else. Or you maybe see at school, you don't think . . ." He rubs final specks of dust from his boots. "We have to stay on our guard or they'll—"

"Now Luc, stop a moment. Your mother's right, in a way," Claude says. "We have to be very careful in matters like this, not get so carried away. Not be bigoted. Or ignorant."

"Yeah, I know, Papa, but we can't just—"

"We have to make distinctions. It isn't the French Jews to worry about, the ones who've been here generations. I fought side by side with French Jews in the Great War, some of them were very brave. Good patriots. Your grandfather," he says to Danielle, pointing his sausage finger at her, "he was a good man, child. An officer. A fine solider. You can be proud of him."

She is startled; in the six months she has been here, been Marie-Jeanne, there has been almost no mention of her other life, of before. But she says nothing, just catches a breath, lowers her eyes and rips, finally, that stubborn bad stitch from the cloth. It could be a test. A trick. Berthe had called her *Danielle* a couple of weeks ago, then scolded when she'd looked up. Berthe hasn't done it since, but she almost wishes she would, it would be nice to hear her name again. That name, her real name. Like roses on a satin bedspread and chocolate, socks with lace, all in one word. Luc is ignorant, that's all, trying to sound like he knows things. And Claude is talking about some other girl's grandfather, clearly. *Marie-Jeanne*'s grandfather wasn't a Jew. She looks down, sees a tiny red bloom on the linen. She hadn't even felt the needle's sting. She'll soak the stain out tonight, so Berthe will never see.

"No, our French Jews are good Israelites. The Marshal has nothing against them," Claude is saying. "And I'm sure this Commissioner . . . ?"

"Vallat, Papa."

"Yes, I'm sure he understands that. It's the foreign ones, the immigrants. They've taken advantage of us. They should never've been allowed to come here in the first place."

"Or become citizens," Luc says.

"You're right about that, yes. But they're fixing that now, I read in the paper."

"Who is 'they'?" Berthe asks. "The Germans?"

"No, of course not. Our own French officials, just as Luc says. French police. They're rounding up the foreign Jews in Paris."

Yes, that's who they're talking about, she thinks. Foreign people. Like in the Marais neighborhood, the foreigners. Their funny beards and beanies and scarves, foreign languages, customs, food . . .

"Rounding them up?" Berthe asks.

"Gathering them together." Claude positions another nail. "To send away."

"Send them where?"

Claude shrugs, hammers. "Away. Back wherever they came from. Poland, Germany . . ."

"Poland's part of Germany now, Papa."

"Well, good, let the Germans have all of them back. How many of their own Jews came running over here in the past few years? Expecting us to take care of them?"

"And we did, too," says Luc. "We just let them come in. And they took over our cities and towns. Our jobs. Stuff that's ours, that we make and work for. They exploit our labor."

"But they live here, they work here, have families. How can they deport so many people?" Berthe asks.

"Not *deport*, Berthe, *resettle*, that's all. They're foreigners at heart, they'll never be true Frenchmen." Claude searches for another nail. "Back to their own homes and farms and factories. And all those jobs will be waiting for our own men when they come home. Like Petain has promised us." He hammers again. "We'll have a France that belongs to the French."

He finishes his hammering, stands back to admire. It is slightly crooked, he decides. He rubs his stiff arm, begins prying nails from the wall. He will hang it again so that it is perfect.

~

**October, 1941**

Monsieur Monzie is delighted. He has been waiting months for a package to arrive from Vichy, supplies for the latest special school project. He gets so excitable about such things, clapping his hands, fussing with his wire spectacles and working his eyebrows. He joins them in singing to the Marshal every morning—

*You have worked ceaselessly*
*For the common salvation!*
*For giving us your life,*
*Your genius and your faith!*
*Marshal, we are here!*

—his hands clutching his heaving chest. "Because our dear Marshal *loves* you children," he quotes from the newsreels, "he *loves* children who work hard and sacrifice and obey!" He practically jumps up and down when students write correct answers on the board: "*Yes, yes"!* he proclaims. Danielle and Genevieve agree he is foppish and odd; they imitate him—*Yes, yes*? *Yes, yes*!—giggling, when they are alone.

For the first project of the new school year each student had to learn and report everything about the saint for which they were named. The younger students were to draw pictures of their saint performing whatever act gained them sainthood, but the older students were to write a story about their saint's miraculous act, and why the saint was so holy he or she deserved to be a saint. Danielle, with a choice between the Virgin Mary or Jeanne d'Arc, chose Jeanne. It would be too easy to make a mistake with Mary, to get a detail wrong about a thing like the *Immaculate Conception.* She had Berthe's old copy of *A Children's Catechism,* mostly endless lists of questions-and-answers she was supposed to memorize so she'd know everything about being Catholic and Christian, *Who is God?* and *What is Hell?* and *How do we keep Sunday holy*? But what was the point of being given the questions *and* the answers, she'd wondered, and then not be allowed to come up with more questions of your own?

But the Immaculate Conception really made no sense. Her mother had told her how babies were made when she was just a child, so long ago it didn't even hurt to remember, how someday she would find blood in her underpants and shouldn't be scared, it would only be her body changing, her monthly courses, her *regles,* it would mean she was a grown-up woman and could conceive a baby, and *pat pat,* Maman had leaned forward and patted Danielle gently on the cheek, smiling, saying Jewish tradition meant she'd get a tiny slap that first time of blood, but only this kind of *pat pat,* it was *a welcome to becoming a woman, cherie, not a punishment.* And she'd explained how babies were conceived between a husband and wife, how beautiful it was, that special kind of love between married people. It had all sounded very medical to Danielle, and queasy-making; when she looks at the grubby boys at school, or at Luc, she can't imagine touching any of them like that, or having them touch her—none of them were *dreamy* at all, not like Spencer Tracy or Franchot Tone. And she could sense, from the way the boys would make jokes she didn't quite understand, and how Monsieur Monzie would tell them to *Settle down, young gentlemen!* that it must have less to do with love or beauty and more with something shameful and unclean. Yes, maybe it would make sense, she supposed, if God gave Mary a baby without any of that kind of touching or blood.

So she'd asked Berthe, who explained No, the Immaculate Conception was *Mary* being conceived without *Original Sin,* so the mother of Jesus would be sinless from birth, more special than all the women in the world. Because we are all born with Original Sin, Marie Jeanne, Berthe told her, the sinful condition of our soul we must always guard against. It's why our Blessed Lord gave us His only son, and why we are always in need of Christ's redemption, even newborn babies. But how could a baby be full of sin, Danielle wondered. And didn't baptism wash away all the sin, anyway, let a person start over sinless and clean? Well, easier not to bother asking Berthe anything more, she'd thought. Easier just to memorize all those questions-and-answers and recite them when asked.

And she already knew the story of Saint Jeanne, of course, how she heard saints and drove the English invaders away and so became the patron saint of France. La Perrine had celebrated her feast day in May, everyone spending the month's ration tickets to make cakes in celebration, and Danielle had felt it made her special, too, given that she—well, Marie-Jeanne—had been named for Jeanne. She switched to Berthe's book of the saints to learn more about Jeanne, but it didn't give any real specifics on what Jeanne's saints said to her. Or explain why Jeanne would even agree to do something so crazy.

So, *Drive them out, the evil foreign invaders! They do not belong here!* Danielle began the story, with the saints' voices booming at Jeanne in the middle of the night, convincing her to leave her tiny village and travel to get the young dauphin crowned King Charles VII, and that way she would become the famous and glorious Maid of Orleans. She wrote about Jeanne cutting off all her hair and riding a large white horse, her suit of armor shining in the sun as she did battle. And she killed so many evil barbarian foreign invaders by herself with a gleaming sword (Genevieve suggested she add the 'gleaming sword,' said it sounded theatrical) she was able to save all of France for the French, the real pure strong French, and that was a holy thing to do. But she was betrayed by the French people who didn't believe in her, who handed her over to the invaders, Danielle wrote, and so the invaders killed her and made her a martyr, thus deserving of beautiful statues everywhere, and our grateful prayers.

She'd shown her story to Father Tournel, who was supposed to help them with the miracles and holy parts. Father Tournel had turned out to be very nice. Funny, how she'd once found him so terrifying, how frightened she'd been all those months ago! Church was nothing to her now, the Jesus on the wall just a piece of bad art, the prayers and Latin bits memorized to rote. The host on her tongue a meaningless wafer, just a bit of pulp. And Father Tournel, with his soft voice and curly black hair, his damp brown eyes and red-rimmed nostrils, his whiff of incense, his elegant *soutane*, he *was* a little dreamy, welcoming her to the congregation, always assuring her Papa and Maman were in Heaven now with God and she was making them so happy with her prayers, her faithful observances. Her second Sunday he'd placed his warm hand on her head after Mass to give her a special blessing, and presented her with a tiny silvered charm, the face of an old man pressed into the metal, told her it was Saint Jerome, the patron saint of orphans, who would look after her now with Jesus and Mary and all the other saints; she wears the charm every single day on a string around her neck, hasn't missed a single Sunday Mass or Confession on Saturday afternoons, and Father Tournel encourages her to come see him anytime, about anything, he and God are always there for her, bless her heart.

The first time she kneeled in the Confessional she felt trapped in an upright coffin, the boxed space smelling of wax and wood soaked in other's people's breath and the odor of well-worn woolen clothing. She felt her heart beating in her ears and fingertips again, the sudden sweat along her scalp and spine and under her arms, in the crooks of her clasped fingers. *BlessmeFatherforIhavesinned*, she mumbled, crossing herself as Berthe had coached, then confessed to being so hungry the previous Sunday before church, she'd eaten a bite of bread Berthe had left out—she had decided the bread-eating sounded appropriately sinful but not too serious, a very venial sin and not at all a mortal one. She could see Father Tournel's nodding silhouette behind the screen, then listened as he explained God understood she was hungry, but how that very hunger would help her identify with Jesus' suffering, his human and bodily trials, and would help open her heart and soul to accept God's grace, and was she truly penitent? She assured him she was sincerely sorry and wouldn't do it again, and Father Tournel told her to say five Our Fathers and five Hail Marys, and she felt a sudden sweep of light and clean air fill and then empty her lungs, and a spirited sense of relief as she scurried out—not for the penitence or absolution, but for how easy it was! She dutifully reports all her sins now, about spilling a bucket of fresh milk or forgetting to obey Claude's directions not to linger at Genevieve's after school, all the wasteful or disobedient sins that spring from Original Sin. If she's been perfect and hasn't made a single mistake, she makes sins up, just as Claire used to: she overslept and rushed her Hail Marys in order to be in school on time; she broke an egg and lied about it to Berthe. These kind of little lies come easily, too, no stumbling over which noun or verb tense or grammatical rules. But how silly, she thinks sometimes, to lie about sins in order to be sinless.

Her story of Saint Jeanne d'Arc was very good, Father Tournel told her. Very imaginative. But . . . perhaps it could use, still, just a few small changes.

They were in his rectory, the small whitewashed room where Father Tournel eats and sleeps and counsels the village's troubled souls. The smell of cold stone and old wood in here, too, and fresh wax, smoky sweet incense in the folds of his soutane, and the faint chemical odor of the mimeograph machine he uses to print out sermons for the sick or old people who can't always come to church. There is the usual portrait of Petain, and another of a bald man with glasses, a red shawl over a white dress, the face of a friendly beagle dog and a brimless white cap on his head like, oh yes, a *kippot*, she remembers from those foreign-Jewish boys and men in the Marais. The wooden crucifix on the wall, Jesus' flesh painted a tender pale pink, the blood at his ankles and wrists and belly a vivid red. Berthe has explained Father Tournel is a living symbol of God's presence, the village is lucky to have a priest who sacrifices everything for their spiritual well-being. Danielle wonders sometimes if he is ever lonely. Who did he share his secrets with, his own little sins?

"What changes?" She was not used to her schoolwork being questioned. Always good grades, for her essays at her old school, always the best in class. And the work was so much harder there, too. The only hard thing about school here is pretending not to know as many answers as she does, remembering it is safer not to stand out.

"For example," he said, "you focus on how Jeanne drove out the 'evil foreign invader'."

"Yes, Father?"

"Well, one might read this and think it applies to the German presence in France. And we all know, of course, that the Germans, unlike the English, have no interest in *conquering* France. Subjugating us. They could have done that easily, if they'd wanted to. Like Poland, or Czechoslovakia. But we have a French leader, a French government."

"But tonton Claude says the foreigners have been bad for France," she explained. "It's why Jeanne was such a brave heroine, isn't it? Why she is so important to us, today?"

"I don't believe your uncle meant the *Germans*, Marie-Jeanne. After all, France and Germany share many of the same values. We have for hundreds of years. The importance of family, and faith. National pride. We aren't really all that foreign to each other, if we look for what might bring us together. And thanks to our Marshal Petain's friendship with the Germans, and Germany's respect for us, France will rise again, to walk hand-in-hand with Germany."

Then why don't the Germans give us back all our prisoners-of-war, she wondered. Why can't Simone's brother and Hortense's father come home? Why do we have to send so much food to the Germans, turn in every bit of metal, and count out little tickets for sugar and salt and tea?

"The Church teaches us to respect and obey secular authority, it's our moral obligation. How we must live together in peace, as brothers, despite any small differences. No, we don't want to confuse the

English with the Germans. Your . . . interpretation isn't quite accurate," he said with a little smile. "*Impious England, fatal executioner of all that France held divine, murdered grace with Mary, Queen of Scots, inspiration with Jeanne d'Arc, genius with Napoleon,*" he quoted to her. "Do you remember who said that?"

"Dumas." An easy question, it had been the answer to a popular newspaper contest held the previous year.

"Yes, very good." He nodded approvingly.

"Why don't I simply refer to the invaders as 'the English,' then?"

"That would be very good," he said, nodding again. "After all, the English are still a problem for us, today. Their betrayal, and now their aggression. They're fighting *against* peace. And this other part, about Frenchmen betraying Saint Jeanne . . . that isn't so important. Remember, she was captured by the English. Killed by the English."

"And so became a martyr."

"Exactly. Because what really makes Jeanne holy, Marie-Jeanne, was her obedience to God. Not denying her womanhood and taking on the role of a soldier. Or seeking any personal glory. It was her belief in the voices of Saint Michael and Saint Catherine and Margaret. *That's* what was brave. Her commitment to follow the word of God. Despite skeptics, or any possible dangers."

"It's a little like Our Blessed Mother then, isn't it? At the Annunciation. Mary didn't question the angel's message. She just accepted the will of God. 'May it be done according to your word.'"

Father Tournel's smile grew wider, his eyes went even more damp, and a richer brown. "How wonderful you can understand that! Yes, both Mary and Jeanne understood the path to grace often involves sacrifice. It isn't belief alone that makes us virtuous, it's our actions. Every decision we make, we have the choice of following the path toward grace, or refusing the redemption our Blessed Lord lived and died to offer us."

"So is that what it means in the catechism, about 'free will'?" She hesitated, unsure if she would seem too ignorant, but Father Tournel seemed so happy with her, so pleased by her questions. "That of all His creatures, God gave us the freedom to choose between good and evil? To decide our own actions, and be responsible for them?"

"That's right. And it *is* a responsibility, an enormous one. But also a gift, His gift, you see? And when we choose to turn away from God, we're rejecting that gift. We're choosing evil instead. Mary and Jeanne could have refused His call. But they didn't, they listened, and believed. They *chose* to accept His will. And that is a perfect obedience."

"So they were good . . . collaborators?" Danielle offered, remembering the word from the newsreels, the radio broadcasts.

"Yes, exactly! Collaborators with God's plan. So you see, the idea of Frenchmen turning on each other . . ." He shook his head in distaste. "No, that isn't right."

"Then perhaps I should emphasize Jeanne's divine mission a little more? And her decision, her choice to obey God?"

He patted her hand, nodded with such happy red-rimmed approval that for a moment she felt guilty about lying to him so often. And for leaving him all alone, too, in his sinless little wax- and-wood room to eat his lonely meager meal, type his sermon, nothing except his Bible, his Jesus and Pope on the wall to keep him company. Dear Father Tournel.

She rewrote the story, describing Jeanne walking through a field of sunflowers, on her way to pick berries, but how all the jam she made would have to be sent to the barbarian English invaders who were trying to conquer France. And how a shaft of brilliant sunlight suddenly illuminated the field with the holy light of saints. And the mellifluous voices of Saint Michael and Saint Catherine and Saint Margaret (Genevieve had suggested the word "mellifluous," pointed out saints' voices are supposed to sound that way) chimed together like beautiful music, and their faces appeared alighted in the centers of sunflowers and berries, and they told her God wanted her to tell everyone the aggressive and hostile English must leave, and how she must inspire France to form an army and drive the English foreigners away. That she alone was blessed with the task of saving all of France. And God and the saints trusted Jeanne to be obedient and do all of this, even though she was a very young humble peasant girl, they knew she would accept her responsibility and wouldn't make any mistakes and would be able to save everyone, her family, her village, that she could save the entire country all by herself as long as she listened and sacrificed and chose to do exactly what she was told. And so Jeanne put on armor and cut her hair so the soldiers wouldn't be bothered she was just a humble girl and that through her they could see the light and follow and obey the voice of God.

"I like the first version better," Genevieve told her.

They were at Claude and Berthe's house, doing their homework. At least twice a week they study together; afternoons at Danielle's Berthe gives them cornbread with a scraping of jam and weak tea and hovers nearby while they work. Lately, though, Berthe has been leaving them alone more, as if finally trusting Danielle not to make a mistake, or perhaps worried it would look odd for her not to have a best friend, sometimes spending those afternoons herself in the village at the little Leroux café where the women gossip over their ersatz tea, asking Marie- Jeanne to remember to bring in some wood from the pile or put what's left of the rabbit stew on the stove for supper. But even if Berthe isn't there, Luc always seems to be going in and out of the kitchen to get a dishrag or tool or wash his hands. He usually makes some comment just mean enough to annoy and make Genevieve turn pink, but not mean enough to snap back at. As if he's spying on them, always watching and waiting to catch her doing or saying something wrong. They both prefer going to

Genevieve's, although Berthe has said it would be rude not to offer their hospitality in return.

"I did, too," Danielle said, shrugging. "I liked the other Jeanne."

"I think . . . maybe Father Tournel has been listening to the radio too much," Genevieve said. She gave Danielle a sideways look, as if testing to see what Danielle would do or say.

"Well . . . this is the story he wants. And I should . . ." just tell him what he wants to hear, Danielle thought, but didn't say. It felt so nice, how he'd praised her.

"It's sort of like going to Confession, isn't it?" Genevieve said.

She was surprised at this, uneasy. But Genevieve simply smiled, and she thought maybe Genevieve did understand something true about her. There was another language they sometimes spoke when they were together, not the truth and not the lies, almost a silent language she could understand in the slight angle of Genevieve's head, the smile-corners of her mouth, how she'd twist a strand of her pretty long hair. And it felt less lonely that way, to feel she didn't have to lie about anything, even for just a wordless moment.

And Father Tournel was right; Monsieur Monzie gave Danielle's Saint Jeanne story the place of honor on the schoolroom wall. A special evening at school, everyone's family there to see the children's artwork and hear them recite. Danielle and the other girls read their stories aloud and everyone applauded after each, Danielle getting even more applause than Hortense and Monsieur Monzie announcing *Yes, yes!* and clapping, everyone saying how proud the Marshal would be if he could see these precious children of France! Father Tournel presented them with holy cards of their saints; Danielle's Saint Jeanne d'Arc was kneeling humbly in prayer, no armor or sword, golden beams poking down from a heavenly cloud and a gold halo over her head. Genevieve's story of Saint Genevieve practicing the *Mortifications of the Flesh* was popular too, people dabbing tears at Genevieve's giving all her food away to lepers, although Genevieve had told her she wasn't even really named for the saint, it was after some relative who'd died long before she was born. Genevieve's father hugged her, kissed the top of her head, whispered something that made Genevieve smile and blush, and Danielle had to look away from them, and swallow hard. Claude and Berthe were there, and afterward Berthe told her the story was beautiful, so touching and poetic, and Claude patted her shoulder with his clumsy hand. Maybe it was all right to stand out, a little, if it made them so proud of Marie-Jeanne. She wondered how many ration tickets that might be worth. How many mouthfuls of bread.

Now Monsieur Monzie is talking about this new project, how much fun they will all have. He looks like a clerk in a bank, Danielle thinks, angling for a promotion, his black suit shiny at the elbows, his shirt collar thready at the tips, too much pomade in his sharply-parted black hair. He hands out to everyone little packages wrapped in brown tissue paper, spreading his smell of chalk and cigarettes and old cheese. They are told to take the booklets home and start working on them during the weekend, as next week in class they will all share. "Work hard, children! *Yes, yes!*" Monsieur Monzie claps excitedly as everyone hurries out to go home.

*"The family is the basis for our society,"* Danielle reads aloud. *"And family honor and strength lie in the bloodline."*

She has torn the tissue from her booklet: *Livret Genealogique,* it says on the cover. Inside is the usual picture of Marshal Petain, and text explaining how the families of France must rediscover their honor and proud history. *Strong families mean a strong nation.*

Genevieve is busy at the stove, and Danielle gets a whiff of baking bread; it is Friday, and she has permission to visit with Genevieve all afternoon, as long as she gets up early tomorrow to make up her chores. She inhales the rich wheaty smell. Chicken, too, she'd spotted the naked bird in a pan when she arrived, stuffed with onions and herbs. She watches Genevieve put the chicken in the oven, then looks back at the little booklet. She hopes Genevieve will ask her to stay for supper, has already told Berthe she might not be back until evening.

"It's a family tree," Danielle tells her. She flips the pages, the many pages to be filled in with family. "We're supposed to list our parents, and their parents and their parents. And their children, and our cousins. Where everyone was born and lived and what they did." Her heart is starting its rabbit rhythm, beat beating, *And Abraham begat Isaac,* she thinks, *begat Jacob begat Joseph . . .* She remembers a big leather Bible, her grandmother Sarah reading to her. She must have been very little. The jagged black letters, like insects crawling across the page. The Old Testament, the Jewish Bible. Her mother and grandmother singsonging the prayers, her grandfather reciting in Hebrew. Her heart is still pounding, she shouldn't listen to those ghost voices, or picture any of it, just sweep it all away. Remembering is dangerous. That's how you get confused, that's how you make a mistake.

But Marie-Jeanne has to remember, she thinks. There are lines and lines on every page, awaiting all of Marie-Jeanne's family and blood.

"*Good blood doesn't lie,*" she reads.

"It really says that?" Genevieve wrinkles her nose.

"Yes."

Genevieve wipes her hands, comes to the table and tears the tissue from her own booklet, examines the text as if she expects it to be different from Danielle's. "Oh," she says. "So what do we have to do?"

Danielle shrugs. "I guess we just have to write it all down."

They look at each other a moment in silence.

"Who cares about any of that?" Genevieve asks.

"Marshal Petain, I guess. And Monsieur Monzie."

"Is he going to put them up on the walls?" Genevieve asks. "For everybody to see?"

Danielle tries a small chuckle. "Maybe the Marshal thinks that's how we can rebuild France."

"I don't know a lot of those answers, who and where for everybody." Genevieve picks up a dishtowel, brushes at invisible crumbs on the table.

"You can ask your father."

"What if he doesn't know? Or can't remember? Sometimes people forget things like that, or papers get lost or destroyed."

"We can leave spaces blank, I guess, if no one knows."

"Let's do yours first," Genevieve says. "If we have time, we'll do mine."

They look at each other again. Maybe it's another test, she thinks. She tries to think of every single thing she has ever said to Genevieve, tries to remember any slips or cracks. She remembers Genevieve showing her a trick with needle and thread, helping her fix a crooked seam on her apron, *I thought your maman was a seamstress, didn't she teach you how to do this?* Genevieve had asked, her face curious. But Danielle felt sure she had smoothed that over, *Oh, yes, but she mostly took in fine sewing, and was so very busy, she was always promising to show me this sort of thing, before she died . . .* She'd let her voice trail off, touched the Saint Jerome orphan medal at her neck, and Genevieve had nodded, squeezed her arm in sympathy, gone back to ripping out a poorly knotted stitch.

"All right," she says. "Fine." She turns to her booklet, tries to look studious and not nervous at all.

*Marie-Jeanne Chantier,* she writes. She writes down Marie-Jeanne's birthday, the same as her own, 25 January, 1929, and Paris, her own real same place of birth. She thinks of the identity card in her pocket, no, it isn't there, she was rushing that morning, but she knows it by heart, she doesn't need to look, Genevieve isn't going to ask for *Your papers, please!* She grips her pencil, writes *Paul Chantier* (no, Marton, *Juif*), and *Rachel Chantier* (Marton, *Juive*), teacher and housewife/seamstress, both born in Paris. She stops writing. She knows the names of her godparents, they're her real true ones, Claire's parents, Monsieur and Madame Beaumont, but that isn't blood, and they want blood. *Good blood doesn't lie.*

Genevieve is looking at her, her sideways look. "Who else?" she asks.

They hadn't given Marie-Jeanne any grandparents. They hadn't planned such old lies. She sees her mother, and Claude, and Berthe that first night at the table, all of them whispering. How could they leave her without enough lies this way? She sees a paper tart, a penciled circle, divided in eighths. Danielle's grandmother was Sarah. Her grandfather was Jacob. Lace, and sweet purple wine passed around in a silver cup. Paschal lamb. Milk and meat, separate. Sarah and Jacob, she can't use those foreign-sounding names. Marie-Jeanne's family is all French, pure French. But Berthe is her aunt, she remembers. And her parents were Bernadette and Louis, yes, they're dead but Berthe talks about them from time to time, she lights candles and says prayers for them in Heaven.

"Write down your grandparents," Genevieve says.

"Bernadette," Danielle says. "My Grandmère Bernadette. And my grandfather was Louis. Both of them born in . . . Lille." She writes the names down. "They, they owned a small bakery. Their children were my mother and tante Berthe. The sisters. And Berthe married my uncle Claude, and there's my cousin Luc. And my grandfather Louis was a soldier in the Great War, an officer, and very brave. Until he was killed." Close to the truth, the part about a brave officer, *Your grandfather, he was a good man, child.*

Now what? Genevieve is waiting. Marie-Jeanne would know

more about her own family, wouldn't she? She thinks suddenly of Jeanne d'Arc's saints, their booming voices.

"And my father's parents were Michael and Catherine. They were from Orleans." She writes those names down, too. She thinks of Berthe's book of the saints, sees their cracking pages, their faded illustrations. Hundreds of saints. So many names to choose from. "And my father's brother was Francis, and he married Margaret. And they have two children, my cousins Thérèse and Jérôme, and they live in Toulouse." A phony family tree. Who will know the difference? The Chantier family goes back a long way, she tells Genevieve, many generations. She tells her which Chantiers fought in which wars, who became a priest or a nun, who started a thriving business in Bordeaux or Marseilles, merchants and teachers and doctors and bakers and farmers, using all the saints' names she can think of, who begat whom begat whom begat whom, then, feeling inspired, she tells Genevieve about ancestors from Scotland, that's probably where her own reddish hair comes from, about distant relatives who still live there and if you go hundreds of years in the past, Marie-Jeanne explains, why, she might even be related to Mary, Queen of Scots, who was a French Queen, too, and full of grace until the English murdered her, and it's a shame there aren't enough lines in the booklet to go that far back.

She stops, out of breath. Besides, Genevieve is looking at her oddly. Perhaps she has gone too far.

"It's wonderful you know so much about your family." Genevieve's voice is low; she is playing with a pencil, rolling it back and forth along the table, the way Danielle has seen her roll a length of bread dough.

"Yes," Danielle says. "It's important to know where you came from. Who you are." She wonders if she'll be able to remember all those lies, if Genevieve asks more questions. "All right, it's your turn."

Genevieve slowly turns to the first page of her *Livret Genealogique.*

She writes her name and birth date down, and her father's name and birth date, and stops.

"What was your mother's name?" Danielle asks.

"Anna," she says. She writes that down, *Anna*, and the birth date.

"Where were they born, your parents? What city?"

"*Rawicz*," Genevieve tells her, pronouncing a strange word with soft, coiled sounds. "It's a village. Near Cracow. They were married there. But they went to Paris in 1922. Then after my mother died, when I was little, my father brought me here to live."

"Why did your parents come to France?"

"It wasn't safe in Poland, my father told me. They thought they would be safer here."

"What wasn't safe?"

"He doesn't like to talk much about that."

"Well..." She isn't sure what else to say. "What about your name?" as it suddenly occurs to her. "*Clermont* is a French name."

Genevieve nods. "My father changed it. His real name, my real name, I guess, is . . ." and she says another word with strange sounds, a *k* and an *l* and a *schwa*, and other consonants all twisted up together. "People couldn't pronounce it." She laughs a little. "But he says it's just a name, it doesn't matter."

"Oh. I guess not. Well, what about your grandparents? Who were they?"

"I don't know anymore. I told you, my father doesn't like to talk about it. He won't talk to me about any of it."

"You probably still have relatives in Poland. You could write to them?"

"I can't. They're gone."

"Where did they go?"

"They're all dead."

"Your whole family? What happened?"

"So many questions, Marie-Jeanne!" Genevieve laughs the tiny laugh again.

"I'm sorry, I just . . . it's the assignment . . ."

"No, it's all right." Genevieve rolls her pencil again. "They were killed. My father told me that part. There was some kind of battle. Soldiers came."

"But who was at war? The Great War?" Danielle tries the math in her head, who was at war with whom, and when. It always confuses her, countries that have alliances with each other one day, then next day they're enemies. Like dogs romping in the street, then suddenly howling and snapping and wanting to tear each other apart. Didn't Hitler and Stalin have a friendship pact, just before the war? And France and Britain were supposed to be best friends, too, allies against everyone else, and now look.

"No, before that. My father was a little boy. He heard soldiers, and people scream. He remembers horses. And guns. He had to hide. That's what wasn't safe. And he was the only one left." Genevieve studies her pencil. "He was just a very little boy," she says, quiet.

"Oh." She looks at the first page of Genevieve's book, the three short lines filled out. A very tiny tree, she thinks. A very little blood. "So . . . do you want to just make the rest up?"

"No." Genevieve looks surprised. "I don't want to lie."

"No, it's like . . . a joke. It's just a joke. It's just a dumb project," Danielle says.

"I know. But . . ." Genevieve shakes her head.

"I'm sorry," Danielle says again.

"That's all right. It doesn't matter." Genevieve closes her booklet. "There, *I'm* all done!" She gets up, ties an apron over her dress.

Danielle nods, smiles. But it doesn't seem enough.

Genevieve opens the stove to remove a loaf of bread, golden, rippled, and the scent of it fills the kitchen, rich, and the chicken smell, too, there's onion and herbs and crisping fat.

Danielle inhales longingly. She loves this smell, has almost forgotten it, wants to bring it inside her, hold it in her arms. Berthe needs her chickens for their eggs, she gets nervous as she counts them to send to the Germans; they only eat chicken when a stringy old one is ready to die. She can taste this fat chicken dinner smell in her mouth. The Friday dinners' smell, yes, dinners with lace and candle wax and silver-sweet taste of wine. She and her mother taking the train to Louveciennes sometimes for the weekend or a holiday. Her father never came with them, always late classes on Fridays or many papers to grade. The special dinner with candles and prayers, her mother reciting along with her grandparents. Her mother lets Danielle sip the wine and say the Hebrew prayer she knows, *Baruch atah Adonai . . . , Blessed are you, Adonai, Creator of the Universe, who has created the fruit of the vine, Amen,* she hears her own little girl voice, and her grandmother's voice, her grandfather's voice, and she lets herself remember, hear their voices, taste the sweet wine, smell the roasted meat and candle wax, her mother and grandmother with lace draped on their heads, hands caressing the air above a candle. And there is her grandfather, slicing the tip of bumpy brown challah away, kissing it, sprinkling salt on yolk-yellow slices to be passed around, her favorite part, that rich bread, bringing the warm golden light of God to their Sabbath heart and home . . .

She opens her eyes, sees Genevieve slicing thick slices for them, thick rich slices, golden yellow, from a fat brown braid of bread.

"You're Jewish," she says to Genevieve.

"Yes . . ." Genevieve says. She frowns at Danielle, at the same time making a crooked smile. "You, you knew that. Everybody knows that." A nervous little laugh. "Didn't you know that?"

"No. I didn't." *Baruch atah Adonai* . . . She shakes her head, eyes on the bread. "But . . . you go to church. You take Communion." She sees

Genevieve sitting across the aisle. Always in church alone, her father working on Sundays, always working, even on the holy Lord's Day. And you go with an impure heart, she thinks, staring at Genevieve. You just go through the motions. With a fake name. The blessed host is the true body of Christ, and that's only for honest and true believers to partake of! You lie about this, and everybody knows, Father Tournel knows, he *allows* it?

"My father doesn't want us to be very Jewish about things," Genevieve is saying, her crooked smile stuck in place. "But it's the same God, isn't it?

"Uh huh," Danielle says.

"So at church I just think about what God wants from me, and how I can do better, be a better person. That's like the *Confiteor,* right? And Communion, Father Tournel says it can just be the heart of it, for me. Like Jesus and the Apostles, just sharing with each other. And at Confession, Father Tournel says I can just talk to him about whatever worries me, with an open heart. He says God loves me exactly as I am, for who I am," blushing, "I don't ever need to pretend anything. I'm not going to be confirmed, though, that doesn't feel right, to say I embrace Jesus that special way, as the Son of God. Although I believe Jesus was a real person, a good person who taught about love and understanding," again, the little laugh, "and we should honor him and follows his lessons. And he was even Jewish, too, right . . . ?" She says all of this too rapidly, too nervously.

And Luc, always glaring at Genevieve, telling her she should get home. Where she belongs. As if he couldn't bear her in his house, infiltrating their family, touching their things.

". . . and we still light candles together on Shabbat," she continues, "me and my father. And I make a special dinner on Fridays, I think that means a lot to him . . ." Genevieve pauses, finally, as if she's out of breath. "Friday is the Jewish Sabbath," she explains.

"Yes," Danielle says, dully. "I know." *L'had'lik near shel Shabbat...*

"I'm sorry, Marie-Jeanne. I thought you knew."

"Well, it doesn't matter. Like you said." She rises from the table, busies her hands putting her *Livret Genealogique* away in her school satchel. "I have to go home," she says. "It's so late, I told tante Berthe I'd help her this afternoon."

"Don't you want this?" Genevieve holds out a piece of bread, of challah, yellow rich with egg, sunflower-bright butter melting on top, a careless fat swirl of butter.

"No, that's okay."

"What about a book? Don't you want to borrow a book?"

"I won't have any time to read this weekend, I have so much to do. But thanks."

"I wanted you to stay for dinner," Genevieve says. "Papa said I could ask you." Her hand is still holding out the bread in offering.

"Maybe next Friday," Danielle says. "Or one night next week. Thank you, anyway. Thank your father for me. I'll see you Monday morning, all right?"

Genevieve's crooked, tiny smile again. And something else, something new in her eyes. "Well, Sunday. At church."

"Oh, right. Bye."

It makes no sense, none at all. It doesn't *matter*? So what is the reason for all the lies she's had to tell, the fake name and family honor and history, the fake blood? A baptism that never happened, sheep dung stuck to her heels, counting her swallows of ration-ticket tea, broken fingernails and needle-pricked fingers and being told, as she hears the little neck go *snap*, that she'll have to learn to kill the rabbits by herself someday? And *Don't make a mistake, don't give us away, the Germans will come, will take you, take all of us away!* But there are no Germans here and she is only three-fourths Jewish, anyway, not like Genevieve, whose parents weren't even born here, aren't even real pure French. And no one cares? So her own mother didn't have to leave her here, didn't have to go Underground? Maybe they didn't even have to leave Paris. Maybe her father didn't have to die! All of this, for nothing. Why can Genevieve be the real her and not have to speak the foreign language all the time, wear that satin bow and live here with her Jewish not-even-born-in-France father, have him hug her, both of them one hundred percent Jewish and observing the Sabbath, chicken and challah and prayers over wine, *borey pri hagafen*, and everyone knows the truth and no one *cares*?

She sees Berthe and Claude's house, further down the road, and she slows, realizes she's been walking fast, is out of breath, her school satchel clutched to her chest so hard her shoulders ache. Why can't she just go into the house, *their* house, it isn't *her* home, tell them she isn't going to lie about anything anymore? No one here even talks about Jews, only Claude and Luc, sometimes, their crazy talk about what's happening in Paris, *Jews and academics, it's who they always come for first*, in the Occupied Zone, foreign Jews, *sale Juif*, being gathered up, *deported, resettled*, and what difference does any of that make, anyway, here in La Perrine, in the middle of nowhere? Everyone's safe here, no one wants to hurt anybody. She'll point all that out to them. Why didn't you tell me about Genevieve, she'll ask, why do you still always warn me to watch every word I say, why do I need to be so scared all the time? No one cares. She thinks suddenly of fat envelopes, extra ration tickets, a suitcase of jewelry.

Well, I'm not going to church or Confession anymore, she hears herself tell them, there's no reason to pretend all of that. You're just my grandparents' old butler and maid, that's the truth, and you're being well-paid, so let's stop pretending, stop acting like we're family, like we're real blood. I don't need to keep lying. There isn't any danger. No one is going to get in trouble, no one's going to get shot just because of me.

How much easier everything will be! She can say anything she wants, now. All the real true things, no more translating in her head, no more *poor Marie-Jeanne*. And they'll get word to her mother, that she can stop being Underground, stop eating rats or wearing wooden shoes.

They can go back to Paris together, back to their real home. Back to Claire! Her real and true friend, like a sister, named for real for a saint, who doesn't lie to you and make you feel ridiculous because you didn't see what everyone else already knows. Who knows you're Danielle. You'll be there waiting for me, won't you, Claire, you haven't forgotten me, have you? She thinks of the Saint Jerome medal around her neck, she'll cut it off, throw it away, that ugly fake charm . . .

"Marie-Jeanne! Marie-Jeanne!"

She turns; she hasn't heard the steps behind her at all, running steps, or Genevieve crying out her name. Her crying.

"Genevieve, what you are you doing?"

Genevieve shakes her head, wipes her nose with the back of her hand. Struggles to catch her breath.

"Don't cry," Danielle mumbles. "You don't need to cry about anything."

"I *was* lying," Genevieve says. "Sort of. I mean, everybody does know, it isn't a secret. But it feels like a secret. I can't talk to anybody about it. I have to act like it doesn't mean anything."

She's shivering, Danielle can see, she should be wearing a sweater.

"But it does. It makes me different. And it's been so lonely, pretending all the time. But when you came . . . you're different, too."

"I'm not!" Danielle tells her. "I'm just the same as everybody else!"

"No, you aren't." Genevieve smiles. "At first I thought it's that you were new in school, but you aren't really new anymore. So I don't know what's different about you, but it means we can both be different together. And that's less lonely. Please don't be mad at me." Her smile weakens, falters. "Please don't think I'm different in a bad way."

"I'm not. I don't." She looks away from Genevieve's odd expression, back toward Claude and Berthe's house; the lights are glowing from inside. It's getting late. She should go inside, help Berthe. Listen to Claude go on about Petain and the latest news, *It's the foreign Jews that are the problem,* listen to Luc read from the newspaper, *It's the Jews, Papa, all the corruption,* all their crazy ideas. She's shivering, too, they're both shaking in the cold.

"I'm glad you finally know the truth," Genevieve says. " You can't be friends with someone if they don't know who you really are, right? Isn't that true?"

Danielle nods. Yes, she should tell her the truth. There's no reason not to.

But there's something in Genevieve's eyes, in the twist to her mouth. The something new. It's fear, she realizes. She's afraid. Afraid of me.

*She doesn't really even look like a Jew,* she hears, Jew, like it meant insect or evil person or some kind of ugly little animal. But she's made in God's image, like Genevieve, they both are. Both different and the same as everyone else. Children of God, and He loves them all, even Father Tournel says. So why is she afraid?

"Marie-Jeanne?"

*My name is Danielle,* the words in her mouth, but something sticks in her throat. Go on, she thinks. Tell her.

"And sometimes real friends don't even have to tell each other everything," Genevieve is saying. "You just understand each other already, without saying. Like being sisters, maybe. Don't you think?"

Danielle nods. Maybe that is true, maybe there's no need to explain. No need to tell everything. Saying or not saying words aloud doesn't change what's really true, inside. What you know is true.

"So nothing's changed . . . has it? Marie-Jeanne?"

"No. No, of course not." She leans, kisses Genevieve on the cheek, watches as she blushes soft pink. "Here," she says. She takes off her gray sweater, puts it around Genevieve's shoulders. "It's cold."

Genevieve huddles in the sweater. "Do you really have to go home," she asks, hopeful. "You could still come back and eat with us. If you want to."

"Oh, I don't know," says Danielle. "You probably burned the chicken."

"I did not!"

"Well . . . okay, then."

"Yes, *yes*?"

"Yes, *yes*!"

"Here . . ." Genevieve helps Danielle put one of her arms in the sweater, keeps her own arm in the other sleeve, they wrap their naked arms around each other's waists, and run, laughing, gasping, squeezing hands, back to Genevieve's.

~

They say a German naval cadet was shot in the Paris Metro by a member of the French Communist Party. They say two Communists stabbed a German solider to death near the Porte d'Orleans, pinning a note to his chest that read *Ten Nazi officers will pay for every patriot killed.* They say another German soldier was shot outside the Gare de l'Est. There were more and more attacks on German soldiers and personnel in the Occupied Zone, German military and supply trains derailed, telephone cables cut, grenades thrown into crowds. Tires slashed, posters defaced. Seditious pamphlets were appearing in cities and towns, in the Unoccupied Zone, too, pasted over official Vichy announcements, stuffed into mailboxes, stacks left on buses and café floors, calling for citizens to *Rise Up!*, *Resist the German Oppressors*, *Don't Believe the Vichy Lies*! In the village people talked of the foolish, brutal assassinations, the petty, pointless vandalisms. They say the local *Feldkommandant* had his throat cut outside the cathedral at Nantes, Danielle heard at the Leroux café. They say an advisor to the German military was shot in Bordeaux, she heard at Madame Richie's grocery. Claude read the newspaper accounts to them in the evening, or they listened to official announcements on Radio Vichy, Petain's quavery old lady voice condemning these cowardly acts: *We laid down our weapons at the Armistice. We do not have the right to seize them up again to shoot the Germans in the back!*

"Why must they do such things?" Berthe asks, snapping beans into a bowl. "A German here, a German there. It's just more killing. We need peace, now. What's to gain?"

"They're mercenaries, Maman," Luc says. "They're part of the Jewish-Marxist plutocratic alliance."

What a child he is, Danielle thinks, always trying to sound so grownup. She leans over her math exercises, hands covering her ears.

But, "Heaven's sake, where do you get that language from?" she hears Berthe ask.

Luc waves a newspaper at his mother, *Je suis partout*, reappeared after years of suppression by the Third Republic. Monsieur Leroux has refused to sell the paper at his tabac—Claude had returned furious from the Legion one night after a fight about it, Monsieur Leroux calling it bigoted right-wing trash and Claude trying to explain to him, *But that idiot Leroux, he won't listen to reason, that we have again, finally, a newspaper that dares to tell the truth, news* from *patriots* for *patriots*! So now Luc bicycles once a week all the way to Limoges to buy it, and Claude is happy to give him the money. He and Claude read it aloud in the evenings, getting foamed up with anger at reports of anti-Petain, pro-de Gaulle demonstrations, while Danielle tries to ignore them, focus instead on her schoolwork or chores. Hortense did better on their last math examination, she isn't going to let that happen again.

"They're paid by the Soviet Union, and England," Luc continues. "They're bankrolling those traitors. And money de Gaulle's been stealing and stashing away for years, he's the biggest traitor there is. They want to destabilize our country. They think it'll lead to Germany's defeat. And then they'll take over all the industry, and the banks and—"

"They're common criminals," Claude says. "All it will lead to is more bloodshed. Honest French citizens will pay, that's who."

And the payments began, the reprisals. (No, the "retaliatory measures," as they were called in *Je suis partout.*) French military and political prisoners, anyone held in custody on suspicion of anything, were henceforth to be treated as hostages. ("Expiators," the papers clarified.) Three French hostages executed for each German killed. Two French hostages executed for each German wounded. Twenty-seven people shot in the prisoner camp in Chateaubriant, twenty from the Nantes jail. Eighty-eight prisoners in Paris, marched out and shot in groups of five. Danielle remembered the Germans on the streets of Paris, in the Metro, taking photos, such nice manners, so clean and polite. It made no sense.

*We are paying a terrible price,* Petain's voice pleaded. *If we are still suffering, it is because we have not yet fully atoned for our sins!* He begged good citizens everywhere to expose such dishonorable culprits, denounce these criminals. To think of our good men still held in Germany, Germany's agreement to return them to us, soon, and our agreement to collaborate with them in the reconstruction of France, as the newsreels showed trainloads of happy and healthy French prisoners-of-war returning to their families and factories and fields, hugging their children and wives and dogs.

Although none of the returning prisoners seem to be returning to La Perrine, Danielle thought, watching Madame and Monsieur Leroux weep silently for their son in the flickering newsreel light, and Hortense take and squeeze her mother's hand. Yes, those conducting such cowardly acts are traitors, everyone in the village agreed. Dishonorable. We can't blame the Germans, they agreed to peace, they've behaved correctly, they've followed the rules. These criminals, they're all Bolsheviks, gypsies, Republicans, Jews (yes, she hears that whispered now and then in the village, no matter, she just keeps her face very still, they aren't talking about *her*, about Marie-Jeanne, after all, although how can Jews be poor immigrant Communists *and* greedy thieving capitalists at the same time?) They're still trying to fight the war, keep the bloodshed going, listening to that crazy de Gaulle on the BBC radio, and he ran away, ran off to England, he's a traitor, too. Leader of the "Free French," ha! It's not up to the British to tell us who our leader is! De Gaulle wants us to keep fighting, easy for him to say, living soft and fat in another country, thinking he can tell us what to do. Whose sons does he wish to sacrifice first?

Yes, this is exactly why Marshal Petain is working *with* the Germans, Claude and Luc insist to each other, to make things *better* for us, for our prisoners-of-war, to keep the peace. Claude has warned Danielle if he ever catches her listening to that rubbish on the BBC, or reading one of those treasonous pamphlets, she will be severely punished for it. No matter to her, what does she care about boring politics? She feels bad for Hortense and Simone, of course, she hopes their father and brother will come home soon. But she hardly listens to the radio at all anymore, usually escapes after dinner to her onion-and-garlic room to study, and Berthe tells Claude to *Let her go,* as she slips Danielle an extra candle, *Marie-Jeanne's studies are important, we should be proud of how hard she's working.* Or to lie on her bed and read that fat novel Genevieve has loaned her. Affairs of state, treaties, decrees, a new Minister of this, a new Minister of that, this Minister replacing that one, she was sick of hearing about it. And it was all so far away, anyhow, none of those things had anything to do with her.

~

A special treat tonight! Everyone is joyful, anticipatory, the whole village gathering in the schoolhouse to watch the once-a-month movie, seats packed and people standing along the walls, like on a special recital evening. Father Tournel here tonight, even, with a smile for Danielle and Genevieve, and mothers with babies, Berthe sitting with Madame Richie and Madame Gaillard, and the old men who rarely go to anything except Legion meetings, Claude sitting with them in the back. Because Monsieur Monzie had promised everyone a rare treat, affixed the poster outside the schoolhouse weeks ago, a brand *new* film is coming, has arrived, is here, a *musical*, the glamorous and charming *Romance de Paris*! Danielle squeezes Genevieve's arm—she didn't often come to the Friday night movies, usually preferring to stay home with her father, but Danielle had persuaded her, how much fun it will be, please Genevieve, music and pretty clothes and how handsome the young man looks on the poster! Genevieve squeezes her back. Like at church, Genevieve always sits next to her now, they hold hands and afterward they walk home together, arm in arm. Like sisters, almost.

Everyone arranges autumn clothing against the chill, breathes onto their fingers, finishes their whispers about the price of salt and reinforcing leather soles and how long one should steep dried carrot tops for tea, while Monsieur Druot sets up the screen and Monsieur Monzie feeds filmstock into the projector. She feels the old eager shiver, no red velvet curtains or plush seats or gilded cinema fixtures here, but there will be singing, dancing, new fashions, men and women in swooning love! Luc turns out the lights and everyone blinks at the first-dark, then sudden-bright as the screen bursts into a flickery square of light, then the cheery music of the newsreel, the double-bladed National Revolution ax coming out at them. The usual Vichy goings-on: Petain touring the countryside, attending church and school recitals, inspecting factories, proclaiming how much *stronger we are now as a people, a nation! Those who say otherwise are lying, and throwing you into the arms of Communism!* Then the blurry, sputtering images of Paris, the images she studies once a month, hungrily, despite the clutch in her belly, for glimpses of a woman with a braided crown, for her old apartment building, the lace curtains of her bedroom, Claire, the Pont Neuf and all the images she's able now to sweep from her mind before her mind even sees them. But it's harder when they're right there, big and black and white in front of her, and is it really all blurry, or is it just her eyes, teary from dust or wind? She blinks, brushes at her face. *Focus,* someone yells, and everyone laughs, Yes, *yes*! Monsieur Monzie says in mock-exasperation, flapping his hands, happy at his important task, and Danielle laughs along with everyone, waiting for the glamour and charm and romance.

The blurriness sharpens, people's hair takes on its curl and shops take on their edges, there are words now, a sign on a building, *INSTITUTE D'ETUDES DES QUESTIONS JUIVES,* the letters tightening clear and bold, and the voice, telling them *The Jewish issue can now be dealt with scientifically,* the problem, *LE PERIL JUIF,* yes, the Jewish Peril! And Danielle thinks *such crazy ideas,* thinks *just don't listen, don't look, sweep it away,* but there are rats now, fat and oily, filling up the screen, rats feeding on bags of grain and scampering through sewer gratings and swarming along dirty gutters ("Monsieur Monzie?" someone says, loudly but hesitantly, "What is this?"), dirty Jewish rats in gutters, because *the Jew is like a rat, cowardly, sly and cruel,* the voice tells them, but she keeps her face very very still, doesn't even cringe at the rat fur and eyes and whiskers in sharp poking focus now, with *their need to destroy, their power lies in their superior numbers, breeding like rats, and a danger to human health, to those of good Aryan blood,* and the rats ("Monsieur le Mayor?" another voice, stronger, and another saying "Boo," a few voices, hissing, "Boo, stop this, *arretez*!", but in the dark she can't see who they are) blur and reshape into filthy men and woman and children huddled together, crawling with insects, *See the dark and repulsive pigsty where this Jewish family lives, where vermin swarm,* and at the Palais Berlitz, the Institute is happy to present a new exhibit, *LE JUIF ET LA FRANCE,* crowds of Parisians attending (she hears applause, yes, a few people *clapping,* here, in this very room, but in the dark she can't see who they are), to learn from the displays, "How to Tell A Jew From a Frenchman," to study charts with measurements of noses and ears and skulls, *We have been overrun by Jews, they plunged our peace-loving country into war, they led France to its worst-ever defeat, such is their destructive power, learn all about the extent of the Peril,* and then a ghoulish, bulge-nosed, sneering man ("Shut this off, please!") is clutching a globe of the world, his long ratlike nails digging right into France.

And there is more clapping in the dark, there is hissing and booing and voices shouting, not the newsreel voices but here-in-the-dark-room-voices, it's Father Tournel's voice, yes, shouting at Monsieur Druot to "Stop this, shut off this filth right now!" and Monsieur Druot's and Monsieur Monzie's voices shouting back, some people are shoving their way across the dark room or out the door, and some are standing and shaking fists and yelling, everything flashing in blacks and whites and ghost grays and glinty dust motes still traveling the room from the projector to the screen, but there is a pounding in her ears, she hunches over, puts her hands over her ears but the pounding is even worse that way, trapped inside her head, and there is a sharp stone in her throat, along her side, a digging into her arm and she realizes it's Genevieve, Genevieve's sharp nails are digging into her arm, and she glances sideways to see, in a brief flick of screen light, the hot spots on Genevieve's cheeks, two hot red spots like a fever, like mortified flesh, and the wet-flash tracks of tears on her face before there is a final shout, and a crash, and the projected light makes a few wild jagged arcs and then dies.

"'From one ancestor God made all nations to inhabit the earth.' Yes, the human race, '*in the unity of its nature, is composed equally in all men of a material body and a spiritual soul.*' This is what our Holy Father tells us. His very words!"

Father Tournel, atop his little stairway, is speaking in his booming voice, the one that echoes off cold stone walls and into Danielle's chest. She clutches the piece of paper, *SUMMI PONTIFICATUS,* it says, *On The Unity Of Human Society,* by Pope Pius XII. A smeary mimeographed copy on every seat when they'd entered the church, a fluttering sea of white squares, Father Tournel must have used up so much of his precious paper and ink.

Everyone is sitting in a loud silence in the milk-bright Sunday morning, holding their paper squares. Danielle bows her head, can't bear to look at anyone, but can't bear not to—she can see sideways some heads bowed, some heads bobbing as they read along, some staring back at their priest. Claude and Luc, their faces impassive, Berthe nodding at Father Tournel and Pope Pius's words. On her other side, an empty space, a sheet of paper lying in the empty seat.

"The '*different conditions of life, of culture, of belief . . . these things do not break the unity of the human race. They enrich and embellish it*'," Father Tournel reads. "'*All men are truly brethren.*' *All* men, equally deserving of dignity and respect!"

There is no coughing, no rustle of clothing or shifting around. A baby cries, one of the baby Philippes, but there is no soothing maternal hush.

Father Tournel shuffles papers before him. "My friends . . ." His voice softens. He grips the edges of the lectern, then looks up from his text. "We already know this, don't we? In our hearts? We don't need a sermon. It's so very simple. God is Love. Our Savior was a man of Love, and of Peace. We mustn't turn to the violence of pride, and arrogance. Of hatred. Of choosing to think we are more deserving of God's love than our brothers and sisters. We can all be tempted by this sin, I know. All of us." His voice drops even lower. He looks shamed. "Because we do this out of fear. We're all so afraid. Of suffering, of death. Of losing what we have in this life, what we've worked so hard for and are afraid we might lose, afraid will be taken from us. So we tell ourselves we are worthier than the people of other nations, other races, other beliefs. We believe that makes us strong. We believe that makes us safe. And we cling to that belief, we clutch at it with both hands."

There is a sneeze, a loud cough.

"But my friends, that is not what God wants. He doesn't want us to live that way. That is a lonely life. That is a life of shame."

She feels Luc shift impatiently in his seat next to her, wipe his hands on his trousers.

"That is a life without love."

Father Tournel raises his head, and gazes at them, but the stern, soul-piercing stare is gone, it's his damp-eyed, red-nosed, pleading gaze.

"The greatest gift, given to us by Jesus himself, is the Law of Love. This is the New Law of the Gospel, our New Covenant with God. And our salvation comes not from anger or pride, but from humility. Not from self-love, but from love of *others*. This is how we show our love for God, how we are truly kept safe. How we find true peace. *As I have loved you, so you should also love one another*. I have seen this love among us, here in our village, haven't you?"

A few nodding heads. She wishes Genevieve were here, next to her. She could squeeze her hand, reassure her they were all safe, all the same, one family, true sisters.

"I've seen us care for each other, help one another, in times of both pain and joy. Those extra steps you take to greet your ailing neighbor, offer companionship or an ear for their troubles, to share a pail of milk? The loaf of bread you put aside for a needy friend? For a child that isn't your own? Isn't that merely love? And doesn't that nourish us all?"

The small nods make tiny waves across the room, more and more of them.

"So, please. Let us act out of love, and not from fear. The love I know we all have in our hearts, as children of God. All of us, as neighbors, friends, as one family. I beg you. Let us not lose our very soul." He wipes his nose, his ears. "I beg you," he repeats. "Let us pray together."

Everyone shuffles to grasp hands, and he leads them in prayers, for those suffering, for their brothers and sisters in Germany and England and America and the Soviet Union, for anyone who has turned away from God, that they might open their hearts and minds and souls to the Holy Ghost and rejoice together in true faith, hope, and charity.

~

"Marie-Jeanne, will you come here, please? I have something to discuss with you." Claude removes his jacket, sits at the table. He brings the smell of cigarettes and whiskey with him, as he always does after a meeting of the Legion.

"Yes, Tonton." She puts down her knitting, on the seat near the stove where she has been sitting for warmth. Getting so chilly in the evenings again, almost winter. Genevieve has recently taught her to knit; Berthe had grown too frustrated with Danielle's awkward fingers and given up. But Genevieve was more patient, and it was so pleasant to sit together, long afternoons, their fingers busy, talking about school or books, although never about some things, never about anyone's funny looks or crazy ideas, about secrets, what was safe or not safe. Yes, except for the always-empty space next to her on Sundays, now, everything is just like before. *My librarian,* Danielle calls her—she never leaves Genevieve's house without a book under her arm, a romance or poetry when she chooses, or something more scholarly when Genevieve selects for her, history or the big novels that take forever to finish. She takes very good care of the books, washes her hands before reading and returns them as soon as she can. She had made a practice sampler, a slightly crooked square of thick wool, and presented it to Berthe as a potholder. But she is making another one, a better one, as a gift to Genevieve; Berthe had grudgingly allowed her a length of fresh yarn, had agreed a present in return for Genevieve's generosity was the kind and neighborly thing to do.

"La Perrine will be having a visitor soon. From Vichy."

"Is the Marshal coming?" Luc rises from where he is setting up his pallet bed on the floor. Monsieur Druot had written a letter to Petain, bragging about the grain and produce the village contributed, inviting a visit. Petain had traveled through Limousin in June, touring Limoges, St. Leonard de Noblat, Ambazac, but not La Perrine, and Luc was bitterly disappointed, but still hopeful.

"No, our Leader has more important places to visit. No," patting his pockets for cigarettes, "this is an official of the *CGQJ*."

"Vallat? Is he coming?" Luc is impressed. Danielle can already see him shining his boots, ironing his shirt, trying to make his hair lie flat. A real Vichy official, he'll consider that a special holiday, use it as an excuse to do no work, to form a parade of the Chantiers de Jeunesse boys, they love any occasion to march around and make a lot of noise.

"All the way out here? No, this is just some minor business . . ."

Claude peers into the old tin can he uses for an ashtray. He has taken to smoking dried sunflower leaves, rolling them up carefully in tissue paper squares when his tobacco runs out, although he always seems even more irritable when he smokes those, to Danielle. "They're taking a Census, that's all."

"They want to know how many people live in La Perrine?" Danielle asks. "We're so tiny." She laughs, uncertain. "Can't Monsieur Druot just fill out a form or something?"

"The *CGQJ* is the General Commission on Jewish Affairs." Luc looks at her with scorn. "Don't you remember? Don't you listen?"

"They want to count the Jews, dear," Berthe explains.

"Oh." *The Jewish Peril.* "But they already did that, last year. They counted all the . . . those people."

"Only in the Occupied Zone," Claude says. "Jews in the Unoccupied Zone must be counted now. And register with our government officials."

They are all silent a moment, looking at her.

She eyes them back, steadily. She shrugs. "So what? That has nothing to do with me, Tonton." The Chantiers have been here many generations, she reminds herself. With our fair skin, our golden red hair. Our good blood.

"Of course not, Marie-Jeanne." Berthe puts down her dishtowel, places her hands on Danielle's shoulders. "This doesn't concern you at all. It doesn't concern any of us."

"It does, in a way. A ha!" Claude discovers a real cigarette butt with some tobacco left. He lights it, careful not to spill any of the loose shreds, and inhales, deeply. "You know, child, we're very proud of you these past months."

"Yes, we are, very much," Berthe says.

"You've worked very hard. And done a fine job. You're a good girl."

"Thank you," she says. Then why is he looking at her like that, why does he sound as if she's done something wrong?

"But you'll need to be very careful right now. Especially careful."

"You mean with the official? I know the right answers to say. And I have my papers to show."

"Yes," he says. "And it's important not to give any information that isn't necessary. About yourself. About us."

"I understand that."

"Or about anyone else in the village."

They are quiet again, looking at her.

"This is about Genevieve," she says. They have never discussed this; there has never been any mention in the house of it. The thing about Genevieve and her father. She knows Luc hates Genevieve, of course. But Claude and Berthe have never said a word. So why talk about it now, why . . .

"Why didn't you tell me about her, before? That they were . . ." the word doesn't quite come out of her mouth, though, ". . . what they are."

Claude and Berthe exchange glances. "We didn't think you needed to know. And it isn't something to be discussed."

"But you're telling me now I can't be friends with her?"

"You shouldn't have gotten so friendly with her in the first place," Luc says.

"But I didn't know!"

"We just think you should keep more to yourself for a while, dear. Stay home more."

"She shouldn't be around here so much, either," Luc says. "You're always inviting her over here, you're always talking about her." He punches his pillow, tosses it to his bed. "It's dangerous."

"But everyone knows about them, and Father Tournel says we're all one human family, didn't he?" She looks at Luc. "Aren't we all supposed to love one another?"

Luc opens his mouth, then closes it, shakes his head as if she isn't even worth speaking to. He violently whip-shakes his blanket.

"Yes, child," Claude says.

"And that's very true, dear," Berthe says. "Yes. Amen."

"So, what's changed? What's so different?"

"It isn't that simple, Marie-Jeanne," Claude says. "We're all neighbors, yes. And we get along fine. But there's still differences between us and them. Genevieve's a good little girl, we have nothing against her. But Monsieur Clermont is a foreigner."

"But he's so nice, he—"

"He's not a bad man, I'm not saying that. That newsreel a few weeks ago, that's just propaganda. Someone trying to make a point and getting carried away."

"We have a new Minster of Propaganda, Papa."

"Another one? Well, there you are, he's just trying to impress everyone. Overdoing it a little. I'm sure the Marshal doesn't believe any of that rubbish, he'll put a stop to it."

"But isn't it Marshal Petain who appoints the Ministers and tells them what to do?" Danielle asks.

"Marie-Jeanne, the point is, no, Monsieur Clermont isn't looking to cause anyone harm. He works hard, we all know that. He's a good neighbor. And we've all been very good to him in return, haven't we? In fact, the Legion feels it isn't necessary to be so . . . official. Even Leroux, that idiot, he agrees. La Perrine's making an important contribution to the National Revolution. We know the truth here, and that's fine, that's enough. We can keep it to ourselves."

"The truth is the village needs Monsieur Clermont," Danielle says. "He helps La Perrine make that important contribution. Doesn't he?"

Nobody says anything.

"He's working himself to death to make the village look good. For all of us. Isn't he?" Claude cracks his knuckles.

"So, you're saying Monsieur Clermont isn't going to register? You want him to break a *rule*?"

"We're only suggesting this to him."

"But what if he did? If he and Genevieve were counted? Would they get into trouble?"

"Nothing would happen, I'm sure. It's just paperwork."

"You said they were rounding up foreign, the foreign ones in Paris."

"That's in Paris, Marie-Jeanne. We're not occupied, here."

"So you want me to lie about them, too?"

"No one's going to ask you. You're just a child. But we don't want anyone to think we're too friendly with them, too close. Like Luc says. Just in case."

"In case of *what*? If we're all—"

"She doesn't understand, Papa," says Luc. "She's too young to understand."

"I *do* understand, but why don't you—"

"Stop asking all these foolish questions, Marie-Jeanne." Claude gets up from the table, grabs his coat from its hook on the wall, struggles to fit his crooked shoulder in. "Just do as you're told. You're to go to school, to church, and then stay home with us. I'm going to the barn. We're not going to discuss this again."

~

There are two new people in church today. Danielle is acutely aware of the older man, red-faced and ill-at-ease in a necktie, and the young man, handsome in the dark blue uniform, his golden hair gleaming like his buttons, his glittering braid. She glances at Genevieve, sitting several rows back, next to her father. Monsieur Clermont's head is bowed, he moves his lips in prayer. Is he praying in Hebrew, she wonders, or Latin? In Polish? His accented French? She can see

Genevieve tug his sleeve when it's time to sit, to stand. His face and hair have been washed clean of chaff, but he looks worn, so tired and old. Everyone paid a careful, careless kind of attention to them when they walked into the square, polite nods, a handshake or two, as if Genevieve and her father always came to church together, as if this happens all the time.

But there was a fuss over the young blond man, the official. He had arrived early on Friday; Danielle, on her way to school, had watched him speed past her into the main square in a dirty black car coughing exhaust, and park in front of the mairie. He was staying in one of the two extra rooms above the tabac, Simone had whispered to them, the only version of a hotel the village had to offer. And he'd made his bed *himself*, had stacked his plates on his breakfast tray, folded his napkin, carried the tray down *himself*! Danielle, sitting next to Genevieve, just shrugged. Everyone had been fussing for days, women weeding their kitchen gardens and making sure to take in their clothesline wash, the Chantiers boys, on Monsieur Druot's orders, working to smooth the main road through the village, to pick up any bits of trash, any of those seditious pamphlets that collected along the dirt paths, at the foot of trees. Even Hortense and Simone wore their best Sunday dresses to school. There was a small commotion at the end of the day, as the door to the foyer opened and Monsieur Monzie greeted the official, clapping his hands for attention, Welcome to Monsieur Bonnard, an esteemed member of the *CGQJ*, we have the honor of his visit from Vichy! She'd felt Genevieve next to her, felt her breathing fast and hard, but she'd smiled at her, squeezed her hand, and they joined in with everyone in a loud rendition of *Marechal, nous voila!,* the second that day,

> *Marshal, here we are!*
> *Before you, the saviour of France.*

*We, your children, all swear*
*To serve you and follow your path.*
*You have given us back the hope*
*That our homeland will be reborn!*
*Marshal, Marshal, here we are!*

while Monsieur Bonnard nodded and applauded politely afterward. She observed him back, as students recited the *Principles of the Community* from the new poster Monsieur Monzie had put up next to the portrait of Petain, replacing the old *Declaration of the Rights of Man.*

"*Freedom and justice are maintained only by the virtues which generated them: work, courage, discipline and obedience to the law,*" Simone read, and,

"*Citizens must work to make society better, and not complain that it is not yet perfect,*" Hortense read, and,

"*The spirit of entitlement delays the progress made by the spirit of collaboration,*" Danielle read, thinking Monsieur Bonnard seemed to have his eyes especially on her, perhaps, and was careful not to stumble over the words, to proclaim in a clear, strong voice. But he was smiling at her, perhaps even a wink? She relaxed, relieved. Hortense caught her eye, *He's dreamy!* she mouthed, and she'd shrugged again in response.

She'd reported his arrival to Berthe and Claude that night, commented he must be a minor official, indeed, to be driving himself from village to village, probably just some kind of common clerk or lowly gendarme. She remembered the German officers in Paris, driven in sleek new cars by young men who never smiled and hurried to salute, to open and close car doors. But Monsieur Bonnard is a Frenchman, Claude pointed out, and our people have no need for such showy displays. And Marie-Jeanne was to stay home on Saturday, away from the village, did she understand? And miss *Confession,* Tonton? she'd asked, in a mock horror. Never mind, he said, just let the Monsieur tend to his own business and be on his way. They would mind theirs.

But he is in church today, the official, seated up front in a place of honor, the first to take Communion. Danielle walks up the aisle in her usual place behind Luc, knowing Genevieve and her father would be coming up at the rear. She remembers her first Mass, the sweat between her fingers, the rock in her throat, the heartbeat in her ears, and wishes she could look back now, give Genevieve and her father a reassuring smile, but knows she must march straight up to the altar to receive the body and blood of our Lord Jesus Christ, like any regular and boring Sunday.

Afterward Monsieur Bonnard stands with Father Tournel and Monsieur Druot on the church steps, Monsieur Druot acting like the mayor of Paris welcoming a foreign dignitary, "Ah, La Perrine is so honored by your visit, dear sir! Please, tell us about Vichy, is it true Marshal Petain takes a daily walk through the park, among the ordinary citizens? How is his health, our dear Marshal? Does he take the waters?"

Monsieur Bonnard, nodding, smiling, shaking hands with gathering around, declares his happiness to meet the wonderful citizens of this lovely village! Of course he will share his impressions with the Marshal! He is invited to dinners, a recital at school, but no, his stay will be too brief, alas, a mere formality, he must leave immediately. But everyone, please know, La Perrine now has a special friend in Vichy, at the *CGQJ*, if there is ever any assistance he might offer, any help he might provide to any of them, why, he would be honored to be called upon.

He looks younger up close, Danielle thinks. Probably glad to be leaving boring La Perrine, for all his ingratiating words, happy to go back to the excitement of the city.

"Monsieur and Madame Morel," Father Tournel says, "their son

Luc, their dear Marie- Jeanne."

Luc salutes the officer. He is hoping for a commission, Danielle thinks, as if he'll be invited to serve at Vichy, be given a proper uniform and real gun to march around with instead of sticks. Claude and Berthe shake hands, Berthe fussing with the Petain silk scarf around her neck. Danielle shakes his hand, too—how clean his hands are, those pink fingernails, smooth cuticles, no farmer's hands there—bobs a curtsy, and Monsieur Bonnard's shiny smile grows wider. The adults chuckle, they all move on. In the square they stop to chat with Madame Gaillard, wearing her ugliest fake necklace and brooch, and Danielle takes the moment to glance back to where Genevieve and her father are finally exiting the church, shaking hands with Monsieur Bonnard. She sees Father Tournel pat Genevieve's cheek, linger his hand there a moment, a reassuring little caress, sees him place his hand gently on Monsieur Clermont's arm. Good, she thinks, it's all over. She will go to Genevieve's house that afternoon, after Sunday lunch. She has spent much of her at-home Saturday working on her knitted potholder. It is almost finished, she is very proud of her work, cannot wait to offer her gift to her friend.

"Mademoiselle?"

She hears the call, is startled, trips on one of the rocks pitting the dusty road. A friendly voice, soft as music, not official-sounding at all. But he was supposed to leave right after church, leave La Perrine behind and drive back to his big city, Vichy and Petain, leave La Perrine to its mountains and farms and farmers and quiet own unimportant business . . .

"Yes, Monsieur?" she says. Look like you're in a hurry, she tells herself, shifting her weight from foot to foot, no, wait, don't look as if you want to run away, get away. She stands up straight, looks him full in the face. "Can I help you?"

"It's Marie-Jeanne, isn't it?" Monsieur Bonnard asks again, polite, as he approaches. So starched and pressed, sharp creases in his trousers and no dust on his shoes, how is that possible, no dust, if he walked out this way from the village?

"Yes, Monsieur." She is halfway to Genevieve's, the newspaper-wrapped potholder and borrowed book clutched in one hand, the other holding her gray sweater closed tight against the autumn wind. What is he doing here? He is smiling, lifting his cap, even, as if she were older, a lady. She resists the impulse to extend her hand to him, too sophisticated or elegant a gesture that would be. No, not with that hand, she thinks, that dry cracked hand of yours. She feels ashamed of her rough peasant hands. Of her tattered sweater, her sunburned cheeks. But no, that's good, she looks how she should, a dusty little village girl, she's no one, nothing. Just a child. But her identity card, where is it, *Chantier, Marie-Jeanne,* she realizes, it's at home, he'll ask to see it perhaps, *Your papers, please?* How could she leave that behind, today of all days?

"Marie-Jeanne, yes, I remember. Father Tournel was telling me about your coming here to live with your uncle and aunt."

"Oh . . ." she says. "Really?"

"I'm so sorry about your parents." She hears Genevieve's voice, *I'm so sorry . . .* He takes his cap off, as if embarrassed he'd forgotten to make the polite gesture, turns it around in his hands.

"Oh, yes. Thank you." She lowers her eyes, tightens her clutch on sweater and package and book. He's being nice first, maybe, to trick her.

"But how fortunate for you, to have family to take you in. Take care of you."

"Yes, Monsieur. Very fortunate." He'll call her Danielle, to see if she responds. *Danielle who?* she'll say, *I don't know a Danielle, there is no Danielle here. My name is Marie-Jeanne.*

But he doesn't, he's saying nothing at all. She waits for him to speak again, trying to breathe like a regular official girl, free of all care, he can't hear her heart beating, can he, in all the quiet? *Your papers, you'll show them to me at once!* But he is studying the mountains that hug the village, the fields with their dead sunflower stalks and withered old corn rasping in the breeze, the dry leaves scuttling along the street, collecting in piles against the long rock wall that lines the road. The sun has almost set, the sky turning dark-jeweled blue; by now Berthe has lighted the fire, and if she turns she will see smoke rising from the stone chimney down the road, the family getting ready for Sunday dinner. There is smoke in the air, from farmers burning their dry fields down, the burning smell of Paris, those early days of German boots, the scorch wandering into her bedroom curtains, clinging to the lace. But home isn't far away in a burning city, it's just down the road now, where it's warm, safe, thick stone walls, her cozy attic room, her clean dress hanging on a nail, her ceramic bowl on its shelf, supper bubbling on the stove. Claude and Berthe there to watch over her. And they do, she thinks, it isn't just the ration tickets, a suitcase full of jewels, I'm safe because of them, they wouldn't let this phony-nice official man trick me . . .

"It's always the children who suffer in times like these," she hears him say. "*Suffer the little children,* indeed."

"Yes," she says. "But as you said, I'm very lucky." *We're so lucky to be here, where it's safe,* didn't Genevieve say that? "And I should get home, I need to help with supper . . ."

"But you were coming this way?" he says, smiling.

"Just an errand, in the village."

"Oh?"

"To return something to a friend."

"How lucky for me, then. To run into you this way."

"Yes . . . but I can do it tomorrow, at school. My errand. It's colder out than I thought. And it's late." She plays up a shiver, *Let me go,* she thinks, let the cold little orphan girl without her papers go home to her nice family, please, be as gentlemanly as you seem. "And it's Sunday," she adds, "I shouldn't have come out at all. I should be home." If she stresses this, maybe, this small sin, out visiting on a Sunday afternoon instead of being home and pious, knitting socks for our brave prisoners-of-war, perhaps he'll be satisfied. Like those lies of sins at Confession, to make Father Tournel happy. That's smart, offering up something little to keep the bigger thing secret and safe.

"It is surprising how chilly it gets out here," he says. "Out in the countryside. It feels warmer in the city, somehow. Maybe it's all the buildings, trapping the warmth. Do you miss Paris?" he inquires.

"Oh no," she says. "I mean, I miss my parents—"

"Yes, of course . . ."

"—but I know they're in Heaven now. And I'm very happy here, really."

"Well, Paris must be very different these days, I'm sure. Don't you think?"

She can't tell if how he means this, *different.* Is *different* always bad, is that a criticism of the Germans? She smiles, shrugs. But he continues, without waiting for her response.

"And the air is so wonderful here. So clean. No car exhaust, no coal dust. Away from the noise. The smell of honest earth, here. And the sky . . . the sky is so . . . tranquil." He gazes upward, and she hurries to take a deep breath, let it out again. "I can just see an early star or two, twinkling. Look, there." He points. "Little diamonds in the sky. How does that poem go, let's see . . . *How sweet it is to see, across the misty gloom, a star born in the blue, a lamp lit in a room . . .*" He laughs, self-consciously. "I probably sound silly to you, don't I?"

An adult has never asked her such a question. He seems to want her to agree, but that can't be the right thing to do—tell a Vichy official he is being silly?

"No, no," she manages, "I understand. The sky here, yes, it's very tranquil."

But he has stopped smiling, is looking closely at her. Blue eyes, pretty eyes, like Petain, like the sapphire sky.

"You know, Marie-Jeanne, when Father Tournel told me about you, I wondered if—"

"Why would he . . ." she blurts out. "I mean, why, what else did he—"

"Oh, he was just telling me stories of the people here. And I thought A *ha*, I knew that girl wasn't from a place like this." He runs his hand through his blond hair, breaking its smooth cast, more boyish now than official.

"Oh?" she says.

"Oh, but I mean no disrespect to La Perrine. These little villages are the soul of our country. *France is our soil and our sons*, as the Marshal says. Not the cities, and what's going on there, now. All this 'official business' everyone bothers with, the foolish politics. No, this is the real France . . ." He pauses a moment, and there's a brief sadness about him, ". . . not Paris. Not Vichy."

"Everyone here works very hard," she says.

"Oh, no doubt! We appreciate the vegetables, the meat and grains you send. It's the hard work of peasant families like yours that's keeping our country going."

*Peasant?* No, she *is* a peasant girl, that's all she is, and that's good . . .

"I wish that were my job, really. Living and working in a beautiful place like this." He gazes around the empty fields, the dotting of farmhouses, the tiny glows of lights. "The honest labor. That would be something real. Instead of all this boring paperwork. It's ridiculous, what they have me doing. Rules and regulations, statutes, submit everything in triplicate, yes sir! Deadlines and files. Reports that disappear into drawers. It never ends. Do you know why the Marshal moved the government to Vichy?"

She shakes her head.

"Because there were enough hotel rooms for all the bureaucrats! And now the city is overrun with them. My office is a converted water closet! My filing cabinet is a bathtub! Everyone so consumed by all this pointless bureaucracy." He shrugs. "Oh, well . . . What are you reading?" he asks, motioning to the book in her hand.

"Oh, uh . . ." She shows him the book, hesitant.

"*Le Rouge et le Noir*! Impressive. For school?"

"Oh, no . . ." Genevieve, urging it on her, ". . . just, just on my own."

"Ah. You're a true reader, then. You read for love."

"I guess so."

"Me, too. Actually, what I wanted to do," he lowers his voice a moment, as if they aren't wholly alone, "well, I wanted to be a teacher."

"Really? My father, he—" *was a professor*, she almost says, then catches herself, "he was a teacher."

"How wonderful. Yes, I wanted to go to Paris to study and teach literature. Poetry."

"That's what my father taught!"

He beams. "Well, there you are. No wonder you love to read, then. It's in your blood." In my blood, she thinks, No, there is nothing in my blood, my blood is clean, pure, yes, my family honor and strength lie in my bloodline . . .

"*You are a pink and lovely autumn sky*," Monsieur Bonnard is reciting. "*But sadness in me rises like the sea. And leaves on my lips, as it retreats, the bitter salt of memory*." He looks questioningly at her, and she shrugs again, shakes her head.

"Baudelaire," he tells her. "I could send you a copy, if you like."

"Oh no, no, thank you!" Baudelaire, one of those writers Vichy has banned from schools and libraries, Zola and Rolland and Gide, books *contrary to the fundamental notion of morality*. Monsieur Monzie had made a production of it, bundling books up and handing them over to Monsieur Druot to lock away in the mairie, to keep everyone safe from their influence. Surprising, that he'd suggest such a forbidden book, an officer of Vichy.

"My parents, well my mother, said I was too young for Baudelaire."

"I'm sure you're mature enough now to appreciate him."

It must be a test. "I *know* my aunt and uncle wouldn't approve."

"Well, perhaps they're right. And now I've corrupted you. With all this decadence." He leans toward her conspiratorially, smiling. "You won't tell the Marshal on me, will you?"

"No, of course not!"

"Good. This can be our little secret."

"All right." Secrets, she doesn't like the talk of secrets. "So . . . why didn't you become a teacher?"

"The war was coming. And my parents, they live outside Reims, a little village like this. That's where I grew up. A wonderful place, some might even say progressive. An appreciation of different cultures. People of many nationalities. Catholics and Protestants, living in harmony side by side. Jews, even."

She nods along with his words, it's just a word after all, careful not to blink or change her breathing or expression, not to move the tiniest muscle in her face.

"But a true community, like here. Everyone looking out for one another. With the war, though . . . everything's changed now. And we have to change as well, do what we must. Life is very hard up North. This way, I can send them money. Extra tickets, if I can get some. Special treats. My father, he misses his coffee, his sausage . . ." He looks worried a moment. "You won't, you won't tell anyone about that, will you, Marie-Jeanne?"

"No, of course not." They're *his* secrets, she tells herself, nothing to worry about. It's like he's lonely. Maybe there's no one to talk to, in Vichy.

"I suppose they're proud of me."

"I'm sure they are," she says. "You're an important man. A Vichy police officer!"

"I'm a glorified clerk. That's all I am." He kicks at a pile of dead leaves. "People see the uniform and think it means something important, but it doesn't. It's just for show. Like so much of this, of what I do . . . Sometimes I'd like to run away from it all. Just run away in the middle of the night. Go home. Work the land. *The virtues of the earth,* as the Marshal would say." He looks sheepish. "Could you see me as a farmer, Marie-Jeanne? Planting my fields? Harvesting the grain?" He poses as if struggling to carry a yoke of heavy buckets, and she laughs, in spite of herself.

"Not really, Monsieur."

He laughs, too. "I suppose not. It's terrible, how you get used to things. A softer life. The easy way. It's not a bad job, I guess. And village life can be very hard, I know. Your mill, for example, what labor that takes! And it's run by a single man, Monsieur Clermont, isn't that right?"

"Yes . . ."

"Yes, I met him. With the accent. He must work night and day!"

Ah. Here it is. The trick. Genevieve's father. And Genevieve. *That's* what this is about, she realizes. Claude was right. Oh, he thinks he's very clever, this young man. Thinking she's just some foolish child. She isn't going to be tricked, no.

"I guess. I don't really know. But everyone here works hard. And . . ." something different, a different thing to talk about, ". . . and some of the boys go help at the mill," she says. "After school. Like my cousin Luc." Luc, always grumbling about having to go, always angry in that hard, simmering way when he comes home, his shadowy eyes turned black. "He's a member of the Chantiers de Jeunesse," she says, proud. "He wants to serve our country. He believes—"

"Yes, Monsieur Clermont, with the pretty daughter. They were at church this morning, weren't they?"

"I guess. But really, I don't know them very well," she says hurriedly. "My family—"

"There, you see? An entire village, working together! It's very true, that's where our strength lies now, everyone joining together to serve the common good."

"*Any citizen who pursues his own good outside of the common good goes against reason, and even against his own interest,*" she recites. That Vichy poster at school, *The Principles of Community.*

"Yes, exactly. But you, I was saying something about you . . ."

"Oh, yes, Monsieur?"

"Lucien."

"Excuse me?"

"Please, I can't stand all the formality! I have enough of that in Vichy. People there don't talk about anything real, about music or literature. Important ideas. Please. My name is Lucien." He looks at her, expectant. Hopeful, almost.

She swallows, nods. "Lucien."

"Yes, when Father Tournel told me you were from Paris, it was funny, that's *exactly* what I first thought when I saw you, walking down the road—"

"You saw me?"

"—and when I heard you recite. How different you were. That you didn't quite belong here. Not just your accent, of course, but something else—"

"Oh, no, Monsieur, really," she says, never mind she's contradicting an official, interrupting him, he mustn't think that, "it's just my hair. They say it makes me look Scottish!" She laughs, awkwardly, holds up a braid. "But that's it, there's nothing different about me."

"Your hair, yes . . ." He studies her a moment. "Ah, *pale girl, with auburn hair, whose tattered dress reveals your poverty and your beauty . . . for me, a wretched poet, your frail and freckled skin is so sweet . . .*" He flourishes his hand through the air.

Is he, is he insulting her now? She tugs at her sweater, *tattered, poverty,* tries to keep her face still but feels the quick frown tighten her forehead, can tell he sees it, too, by his sudden face of regret.

"Oh, Mademoiselle, forgive me! I didn't mean, really . . . the poem goes on, you see, the speaker is addressing a little red-haired beggar girl, yes, and she's poor, but he can see past that, because he sees how she carries herself. How special she is. *You wear your wooden shoes with more elegance than the Queen of a romance wears her velvet robes,* the poet tells her. And it's true, there's an elegance to certain women. A natural grace, no matter what the circumstances. You know what I mean, don't you?" He looks at her, distressed.

"Well, maybe." She sees her mother's red crown, the jeweled combs, the gleam of gems at her ears, her throat, her soft creamy hands, then no, it's swept away. She smells roses, too, but there are no roses here, all the roses are gone, everything's dead now, and her mother wasn't a queen. She stands up straighter, *A lady always stands up straight, cherie, think of the line you create . . .* He's right, it's all in how you carry yourself. "I think I know what you mean."

"You're how old, Marie-Jeanne? Fourteen? Fifteen?" He is smiling at her again.

"Oh, no. I'm twelve, Monsieur." Her birth date, that's real, hers and Marie-Jeanne's. That isn't a mistake she can possibly make.

"Only twelve! Really?" he says, his pale eyebrows raised. "Ah, so you're just a child, then!" She feels disappointed, as if she's failed a test, but no, she's doing well, doing everything right. Graceful, but a child, it's good he thinks that.

"But there you are," he continues, "you can already see it. There's a maturity about you. A sheen. It's a lovely thing, really. It's lovely to see in a young girl." He takes a step closer, skims his hand along the top of the stone wall.

"Well, thank you, Monsieur."

"Lucien."

She pauses. "Lucien."

"Yes. It's . . . well, again, we could say it's in your blood."

My blood, my blood, she thinks. Then this *is* about me. About my blood. But my blood, *Marie-Jeanne's* blood, is pure, it's clean one hundred percent Christian blood, for generations, honorable blood that doesn't lie.

"I'll be thirteen in a few months, though," she offers.

"Ah. Almost thirteen! Well, that's very different." He takes another step toward her, so close, too close, she backs up to lean against the stone wall, the leaves crunching under her feet. He looks even less official, this close, less like a policeman or bureaucrat and more like a regular boy. But not one of those grubby boys at school, no, like an older boy you could go for a walk with, go ice skating with, drink hot chocolate and talk about important things with, poetry and music, a grown-up mature boy you could imagine holding your hand. *Dreamy*, yes, a little. She looks away from his hot-chocolate-boy face, glances down. There's a bright white among the leaves, a piece of paper, maybe one of those seditious pamphlets, or that sermon of Father Tournel's, the *Unity* of something. But she can't make out the words. She hopes Monsieur Bonnard doesn't notice it. She tries to casually brush a few leaves over it with her foot. She feels a shift against her spine, the stones must be loose in their cement.

"And the Bishop will be coming to La Perrine next spring, my friends and I, we're all getting ready for our Confirmation," she says.

"We're all so excited."

"All of you together!"

"Yes, Hortense and Simone, you met them at church, and some of the boys—"

"The sacrament of Confirmation is such a joy. To make the choice to accept the Holy Ghost, become a true member of our community. That's the real test of strength. Maturity."

"That's what Father Tournel says."

"And to accept the responsibilities that come with such enlightenment. Having the courage to share and defend our faith."

"Of course."

"That's another thing, about these small villages. You see the Holy Ghost everywhere, in that feeling of community. Maybe that's what I mean about the air, the sky . . ." He waves at the air again, gazes up and around at the sky, and she slides her hand under the string around her neck, furtively pulls her Saint Jerome orphan medal from beneath her dress, lets it drop at her breast, on top of her sweater, there.

"*Love thy neighbor*, to me that's the truest spirit of Jesus Christ." He looks at her, as if it's a question. "Is it not?"

"Oh, yes! That's . . ." she thinks a moment, too many slogans and sayings tangled in her head, it's confusing, he's *testing* her, and Marie-Jeanne would understand this, would know, ". . . that's our *unity*, under God. That's the *New* Law," she says, remembering, grateful for remembering. "From the Gospel. From Jesus. It's the greatest gift we have from Jesus. To love one another, to always act out of love."

"Exactly!" He is smiling at her, nodding in approval, like Father Tournel. "And part of that love, of course, being a member of the community, is having respect for the community's laws. Don't you agree?"

"Well yes, that's . . . our moral obligation. Doing that."

"Although they seem so silly sometimes, don't they? All those rules and regulations?"

"I suppose," she says. A shiver surprises her, a real one. The chill of the stones, it must be. She should have worn her coat, the old white coat, so tight now in the shoulders, the elbows, it hardly fits anymore and what will she do, this coming cold winter? The sun has fully set and the light, the very air, are turning a dusky ink. She sees herself standing on a bridge, sees the shifting colors of sky,

*Entre chien et loup.*

Twilight, she thinks. The hour between dog and wolf.

"Look, you're cold. I don't want to keep you, your errand, was what . . . ?"

"Oh, just to return this book. Yes, I should—"

"There is a library here?"

"No, to my friend, Genevieve."

"Yes. The pretty little girl. Monsieur Clermont's daughter."

She nods.

"It's just the two of them, isn't it? Another sad story, Father Tournel told me, to lose a mother so young. But it's good the village helps them. Stands by them. So, she isn't getting confirmed, then?"

"Excuse me?"

"Your friend? Genevieve?"

"No, she's—" she starts to say, but stops, confused.

"Yes, she's your best friend, isn't she? Your teacher, he told me. The two of you are very close."

"Oh, not really, I—"

"*Like sisters*, you wrote."

"What?"

"Yes, Monsieur Monzie showed me some of the wonderful projects you've all done. *And we share all of our secrets*," he says in his quotation voice.

*And we promise we will always be like sisters.* She closes her eyes for a moment, sees those words. Written down, made official, those words. In her hand.

"You wrote that. Didn't you?" He smiles, waiting.

"But that was, it was just some assignment for school. I hardly know her at all."

"I understand," he murmurs. "She's very fortunate to have a friend like you. Someone with your maturity, your sophistication. Your faith. You understand what's important and what's not. Forms to fill out, reports to file. Assignments to write. None of that means anything, really. But at the end of the day, following the rules is how we show our love for one another. Isn't it?"

"I guess . . ."

"It's how we show our strength. It's what will save us." He reaches for her hand, the hand clutching at Saint Jerome; she drops the charm and his hand taking hers feels like a man's hand, warm and clean and smooth, and she's so ashamed of her own roughened hand, she hopes he doesn't look closely, hopes her hand isn't dirty, doesn't reek from stringing onion or garlic, and she squeezes her fingers around his without thinking.

"I'm sure you want what's best for her. What's best for everyone." He squeezes her hand in return. "The whole village. Your own family."

"Of course."

He interlaces his fingers with hers. "So it doesn't really matter, does it?"

"What?"

He smiles. "That she's Jewish?"

She blinks. "Oh, but she isn't, she's—" She stops herself.

He frowns at her. "Isn't that the truth?" He waits for her to speak. "*Love thy neighbor,* you said. You *do,* don't you?" He peers, searches her face. "You accept His gift, don't you?"

She swallows, nods.

"And we can all still love one another, be united in God. Don't you feel that way?" His frown deepens. "I haven't . . . *misjudged* you, have I?"

"No, no!"

"And you still love your friend, don't you? Even though she's—"

"Yes, of course she is!" She nods, vigorously. "Of course I do! Yes!"

His frown relaxes back to a relieved smile. "Thank you, Marie-Jeanne."

"For what?"

"For confirming my . . . impressions. It's just as I thought."

"But, Monsieur—"

"I see so much in you, Marie-Jeanne. How you understand things. Although you're much prettier than she is, you know. What a beautiful young woman you will be." He reaches, takes one of her braids in his other hand. "Thank you for making my business here so pleasant." He drops her braid, abruptly presses his mouth to the back of her hand and she almost gasps but catches it from making a sound. How briefly warm his mouth is, warming her cold hand. "You should be very proud of yourself. Helping me this way." He lets go of her hand, and it hovers a moment between them, extended, waiting. But he backs away from her, smiling. "I hope to see you again someday, Marie-Jeanne. Please know I am always at your humble service . . ."

He offers a little bow, replaces his cap on his head. He turns, strolls to behind the stone wall, and she realizes his car has been parked there. No wonder there's no dust on his shoes, she thinks. He must have driven out this way and stopped, for some reason.

"Good bye, Monsieur!"

"Lucien!" he calls.

"Lucien."

*"One special time, my sweet and lovely friend, your smooth arm on my*

*own was laid . . . Deep in my spirit, where the shadows blend, that memory will never fade!*"

He laughs, waves his hand at her with another flourish, and she turns away, quickly, before she has to hear his car engine growl, has to watch him drive away. It's so dark, hurry, go home, the light is all ended and gone, such dark air now, sudden night everywhere. Too late to see Genevieve now anyway, she can return the book another time. And the knitted potholder, she'll just give that to Berthe, replace the misshapen one with this perfect new version. Watch your step on the road, she tells herself, hurrying, book and potholder pressed to her chest against the chill, breaking into a clumsy run toward home.

## *MY FAITH*

*by Marie-Jeanne Chantier*

*10 February, 1942*
*La Perrine, France*

*I am very excited about my Confirmation this spring, with my best friends Hortense and Simone, now that I am thirteen and will become a mature member of our community in the presence of the Holy Ghost and receive all the gifts of this very special sacrament! You see the Holy Ghost everywhere in our village, all of us helping each other and being faithful to God.*

*For example, last fall my dear cousin Luc became very ill with a mysterious bad fever. Monsieur Leroux gave us medicine without charging, and Madame Gaillard even gave an orange for Luc to eat, so he could have all those vitamins. Father Tournel came over every single night to pray at Luc's bedside and offer comfort, and Sundays he led the entire village together in prayers to make him well. I prayed especially hard to our Blessed Mother to intercede to Jesus, and I'm sure she heard me and everyone else because finally Luc got miraculously all better and is fine and strong again, thank Heaven!*

*My tante Berthe is making me a new white dress for my Confirmation, and also promises she'll give me my dear Grandmere Bernadette's rosary to keep for my own. It is delicate and beautiful, made of the tiniest dried rosebuds. Tante Berthe keeps it in a trunk with all of her most treasured things, and I've promised I will treasure it and be very careful with it, always.*

*Yes, the sacrament of Confirmation will be such a joy!*

~

**April, 1942**

How wonderful to be in a city again! Even a small provincial city like Limoges, she thinks. She admires the ornamented buildings, the elegant shops displaying creamy porcelain and enamelware, many of the pieces glazed with Petain's benevolent face. Any place would be a wonderful change from La Perrine, where she knows every narrow dirt street by heart, every bleached-out shop sign, every crumbling stone wall and tattered, color-drained poster, every worn shutter and weathered face. And anxious faces, too, everyone in such a bad mood at the tabac, the café, the grocery, grumbling at each other and about each other and full of worried *They says* . . . They say English bombs falling on the Renault factory outside Paris killed hundreds of our innocent people. They say the Americans have declared war on the whole world, have joined up with the English and the Soviets against us, blood and death marching toward us again, and can the Germans keep us safe from the Communists and hostile aggressive forces who still want war, want blood, still want to bomb us and conquer and crush? They say the Americans and the English will invade North Africa, to gain a Mediterranean foothold, no, they say they're really planning a Channel crossing, an attack on our northern shores. They say Marshal Petain can't convince the Germans to release our prisoners-of-war, why can't he, didn't he promise us? They say Vichy is going to cut our rations again—haven't we atoned enough yet for our sins? And why are we still paying for the privilege of being *occupied*, how much more of our money, our food, our art, our treasures, can we send off to Germany, how much more of our blood and sweat can they take? Our own countrymen making trouble, too, becoming profiteers and speculators, *saboteurs* and *resistants*, printing their rabble-rousing pamphlets, setting off a stick of dynamite here, cutting a power line there, chalking those big *V*s for *Victory* on walls like that Churchill is urging over in England. Communists and anarchists and Jews (not the slightest muscle twitch, when she hears that word, not even a blink anymore), gypsies and Gaullists and democrats and Republican Spaniards fleeing their civil war and bringing their problems and dangerous ideas here, to us, all those troublemakers and criminals determined to keep Marshal Petain and the Germans from creating peace and prosperity for everyone.

Maybe it was all or mostly rumor lately, anyway. No newspapers or radio at home for the past several weeks—Claude had decided they would give all of that up for Lent, there was so little else to give up these days and that would be a true sacrifice. And she'd enjoyed the peace in the house, none of Claude and Luc's boring discussions about propaganda or statutes, just all of them working quietly at their chores. Although she'd recently heard voices in the middle of the night, seen the small flicker of a single candle; she'd crept downstairs to see Luc huddled at the kitchen table, his ears close to the radio, a word or two of muffled, staticky English drifting upward to her. The BBC, it must be, in spite of Claude's admonitions about listening to that rubbish. She saw Luc listening intently, scribbling notes. Keeping track of what de Gaulle and the Allies were up to, she'd thought, going back to bed, wanting to impress his papa with a show of knowledge, prove himself grownup enough to understand the whole world.

But she isn't going to worry today, not on this special day. How lucky she is to be in this safe pretty place, far from Paris and what's going on there now, the shrieks of air raid alerts, flames and smoke in the sky, stories of Germans behaving less like friends, they say, and more like conquerors, like *occupiers*. And all the worrying about Claire and her parents, and sending her special thoughts, You are my only true best friend in the world, Claire, I promise! I miss you even more these days, it's like when I first got here and there was no one but you to talk and think to and remember things with . . .

Just maybe not today, no worrying and remembering and thinking. A day to chalkboard sweep everything sad or throat-burning away, although she hardly ever has to do that anymore. And it's too wonderful to have new things to look at right now, and new city people, hurrying in their jackets and pressed ties, crisp pleated skirts and high heeled shoes, their carefully-combed hair, their clean hands, a touch of rouge on lips and cheeks, jewelry, even, she can spot here and there.

And city smells! Few automobiles on those paved streets, but the whiff of exhaust is a rare perfume, and there's the scent of fresh paint, and wood and metal and rubber and coal, no pervasive odor of animals or soil or chaff. And all the sounds, the *clomping* of horses' hooves and hard-soled shoes on cobblestones and the friendly *whirr* of bicycles, the *pling* of their tinny bells, a friendly traffic whistle and the piano music floating from an open window, somewhere. Even the bright colors of posters affixed to windows and walls everywhere are pretty, the fresh red-white-and-blue, double-axe'd recruitment posters offering good wages to men willing to go work in Germany, technicians, mechanics, factory workers, contribute your skills, bring honor to your people, show your patriotism, make German friends, do your share for your country! *France, Remember Yourself!* the posters exhort, which puzzles her—how could a whole country not remember who it was?

And what a beautiful day! That morning, when she and Berthe left

La Perrine, there were dark clouds bunching over the mountains and she'd worried Berthe would change her mind, march her back inside for a day of sewing, or clothes-washing or bean-sorting. But *Nothing's going to spoil our special day, Marie, here we go!* she'd said, bustling off happily to the bus stop. And they rode down the mountain, bouncing in their seats along steep curving roads (had she really *walked* all this way once, in the dark of that icy long-ago night? Climbed all this way to the hidden hilltop valley that was La Perrine? And had she really thought about running away, escaping, a little girl would be so lost out here, wandering through the dark mountains, all alone) and jouncing out suddenly into stretched-out flat fields just beginning to reveal their mist of yellow sunflowers and green corn, the sun bright in the cloudless spring sky, no smoke here, no bombs.

And the hats! She can't believe the hats on ladies everywhere. Hats trimmed with odd buttons and mismatched bows, knitted berries and flowers, dangling acorns, seashells, a spray of pigeon feathers, one with a tiny cardboard airplane, even. How proud they look, all those women, dressed up and oddly elegant, as if they're strolling down the rue de la Paix!

She and Berthe are seated at a corner café at the Place de la Motte, near the humming market square, sipping weak tea, nibbling slowly at tiny, ridiculously expensive pastries (*Now Maire-Jeanne, you've worked so hard, of course you deserve a special treat!*) to make them last. They're dry and stale and remind her of the vitamin cookies they're given at school. But how lovely, to eat something *purchased,* and served on a flowered porcelain plate, food made by strangers and with an actual sprinkling of crystal sugar, to sit here free of all care. A special day, the special treat Berthe had promised for all her hard work, the two of them running errands in Limoges and then a visit to Berthe's dear friend Madame Arnaux. The pastries will be gone soon, though, and she still feels hungry. But she won't ask for any more; she knows exactly how many coins Berthe has left in the pouch of her old black purse. And women are standing for hours in lines for food up north, they say, demonstrating for bread because they can't feed their children, and it's good to always remember that, to be grateful.

She sees Berthe adjust her own dowdy hat, one of the two she possesses, one for everyday and the good one for Sundays, although both look much the same, black straw or black felt, small-brimmed, both fraying and out-of-date. Danielle thinks of her own hat, a yellow one Berthe made from straws she'd soaked for days in a tub of water, braided into a golden cord that coiled at her feet, then sewn around and around for its shape. There's a pink flower on it Berthe fashioned from purloined scraps of glove leather, petals and leaf veins painstakingly embroidered in green floss and, watching these chic women hurrying past with their colorful bangles, the artful elegance of their make-up and hair, Danielle is suddenly ashamed of her unstylish country-girl hat with its crude little flower, the unbecoming yellow straw matching the Sunday yellow ribbons on her braids. She is ashamed of her new shoes, her handmade country-girl shoes, although at least they fit. Her old ones, finally, were so cracked and squeezing, and it had occurred to her maybe Genevieve had left some nice shoes behind when she and her father moved away, shoes she could maybe borrow. She had started walking to the mill but then felt the sharp rock in her throat, how it always hurt to think about Genevieve, whenever she forgot to forget. All of Genevieve's things probably belonged to the French state now, anyway, she thought, her clothes and books, just like the mill, so maybe it wouldn't be right to take them for herself, and she'd turned around and gone home.

But sometimes the hurt was there in sleeping, too, when she couldn't sweep it away, where she'd see a girl with purple hollows under her eyes and temple veins pulsing blue through gray skin, a ragged pink dress, long greasy dark hair falling from a dirty satin bow, the girl crying *Help me, save me!*, grabbing her hard with a bloodied waxen hand. She'd wake up crying, *I'm sorry, I'm sorry!* and suddenly warm strong arms would be there, *I'm here, Marie dear, it's all right, I've got you,* holding her close and she'd finally slip away into regular safe sleep. But there was no slipping away from it during the day sometimes, so she'd poke and worry at the blisters on her feet with a fingernail, make them pop and bleed. *Mea culpa.* But then Berthe had seen her limping, and become upset with her for not telling about the hurting shoes and blistery raw feet.

And so new shoes, the special birthday gift from Berthe and Claude. He'd carved wooden soles and jointed them, cut up a pair of his old worn boots to put leather on the sides and tops, and they work fine. She stretches her toes, scabbed over and healed now, reminds herself to be grateful for these sturdy, crude shoes. Funny, to think how many pretty shoes she used to have. Patent leather party shoes, and oh, those embroidered satin green ones, Claire, she thinks, do you remember those? You loved those but I wouldn't ever let you borrow them, I'm sorry about that, forgive me? I was so spoiled back then, like how Claude says our country became spoiled, with bad values, and we deserved what happened to us. But there's nothing wrong with wearing wooden shoes, if you carry yourself with elegance and grace. Sometimes I wonder what happened to all those pretty things I left behind, I hope they're all yours now, Claire, take anything else of mine you want, take it all . . .

She looks down at the fraying yellow ribbons. Maybe she's too old now, at thirteen, for braids, she thinks. Maybe when they pick up the newspapers for Claude at the tabac there will be a fashion magazine she can look through. Maybe Berthe will even let her cut her hair. Like Jeanne d'Arc, but more chic. Or start putting it up, maybe at least let her pin a braid up on top and around like a crown. Maybe after she's confirmed. She'll have to ask, later, when Berthe is in a good mood.

Because right now, Berthe is jutting her chin in a new way as the fashionable ladies *click clicking* past and she imagines Berthe must feel jealous of these ladies, too, and ashamed of her own dreary hat, also of straw, so obviously homemade.

"They look beautiful, don't they?"

"Who, Berthe?"

Berthe motions to a woman wearing a turban twisted of gray fabric. "Look, that's probably made from an old suit. The folds can hide stains or worn spots. Very clever. And that lady, there," she indicates a young woman juggling packages, leading two small children by the hand, all of them in matching multihued berets, "she knit those hats from leftover yarn, I can tell. Maybe unraveled an old sweater or two. And look how pretty and colorful they are. Any woman who knows what's what can still look like a proper lady."

*Any woman can be a lady, cherie, if she behaves like a lady.* And Danielle nods, agreeing. But did Berthe really just say that? Sometimes she hears a woman's voice, *You'll be sure to thank Madame Gaillard for that extra salt, won't you, dear?* and of course it is Berthe speaking, it is Berthe who is there, but they are also things a mother might have said, about manners and right and wrong and what is proper behavior and what isn't. And she has to stop a moment, sort through the voices to remember which is the real one she is hearing, and which is just a memory of a voice. Or an imagined voice, a figment, like in a ghost story.

But Berthe is here, nodding, head held high, and Danielle realizes it isn't shame on her face, it's pride. She watches her aunt sitting up straight and holding her porcelain teacup so carefully in her callused hand, her knuckles bulging out hard; she's seen Berthe examine her fingers in the lamplight, her left middle finger that is crooking at the joint, and wince as she tried to pull it straight. She thinks of all the things Berthe can make and do with those thick crooked hands. How many onions sliced, birds plucked, blouses scrubbed free of berry juice, cooking pots scoured with sand? She's watched Berthe's hands swell from wringing the icy or boiling water from a pile of wet laundry, from slapping the hard round rinds of cheeses she must make only to send away; she's seen those fingertips grow furred with needle pricks from the hours of sewing she does, for just those few extra francs. And still, she thinks, she's making *me* a new Confirmation dress, is spending hard-earned coins to take *me* to the city for tea. She feels ashamed of her vanity. Of still being hungry. Of judging Berthe, not being mature enough to see past that dowdy hat and those worn hands to the good person inside, all the good works she does, a natural lady, a woman of true grace. How many hours did Berthe work for this cup of tea and bite of dry pastry, how many glove fingers did those tired fingers stitch, her eyes strained by squinting to see in dim lamplight, the wick cut down low to save precious oil? Berthe holds on her lap a package of those embroidered gloves they will soon deliver to the milliner's shop down the street, gloves that will be sent north to fill the orders of German wives of German soldiers, to adorn the creamy soft hands of German ladies. (No, *they* aren't ladies, *real* ladies, those German women, she's heard people in the village whisper.) Or they'll be slipped onto the hands of those French women who have taken up with German soldiers, and they aren't ladies, either, no matter how they behave, they're even worse, French women prancing around in velvet and silk and getting plump on our cheeses and pastries, our beef, the fruits of our labors, sitting on fat German laps, bringing shame and dishonor to everyone, they'll pay for their sins when the war is over! She's heard Madame Richie and Madame Gaillard say that to Berthe, they love to mutter about such terrible French women, how could they *do* such a thing, let a kraut touch them, think of all those little kraut bastards we'll be seeing soon! But she's seen her aunt just shake her head sadly, as she tugged at silken threads, *No, Celeste, Therese, dear, we mustn't judge. Not every woman is strong as the both of you, without your brave husbands here. We must pray for their weakness, for their souls.*

Yes, she thinks, we *are* ladies, sitting in a café, having tea. She sits up straighter. It doesn't matter they live in a grubby little village and eat scrubbed potato skins and wear handmade wooden shoes, sweaters knit from their own smelly sheep, hats sewn from those sharp broken straws from their own fields. She should be proud of such things. Berthe is the one who deserves a treat. She'd been working so hard these past months, been so worried. Like everyone, worried and anxious. The rumors, the stories, that German progress against the Soviets was not going well as expected, that Petain's call for volunteers to join the Germans in their crusade against the Red Army might soon not be so voluntary. They say Alsace-Lorraine has already been annexed as German territory and young Alsatian men are already being conscripted to the *Wermacht,* are already wearing German uniforms, why, the Germans may even be eyeing our own boys from the Chantiers de Jeunesse to replenish their army, and hearing that, Danielle knew, made Berthe worry far less about bombs or the threat of Communism or godless Bolsheviks taking over the world, and far more about Luc. Sixteen years old now and passing for older, taller than Claude, angry and itching to leave behind the silly camping-out games and marches and acorn-gathering of the Chantiers de Jeunesse for a real uniform and real gun of his own, to strike a real blow, fight a man's fight, to answer Marshal Petain's supreme call.

Especially since he'd gotten all better, after his strange fever last autumn. Last November it started, right after Monsieur Druot and Father Tournel had come running to shout how Monsieur Clermont and Genevieve were being taken away. There were men in uniforms, Monsieur Druot had gasped. A truck. Guns. No, not Germans, they were *French* police! Claude shook his head, angry, and Luc's face went a sudden potato white that showed his dark eyes even darker, Berthe crossed herself and began to weep and Danielle busied herself with the coffee mill, grinding roasted acorns, round and round, she swallowed hard, grinding, tried to keep his voice from her ears. It had nothing to do with her, she reminded herself, just some pointless bureaucracy. Although Monsieur Druot, breathless and babbling, reminded her of Monsieur Beaumont, Claire's papa, rushing in to tell about other men in uniforms, other guns, the end of someone else. But so long ago, that was in the past too, and now these acorns needed to be ground.

Claude and Luc hurried to the mill, returned later with the news: Monsieur Clermont and Genevieve were being escorted to a camp, that was all, on their way to a new home. Nothing to worry about. Vichy officials had simply arrived to oversee the transfer. (Monsieur Bonnard? Danielle wondered, briefly, Lucien?, her breath catching, remembering his warm mouth pressed to her cold hand, but it couldn't be him, Monsieur Druot would have said if he'd come back, and he would have come to visit her, wouldn't he? But then, such a surprise, a gift arrived a few months later, all the way from the *CGQJ*, the pearly white leather prayer book and her name, *MARIE-JEANNE*, in large gold letters, *There is poetry in these beautiful prayers, too, Marie-Jeanne! Happy Birthday, your friend always, Lucien Bonnard*, the note read, how nice to be remembered . . .)

Yes, Clermont must have registered with the authorities after all, Claude had grumbled. Behind our backs. You can't trust those people, that's the truth. The whole village could have been blamed, harboring a man like that! And what will happen to the mill, who will serve as trustee? Yes, Berthe, he said, Clermont and Genevieve will be fine, it's just a camp, like staying at a hotel, they'll be resettled back in Poland soon. But a terrible thing for that Clermont to do, hurry off and leave things in such a mess! Oh, here, Marie-Jeanne, a letter for you, Luc found it in the little girl's room . . .

*10 November, 1941*

*Dear Marie-Jeanne,*

*Police are waiting outside, we have to leave. They found out about us, somehow. They came and made my father sign that he was non-Aryan and to give the mill to the state. They say they're taking us to a camp near Gurs. My father's worried they'll send us back to Poland, but I told him it couldn't be so bad there anymore. Maybe I can find some of my family, and I'll be able to finish my Livret Genealogique! I'll write you, from wherever we're resettled.*

*I've been knitting white lace, a surprise to hem your Confirmation dress! I'll take it with me and send it when I finish. Take anything of mine you want, and the books, my father says you can have all of them. And the last two jars of sunflower oil for your uncle are ready, they're here, don't forget those.*

*You're my best friend in the whole world, Marie-Jeanne. Please don't ever forget me,*

*Genevieve*

She'd lain in bed all that night trying to sweep away a shivering, hand-squeezing, pink-cheeked girl, finally tore the letter in tiny shreds, in the morning toilet-flushed the pieces all away. It's in the past now, forgotten, that's always what's best. Just a camp, like a hotel for a little while, not a prison or someplace terrible. Monsieur Clermont must have registered anyway, like Claude said, that's why it happened. There was nothing to worry about. And after all, everyone, the whole village was safer now, really. She had to work harder to remember that.

And there was even a bit more flour in the house, more bread, since Claude became trustee of the mill. There was a huge fight at the Legion about it, Claude told them—Monsieur Leroux angry that Clermont had to leave and the mill was "Aryanized," he said it was a disgrace and a shame and Father Tournel was upset, too. But Claude said better Aryanized than Germanized, and Monsieur Leroux probably just wanted to be trustee himself. So now Monsieur Leroux and Father Tournel didn't go to Legion meetings anymore, another thing everyone seemed upset about. Maybe because it was getting so cold out, everyone mostly staying home and separate.

That was when Luc suddenly seemed to stop speaking, and eating, always hunched over, and she'd seen the veins in his temple twitch sometimes, seen his jaws grind inside his shut-down pale face as he listened to Radio Vichy, and the violet smudges under his eyes were turning a darker plum. Then she'd heard, in the middle of one icy night, a choking kind of breathing sound that rose all the way to her room. She'd crept down to find Claude slumped at the kitchen table, his face in his hands, Berthe sitting next to Luc's pallet bed on the floor, pressing a damp cloth to Luc's forehead as he lay twisted in his sheets, eyes closed tight. She'd looked up and seen Danielle.

"Go back to bed, Marie dear, it's cold."

"What's wrong?"

"A little fever, that's all. He's been working too hard. He'll be fine in the morning."

But he wasn't. For weeks he lay in bed without speaking, pushing his face deep into his pillow with soft moans or lying still as stone, sometimes sweaty and feverish and crying as if his head would break open with pain. They feared consumption, diphtheria, typhoid, but

*No,* Father Tournel had said, feeling Luc's pulse, studying his face, *I'm afraid there's something else. A sickness of spirit or soul . . .*

And he'd asked to be alone with Luc, to offer spiritual comfort, which caused Berthe to gasp and fear Father Tournel meant to perform Extreme Unction, before he assured her No, this would pass, Luc would heal, but he believed Luc wished to unburden his heart about something, and nodded to Danielle as she gently led Claude and Berthe from the room.

Maybe he really *was* dying, though, and she felt a brief, happy hope—how wonderful, if Luc were gone! All his anger would be gone, too, that smolder always about to spark and flame and burn, it would just drift away, the air in the house would be easier and light and her shoulders could unknot. No more nasty snaps from him, or complaints how she was always in the way and why was she still such a spoiled baby, why is it she still couldn't even kill a stupid rabbit? It was so pleasant when he was working at the mill or in the fields, just she and Berthe together and Berthe would ask her to read her lessons aloud, ask questions about school. Or they would sew together, Danielle trying to help with the easier bits of glovework for the shop in Limoges, threading needles and making the French knots. Or Berthe would rehearse with her the Confirmation ritual (how funny, Claire, she'd thought, if I were still a Jewish girl I wouldn't have to be Bar Mitzvah'd like boys, but now I have to go through that silly Catholic ceremony, oh Claire, I wish we could be confirmed together, you'll be so pretty in a white dress, your dark hair and all that lace, like an angel) and she'd recite for Berthe the gifts and fruits and virtues she would receive from the Holy Ghost, while Berthe would nod, tell her she was so happy and proud. Or they would figure out a meal for four on the scraps of vegetables and cheese they were able to keep these days, the increasingly meager rations their tickets still bought at the grocer, so little food to be had now, even with the extra bread Claude brought home from the mill.

But they'd have even more food if Luc died, one less mouth to feed. She pictured a tart divided into thirds—the pieces would be so much larger than a tart divided into fourths. And Berthe was always saving the biggest and best pieces of things for him, and with Claude's blessing. She'd seen Claude give Luc his own portion sometimes, even, as if their precious son was worth sacrificing anything and everything for.

But if Luc died, other things would be harder. Their meat mostly came from his snares now (illegally, all wild game was supposed to be packed up and sent away, but that was another rule Claude was willing to break . . .). He caught wild rabbits so their own rabbits could grow bigger and make more babies, and carp and frogs in the lake (illegal), quail and partridge he'd slingshot down with a sharp stone (illegal). He gathered and split all that kindling and wood to keep them warm. And how could Claude possibly run both the farm and the mill if he were gone, Claude, too, already working eighteen hours a day, doing by hand much of the work he once had equipment for, that equipment old and breaking down and unable to be repaired? And they'd lose his rations, those paltry calories and pitiful grams Vichy officially allowed a teenage boy. There was a rumor about a family in Lille who had lost their little boy to tuberculosis but kept his death a secret for months, to keep his ration tickets coming, and they'd been thrown in jail when their mayor had found out. No, she felt guilty, having wished, even as a small dark secret no one would see, that Luc would die. She couldn't bring herself to tell that at Confession, though—how disappointed Father Tournel would be. And she didn't want him to know she'd wished for something so terrible and unChristian.

So she offered to give her attic room back to Luc, she could sleep in the kitchen and maybe that would help him get better, and that would be more good atoning works she could do to show and prove her faith and so earn God's love. But at the sound of that Luc became agitated, crying, *No, no, I want to stay here,* and Berthe said it was warmer in the kitchen, anyway, they should let him be. He wouldn't even allow them to change his linens, breaking into tears and clutching passionately at his pillowslip when they'd try. There was talk of the hospital in Limoges, a doctor from Ambazac or Razes, but Luc begged to be left alone, just let him alone, only Father Tournel could help him now.

Berthe sponged him, tried coaxing him to swallow broth, stewed the last of their onions to make a poultice for his chest, sat by his bed all day praying the Rosary and special prayers to Saint Bernadette, her eyes red-threaded and damp. No more sewing together, no more gossiping about the village goings-on or praise for Marie-Jeanne's hard work. One day Danielle impulsively got down on her knees with Berthe in front of the picture of the Virgin Mary Berthe had moved downstairs, next to the portrait of Marshal Petain, so their Mother could be with all of them every moment of every day. She placed her arm gently, hesitantly around Berthe, and Berthe had stopped in mid-*Hail Mary*, startled, then rested her big head on Danielle's shoulder, as if it were suddenly too heavy for her to lift, until Danielle chimed in with the prayer, prompting, *Blessed art thou among women* . . . Why not, if it makes Berthe feel better? Not any different from chanting all those prayers in church. Or singing *Marechal, nous voila!* at school. And she and Berthe prayed together, side by side, their voices rising and falling, reciting the *Our Father*s and the *Hail Mary*s and the *Glory Be*'s, their fingers counting out the decades on Berthe's rosary, and it felt lulling and peaceful to be there like that, together. She looked at the portrait of Mary gazing down at them, golden and blue, her gentle smile, warming them, blessing them. Listening. Maybe. After all, Jesus was a real person, even if he wasn't the Son of God. And so Mary was a real mother, wasn't she? And if she was only a regular mother, not the Mother of God or Queen of Heaven, does that really matter, when there's that sweet warmth in the room? Like when you think to Claire, Danielle reasoned, when you write to her in your head and heart, just because she isn't there for real in the room doesn't mean the thoughts and feelings aren't real. Isn't that just like prayer? So she sent her real mind thoughts, her real heart prayers, to Mary, asked her to watch over Luc. And Berthe and Claude. And Father Tournel, too, and Simone and Hortense, and Monsieur Monzie, everyone in La Perrine. Oh, and the prisoners-of- war. And Monsieur Bonnard, and Claire and her parents, of course. Who else? Oh, just watch over everyone, dear Holy Queen, our Blessed Mother, to you do I send up my sighs, mourning and weeping in this vale of tears, thank you very much, Amen!

Coming up from the root cellar with a basket of carrots and rutabagas (not allowed to keep their potatoes anymore, just rutabagas all the time now, they're horrible, and they keep cutting them up in smaller and smaller percents . . .) she found Berthe sitting at the kitchen table, her head resting on her arms, hair in a long spine of braid down her back, shoulders rising in deep sleep breaths. She set the basket down quietly, she could put the beans to soak, could cut up the rutabagas herself. Luc was murmuring on his pillow, she could hear the rasp of his lungs. What if he actually *did* die? This strange mean boy, this pretend dear cousin of hers. Like a brother, he was supposed to be. What would that be like, if it were real and true? To have a brother, an older brother, who would tease and play games with her, listen to her stories and problems, help her with schoolwork, who she could go to for comfort and advice and would always understand? Luc had never done any of that. But—look how little room he has, lying there on the floor, how uncomfortable he must be—what had she ever been to him but an intruder, an annoyance? A spoiled girl-stranger full of complaints, a phony cousin and niece and *ersatz* sister who brought danger with her to the whole village, another mouth to feed, and a Jewish mouth at that, the sudden new foreign child in the house who got the attic room all to herself, the little girl his own mother had always been so hungry for, who she could stitch pretty things for and fuss over, whose hair she could braid and tie ribbons on. Dear God, dear Blessed Mother of Mercy, mea culpa, I'm so sorry! She looked up at the picture of Mary, kind and smiling and forgiving as always, *Yes, Marie, you must love him as you love yourself,* she heard the voice say, *You must comfort him, care for him.* And she blinked, startled. Did she really hear those words, or just think them? Whose voice was that, soft and firm, or was it just a figment, the idea of a voice? But yes, she should do something to comfort him, care for him. Change his pillowslip, at least, it was so darkened now with tears and sweat. The *Annointing of the Sick,* bringing comfort to the ill and suffering. Luc wouldn't even notice, but God would. And Jesus and Mary, they would see, they would know and understand she never meant any harm.

She crouched at his bed and lifted his head carefully, surprised by its weight and the thick rough feel of his hair, the hot flush of his skin, surprised to realize this was the first time she'd ever touched him. Or been this close to him—even at church, sitting side-by-side, he sat slumped away from her. Now he was asleep like a very little boy, his head tilted back against her arm, mouth open, breathing coming congested from deep in his chest, and when she touched his hot sticky forehead he pressed his head against her chest like a baby in his sleep, that's how a baby must feel, his hand reached up to clutch at her apron, and her heart hurt all of a sudden about his being so helpless and sweet, about his sour unwashed smell of onions and used oil and damp wool. She rocked him slowly for a moment. Like a mother with her child, she thought, almost like he's my own baby boy, like the statue at church of Mary holding baby Jesus. Please help him, Holy Ghost, please, dear Blessed Mother . . .

She gently tugged the pillow free, trying to hurry, what is that small lump down at the bottom? She reached into the greasy pillowslip and felt something soft, a small knot (fabric?) buried deep down in the corner. She fumbled, drew it out—yes, a scrap of twisted cloth (a bow?). A sheen, and in the weak lamplight she could see it was pink, satiny, a bow, yes, a pink satin bow. With a long dark strand of hair woven through the knot. Genevieve's bow. *Luc found it in the little girl's room*. For a moment she was holding Genevieve's hand, could see her pretty dark hair and pale skin, one of those quick shy blushes coming on her cheek the way they do, when her father praised her, when she was embarrassed reciting in school, whenever Luc was around.

Whenever Luc was around. Always, around. Whenever Genevieve was there. And she could see the flush of red on Luc's face, too, a red she'd always thought was an angry red, to match his mean words and black eyes, and the way he breathed harder and distressed and moved in a clumsy way whenever Genevieve was around. Used to be around.

She thrust the thing back down and away in the pillowslip, hide it, quick, hide it away, stuffed the pillow in after, tucked it carefully beneath Luc's heavy head. He moaned, purple eyelids twitched. She backed away on her knees, slowly got to her feet, the soup, that's what she should be doing, you need to work harder, try harder, do your best better, everyone is safe now and that's what's important. She returned to her basket, emptied her vegetables without a sound.

"More tea, dear?"

She is startled back to the café, the sparkling city, special day, sees Berthe watching her, holding up the pretty porcelain teapot.

"Yes, thank you, Berthe."

"I believe there might be real tea leaves in this." Berthe smiles, pours more tea, hands Danielle the cup. She sits up straight, sips delicately, like a lady.

"Marie-Jeanne? Have you been feeling all right lately?"

"Yes, of course. Why?"

"Well, when you first came to us . . . those first few weeks you sometimes woke up crying in the middle of the night, you know.

Sometimes I went to you."

"Oh, but that was so long ago." If it ever really happened, her crying like a baby in the dark that way. She swallows more tea, it's tasteless but warm. "I'm much more mature now."

"Yes, you're becoming such a young lady! And you're so smart, dear, I'm so proud of how well you're doing at school. How beautifully you're getting along."

"Thank you."

"But I've wondered if anything is bothering you, again? Any trouble sleeping, like that?"

"No, not at all."

"Maybe some bad dreams . . . ?" Berthe is looking at her strangely, questioningly.

"I don't think so, Berthe. No."

"Well, if there's ever anything you'd like to tell me . . . I'm always here, dear. If there's something worrying you . . . ? If you did something that—"

"No, no, of course not! I'm fine."

Berthe pauses, then leans closer. She can smell Berthe's familiar smell of homemade soap, fresh cheese, warm fleece. And the unfamiliar scent of sugar on her breath, sweet.

"I'm sure she's all right, Marie."

"Who?"

Berthe blinks. "Why, your mother, dear."

Your Mother. She sees a blue robe, a golden light, smiling gentle eyes, hands reaching out to smooth her hair, stroke her face, so heavenly, so sweet . . . No, not her *Blessed Mother*. Just *Maman*, that's all, that's who Berthe is talking about.

"We would have heard something, someone would have gotten word to us if she was . . ."

Her low voice trails to an empty space, a missing word. *Gone*, that's what she means, Danielle thinks. *Dead*, maybe. Lying in a gutter, covered in blood and broken glass, shattered by an English bullet, an American bomb. Those envelopes, how long now since one's arrived? And not every month like they used to, Claude unhappy when he comes home empty-handed from the tabac. No envelope in a long time now, too long to still maybe happen again, like a chore someone's let slip their mind, forgotten all about. *I'll be thinking about you every moment of every day.* Missing, gone, dead, she must be, your mother, that other mother, that's why there's been no note . . .

Maybe that's better, she thinks. Better than being forgotten.

"I don't think about that," she tells Berthe. "Not at all. Please don't worry about me."

Berthe squeezes her hand. "We're so glad to have you, Marie."

She squeezes Berthe's hand back. They sip their tea, how soothing that is.

"Berthe, you said you'd always wanted a daughter, so why didn't you . . . ?"

"Oh, well . . ." Berthe fusses with her Petain scarf. "That was long ago. Back when I was working for your grandparents." She lowers her voice again. "Do you remember them, dear?"

Grandparents. Bernadette and Louis. No, the other ones, Berthe means. The frowning old lady with lace draped over her head, asking about milk and meat. An old man who only smiled when she recited meaningless Hebrew words. *Baruch atah Adonai* . . . But she isn't supposed to remember any of that, anyway, is surprised Berthe has even asked.

"Is that when you met tonton Claude?" she asks instead.

"Yes, back during the war. I needed work, and I couldn't be a teacher, or governess, or anything like that, I didn't have that kind of schooling. I wasn't used to being a maid in a fine house, either, but your grandmama was very patient. It was good of her to take me. She was always so proper about how things should be done, you know, very strict about the rules"—*Milk and meat mustn't touch*—"and so many foreign customs, of course, because they were—" Berthe catches herself, glances around the café.

"What?"

Berthe leans in close. "Well, because of what they were."

"Oh. Uh huh." She nods.

"I was used to a good Catholic home. But I learned. And your grandmama always gave me my Sundays off, and feast days, and holy days of obligation. So I didn't even mind about your grandparents. The truth is, they were very devout, good people of faith. I respected their observances, really. And I prayed for them every night, that they would open their hearts to the mystery of our Blessed Lord, and to His love."

"Yes, of course."

"So, your grandpapa came home from the war and he brought a wounded soldier with him, from his regiment. It was a dreadful wound, a shell ripped much of his shoulder, they'd tried to stitch the flesh and muscle back into place in the field hospital, but oh, it was terrible, very infected, the smell of it. He was in agony, the soldier. But he was very brave. I never once saw him cry. I worried he'd lose the arm. That we'd lose him. Your grandmama even allowed me to call in a priest . . ." Berthe pauses, both somber and proud. "It still hurts him, you know, to this day. Sometimes he's in terrible pain."

"I didn't know that."

"No, he's not one to complain, your tonton. Don't tell him, but I'm glad about that broken plow, it's forced him to let a few of the crops go. If the Germans want our grain, let them buy us a new plow!" She chews a bite of pastry. "But he did get better, thank Heaven. Such a strong man. He valet'd your grandpapa, but he also worked in the garden, with the horses, fixing things. Whatever was needed. Very clever with his hands. Even helping me, lifting things in the kitchen. Not much for speaking, or much education, but he was very devout, a good Catholic man. And well, I suppose you could say he began courting me."

Berthe smiles, is suddenly girlish. Her cheeks are flushed and she looks like Hortense does when she calls Father Tournel *dreamy*. Or Genevieve, when Luc was around. Cheeks flushing pink . . .

"Go on, please!" Danielle says. "What did he do, tell me?"

"Sometimes we'd walk together to evening Mass, just the two of us. There was a footpath through the trees, and when the moon was out, oh, it was so beautiful. One night he gave me a present. He'd carved a set of hairpins. Hours and hours it must have taken him! I still wear them." Berthe's hand flutters toward her knot of hair. "And when he asked me to marry him, well, I just couldn't believe . . . He knelt down, very formal and proper, but I could see him shaking . . ." Her voice softens in memory, a smile sweetening her face.

She can't imagine Claude doing such a thing, presenting a present to his lady fair, asking for her hand in marriage. Like a prince in a story. "And you said yes, right?"

"Well, I was almost thirty years old! I thought my chance was long past. And here was this fine man, a good, devoted man. We talked about a place of our own someday, a small village farm, he'd been saving his wages . . . Our dear Lord answered a prayer I didn't even know I'd said. A prayer I hadn't even dared. He does that, you know, He sees into our hearts and our souls, and He is always there to provide what we need."

"Even if we sometimes don't know what that is," Danielle says. "The thing we need most. Father Tournel says that."

"Yes, very true. He knows us better than we know ourselves, bless Him!"

"Do you mean Father Tournel or our dear Lord?" Danielle asks, teasing, and Berthe chuckles.

"Well, bless them both, I say! Anyway, we were married. And your grandparents approved, thank goodness, that isn't always the case, with servants. I was so happy. And then, years later, another prayer was answered, when I discovered I was going to have Luc. At my age! Such a miracle."

"A little like Saint Elizabeth, maybe?" Danielle says. "To be blessed with a child in her womb, after so long?"

"What a beautiful thought, dear, thank you!" Berthe touches Danielle's hand. "But I was worried. Employers don't like that, a servant's child running around. And I was feeling sick and sometimes I'd bleed a little. I was worried I'd lose the baby, and I was still doing all my work, trying to hide it, letting out my apron to keep covered up. We didn't have nearly enough money for our own home yet. I was hiding in the larder one day, feeling so ill and crying. Your grandmama was good to me, but she was so strict. I feared we'd be out on the street."

"Would she really have done that, Berthe? That's terrible."

"I thought maybe. There was one time, when I'd chipped a bowl. A soup tureen. An accident, just the rim, you could barely see it, but she was so angry. She'd asked me to be very careful with that piece. And she took the cost of the repair from my wages."

"That's so mean!"

"That's just how those people are, dear. About money, you know. But I was crying that day, so worried about the baby, and then your mother came in, and—"

"My . . ."

"Your mother, yes." Berthe catches herself, then shakes her head. "Oh, it's fine to tell you this, I'm sure. Your mother heard me crying, she must have been seventeen or eighteen. Just home from school. A young girl, really, not much older than you are now, Marie"—a schoolgirl *Maman*, knee socks and braids, no, just some other girl's mother, just the daughter of the lady Berthe used to work for, is all—"and she said 'Berthe, tell me, what's wrong?' And I found myself telling her everything. I'd known her since she was just a tiny little thing, running around. She liked to give all of us orders, such a little princess. And she went marching off to her maman and papa, she said we're to have a miracle from God, wasn't it wonderful! And Claude and Berthe must stay, she would even help take care of the baby, and how lucky we all were to celebrate such a blessing in the house! And your grandparents, well, they weren't happy about it. But they always gave in to whatever she wanted. They even gave us some extra money, to put aside. And Luc arrived, Claude was thrilled it was a boy, of course, but I suppose every woman wants to have a little girl. And I hoped it would happen again, someday, but Luc's delivery was hard, my labor was very long, the doctor was worried he'd have to go inside me, take the baby. I heard Claude tell the doctor he couldn't lose me, couldn't live without me, begging him not to let that happen . . . I'd never seen him cry . . ."

Berthe stops, a smile still on her face, but Danielle can see her eyes glisten, her lip quiver.

"Afterward the doctor said he had to do something to my insides, to stop the bleeding. That we probably wouldn't be blessed again. And we weren't."

"I'm so sorry, Berthe." She reaches, squeezes Berthe's hand again.

"Oh, but we had Luc! Such a beautiful baby, with those black curls. Those big dark eyes, always gazing at me. The sweetest baby boy. We stayed a while longer at your grandparents. I saw your mother marry your papa"—*My papa*, no, just that young woman's husband—"I was so happy for her, although you know the terrible difficulties about that. But she had her way in that, too. Then you were born. And later we were finally able to move here, to our own home. Yes, I owed your dear mother so much, Marie-Jeanne."

*Owed*, she said, like a debt to pay . . .

Berthe sips her tea, takes a bite of the pastry. "Of course we *were* blessed again, when you came to us! Another miracle!"

But . . .

"Berthe, what do you mean, 'difficulties'?"

"Hmm?"

"What you said. About 'the terrible difficulties.' What was so terrible?"

"Well, you know. About that." Berthe chews pastry, her mind walking along a moonlit path with her miracle suitor prince, holding her blessed baby boy.

"I *don't* know. What are you talking about?"

"Well . . ." Berthe glances around the café again, hitches her chair closer. "You know, how your grandparents didn't approve of your father."

"Oh. Yes, I guess . . . Why, though? Because he was older?"

"Oh, no . . ."

"Because he was . . . " she lowers her own voice, ". . . he was a professor?"

"Well, that was part of it. I'm sure they wanted your mother to marry, oh, someone important. A count, maybe. A captain of industry. The son of one of the gentlemen your grandfather did business with. She had so many suitors. She was so beautiful, your Maman"—*Was*, used to be . . .—"she could have chosen anyone, I imagine. But she wanted your papa. And your grandparents were so distressed, they said no, absolutely not."

"But what's wrong with being a professor, really? Just because he wasn't rich?"

"No, it wasn't that, dear." Berthe drops her voice so low Danielle can barely hear. "They didn't approve of his religion."

"But . . ." His religion? "But he was *Jewish,* wasn't he? He was—"

"Marie, shh, please! We shouldn't even be discussing this!"

Danielle mumbles, "I don't understand . . . ?"

"Well, only his father was a Jew, it seems."

"I know that." *One-half. Fifty percent.* "So?"

"Yes, and his mother was a good Christian woman. So I think that means he *wasn't* a Jew, not really. Now, in our faith any soul who wants to open his heart to our Blessed Lord, we welcome them, of course. To start a new life, with God. But the Jews have other ideas about that. Who can belong. Who they think is good enough or not, I suppose."

"That's why they were upset? Because he wasn't all Jewish? He wasn't Jewish *enough*?"

Still, *sale Juif . . .*

"Your grandmama felt it was wrong."

"But they loved each other! They did, didn't they? My . . . those two people?"

"Oh yes, anyone could see how happy they were. But your grandparents were so angry, they said if she married your father, she wasn't their daughter anymore, they'd wash their hands of her. And she said if they wanted to behave like that, she would just run off and marry him, anyway. And that's exactly what she did. But after you came, well, you were their grandchild, of course. Their blood. They couldn't bear to see you and your mother living on just what your papa could provide. So, they came around. I know they were very generous. Fancy clothes and things for both of you. A maid, even! And your mother's jewelry."

All those gleaming jewels, a small treasure. *A small fortune, there.*

"But your grandparents were so hurt. It was very painful for them, always."

"But that was so . . . bigoted. That was very bigoted of them to be that way!"

"No, try to understand, dear. I'd feel exactly the same way."

"But—"

"Marie, marriage is a sacrament. You know what that means, I know you do."

"Sacraments are sacred signs through which Christ's love is made visible in the world, and the means through which our faith is expressed and made strong," she recites.

"Yes, exactly. And Jesus is especially present in the love between two people, two baptized people, who marry and declare their commitment before God. But if *one* of those people isn't close to God, isn't open to receive His love . . . And to bring up children in a home like that! That isn't a *real* home in God's eyes, it just isn't. Why, if Luc wanted to marry someone who wasn't a good Catholic girl, well, even the idea!"

"Oh," she says. She looks down at her plate. "I see."

"I remember, when Luc was very little, maybe seven or eight, he came running home one day and told me there was a new little girl in school and she was the most beautiful wonderful girl ever and he was going to marry her when they grew up. It was very sweet. So I humored him, you know, how you do with children, and said Well, tell me all about her, dear! And, of course it was your friend, Genevieve—"

"My . . ." *And we will always be like sisters.* She quickly swallows tea.

"And so I had to explain, how this little girl and her papa were different. Yes, they were our neighbors and we should be kind, but no matter how pretty or nice she was, he just could never think about her that way. It was just wrong, in God's eyes. And one day he'd meet a good Catholic girl who was every bit as pretty and special. And they would make a happy home together, a real home we could all be proud of."

"You . . ." She fusses with the crumbs left on her plate.

"What, dear?"

"Sometimes, Berthe . . . sometimes you sound like only someone who is Catholic or Christian can be a good person. Someone God can love."

Berthe frowns. "Marie-Jeanne, you know me better than that! Have you *ever* heard me say anything, well, *anything* like what some people are saying these days? That terrible filth?"

"No . . . I guess not."

"Of course not. *Love thy neighbor*, didn't I just say that? No matter who or what they are. My heart goes out to those people. Look how they suffer." Berthe shakes her head, sorrowfully. "Your grandparents were only worried about your mother, dear, and you. About your very souls. I understand how they felt. Look at your parents, all the pain and trouble that caused."

"But you said they loved each other and were happy? And you were happy they got married?"

Berthe shrugs. "Well, she did run off and marry him. She was a dear girl, but she always did exactly whatever she wanted, your maman. No matter who it hurt." Berthe drinks the last of her tea. "And, after all, she wasn't *my* daughter."

"No . . ."

Berthe gathers her purse, her package of gloves, readjusts her hat. "I'm sorry, dear, I didn't mean to upset you."

"Oh, I'm not upset, Berthe. I promise."

"Well, good. Let's just put all that behind us, all right?"

"Of course. We can forget all about it. That story."

"Heavens, it's late. I don't want to miss the tram to Oradour. Juliette is so excited to meet you! Why don't I deliver these things while you get the newspapers?"

"All right."

"And, you'll be careful, won't you? With Juliette? After all, she believes . . ."

"Yes, of course. Don't worry, Berthe."

"Oh, I'm not. You're so smart about things." Berthe pushes herself to her feet.

"Thank you for the tea, and the treats."

"You deserve it, dear. Here, have this last little piece." Berthe offers her the last dry bit of pastry.

"No, I couldn't eat it," she says. She is still hungry, but the sugar taste has gone sour. Maybe Madame Arnaux will have some more food for them. "That's for you, tante Berthe."

"Oh, Marie . . ." Berthe leans, kisses Danielle on the cheek. "My dear Marie-Jeanne!"

She buys *Je suis partout, L'Action Francaise* and *Les Nouveaux Temps* at the tabac for Claude, newspapers with the cheeriest headlines, the largest pictures of a smiling Marshal Petain, statistics on robust agriculture production and troop deployments and photos of German troops buying flowers on the street, or the German Red Cross ladling soup to victims of the Allied bombings up north. She peers down the street—no sign of Berthe, maybe she and the milliner are still discussing price, or going through the next pile of piecework. She glances through the papers. Boring politics and current events, Claude will be happy to catch up on everything. Something on the *CGQJ* in Vichy, Luc talked about that, but Xavier Vallat has been fired now, something about his not getting along with the Germans, his resistance to their interference in French policies. Monsieur Bonnard, she remembers, he's with the *CGQJ*, isn't he? She reads more carefully. The *CGQJ*, that's the General Commission on Jewish Affairs. Oh, that's right. That's what it stands for. Yes . . .

She hurriedly looks elsewhere on the page, a small article catches her eye, about a camp, all this talk of camps these days, this one just outside Paris, a place called Drancy. Thousands of men being held there, most of them foreign Jews or prisoners, political undesirables, hostages taken in reprisal for all those criminals engaged in sabotage activity. More Jews will be gathered up and sent to Drancy, soon, the dedicated police of the *CGQJ* hard at work, all those foreign Jews, from other camps throughout France, even from the Unoccupied Zone, too, from Le Vernet and Les Milles, and Gurs (*I'll write to you, from Gurs*), and then they'll be sent onward, the resettlement has begun. They're being sent away from France to work in those camps, in foreign factories or farms in Eastern Europe, the first trainloads heading east through Alsace-Lorraine then continuing on under German guard to a place in Poland called Auschwitz.

She rolls the strange word in her mouth a moment, the soft, coiled-up letters. They're going to more *camps*, then, the foreign Jews, not back to their homes, their own villages and farms. Well, when they're done with the work in all those factories and camps, that's when they'll be sent home, of course. Auschwitz, maybe that's near where Monsieur Clermont is from, what was the name of that village? The newspaper is trembly in her hands, words dancing, she tries to grip harder, shake it straight. It means they'll be home soon, then, resettled and relocated, they'll be fine and happy and safe, be together. Be back where they belong. Free of all care. Nothing to worry about, no.

She quickly turns the page again. News of Paris. The University, an awards ceremony in Paris for distinguished, patriotic academics, a small grainy photo. A family, a man holding a plaque with one hand, shaking the hand of a swastika'd German official with the other, his wife and young daughter standing next to him with posed smiles. The daughter is pretty, about Danielle's age, a pretty dress, long dark hair, all of them with round, well-fed faces. Monsieur Georges Beaumont, Dean of the University, *Beaumont*, like Claire's father—that's *him* in the photo, that's *Claire*—honored for his excellent service to the Third Reich, his outstanding work in helping cleanse our academies and universities of the polluting Jewish influence (*And he reached out, your father, he was yelling, and he hit one of the soldiers,* a babbling, breathless voice, *incredible, he did that, was he crazy?,* yes, that *was* incredible, her gentle father who never raised his voice), Monsieur Beaumont's discovery and delivery to the Reich (*And the other soldier shot him, right in the belly, and I tried to help, their guns pointed right at me!*) of the most treacherous and dangerous of French academic Jewry (*And they took him, they dragged him away!*). Such a happy photo, the whole family together. His face looks so kind, that nice distinguished honored papa. The daughter looks so proud.

*They found out about us, somehow.*

The newspaper is shaking, again, faces and words scattering around the page and impossible to read. She blinks. Her fingers are damp, smeary with newsprint. Too much news, too many things happening, everything too fast, and her heart going rabbit quick again, all that sugar, probably, so bitter in her mouth, she's not used to it. She swallows, closes the paper, folds it up tight. None of it has anything to do with her, all so far away, and she's just a child. She looks around the tabac for a fashion magazine, a movie magazine. But her hands feel so dirty. She'll go find Berthe, look at the hats for sale, the gloves, that will be fun, the milliner will have something she can wipe her hands clean on. This is a special day, after all, a treat, something to enjoy. Not a care in the world.

Another photograph, another happy one, framed and on display. A photo of two young people with fresh-love smiles, seated on a grassy river bank, squinting into the sun. He is a young soldier, proud, his uniform crisp, his arm holding the young woman close. She is so pretty, blond hair swirled atop her head, holding an apple, a knife—there is a picnic spread out before them, she is obviously about to serve. Danielle imagines the young soldier stopped the young woman in the midst of unpacking their lunch, having positioned the borrowed camera on a nearby rock. The girl probably protested, laughing, *No, darling, let's eat first,* but he would have wanted to capture that exact moment the sun reflected off her hair, her bright smile. Keep that moment, forever. Keep it in a silver frame on the mantle. Show it to the baby, someday.

"And here is his medal." Madame Arnaux opens a small case, shows Danielle a square cross with two crossed swords, a bit of red and green ribbon, lying on a bed of velvet. Madame Arnaux touches it, a brief smile. "His *croix de guerre*. For acts of heroism in battle."

"He was a brave man, your Francois," Berthe says, chewing, from the table. She is eating. Madame Arnaux had indeed laid out food for them: cheeses and jams, apples, bits of crusty bread, and oh, what a delight, strips of smoked pink ham—*ham*!—sliced razor-thin. How many ration tickets she must have used for all of this! But Danielle had been too occupied with the baby to eat, the chubby little girl with white-blond curls, who, when Madame Arnaux met them at the tram stop, had pulled away from her mother's grasp, toddled a few steps across the grass and flung herself into Danielle's arms. They'd all laughed, Berthe and Danielle and Madame Arnaux, *No, Marie-Jeanne, you must call me Juliette, how wonderful to meet you!* The baby, Gabrielle, grabbed hold of Danielle's braids with sticky fingers and refused to let go, and Danielle has been carrying her ever since. Although her arms are beginning to ache. But how sweet, to hold a baby, how nicely she fits against her hip. It's nothing like holding a doll, a pretend baby, stiff and lifeless. She can't remember the last time she held a doll, anyway, so long ago that she was a little girl playing with dolls. What was that baby doll's name, the one she used to sleep with? It doesn't matter, it was just an old doll, and this baby is real, heavy and warm and full of squirms, the smells of milk and jam, the slightest whiff of urine, even, but a clean and nutty human smell. She thinks about Original Sin, no, this innocent squirmy thing has no guilt, no sin. The food, the tea, she would get to that later. And how nice to be in this pleasant room, the sound of the river floating through the lace curtains. Berthe was right, Oradour-sur-Glane was a pretty village, with happy air, a broad open sky. A short tram ride from Limoges, gliding along the side of green hills and across the little bridge over the Glane river to the center of a cheerful square. A hotel or two, restaurants and cafes where people were chattering pleasantly, hairdressers and bakeries, little girls playing hopscotch and boys fishing along the river's edge. Madame Arnaux's little apartment is lively with flowered wallpaper, a lace tablecloth, embroidered cushions. A sewing machine in the corner, bolts of fabric, a dressmaker's dummy half-clothed in folds of pink wool. Madame Arnaux is wearing a ruffled dress printed with daisies, her puffs of fresh blond hair like petals atop her head. Lipstick, even, and a light cologne, is that lilac, or lavender? And a phonograph! She hopes Madame Arnaux will put some records on later. It would be nice to live here, Danielle thinks wistfully, then guiltily, that's unfair to Berthe and Claude, after all.

Berthe is stirring a cube of sugar into a steaming cup of tea. "You can be so proud of him, Juliette. A dedicated, patriotic young man."

"Yes," Madame Arnaux says. "I tell that to Gabrielle, all the time. That she should be proud of her papa."

"Papa," the baby says. She grabs toward the photo of the young couple.

"Yes, darling, that's your papa, see?" Madame Arnaux says. "Are you sure she's not too heavy?" she asks Danielle. "You don't have to carry her all afternoon."

"No, please, I like it. I've never held a baby."

"Really? No little brothers or sisters?"

"My sister and her husband only had their dear Marie-Jeanne," Berthe says quickly.

"They hoped it would happen," Danielle says, a nod to Berthe, telling her not to worry, "they hoped they'd be blessed with more children someday, but . . ."

"Of course," says Madame Arnaux. "I always wanted a large family."

"Yes, well . . ." Perhaps the story needs more, the reason there weren't more blessings. "Maman's labor with me was very long and hard, you see. She was bleeding a lot. The doctor had to do something to her insides. She almost died, having me."

"Oh." Madame Arnaux glances at Berthe, who blinks. "I'm sorry, I had no idea . . ."

"Afterward the doctor told her they probably wouldn't be blessed again, and," hearing Berthe cough a little, "and they weren't. Because of me. And now they're both gone."

"I'm so sorry, Marie-Jeanne." Madame Arnaux places her hand on Danielle's shoulder. She looks so sad, Danielle thinks, *I'm sorry about your parents,* the memory voice in her head whispers. "But it isn't your fault," Madame Arnaux is saying. "You know that, right?"

"Yes, thank you," she says, polite. "And I know they're in Heaven, with God."

"That's what people say about Francois. He's watching down on Gabrielle and me now. And he died for France, and he was a hero, all of that . . ." Her voice thins out.

*A hero, Danielle, he died for the Jews and freedom and for France, he died for you . . .*

"That's, that's what my mother told me about my papa. What he died for."

"Your mother?"

*The polluting Jewish influence, they dragged him away . . .*

"Excuse me, Madame, I'm sorry, what were you saying?"

"I thought they were together, your parents, when . . . ?" Madame

Arnaux looks questioningly at her, at Berthe. Danielle sees Berthe stop in mid-chew. A mistake, that was a mistake, she thinks, why did you say that, when did you last make a *mistake*?

"Marie-Jeanne means—"

"I meant my *grandmother*," she interrupts. "She used to tell me that. After they died, together. My Grandmere Bernadette loved my papa very much, didn't she, tante Berthe?"

"Oh yes, dear. Of course she did."

"She was always talking about what a good man he was, always helping people. And very devout, so much faith. Grandmere Bernadette and I always went to church together to light candles for him and my mother, all the time. Before I came here. Right, tante Berthe?"

Berthe pauses, then goes back to chewing, nodding. "Yes, that's very true, Marie."

"And that's why God called them, my parents, because they were such good Christian people, He wanted them with Him forever in Heaven." Stop, she thinks, stop talking. She fusses with the baby, sways her a bit to ease the ache in her arms.

"Yes," Madame Arnaux says. "They're all with Him in Heaven. But it doesn't always help, does it, when people say that?" She looks at Danielle, and there's something in her eyes that's familiar, reminds her of Genevieve, that look of knowing Danielle is thinking and feeling things inside she isn't supposed to, the things she feel churning sour sometimes, even now, in her belly, her throat. Tea, she should drink some tea, that might help . . .

"Does it help you, Marie-Jeanne? When they say things like that?"

"Oh, I don't know . . ." She clears her throat. "*Blessed are they who mourn, for they will be comforted*," she quotes, hesitant. Did she get that right? She glances at Berthe.

"Yes," says Berthe, nodding, "how comforting it must be, Juliette, to know your Francois is with our Blessed Lord."

"I think our Blessed Lord has enough company these days," Madame Arnaux says, a bit sharp.

"Oh, Juliette . . ." Berthe puts down her teacup, opens her mouth, then closes it.

"I'm sorry, Berthe, I didn't mean . . . yes, you're absolutely right. And the two of you didn't come all this way just to listen to me being sorry for myself! There are so many other women here with the same story. And the poor children, all the children . . ."

*Suffer the little children, indeed,* she remembers.

"But today, we have a party!" Madame Arnaux refills her kettle with water, sets it to heat. "Please, Berthe, Marie-Jeanne, help yourselves. The butcher in Limoges is very kind, he tries to set aside some luxuries for us. And I'm still nursing, so I get extra rations." Her mouth makes a smile, but it's just the lipstick shape of one, a drawn-on smile. "My reward for motherhood. Doing my duty."

"Thank you, dear." Berthe carefully folds a limp strip of ham onto a piece of bread. "Everything is delicious!"

"What a pretty hat, Marie-Jeanne."

"Thank you," she says, proud. "Tante Berthe made it for me. And Tonton Claude made me these new shoes." She holds up a foot, to show.

"And how do you like school in La Perrine?"

"Very much. Our teacher, Monsieur Monzie, he likes to give us projects. That's fun."

"Marie is so smart!" says Berthe. "She writes wonderful essays and stories. Such beautiful penmanship."

"Hortense really is much smarter than I am, tante Berthe."

"Is she your best friend?" Madame Arnaux asks.

"Yes, her and Simone. Hortense is mostly just smart about school things, memorizing equations and history dates, and she gets good marks, but Simone is much funnier. They're both my best friends, really." *You're my best friend in the whole world,* she shakes that away.

"And what are the boys like?"

"Oh, Juliette," Berthe laughs. "Marie's too young to think about that kind of thing."

Madame Arnaux raises an eyebrow at her. "Are you too young for that, Marie-Jeanne?"

"I don't know . . . I think it's the boys that seem young, maybe. They aren't very . . ."

"Sophisticated?"

"No, not at all. And they aren't interested in talking about books or ideas or anything important. Just the war. I mean, I know that's important, but they're always yelling and running around with sticks, pretending they're guns."

"Little boys being soldiers." Madame Arnaux glances again at the photo on the mantel. "Men do that too, though," she says. "They want to prove how strong and brave they are."

"They *are* strong and brave, our men," Berthe says.

"Yes, of course, but sometimes the show of it means so much to them. Showing how they can take care of us, protect us." She sighs, with a small laugh inside of it. "It's funny, that photo. He'd told me he was leaving to fight, even though he didn't have to go yet, he was too young. I said he could wait six months, they'd allow that, but I really thought there wouldn't be any war. Or it would be over soon and he wouldn't have to go at all. But he wanted to fight. He showed up for our picnic in that uniform, thinking he was all grown up. And he surprised me with that camera, he wanted a picture of us together before he left. It looks like I'm smiling, doesn't it?"

"Yes."

"But I was so angry. It isn't a true smile, just how the camera caught us. So it's funny, to look at the picture, we look so happy. It's easy to forget the truth. Sometimes even I think how happy we were, when I look at it. I guess the lie is nicer to remember."

"That isn't really a lie, though, is it?" Danielle says. "To remember things just a little . . . rearranged? Or only remember what was happy, and forget all the rest?"

"Sometimes remembering what was happy hurts even more. Sometimes it's easier to remember the bad things. So you can be glad they're gone." Madame Arnaux pauses. "Do you ever feel that way?"

"I try not to think about any of it, I guess. I try to just . . . sweep it all away." Her throat is hot, a hot dry patch in the back. She glances at Berthe's cup of tea, a sip of tea would be good.

"When Francois was captured, that's when I was most happy, really. Better a prisoner-of- war than a casualty, right? The Germans would put him to work in a factory, they'd take good care of him, if he was useful. Let him repair their tanks, help them build their bombs, I don't care. He'll survive. He'll come back. My husband, he was training to be a mechanical engineer before the war. In Limoges," she explains.

"Oh."

"And then I heard he was still in France. Someone had denounced him, said he was a Communist—"

"Oh, how awful!" Berthe says.

"But he wasn't, really!" Madame Arnaux says, hasty. "Someone said they'd seen him at a meeting, before the war. And maybe he did go to a meeting or two, so what? It wasn't against the law, back then. He was just curious, he wanted to do something good. But they arrested him. They sent him to a camp at Chateaubriant, for political prisoners. I was happy again, though, I thought Good, at least he's here in France, it can't be so bad."

"No, not so bad," Danielle says. "Just a camp. That isn't a prison, or anything like that, right? More like a hotel."

Madame Arnaux smiles, the uncomfortable lipstick smile.

"Maybe."

"How did he . . . did he get sick?" Danielle asks.

"No . . ." Madame Arnaux offers a bit of bread to the baby, who takes it, sucks. "It was last fall. After that German officer was killed in Nantes. Francois and some other men were taken out and shot. Five of them. The first five names on the list, I suppose." She shrugs. "*A* for *Arnaux*."

"Oh . . ."

"A 'retaliatory gesture'. Our 'expiators.' The sacrifice we must make for our sins, as they tell us."

"I'm so sorry, Madame." She shifts the baby to her other hip, puts her own hand awkwardly on Madame Arnaux's shoulder. "But . . ." she gropes for the right kind of words, ". . . our sacrifices unite us to Christ, don't they?" She looks to Berthe, sees her nod. "So, maybe your husband's sacrifice brought him closer to God. In the end."

"Sacrifice, yes." Madame Arnaux moves away from Danielle, fusses to rearrange pieces of bread in their basket. "I get angry with him all over again, when I think about that. How he wanted to go off and be a soldier. And *sacrifice*. That he wanted to go off and do all that rather than be with me."

She feels her throat tighten again, begin to burn. "I'm sure he didn't really want to *leave* you, Madame—"

"I even yelled at his photo once, Fine, you got yourself killed, I hope you're happy!"

She looks away from Madame Arnaux's flushed face, presses her cheek to the baby's fine waxy hair.

"Juliette, dear, he *is* with our Blessed Lord now, he *is* watching over you and little—"

"Oh, Berthe, what difference does that make? When he's dead because some clerk somewhere had to fill out a form? Check names off a list?" She turns to Danielle again. "What kind of brave, noble sacrifice is that, to die as a *number*?"

"I don't know, Madame—"

"And Gabrielle, she gets a bunch of stories, a piece of old metal? A photograph that's a lie?" She takes the baby roughly from Danielle's arms, squeezes her hard. "What's God punishing *her* for?"

"I don't think God is punishing any of us, exactly . . ." she mumbles. "Why would he do that, want us to suffer? He gives us so many beautiful things, too, there's flowers and shells. And poems. And the cello . . ." she swallows again, hard, to push the burning away, ". . . but He has to allow the ugly awful things to exist, too. Because of, of free will. He gave us the freedom to choose between good and evil, that's how He shows His love and respect for us."

"Francois didn't have any *choice*. He had a German gun at his head! God made that choice, *He* chose the evil right then, didn't He? And left me with *that*?" She nods at the mantel. "What's a photograph? It can't talk to me. Touch me. It can't hold Gabrielle or tell her he's proud of his little girl. It's just another dead thing, that photo. It's a piece of junk!" She sets the baby down, to a wail, seizes the silver frame. "I don't want Gabrielle to look at it. I should throw it away, just get rid of it—"

"No, don't do that, please," and she's grabbed the frame from Madame Arnaux's hand, is clutching it to her chest, "it's beautiful to have this! I wish I could still have his face this way. My father." She crosses her arms around the frame. "I don't have a photo to look at. I don't have anything. I can't even see . . ."

Madame Arnaux abruptly stops pacing. "I'm so sorry, Marie-Jeanne. I wasn't thinking."

But she shakes her head. "Even if I want to, if I try . . ." and she does try, squeezes her eyes closed, looks and looks, but there's just a white smudge for skin, dark streak for hair, like a blurred newsreel face, "I can't see him anymore. It's shadows, is all." She opens her eyes, looks to Berthe. "Everything from before, Berthe, like you said. It's gone," she says, blinking. "It's all gone away. Disappeared. When did that happen?"

"Oh, dear, I didn't mean . . . I never meant you should—"

"I didn't *want* to see them, for so long, I didn't want to remember. And I used to *blame* him for getting killed, the way he died, that he would actually go and—"

"Marie-Jeanne, stop! I don't think you—"

"No, Berthe, don't worry. Don't worry, I just . . ." She wipes at her eyes, clears her throat. She turns to Madame Arnaux. "I only mean, you're right, Madame. It doesn't matter how he died, or for what reason. My father is dead, that's all. He's gone forever. And my mother, she's gone forever, too. She left, and I was so angry at her, also. And she's never coming back for me. It's true. I see that now."

"Oh, Marie . . ." Berthe presses her hand to her mouth.

"And I wish I believed they were in Heaven, watching over me, but I *don't*. I'll never see them again."

"Marie-Jeanne, now that isn't so! God wouldn't—"

"No, Berthe, you don't understand! God isn't *punishing* me, it's a gift, what He's done! It's better this way, I don't have to be waiting and hoping all the time. I can just . . . *be*, from now on. Be myself, for real." She blinks, amazed. "And it's *wonderful*. I was like you, Madame," she nods at Madame Arnaux, "I was so angry, before, when they were first gone. And God let me be angry, He didn't judge me for the terrible things I thought and felt because He knew I was just afraid. I thought being angry was better than feeling something more awful, and He was just waiting for me to see and understand, too. And I do now. Because when I pray and trust Him, when I let Him in to myself, I don't feel hateful or afraid anymore. I just feel . . . love. His love. And it fills up everywhere, like hot chocolate, like candles are glowing inside, here," her hand pressing the frame to her heart, "or like the sky, when it's twilight, all the darkness and light are still together and that way they make every color in the painting. And He'll always be with me. And Jesus and Mary, too, they won't ever leave me, I won't ever be left alone again. I used to think that was crazy, like a fairy story or a lie, I didn't *want* to believe any of it. But I believe it all now. Tante Berthe, I *feel* it. It's true!"

And it is gone, the pain in her belly, her eyes and throat, the heavy hot rock handed over to someone else and she is lightened and free of it, unburned.

"So Madame, maybe this photo, and his medal, I know it isn't your husband, but it's still a real thing God has given you, that you can hold in your hand," she reaches, presses the picture frame back into Madame Arnaux's shaking hands, "like when you hold your rosary or feel the music in church, those are all the little candles everywhere inside you that's *God*, our Blessed Lord. That's His real gift, if you can just open your heart and soul to accept it? Please do that? You need to do that. Please?"

She closes her eyes again, to see all the glowing satin colors and lights, like arms wrapped around her, and there are real soft arms around her now, holding her close.

"And that's the most beautiful thing," she whispers, "feeling that. Isn't it?"

"Yes . . ." Madame Arnaux is saying, nodding into her neck. "Yes, maybe . . ."

She feels the warm skin, the golden hair against her face, wet tears against her throat, the scent of lavender. She hears the baby fussing, Berthe trying to soothe her, but Madame Arnaux is still holding her, their breathing and heartbeats weaving together, and they sway a moment, as if the breeze through the lace curtains has draped itself, embraced itself around them.

Then Madame Arnaux leans back, brushes the damp from Danielle's face, smoothes a strand of her hair.

"Well. It really is a day for special gifts, isn't it?"

Her hand is cool against Danielle's cheek, and her smile comes from deep inside, not the painted-on kind, and Danielle nods, grateful. "Yes, Madame."

"Gifts for everyone!" Madame Arnaux releases her, sets the picture frame carefully on the mantel. She takes from a drawer a small package and hands it to Danielle. "For you."

"What's this?"

"Berthe wrote about your Confirmation, how excited you are, and I just wanted to make this for you."

"Oh, thank you, Madame, but really, you don't need to . . ."

She unwraps the tissue, and a delicate white foam unfolds, spills over her hands—

"Do you like it?"

—yards and lacy yards of it, knit in the finest thread.

"It's beautiful . . ."

*I've been knitting some white lace for you . . .*

She quickly holds it back out to Madame Arnaux. "But, I can't, I can't take it."

"Of course you can, why not?"

"You should save it for Gabrielle. For her first Communion." She motions toward the baby with it, she's deserving of this clean whiteness, she's so innocent and pure, so without sin. Gabrielle, squirming on Berthe's lap, holds her arms out to her mother.

"Well," Madame Arnaux laughs, "I have a few years to make some more for her. You could use it to trim your dress." She picks up the baby, wipes spittle, cuddles her.

*You can hem your dress.*

"No, please, I don't deserve this!"

"What do you mean?"

*Take it away please,* she wants to say, but she can't, can't explain, doesn't know why the lace is burning so blinding and white in her hand. She closes her eyes to it. There must be something, a bad thing she has thought or done but still hasn't confessed or atoned for. Ashes on her forehead. Confess, repent, *mea culpa,* and all will be forgiven. Swept away clean. But what is it? What could she have done that is so terrible? How can this be a punishment, this beautiful gift?

"It's all right, Marie-Jeanne," Berthe says. "You can accept it, really."

What if it's a *sign*, perhaps? A symbol of His grace, of His understanding and forgiveness, for any of her mistakes? Maybe it's a special blessing He has sent, for all her trying and doing her best, all her hard work? An expression of His love. And how terrible it would be of her, not to trust Him, not to accept such a gift . . .

*You accept His gift, don't you?*

She nods, closes her hand around the lace, yes.

"Thank you, Madame." She puts her arms again around both Madame Arnaux and the baby. "It's so beautiful, so good of you! Thank you so much!"

"My goodness, you're welcome, Marie!" How lovely, to feel Madame Arnaux's soft arms again, stroking her hair. "And I'll come celebrate with you in La Perrine. And maybe you'll come back here to visit Gabrielle and me again sometime? If it's all right with Berthe?"

Over Madame Arnaux's shoulder Danielle sees Berthe, smiling. "Of course, dear. Anytime. That would be nice for all of you."

~

*"Spiritus Sanctus superveniat in vos, et virtus Altissimi custodiat vos a peccatis."*

*"Amen."*

She is kneeled down, holding hands with Hortense on one side,

Simone on the other, and gazing up at the bishop. He is tall, made even taller with his standing and their kneeling and his tall pointed hat, although he is frail-looking, with loose waxy skin. Father Tournel stands near him to assist, his face and eyes shining. She breathes in the incense, the clear warm light from the windows, the fresh soap of her white dress and the starched white lace so immaculate against the dark stone floor. Her own rosary at her waist, the precious gift from tante Berthe, that belonged to her Grandmere Bernadette and now belongs to her. The bishop makes the sign of the cross, and she breathes in the Holy Ghost and the light of His grace. She knows the entire village is there, behind them, and Juliette is there with Gabrielle, too, she can hear the baby's fussing, the community united for this blessed event for the children of La Perrine who are ready to undergo the sacrament of Confirmation, to complete and confirm the grace they received in baptism, she did, yes, she *was* baptized, in her heart and soul, God knows that, and she has the certificate to show, doesn't she? Attesting and official, embossed, her name on it, *Marie-Jeanne,* like her prayer book, *MARIE-JEANNE,* a true child of God in those beautiful gold letters.

The bishop extends his hands over the confirmandi, is praying for the sevenfold gifts of the Holy Ghost to come upon these children, His wisdom, understanding, judgment, courage, knowledge, reverence and awe of Him, and she prays, too, that she might prove worthy of such gifts. The bishop sits and one by one the confirmandi rise and go to him, and, waiting, she prays again, to always have the courage and strength to serve Him and accept the responsibility of His love and enlightenment. It's her turn and she kneels again before the bishop, hears the bishop ask *Are you ready to do this, as an adult?* And she bows her head, says *Yes.* The bishop dips his thumb in a small bowl Father Tournel holds for him, the holy oil, the *chrism,* traces the sign of the cross four times on Marie-Jeanne's forehead, the seal of the Holy

Ghost, the indelible spiritual mark, and she is anointed, cleansed, strengthened, the thousand candles of His love making radiant and warm her soul, her heart, her blood.

"*Signo te signo Crucis. Et confirmo te Chrismate salutis. In nominee Patris, et Filii, et Spiritus Sancti.*"

"*Amen,*" she says.

And she feels the slap, the quick sudden burn of it—

"Peace be with you."

"And also with you."

—but not a burn, it's just a *pat*, it doesn't hurt, it isn't a punishment, it's a *welcome* to being truly grown up and mature, a member of the community, to show she is ready for the challenge and accepts the call to righteous action, open to the full true love and light of Jesus and the Father and the Holy Ghost, to the promise of His divine protection, His enduring love, His eternally safe embrace.

## *MY FAMILY*

*by Marie-Jeanne Chantier*

*1 September, 1942*
*La Perrine, France*

*I am so grateful for my wonderful family! Tante Berthe and tonton Claude sacrifice so much to keep me happy and safe. And my cousin Luc is the best big brother ever, I look up to him so much. I try hard to be a good daughter and sister back to all of them.*

*But family can be more than just blood—France is like one big family of fellow countrymen, or like neighbors here in La Perrine, how everyone helps one another. And my good friend Juliette Arnaux and her little daughter Gabrielle are almost a big sister and little sister to me now. Juliette teaches me sewing, I read stories to Gabrielle, and sometimes we go for picnics down by the river, when I visit them in Oradour-sur-Glane.*

*Our Heavenly Father and Blessed Mother are family too, of course, and all the saints who listen to our prayers, who think about us and look after us every moment of every day.*

*Being part of a family means you must work hard to look after each other and deserve their love and care. Even if that involves sacrifice, just as our dear Lord Jesus sacrificed for us, because it's often by what we sacrifice that we can best show our love.*

*7 September, 1942*
*M. Lucien Bonnard*
*c/o Commissiariat General aux Questions Juives*
*Vichy, Auvergne*

*Dear Monsieur Bonnard,*

*I still treasure the beautiful gift you sent me last year! Every morning I read the Gospel of the Day to my tante Berthe—you were very right, those beautiful prayers are like poetry, and give us such strength in these trying times.*

*I hope this finds you at the CGQJ, and that all is well in Vichy. It must be exciting there, although we hear about troublemakers attacking recruitment offices since Monsieur Laval created the "Releve," or ganging up to do sabotage and be seditious. Demonstrators shouting Death to Petain, even! Terrible people like that don't understand sacrifice and duty. Although I didn't understand the "Releve" either—it didn't seem fair that three of our people had to go work in Germany for only one of our prisoners to come home. Then tonton Claude explained how not enough of our people were volunteering, so Monsieur Laval was smart to make a deal where we get something back. And when Monsieur Laval said "I hope for a German victory!" on the radio, when the Germans begin sieging Stalingrad, Tonton has us pray for that too, so we can defeat Communism. But only at home - Father Tournel doesn't like us praying for "victory," he wants us to pray for an end to all the fighting and killing. But I think tonton Claude is right when he says the only way to have peace is if the good people fight hard and win all the battles, first. And then we can have peace.*

*But tante Berthe is upset how boys from the Chantiers de Jeunesse are being conscripted into the German army now. Tonton Claude says we all have to sacrifice, and it would be an honor for Luc to serve. She would still rather Luc work in a factory than go into the army, though.*

*So, I wonder if there is perhaps some way you could help with that, when Luc is old enough to volunteer? I'm sure you have many more important things to do. But you once said you would always try to help us. And I promised my family I'd ask you.*

*Thank you, and my very best regards,*
*Marie-Jeanne Chantier*

27 September, 1942

Mlle. Marie-Jeanne Chantier c/o
M. Claude Morel
La Perrine, Limousin

Dear Marie-Jeanne,

How wonderful to hear from you! You must be such a grown-up young lady by now! It's good to know you and your family are doing so well. And it's gratifying to hear of such commitment from a young man like your cousin Luc. I do hear of interesting opportunities from time to time in my position, and I promise I'll see what I can do to get Luc a good assignment.

Please write again, and keep me up-to-date on all the goings-on in La Perrine. I so enjoy hearing what everyone is up to, especially you. It is valuable for me to understand what goes on in the hearts and minds of our young people these days, and I am always impressed by your observations and insights.

Always remember, you are the future of our beloved country.

Your special friend, Lucien Bonnard

*15 October, 1942*
*M. Lucien Bonnard*
*c/o Commissiariat General aux Questions Juives*
*Vichy, Auvergne*

*Dear Monsieur Bonnard,*

*Thank you for writing me back! And for helping my cousin Luc, if you can. I'm very honored to know that you read and like my letters, and are interested in our little village.*

*Life here is very peaceful, with our nice air and tranquil sky. Although some people are unhappy about things on the radio. Like the round-up of foreigners at the Velodrome d'Hiver stadium—they say there were thousands of people packed in for so many hot days, that there wasn't enough food and water, and people were getting sick and babies crying, and some people even died. But I'm sure our police were doing their best to get everyone on the resettlement trains.*

*Tante Berthe was upset Jewish women and children were rounded up this time, not just the adult men, and she wondered what good will those little children be in the factories?*

*And most of the children are French citizens, she said, born here, even if their parents were foreign. Although we heard most of the grown-up Jews weren't foreigners this time, either, but French citizens. Or, they were citizens, before our leaders decided those people can never really be French at heart.*

*Tonton Claude said it was good of Monsieur Laval to round up the women and children and old people, because that way families can work and be resettled and stay together. It would be heartless to take parents away from all those innocent children—and I think he's right, those poor children would be so alone and frightened, to be left behind!*

*Father Tournel was also unhappy the Jewish people in the Occupied Zone are wearing yellow stars on their clothing now. But that makes sense, to ask the Jews to wear that star, because many of them look like regular people, so how else could you tell? And it's a sign of their faith, isn't it? So I think they should be proud to wear those stars. It isn't any different from good Christian people wearing a cross or a saint's medal, is it?*

*We're all hoping you might visit again, sometime? But we understand how busy you must be. And again, if you could help my dear cousin Luc, that would be wonderful.*

*Your special friend,*
*Marie-Jeanne Chantier*

~

**November, 1942**

It isn't that bad, really. Not nearly as bad as she'd feared. She's learned, the trick is to do it fast. Or you begin slow, you come up quietly to the pen, so it stays calm and unafraid. And you reach in, slowly again, and pull it out. She sometimes even pets it a moment, first, enjoying the soft fur between her dry fingers, the quick little flutter of its heart, the twitch of the tiny nose. It's easier to get it in position that way, when it stays calm, you don't want it to know you're the one who's afraid. Then you grip it by the hind legs—now you go fast, the faster the better—and you tuck the body under one arm, tight so you can feel its thin ribs, so you can't see its wet brown eyes, you grab the back of its head with the other and give a good hard twist. And the break is so quick, it's always a surprise, it makes you gasp a little, which reminds you you've been holding your breath the whole time, ever since you opened the door to the pen and reached inside and touched the soft fur, but it bursts out of you now, at the moment of the *snap*, and you feel all of a sudden relieved because it's over and dead and now you can breathe.

The first time was the worst. Tonton Claude spent long hours away at the mill, and Luc, too, working to collect every last sunflower seed, grain of wheat, cob of corn from the fields.

Luc was hardly ever around now, leaving before dawn, returning late in the day stained with sunflower oil and dusted with wheat germ, to bite at a sandwich then rush off with the Chantiers boys or disappear on his bicycle, coming home well after Marie-Jeanne was already asleep, and sometimes in the morning there would be an iron bolt for tonton Claude, an apple, or a small tin of smoked fish, and tonton Claude would smile, proud, and tell them not to ask Luc any questions. And tante Berthe's poor hands were so twisted and swollen, Marie-Jeanne was doing more of the gardening and cooking herself now, and the sewing, even the fine embroidery, she was so much better at it thanks to Juliette's teaching, and how proud she felt, being allowed to skip school one day a week and take the bus to Limoges all by herself, to hand over a package to the milliner, to be handed back those precious coins, to use those coins, the money she earned, to purchase salt, a tiny pouch of tea, sometimes a bit of ham from the friendly butcher, who would smile at her and sometimes wink.

But *Could you bring in a rabbit, please, for supper, Marie-Jeanne?* tante Berthe had asked, distracted, in pain, clearly forgetting this was a task Marie-Jeanne had still never done. She couldn't tell her *No*, couldn't say *Please, tante Berthe, I can't, I'm frightened*. It was time to stop being such a baby, making a fuss about everything. Almost fourteen years old! At fourteen Saint Jeanne d'Arc led an entire army, all by herself! And here she, Marie-Jeanne, was scared, of what? Where were her courage and fortitude, those Holy Ghost gifts so recently bestowed upon her, the responsibility she'd embraced? So *Yes, of course, tante Berthe*, she'd said, took a deep courageous breath and marched right outside, strode right up to the pen with fortitude. But she'd hesitated then, felt her heart pound like inside the brown rabbit, she could see it, the slight rapid beat inside the white chest fur. Their rabbits were hungry, too, and so thin. You can do this, she told herself. The first time you do anything, it's hard. Remember all the times you've seen Luc do this, and tante Berthe. Remember you're doing this for your family, to feed everyone, to keep them happy and healthy and safe. Such a small sacrifice to make, such a little thing to do. Saint Jeanne saved an entire country! A quick prayer of petition, and she'd reached in the pen, startling the rabbit so it darted back and forth, she grabbed at the soft long ears, heard the frightened rabbity squeal as she dragged it from the pen and she stopped, hesitated again, it's awful, and it kept squealing as she stood, frozen, gripping it squirming by its ears, and another squeal was so loud and hurtful, make it stop, make it be quiet, she grabbed at the little head with one hand and the neck with the other and twisted, slowly, trying to twist hard and steady but it panic-squirmed and scratched, she felt its tiny nails catch on her sweater, tiny stings on her arms, squealing piercing her ears, and she twisted and twisted until finally at last there was the crack of bone in her hands and it hung from her fists, all warm and limp and quiet swinging dead weight, and *thank you, God, for your blessing on my task, for the gift of this precious food, amen!*

Yes, she's learned the trick is to do it very very fast, almost without thinking.

~

"Marie-Jeanne? Is that you, dear?"

"Yes, tante Berthe."

"Oh, thank Heaven!"

She hurries into the warm kitchen, struggling to close the heavy door behind her against the outside chill, fumbling with packages and basket held tight to her chest like a shield. Another cold winter, were winters always this early, this icy and sharp? The winter night falls so fast each day now, an eye blink between thin afternoon sun and a sudden opaque dark. Walking home from the bus stop early evenings it feels as if there's her coat, then her sweater, then her dress, but beneath everything is a thin layer of hot ice, worn right up against her skin.

"We were so afraid you missed the bus!"

Tante Berthe and tonton Claude are seated at the kitchen table, eating a thin gray stew, or what Tante still calls a stew, mostly rutabagas and beans and the picked-clean remains of a rabbit carcass boiled in water with a touch of milk, sometimes a gristled scrap of ham. Good to be home, the cozy warmth, flickering oil lamps, music on the radio, their faces so relieved to see her. That icy air outside, she should be grateful for it, how it reminds her to appreciate this.

"It was late leaving Limoges, that's all. I'm sorry you worried." She kisses tante Berthe on the cheek, then tonton Claude, smiles at his pat on her shoulder, removes her coat, the clumsy mittens Tante had made for her from a worn out pair of Tonton's socks.

"I still don't like you taking the bus by yourself." Tante Berthe scrapes stew onto tonton Claude's plate. "With what's going on these days. Wandering around the city, a girl your age."

"Berthe, it's fine. She's a big girl. Tell her, Marie-Jeanne, tell her you're very careful."

"I'm very careful, tante Berthe." She and Tonton exchange amused glances—it's a familiar routine now, their reassuring Tante, their private joke. "I'm a big girl. It's a small city." Tonton Claude chuckles, nods. She unloads packages from her basket.

"Well, I wish Juliette would go into Limoges and meet you there."

"Yes, you always say that. She does too much for me already. Here's the liniment, the pharmacist said it has wintergreen oil. He was sorry it took so long to get."

"Thank you, Marie." Tante Berthe struggles to twist the cap, holds the bottle to her nose.

"Here . . ." Marie-Jeanne opens the bottle for her. "And here . . ." She proudly places a handful of coins on the table, some unused ration tickets. All the more precious now, those tickets, ever since those once-monthly envelopes had entirely ceased to arrive.

"That's very good, child," Tonton Claude says. "Very good."

"No tobacco, though. Not anywhere."

He shrugs. "Maybe that idiot Leroux will have some this week."

"Simone says the tabac is overdue for a big delivery. And Hortense says her mother ordered things weeks ago that still haven't arrived, so yes, maybe soon."

"The pharmacist was happy with the eggs?"

"Yes. But he said next time, maybe if we had some potatoes . . ."

"Potatoes!" He grumbles. "Who still has potatoes?"

"And the milliner? Did he give you more work?"

Marie-Jeanne holds up a package. "A collar and cuffs to embroider. That's all, he said orders just aren't coming in anymore."

"Well, it's something. Come sit by the fire, dear, you must be so cold."

"I will, I'm fine. But here, look what else I got!" She holds up her prize.

"My goodness, Marie-Jeanne!"

She sees their eyes glisten at the scrap-end of sausage. "I traded the butcher for it."

"What in the world did you have to trade?" Tante Berthe takes the sausage, inhales.

"I knit a hat for his little boy."

"With what? Where did you get the wool?" No more yarn to be had, since tonton Claude had butchered the last sheep, the last of the sheared wool knit into a scarf for Luc. The taste of that mutton, even the bones boiled for soup, long gone now, barely remembered.

"Remember my old sweater, the green one? It was all coming apart, so I unraveled the yarn, remember, like you said? And knotted the pieces together. Juliette showed me how."

"That's my smart girl." Tante Berthe wields a knife on the sausage, winces at the pressure on her hands.

"Berthe, here." Tonton Claude takes the knife and sausage from her, cuts small slices. "Are you hungry, Marie?"

"Oh, no, I ate supper at Juliette's. That's for the two of you. And for Luc, is he home?"

"When is Luc ever home these days?" Tante Berthe accepts the smallest slice of sausage, leaves the rest on Claude's plate. "I never know what he's up to anymore, out riding around in the dark all night . . ."

"He's fine, Berthe. He's doing what needs to be done."

"I know. But a boy also needs his rest. Not out running with those

Chantiers boys."

"He's over at the rectory tonight, he said." Tonton Claude puts sausage in his mouth, chews. "Some repair for Father Tournel."

"Well, that's good to hear. It's nice them spending so much time together. There's a piece of cheese for you, Marie dear."

"No, really, thank you, I'm fine. You two share it."

"Have a glass of milk, at least. I saved some for you. You aren't drinking enough milk, you need those vitamins."

Marie-Jeanne and Tonton smile at each other over Tante's head. That's a recent new one, *Drink more milk, Marie-Jeanne, you need those vitamins,* ever since she'd heard reports of children dying of malnutrition in Lyon and Bordeaux. *I'm fine, tante Berthe,* she always reassures her, *Don't worry, I'm perfectly healthy and fine*!

"All right, tante Berthe, thank you." A glass of milk, good, she *is* hungry, she and Juliette had given the last of the milk to Gabrielle and their supper was only a few bites of bread, some stewed onions, even in Oradour food was becoming harder to get. The radio music switches to voices, a broadcast, she pays no mind. She lifts the pan of milk up to a stool, it's light, the cow giving less these days, and reaches for the cream separator, hurrying, eager to go upstairs. She washes her hands at the sink, glances in the tiny mirror on the wall, smiles at her reflection. It's still a happy surprise to see herself this way, since she'd persuaded Tante to let Juliette cut her hair, a bob that curls now just below the tips of her ears. Easier to wash and keep clean if it's short, she'd told her, knowing that was a winning argument. She'd brought the long shorn braids home as promised, and Tante had wrapped them in tissue, sniffling, and put them away in the trunk with her treasured keepsakes.

"Dear God in Heaven!"

She turns, sees their intent, listening faces, jaws still. "Tante Berthe, what is it?"

Tonton Claude twists at the radio volume.

"*. . . invasion began in the early morning, an amphibious landing at key ports, followed by an aerial assault by Allied troops. French batteries and the invading fleet exchanged fire throughout the day, with the loss of multiple Allied landing crafts . . .*"

"Tonton, what is that, what's happened?"

"Hush, Marie, listen—"

"*. . . while our brave fighting forces have resisted the aggressors, we have reports they have nevertheless seized the ports of Oran, Algiers, and Casablanca . . .*"

"Dear Lord!" Tante Berthe crosses herself.

"What does it mean, Tonton? They've 'seized ports'?"

"They've attacked North Africa," he says. "The Americans and the English have landed in Algeria, and Morocco."

She tries to picture the map at school, there's a whole sea between here and there, isn't there, the Mediterranean?

"But that's so far away. Isn't it?"

"Those are our territories, dear."

"Yes, but—"

"It's an attack on French soil," he says. "And they're headed toward Tunisia, quiet!"

An *attack*, an invasion, again, she crosses herself, too, *Please Jesus, please Mary, please Holy Father please keep us safe, amen,* but is this *it*, then, the *end*, the real end, marching toward them? She remembers drums and boots, the boiling oil, the smoke and poison gas . . .

"But what does it *mean*?"

"*. . . and the situation remains precarious. While it is too early for casualty reports of our own fighting men—*"

"Claude, please. I can't listen to any more of that!"

"*—we estimate that thousands—*"

Tonton Claude switches off the radio. They sit for a moment

without speaking. Tante Berthe gets to her feet, gathers the dishes, but tonton Claude rests his hand on her shoulder.

"I'll do that, Berthe, just sit."

Tante Berthe sits again, wearily, as tonton Claude carries dishes to the sink. He stands there, his back to them, bowed. Marie-Jeanne can see the crooked line to his shoulder, its awkward pull on his shirt. His hands drop to his sides, trembling, as if they're waiting to grasp at something they can do. He takes a handkerchief from his pocket, she can see him wipe at his eyes. He blows his nose.

"Tonton? Will they, will they bomb us?"

"No, no . . ." He turns back to her, brushes away her concerns. "They bomb cities, child. Factories, supply depots. Military bases. No, they just want to distract the Germans from the fighting in Russia. Waste our good men, our supplies. Out in the desert." He laughs, a little. "They've conquered *sand*, that's all!"

"Will they come to La Perrine? The invaders?"

"All the way out here? No, it's just a minor battle. Nothing to worry about. Our leaders know what they're doing." His eyes wander up to the portrait of Petain, his bright blue gaze, his kind yet stern face.

*We are here, Marshal, before you, the savior of France!*

He pats her arm again. "There's nothing to worry about, child."

Child, yes, she's acting like a frightened little child. She's just worrying *him* now, making him worry about her. And look, she's frightening tante Berthe with all these questions. She picks up the cream separator, do something, make yourself useful . . .

"Why don't you go to bed, dear? You have school tomorrow."

"Well, I should . . ."

But tonton Claude takes the separator from her hands. "Go on, Marie-Jeanne. Your aunt is right. Get some sleep. You've been doing too much."

"Well . . . all right, then. Good night."

She kisses Tante's cheek again. Then goes to Tonton, puts her arms around him for a hug. He embraces her awkwardly with his stiff arm, his other arm still holding the separator. But he holds her tight, for a long moment, she can feel his bristly chin nodding against the top of her head, hears him sniff and clear his throat.

"Good night, child."

She fills a water pitcher, takes her last package, a candle, and climbs the stairs to her room. When she glances back she sees Tonton has set the separator down and returned to the table. He opens the bottle of liniment, pours a few drops to his palm, and carefully, gently, begins rubbing the oil onto Tante's hands.

"Our Father, who art in Heaven, hallowed be thy name. Thy kingdom come, thy will be done . . ." she hears them recite together, their hands together, and she joins them in her heart, *on Earth as it is in Heaven . . .*, as she quietly goes upstairs.

It's so cold, the attic air raw against her bare skin, but she wants to look at it, try it on one more time. She unwraps her package. The dress is so pretty, a lady's dress, a woman's dress! With a woman's shape, a snug waist and wider at the shoulders, darts at the bosom. A gift from Juliette, *Really, Marie, it just doesn't fit anymore since the baby.* She'd tried it on at Juliette's, shy, at first, about slipping off her old gray dress, the long-ago dress tante Berthe had let out, once, twice, then finally taken completely apart, ripping and re-sewing the pieces back together again in a more shapeless way so it would fit, although you could still see the faint lines of old seams if you looked. But she'd taken the new/old gray dress off, stood in her underpants and undershirt, hungry for the new one—a new dress! Soft blushing linen with a pattern of pink and violet flowers, a becoming sweetheart neckline, smelling faintly of lavender. *I just need to take it in a tiny bit, there,* Juliette said, smiling, nodding at her chest, *but how pretty you look, Marie!* And she'd twirled for Juliette, giggling like a little girl, never mind she's wearing a grown-up lady's dress, both of them laughing and Gabrielle laughing with them, too, although she didn't know what was funny. And she twirls again now, gazing at herself in the little kitchen mirror she's hung on the wall, next to a braid of garlic. She musn't forget to take the mirror back downstairs in the morning, before Tante notices and chastises her for such vanity.

She and Juliette had spent the afternoon like so many others, sewing and chatting about school and the goings-on in Oradour-sur-Glane, in La Perrine, teaching Gabrielle her letters, such a bright little girl. Juliette tells Marie-Jeanne stories of Francois, thrills her with the details of their first embrace, first kiss, and it's like a romantic scene in a movie, picturing the young couple swept away in a moonlit ecstasy. Marie-Jeanne tells Juliette how it's awkward being friends with Simone, now that Tonton and Simone's father won't even speak to each other, and Simone gets a little too sharp with her jokes these days, they're like tiny needle jabs, but she tries to always forgive Simone and turn the other cheek. And how Hortense really is putting on too much weight, even while everyone else is getting so thin, probably because her mother runs the grocery and can still get her extra food. And she tells Juliette memories about her dear maman and papa and their old life together in Paris, how Sundays they walked to church with Grandmere Bernadette and Grandpere Louis, how thrifty her mother was, on a schoolteacher's salary, how Grandmere Bernadette would bake cookies with her on chilly days, how jolly Grandpere Louis was, his silly stories and practical jokes.

Sometimes Juliette shows Marie-Jeanne how to apply lipstick or rouge, and she loves returning to Limoges on the tram that way, strolling along the streets like the other elegant ladies, with her bobbed hair and rouged lips, although her wooden shoes go *clop clop* and not the pretty *click click click* of high heels. But she is always careful to wipe her face clean before arriving home, Tante wouldn't like that at all. Sometimes Juliette puts a record on the phonograph and shows Marie-Jeanne how to foxtrot or waltz or do a bouncy dance called swing, never mind dancing was against the rules these days, *Believe me, Marie-Jeanne, when the war is over, the first thing everyone will do is dance, and a young lady needs to know how!* She lets Marie-Jeanne try on a pair of high heels for practice, although they're too big for her, and they teach Gabrielle to dance, too, all of them laughing, watch her bounce around on her chubby baby legs.

She takes off the pretty dress, shivering, hangs it on a nail between the yellow wool dress and the summer blouse and skirt Tante had made her, her initials, *MJ*, embroidered on the blouse in Tante's painstaking handiwork. She sets her underpants aside for washing in the morning, hurries into her nightgown. She pours water into her washbasin, wets a rag, washes herself modestly beneath the warm flannel. Tante will think the dress is too grown-up for her, she knows. Tante likes to think of her, still, as a little girl. Braids, and a little girl dress, a little girl undershirt. Even the white Confirmation dress, pretty but made without a tucked waist or any room in the chest, more like a First Communion dress than a mature grown-up girl's. She scrubs her face, looks at herself again in the tiny mirror. She'd been too embarrassed to go to Tante when it started, a few months ago, her *règles*—she'd felt vaguely ashamed, as if she'd done something wrong. The blood on her underpants reminded her of all those times she'd pricked her finger when learning to sew, how she'd soak the linen overnight to get out the stain, so Tante would never know. Or it looked like, yes, picturing the painted crucifix in Father Tournel's rectory, like that bright slash of red on Christ's naked white belly. So maybe her bleeding, now, and the odd cramps that came with it, the feeling of her insides crumpling up low and hard, were a thing that could bring her closer to Christ and his bleeding, his suffering? Like being hungry so much of the time now, her bodily trials a sort of sacrament, her blood a symbol of her grown-up love for Him.

Why *isn't* that one of the seven sacraments, she wonders, a woman bleeding every month like Christ? It *felt* like a sacred sign, both more mysterious and more real than Anointing the Sick. It didn't feel like anything having to do with boys, or babies, or sexual relations and married love. No, that blood was something precious, a holy thing that belonged to just her, her and Jesus. There had to be a special kind of prayer or blessing about it, but she couldn't ask Father Tournel. And tante Berthe wouldn't see it that way, either, she knew. Tante had never brought up a woman's règles to her; anytime she'd heard her and her friends mention their monthlies, *Je suis indisposée,* they'd say, with a telling, weary sigh, or *I have les fleurs,* or *Les Anglais ont débarqués*—a phrase that made no sense at all to her, frightened her, even, thinking they were discussing the war, that English invaders had landed on the northern coast of France, until Juliette had explained, *No, Marie, that's just an old-fashioned expression, 'The English have arrived,' the Redcoats, you see?*—Tante would hush them as if it were a thing not to be discussed, even in front of an almost-woman girl. They didn't understand it was a gift from Jesus. She is happy when it arrives every month, looks forward to it, the way she once looked forward to that envelope of little colored tickets. No, it wouldn't be a happy or holy thing for Tante, her becoming a woman.

Thank Heaven for Juliette! She hadn't been sure what to do about the practical side of it, how to keep herself tidy, had finally mumbled about it one day during her visit to Oradour. And Juliette had hugged her, congratulated her, then given her a rigging of safety pins, string and elastic called a *sanitary belt,* matter-of-fact and no silly euphemism, shown her how to fold the cotton rags, told her she might have stomach pains now and then, but it was nothing to worry about. She said she'd been meaning to ask Marie-Jeanne about this, she'd been concerned, Marie was so very thin, and she knew other women whose regles had gone irregular or stopped completely, not getting enough to eat or all the worry, her own still hadn't come back since the baby, and she was so relieved to know Marie-Jeanne was healthy and fine. She'd given Marie-Jeanne a tiny cake of soap too, a wonderful fatty soap made with rose water, soap was so hard to get, and she knew how Marie-Jeanne liked to keep herself clean. How lovely it smelled. She loved going to bed with her rose-washed hands tucked beneath her clean face, the lingering scent of rose so sweet, like the sweet flower breath and soft voice of her Blessed Mother, blossoming over her as she slept.

And today Juliette had given her a brassiere, as well. Peach silk with a touch of lace, still a little pouchy in front but *You'll fill that out soon, Marie-Jeanne, don't worry,* she'd said, smiling. She doesn't want Tante to know about the brassiere, either. She dries her hands and face, hides the brassiere beneath the yellow wool dress. She'll start wearing it tomorrow when she goes to school. She wonders if Hortense and Simone are wearing brassieres yet. If their mothers have told them about their *règles,* if they already know about sanitary belts and cramps. They usually just talk about schoolwork and which of the older boys are dreamy, when Monsieur Leroux might get new magazines at the tabac, when Madame Gaillard might get some baking powder in. Sometimes Hortense and Simone read letters from their prisoner-of-war father or brother and she listens politely, but those are so boring, just the weather in Germany and how much they miss home, assurances they're fine. She is sorry for them, that must feel so sad, to always be waiting and hoping for someone to come back. And they don't have a Juliette to teach them about important things, share such lovely gifts. Although she hadn't mentioned the special sacrament feeling of her private blood to Juliette, either—there were some things that felt so sacred and holy she only wanted to share them with Jesus, and with Mary and Jeanne. Say your prayers, go to bed, it's so cold . . .

She takes off her Saint Jerome medal, kisses it, sets it on the shelf next to her prayer book and *Livret Genealogique*. Her copy of *Le Rouge et le Noir* she'd given to Tonton ages ago, so he could use the pages to roll his dried sunflower-leaf cigarettes. She smooths the flannel nightgown against her bare hips, sees the nightgown flash white in the tiny mirror. She hesitates, then shrugs it back off, lays it on the bed. She takes off her socks, feels the cold burn of the floor on her bare feet. She walks back to the mirror, never mind she's being immodest. Or prideful, that's a sin, but . . . well, it's just very different, to see her naked body reflected back at her. It's different from glancing down at herself when she gets dressed or undressed, when she bathes twice a week in the old white bathtub downstairs. More like seeing herself as someone else might. How would she appear, to someone else looking at this strange girl? It *is* a strange girl, a stranger's body, this body, temple of the Holy Ghost, yes, thinner but still rounder at the same time. Cheekbones showing on the sunburned face, ruddy arms and legs, she can see muscles on those limbs, can see the startling pale-to-brown shifts at the ankles, the neck. She looks lower. Too old for an undershirt, definitely, this girl has a bosom now! Well, the start of one, anyway. Not like Juliette's, the pretty round woman breast she's seen her nurse Gabrielle with, back when she still had milk, humming a little to the baby and the two of them looking so lovely, like a portrait of the Virgin nursing the infant Jesus. Someday. She stands sideways, admires the swells of flesh on her chest, like apricots, she thinks, touching them, or like little pears, they're so soft. And yet she can count her ribs just below, like the thin bony rows you can feel on a rabbit. Is it her waist that is smaller, or her hips that have broadened, curved outward? And yet the two hip bones stick out sharp on either side of the stomach. Tante always so worried she isn't getting enough calories and vitamins, that she'll get sick or have deficiencies when she grows up.

But she *has* grown up, hasn't she? She's grown taller, bigger, her dress and skirt hems rising above her knees, her old white coat slashed to give room at the elbows, the shoulders, and patched with flour sacking. And she's grown hairs down there now, too, like the hairs under her arms, a darker red than her bobbed hair, she has to stand all the way up on tiptoe and tilt the mirror to see the ones down below. That brown mole on her belly, has that been there forever? And a tiny white scar on her right knee . . . when did that happen? She must have fallen as a child . . . but where, how? She can't remember, those things that belong to another time, to braids and babyhood scars and plump white cheeks. Where did that girl disappear to, and this girl, no, this young woman, this body, happen, appear? When she first held her *MARIE-JEANNE* prayer book or her carte d'identite, wore a blouse embroidered with *MJ*? When she cut her hair? When her regles started? At her Confirmation? Or earlier, before that, back during all the *firsts* of things, first garden weeding, first cow milking, first prayers to Christ and the Holy Ghost, the first time she prayed the Rosary, gave a rose to her Blessed Mother?

And the *first* first would also have been an *end* to something else, wouldn't it?

*Danielle.*

The sound of it in her head startles her. *God is my judge.* It isn't written anywhere. No certificate, no embossed or stitched letters. Danielle is just a word, a *she,* some unofficial *her,* a figment girl, when was the moment of that? It slips, shifts around in her mind, but *Marie-Jeanne* is me, is *I,* blessed by holy water and the Holy Ghost and the state, the real girl in the mirror now, tall and naked and white and sunbrowned, short hair wild from the wind. Marie-Jeanne, named for saints.

Hurry up, it's so cold, you're being silly, say your prayers, go to sleep. She pulls her nightgown back on, gathers her rosary, kneels before her bed. She and Juliette had already prayed together today, at the church in Oradour, larger and more beautiful than La Perrine's, with its tall tower and cross welcoming as she approached the village on the tram, high arched windows that let in creamy jeweled light, the soft marble Virgin and Saint Bernadette, the fine stone altar and lovely Jesus hanging on a scrolled ironwork cross. She loves praying there with Juliette and Gabrielle, the three of them kneeling together in the cool sunshine, counting their beads, their voices blending with the other women's *Hail Mary*'s and *Glory Be*'s . . . She should be praying more, asking for victory in battle so there could be peace, so everyone would be safe forever from the bayonets and the bombs. She looks at her Jeanne d'Arc card pinned to the wall, *she* was a brave and strong girl, she heard the real voices of real saints, not old memory-voices. She didn't waste time on peach-silk vanity or personal glory. She didn't question who she was when, didn't worry about such things. She was obedient to God's will. A soldier for God. She bows her head, presses her beads to her lips, inhales the faint dusty sweet wafting from the tiny rosebuds of her rosary, the gift from her dear Grandmere Bernadette, smell the rose water on her fingers, the sacred gift to remind me my Blessed Mother is with me, always, *Hail, Holy Queen, Mother of Mercy, please help me, inspire me to make the right choices and collaborate with God's plan and help keep everyone safe . . .*

~

She was right, the Mediterranean *is* huge, a whole entire sea, nothing to worry about. Just look at the map on the wall. Two maps, the map of France and the big map of Europe covered with inky lines where Monsieur Monzie has redrawn borders, flecked with little flag pins he sticks in to mark German progress on the Eastern Front, dotted with tiny holes from moving the pins back and forth. And a big red flag stuck right into Stalingrad, ever since the Germans launched such a successful attack.

But No, the Allied invasion was only the first step in a *new military strategy*, Hortense recited carefully to them, like a civics lesson, to *clear Axis forces from North Africa*, to *establish supply lines and neutralize French airfields*. And maybe recruit French troops to their side, attract some of the resistants.

"How do you know all this?" Marie-Jeanne whispers. They are all whispering, she and Hortense and Simone. Monsieur Monzie had left the room, earlier, when Monsieur Druot waved from the window, urgently motioned him outside, and everyone was supposed to work on their projects while he was gone, No talking, children, yes *yes*? The latest Minister of Education had announced a new theme for the school year, *The France We Love*, which Monsieur Monzie found very exciting. *Our historic French heroes can inspire all of us*, he'd announced, reading the dictate from Vichy. And so each student was to write the story of a famous French military expedition. But there hadn't been enough famous ones to go around, and paper was in such short supply, anyway, so the three of them are working together on Napoleon's heroic advance against Russia. If Monsieur Monzie returns, Marie-Jeanne reasons, they can simply tell him they're discussing inspiring military strategy.

Hortense has on her best-student-in-class face. "The BBC. My mother and I listen every night now. I take notes."

"Shh!" Marie-Jeanne glances at the other children, all of them studiously bent over their books, blowing onto their cold fingers. None of the older boys in school anymore, they're all off with the Chantiers. "Not so loud."

"Oh, Marie-Jeanne." Simone rolls her eyes. "You're such a goody-good."

"You aren't supposed to listen to that. It's illegal." She thinks of Luc, his ear to the radio, scribbling by candlelight. But that was different, she tells herself, that was Luc staying informed and educated about their enemies. This was just Hortense showing off.

"We've been listening, too, me and my parents," Simone whispers. "They say the Germans got caught off-guard, Hitler's too busy conquering Russia and Egypt. My father says the only way Hitler could beat the Soviet Union is if he'd gone there right after invading Poland. Instead of invading us. He says only a moron would invade Russia in winter. Like Napoleon." She taps at the papers on their desk.

"And they say our aircrafts and tanks are rusty and too old, and if the Germans had let us keep more troops and our military things more modern, this wouldn't have happened," Hortense informs them.

"We shouldn't be taking about this," Marie-Jeanne whispers.

"My father says it shows we aren't really partners, the Germans've only been using us. Making us give them our food and pay them too much money. They've bled us dry, he says."

"My mother says it's our food keeping the German monsters alive. So they can do terrible things."

"And they've gotten our leaders to do awful things, too, my father says."

"What 'awful things'?" Marie-Jeanne asks, annoyed. The two of them, always bragging about their parents, always trying to best each other, and her.

Simone pauses. "Well . . . sometimes my father reads those other newspapers to us, the banned ones. He read in *J'accuse* about how—"

"That's a Communist paper, Simone, your father's not supposed to sell that!"

"He doesn't sell it. He just reads it. He read all those round-ups of the Jews they're doing, that when they get them to those camps they . . ." She hesitates.

"They resettle them," Marie-Jeanne tells her. "Everyone knows that."

"No. He said they use gas on them."

"What do you mean?" Hortense asks. She looks at Simone, then Marie-Jeanne, unhappy at not having the answer, but curious. "What does that mean?"

"I don't know," Simone says. "He wouldn't explain it to me."

Hortense frowns beneath her heavy bangs. Simone studies her fingernails. Marie-Jeanne glances again at the map on the wall, smooths pages of their story, darkens an exclamation point.

"It's just for delousing," she explains to them. "Those people, they aren't always as clean as they could be."

"That isn't a very nice thing to say, Marie-Jeanne," Simone tells her.

"No, I don't mean it that way," she says. "I know they're our brothers and sisters, but they really are a health risk. That's all the gasoline's for, to kill vermin. It's just good hygiene."

"Oh, of course," Hortense says. "That's what I thought."

"That's all just British propaganda, anyway," she tells them. "About the Germans being so awful. Those camps are like big hotels. Until they get resettled. Tonton says the Allies and de Gaulle are playing on fears, and spreading ugly rumors and lies, and only frightened unpatriotic people believe that rubbish."

"It's better than *Vichy* propaganda," Simone says. "My father says we can't believe a word *they're* telling us anymore. He says that stuff's for the bigots and right-wing fanatics."

"Tonton isn't a fanatic. Or a bigot. He's a patriot. He fought in the Great War."

"Well, so did my father."

"He ruined his shoulder fighting the Germans. It still hurts him, all the time."

"Ooh, his *shoulder*!" Simone rolls her eyes again.

"He did! It was a dreadful wound, and got infected."

"Who cares about a *shoulder*? My father lost his *leg*!"

"Well, Tonton almost died! He was given Extreme Unction!"

"Shh . . ." Hortense says.

"Who cares about *almost dying*? My cousins did *die*! And Hortense's brother!"

"Marie-Jeanne, Simone, please . . ." Hortense looks at both of them, pleadingly.

"Well, *both* of my parents are dead!"

"But they didn't die in the *war*!" Simone snaps.

Oh, she's right, they *didn't*, they died trying to help the poor orphan children, such good devout Christians. But she's annoyed again, like whenever Simone out-argues her, she just wants to slap her, slap it all away. But she sees Simone's face, miserable. *Turn the other cheek*, she hears in her head, and *Forgive her her trespasses*, yes.

"I'm sorry, Simone," she says. "I don't want to fight. We're best friends, all of us."

Simone nods. "I'm sorry, too. That was an awful thing to say. Really."

They look down at their work, but the air is still heavy and wrong somehow. She feels the unfamiliar brassiere strap loose on her shoulder, too big for her, Juliette will need to give that a stitch or two.

"You still shouldn't listen to foreign radio, though, you know," she mumbles. "It's very wrong. You could get into trouble."

Simone makes a face of mock-fear. "Ooh, are you going to *denounce* us, Marie-Jeanne?"

Hortense giggles, and Marie-Jeanne gives her a shove.

"Go ahead, write a letter to Petain. Say 'It is my duty as a citizen of the French State to inform you the Leroux family of La Perrine listens to the radio'. I'm sure they'll send a bunch of tanks or something."

But she is relieved to see Simone is smiling, just normal friend-teasing. "I really think the Marshal has more important things to do than bother with *you,*" she says loftily.

"Well, then also tell them my little sister colors outside the lines in her Marshal Petain coloring book. Maybe Laval himself will come arrest her."

"Yes, good idea. I'll be sure to mention that."

"Denounce me too!" Hortense giggles again.

"All right. 'It is also my duty to report that Hortense Gaillard is always off-key when she sings *Marechal, nous voila'*!"

"'And she complains about her morning calisthenics'," Simone offers. "'She doesn't realize it's very unpatriotic to be so flabby!'"

"That isn't so funny," Hortense says.

"She's just teasing," Marie-Jeanne reassures her. "So, what should I denounce you for?"

"Well . . . I hate rutabagas."

"Everyone hates rutabagas," Simone says. "I bet Petain and Laval won't even eat them."

"Oh, wait!" Hortense says. "Say 'Hortense Gaillard complained unpatriotically when her mother smashed their Marshal Petain statue on the floor and she had to sweep it all up!'."

Marie-Jeanne and Simone exchange glances, and Hortense's giggle shifts to a nervous smile.

"It was an accident. After the newsreels showed those prisoners coming home. She thinks it's a lie our men'll come back. She thinks we'll never see my father again." She shrugs a little. "She was just upset."

"They *are* lying. Petain and Laval see the end coming and they're lying about everything now," Simone says.

"What 'end'? The end of what?"

"The end . . ." Simone hesitates, unsure. "Well, the end of the war. Isn't that what everyone's waiting for?"

"I don't even remember what that's like," Hortense says. "No war. Except more food."

"Pastry," Simone says. "And omelets cooked in butter."

"And butter on white bread. And chocolate!" Hortense says.

"I can't remember the last time I had chocolate," Marie-Jeanne says. She tries to imagine the creamy darkness in her mouth, the melty sweet, but there's no recollection of it, none at all. She shrugs.

"And chicken!" Hortense says. "We had chicken all the time. Every Sunday, at least."

"We did, too!" Simone says. "For Sunday dinner, after church. Roasted with potatoes. Marie-Jeanne, what about you?"

"Yes, we had chicken every, every . . ." The memory gets stuck on something, a piece of lace, a silver cup of wine, ". . . sometimes. Every now and then." There's a twist in her belly, hollow, just hungry. She shakes her head. "I don't really like chicken, anyway. I don't miss that at all. Let's not talk about food."

"I miss my father. I remember him being here," Hortense says. "I remember that."

"He'll come back," Simone says. "My brother, too. And our families will all be together again."

They fall silent, Hortense and Simone glancing apologetically at Marie-Jeanne.

"Of course you will." She smiles at them, reassuring. "It's OK, really. I have a wonderful family, right here. And you're right, we'll win the war soon, and your families will be back together. Everything just the same as before."

Hortense shakes her head. "But Vichy's not telling us the real casualties. How many, I mean. A lot more than they say."

"They died with honor. Keeping the Americans and English from invading us," Marie-Jeanne says.

"My father says the Allies are our only hope. And we should all be resisting the Germans more, and fighting against Vichy, too."

"Oh, Simone, what're you going to do, blow up a truck? Pass out those silly pamphlets?"

"No . . ."

"What difference do those victory *V*s on everything make? That's so childish."

"My mother says the young men doing the sabotage, stealing weapons from the Germans and standing up to them, she says *they're* the heroes," Hortense says. "She wishes my brother died that way."

"They aren't heroes," Marie-Jeanne insists. "They're traitors. They make everything worse for everyone else. And they just get arrested. Or killed, doing stupid things like that. Your brother *was* a hero, Hortense, the way he died."

"But he *did* die fighting the Germans. It was at the front, that's all. What's different?"

"I think there's a big difference between being a *real* soldier, going and fighting where your leaders tell you, when it's patriotic and official, and just . . . making trouble. Yelling and fighting in the street. That doesn't help anyone."

"De Gaulle said it's the sacred duty of every man to contribute all he can to the liberation of our country," Simone says.

"'Our country'! He doesn't even live in France," Marie-Jeanne says. "De Gaulle's a big fake. He's a coward."

"He is not, he *had* to leave. If he'd stayed he'd be—"

"He *abandoned* us, Simone! He just wants everyone to think he's a big hero and loves his country, like he did that all for *us*, and he's thinking about us all the time, every minute of every day. That's a big lie. You don't do that, just run off and leave. Not if you love someone!"

The younger boys glance their way; she bends her head over their work, grips her pencil.

"It's crazy, people always waiting and hoping for him to come back and save everyone," she whispers. "He wanted to save himself. That's all he cared about. He's a joke."

"He'll come back," Simone whispers, stubborn. "With the Allies. Then we'll be liberated."

"No, then we'll be conquered."

"We're already conquered. We're *occupied*, what do you think that means?"

"Not here, we're not. Not in La Perrine." She looks up at them. "Right?"

"Well, that's true . . ." Hortense says.

"You're right, I guess." Simone nods.

"We're autonomous. We're strong, all on our own. And we're going to be victorious, despite what the skeptical people say. We just have to stop doubting and complaining all the time. Having faith in our leaders is what's patriotic."

"Children! Children!" Monsieur Monzie hurries into the room, clapping his hands. "I have news! It's been decreed . . . our dear leaders in Vichy are announcing that in response to Allied aggression on our North African shores, our German friends have decided to commence an active presence here in the Unoccupied Zone." He clears his throat. "Henceforth, the French State will be entirely occupied by the military forces of the Third Reich. Yes, *yes*!"

~

**January, 1943**

She unlatches the front door, peers outside. Habit, now. She listens first from behind the closed door for the *drum drumming*, the foreign accents, but hears nothing. It could be a trick. They could be lying in wait, just outside the door, down the dirt path to the woods, hiding behind the stone wall that leads to the village, sharpening their knives, guns at the ready. La Perrine could be encircled. They could siege, at any moment. The blasted-apart limbs, boiling oil, horses screaming. Little children speared on bayonets, hoisted overhead like flags. Fires streaking through the air, and do they have enough butter to soothe all that burning flesh? Are there enough gas masks, to keep throats and lungs from the blistering gas? She sticks her head further out into the cold morning air, peering. Nothing but the hushed sound and icy smell of winter. No black smoke twisting through the pale sky. No scent of poison gas or gunpowder. No American troops, bayonets drawn. No English soldiers, ready to throw grenades. And no German troops, either, no muddy green uniforms or soup bowl helmets or shiny boots. No chess-piece parades through the town square, cracking the shallow panes of ice with their hard heels. And none of those marauding local thugs everyone is talking about now, gangs of resistants sneaking into villages in the dark of night to steal food from shops, raid barns for livestock or machinery, an old hoe or scythe they might convert to weapons. She is supposed to watch over the cow when she grazes; Luc brings his precious bicycle in the house after dark and tonton Claude has moved the rabbit pen inside the barn, is careful to keep his equipment locked away. Everyone locking doors now, even Father Tournel locks the rectory at night. But it's safe here, of course. Don't be silly. There is no danger, here. She leaves the sleepy warm house, careful to lock the heavy door behind her, hurries to the barn with her milking pail. Like every morning. Nothing's changed, everything is exactly the same as always, as it will continue to be.

That's what Monsieur Druot had assured, them, anyway. They'd waited for German troops to appear in La Perrine, with their pressed uniforms and gleaming, well-oiled guns, to come striding superhumanly through the woods or rumbling up the road in their sleek tanks. To pull down the tricolore and hang their swastika-scar flags, billet in everyone's homes, eat the last of everyone's bread and cheese and meat, forbid the speaking of French. It won't be like the newsreels, no, it won't be German soldiers handing out flowers and chocolates, German Red Cross ladies making us soup. Those happy, peaceful days are over. Another failure, from Petain. *Occupied,* we're *all* in the Occupied Zone now, aren't we?

But *No, no,* Monsieur Druot had insisted. *Nothing to worry about, nothing will change.* He'd addressed them at church last fall, after the announcement, standing at the altar before the beginning of Mass. Thank you to Father Tournel, for allowing me to address the congregation this way, but it is so important! More news from Vichy, very *good* news to share! He rubbed his hands together, his chest barreled out.

"Yes, the Germans are now officially in charge, that's true. But they have more important things to do than bother with every single city and town, every hamlet and village! Not just our fight against Soviet Bolshevism, of course, now we have the Allies and their sneak attacks, why, the Germans are *protecting* us, defending French soil, citizens of the French State should be grateful for their presence throughout our country! Limousin, all of the Haute-Vienne, this won't be an *Occupied* Zone, like up north, merely an *Operational* Zone!"

Monsieur Monzie had applauded excitedly, a few villagers joining in, but their claps had silenced out before Father Tournel's solemn gaze. Even tonton Claude looked upset, he hates the Germans, it's true, Marie-Jeanne thought, he doesn't want them here, he wants the *French* to defend French soil, our own Frenchmen to do all the protecting. Father Tournel looked miserable, too, impatiently shifting his weight from foot to foot. She wished Monsieur Druot would hurry and move away from the altar so Father Tournel could lead them in prayer, offer the precious blood and body of our dear Blessed Lord.

"So, yes, the Germans will be moving into some of our larger southern cities," Monsieur Druot had continued. "Establishing military bases, searching out the dangerous foreign element. And we have our own internal threat to worry about now, those traitors, those cowardly agitators terrorizing our villages and towns. They're calling those groups something now, I hear, the . . . ?" He'd paused, trying to remember.

"The *maquis,*" Monsieur Monzie offered from his seat. "The *maquisards.*"

"Ah yes. The maquis." Monsieur Druot shook his head in distress. "Stealing from their own people, from law-abiding French citizens! Encouraging sedition and dissent! And to think there are those who sympathize with these *terroristes,* who share their dangerous views!"

Monsieur Druot stopped, then, and studied the congregation. Is he staring extra hard at Monsieur Leroux? she wondered, at Madame Gaillard? They stared back at him, stone-faced, Madame Gaillard fingering the ugly paste pearls at her throat, Monsieur Leroux's head high.

"Yes, we must all be on our guard. I remind all of you, it is your *duty* to keep your eyes and ears open! To report immediately about any such treason! Even among neighbors, and friends, we cannot be too careful—"

"*Amen,*" Father Tournel said at that, with a stern cough, a prompt rather than a blessing, and Monsieur Druot had nodded, ceding, it was Father Tournel's altar, after all.

"Yes, amen! Thank goodness we have no such traitorous activity here, of course . . ."

Father Tournel nodded toward the back of the room; the young boys of the choir began to sing, their voices rising up above Monsieur Druot.

*Lord, make us an instrument of Your peace,*
*Where there is hatred, let me sow love . . .*

"No, none of that concerns us here, in La Perrine," Monsieur Druot said, hastily. "We'll just all go about our business, won't we? Nothing will change. I assure you . . ."

And he'd crossed himself, hurried to his seat.

And he was right, nothing changed, not really. Reports of Germans in Lyon and Bordeaux and Grenoble, and Marie-Jeanne saw them sometimes in Limoges, the German soldiers, when she hurried from the bus depot to take the tram to Oradour, but she just kept her head down and hurried about her way, trying to appear law-abiding and invisible. And they looked hurried too, not like the happy German tourist-soldiers she remembered strolling the streets of Paris, or the cheerful newsreel-Germans. And different colors of them now, not just the ugly muddy-green of regular army troops, but soldiers in golden-brown, and dove-gray, and a splotchy beige-and-olive, with big buckles that said *Gott mit uns—'God is with us'*, the Limoges butcher translated for her in a scornful mumble, nodding at a gray-uniformed officer sniffing a cut of ham, *They're Waffen SS, special units they're bringing in now.* But these special new Germans looked anxious as well, too harried to pay attention to her, thank goodness, looked like businessmen worried about being late for meetings or losing an important contract. Except for the guns.

But just as Monsieur Druot said, there was no sign of them in La Perrine, their presence was limited to the cities and larger towns, and they were mostly bureaucrats and minor officials, anyway, their regular troops were needed in the fight for Stalingrad, and they need our good Frenchmen to fight alongside of them, to keep building those tanks and planes. But they say more and more of our own men are refusing to go. They say those guerilla gangs are getting larger, too, the maquis, young men refusing to sign up for the Releve and fleeing to the countryside, taking to the mountains and woods, abandoning their families, getting more brazen in their theft of clothing and food, medical supplies and fuel, robbing railway stations, post offices, banks. And they're better organized, ever since that Jean Moulin became some sort of folk hero, de Gaulle's deputy on French soil, Moulin has been scurrying all over the country with foreign money stuffed in his pockets, attempting to build an army out of a squabbling bunch of partisans, styling himself as some dashing espionage character! Thank goodness there are so many patriotic citizens refusing to help such a traitor, willing to denounce those criminals, hundreds and hundreds of letters pouring into mairies and prefects and government offices, reporting on the local baker's failure to renounce his connection with Freemasonry, the doctor who falsifies medical records and hands out too many certificates of exemption to healthy young men that should be signing up for the Releve, the schoolteacher *who resides at 41 rue de Brettes, and, it is my duty to bring this to your attention, is well known by everyone in town to harbor Communist sympathies. And, if I may report my personal suspicions, may well be hiding several foreigners in his attic, likely of the Jewish race, whose presence I have detected by the glimmers of light sometimes emanating from its windows. Signed, a loyal Frenchman,* as printed in proud example in *Je suis partout.*

Sometimes she heard the sputtering roar of planes overhead, the sound that made her want to run inside the house or under a tree, *run, hide,* more and more of them, are they German aircraft, American, English? No matter, they aren't bombs, no bombs are falling here, although Monsieur Druot decided La Perrine should have a proper air raid shelter, just in case, and set Luc and the Chantiers boys the task of digging one beneath his mairie/café. And sometimes in the early evening hours or the still-dark mornings Marie-Jeanne saw tiny white blossoms dropping from the sky, floating far away over the mountains, was frightened until Tonton explained they were parachute drops, the Americans and English thinking they can lure our good men to their side just by dropping in food, weapons, supplies. Seditious pamphlets and leaflets still appearing in odd places—a stack beneath the bus stop bench, loose sheets left pinned beneath rocks along the roads or under trees—and the meager deliveries from Limoges sometimes came wrapped in pages of newspapers with titles like *Liberation* or *Defense de la France,* or *Le Resistant Limousin,* actual newspapers now, more sophisticated and better funded and bragging about successful sabotage efforts, sometimes a photo of Jean Moulin (handsome, she thought, with that angled fedora, a debonair scarf), stories of Germans afraid to roam city streets for fear of attack, the imminent, inevitable return of a new, democratic République, the truth about German military blunders and their violations of the Armistice agreement and the brutal treatment of French prisoners-of-war, the exploitation of French workers in German factories, the desperate situation of those deported to eastern camps.

Monsieur Druot posted warnings against reading such trash, and Luc offered to patrol the village, collect those pages to bring home and hand over to Tonton, who burned them in the fire, furious, mumbling how Leroux must have a hand in that, maybe Madame Gaillard, too, in league with those resistants to spread misinformation and lies, they're not to be trusted, we all know their sympathies, I need to have a talk with Druot about this, we must do something, notify the authorities, perhaps, and Marie-Jeanne was not to play with Simone or Hortense at all anymore, is that clear?

On the other hand, Tonton had said, musing, they might *tell* her things, they might slip up or confide to her some of what that idiot Leroux or Madame Gaillard were up to, yes, she's to listen and ask them questions when they play together, and she is to inform him immediately of anything seditious, does she understand?

But who *plays* anymore, Tonton? she'd thought, we're all too old for games, he sounds like tante Berthe, like we're still little girls. And she and Simone and Hortense had stopped talking about de Gaulle or traitors and patriots, anyway, as if by silent agreement, focusing instead on finishing their Napoleon project, although the two of them would whisper to each other, sometimes, and stop abruptly when she drew near. And *We should be learning English instead,* Simone had mumbled when Monsieur Monzie decided they should all learn German, drilling them in *Ich bin, Du bist, Er ist,* but most of the children fell suddenly tongue-tied and mind-blank at reciting *en Deutsch,* their *Ichs* turning to coughs in their throats, and he'd given up in exasperation. But she didn't want to report that unpatriotic comment to Tonton, or tell him about Simone and Hortense's whispering, or their families listening to the BBC radio or reading those traitorous newspapers, either—she felt guilty for lying to him by her silence. But they were her dear friends, and were just showing off, trying to act important.

Occupation costs were raised yet again—no, "rebuilding costs," they were supposed to say—the millions of francs feeding the German war machine, quotas increased and official rations were cut once more, but nothing new about that, and there was so little to trade those tickets for anyway, everyone was mostly living on whatever they could barter or scavenge or grow. And those posters Monsieur Druot pasted to the walls of the mairie and the schoolhouse, bearing the Vichy double-bladed axe and announcing

**ALL JEWS IN THE SOUTHERN ZONE MUST HAVE JUIF/JUIVE STAMPED ON ALL OFFICIAL DOCUMENTS**

the first sight of those words startling her as she walked to school, causing her to stumble in her wooden shoes then catch herself, catch her breath and glance around to be sure no one had seen her trip and almost fall. Just Monsieur Druot passing by, with his brush and bucket of paste, "Of course there *are* no Jews here, in La Perrine, Marie-Jeanne," he assured her, smiling, pasting a loose corner flat. "Just a formality. That nasty business doesn't concern us at all!"

Except at Christmas, everyone hurrying across frozen paving stones toward the church, illuminated for Midnight Mass, the very young children carried and sleepy and the older children excited to stay up so late, everyone shivering, desperate to be in the holiday spirit, *Joyeaux Noel to you, yes, Joyeaux Noel!* She saw Madame Gaillard smile pleasantly at Monsieur Druot, and Tonton even shook hands with Monsieur Leroux—although she could see tante Berthe nudge him to do that—as everyone hurried into the glowing church, pausing to admire Father Tournel's precious crèche, the fresh new robes he made so carefully every year for the tiny clay Joseph and Virgin Mary and Baby Jesus, fresh new straw arranged strand by strand for the clay manger animals. But this year a tiny bit of yellow caught the eye, a bright star, a tiny bright yellow star pasted to the little baby Jesus, the star's six points snipped precisely and clear, and

***juif***

it said in tiny black letters.

And there was silence, dead and frozen, no one dared say a thing. Her heart began its rabbit-pound, she could see Monsieur Druot tighten his mouth, Monsieur Monzie wipe nervously at his spectacles with his stained handkerchief, could hear Tonton crack his knuckles and the creak of shoes against stone as everyone shifted their weight, and shuffled along. She saw Father Tournel's inscrutable face as each of his parishioners paused to shake his hand; she saw Tonton wobble his head in a confused way, saw Tante wipe at her eyes and give Father Tournel a brief smile and nod. Luc was returning Father Tournel's steady gaze, his face flushed and jaw clenched, then abruptly looked away as if he couldn't trust himself not to speak out. How betrayed he must feel. And she'd dropped her own eyes, too, away from Father Tournel's face, horrified, wasn't that a sacrilege, a desecration? *But Jesus was Jewish too, right?* says the memory-voice in her head*, and a good, real person who preached about love and understanding,* yes, maybe, but to do that to precious, innocent baby Jesus, to the Holy Family!

But they'd all gone in to celebrate Mass as usual, and she'd prayed and prayed, as His flesh and blood entered her body, her heart and soul, that while God gave everybody the freedom to choose between good and evil, sometimes people had a hard time accepting His will and collaborating with His plan, she shouldn't judge, she should instead examine what she could do better, how she could serve God by always making the right choices and following the path toward grace, Amen.

Yes, just as Marshal Petain said. *Meditate on your misfortunes,* his quavery voice told them in his Christmas address. He was hardly ever on the radio anymore and it was odd to hear his voice, like an old song you'd forgotten and are surprised you still know all the words and melody to, even at just the first few notes. *Try to understand what you were, what you are, and who you must become!*

And the Holy Father, too, Pope Pius XII, reminding his crusaders to live up to the call for moral and Christian rebirth, to listen to the message of Jesus, for only His light can overcome the darkness which comes from deserting God.

Pray, keep the faith. God is with us. Everything will be fine.

But she still always looks out the door, first. There's that old feeling of an *end* rushing at her, again, the threat of another, bigger end, the kind that drops from the sky or bursts into your room without knocking, or grabs the back of your head and twists. And though you clutch and squirm there's nothing to hold onto, no matter how hard you pray you still feel flung through the air and to the ground somewhere else, where nothing and no one is the same, the *same* is what is ended, is gone forever. But maybe if she looks first, she'll see the end in time, marching up the road toward her. Maybe this time she'll be able to take the right action, keep it from happening, shut and bolt the door closed. Maybe she'll be able to keep it from coming in.

**March, 1943**

It isn't a proper uniform, really, just a black beret, dark blue trousers and jacket, a brown shirt, an empty leather holster he's stuffed with old newspaper, his medals from the Great War stuck to his lapel. But he looks so proud. He adjusts the beret at a rakish angle in the little mirror, tugs at his tie, then stands up straight, as straight as his crooked shoulder allows. It's good to see him stand so straight, so tall. She remembers how huge he'd once seemed to her, all the space he took up in the house. Everyone was thinner now, less fleshy, even tante Berthe, but with Tonton it seemed something was shrinking him both inside and out, as if his insides were deflating while an outside weight was also bowing him down. The invasion, the loss of North Africa, the increased occupation . . . And reports on Radio Vichy of the maquis gangs becoming the *Maquis,* the resistants becoming the *Resistance,* that a gang right here in Limousin had destroyed a railway bridge with plastic explosives between Limoges and Usell . . . Rumors of Jean Moulin's success in unifying those terrorist groups throughout the Southern Zone, gaining their sworn allegiance to de Gaulle and the Free French, the formation of the *Mouvements Unis de la Resistance* . . . And the humiliating defeat at Stalingrad in January, that terrible blow . . . Yes, Tonton had grown smaller, all of it piling in a hard crush upon his back.

But now, things are finally turning around! The announcement of the *Service du Travail Obligatoire,* the *STO,* the *requirement,* now, that our young men register for a compulsory two-year term of service in Germany! No, Berthe, don't cry, this is *good,* our young people *should* understand the meaning of sacrifice and duty. But tante Berthe was distressed, the dreaded time had come, she must lose Luc, her little boy, how could a mother send her child off to a hostile foreign country to fight a war, someone else's war, and fight a losing battle, at that? Marie-Jeanne had never heard them quarrel before, never heard them even raise their voices to each other, and it was terrible, their distress bursting out over dinner or floating up to the attic at night like the smell of long-boiled vegetables. Tante so upset, *Don't tell me it's service, Claude,* she'd say, *It's forced labor! Wasn't your precious Petain supposed to shield us from such a thing? Slave labor, that's all it is, like deporting all those poor Jews!*

Her argument infuriated Tonton, *That's rubbish, Berthe, no one is deporting my son!*

And she'd snap back, *I don't care what word you use, resettle, relocate, I won't sacrifice my son that way!*

And he'd plead, insist, *This is Luc's chance to serve, like my generation did, fighting in the Great War, it made men of us, didn't it?*

Luc stayed silent and miserable and hunched in the middle of it all, and she felt bad for him—it was obvious how much he agreed with his father, how edgy and anxious he was to leave, to go off and serve in a big, important manly way somehow, but of course he didn't want to upset his poor maman.

Thank Heaven for the letter from Monsieur Bonnard:

> . . . and I've been able to arrange a position for your cousin Luc with Organisation Todt under the authority of Albert Speer, Germany's Minister of Armaments and War Production. They're building the

Atlantic Wall in Normandy, to fortify our coasts against an Allied attack. It's a very prestigious assignment for such a young man. They'll send your Mayor the paperwork, so your cousin can report as soon as possible.

*You see, Berthe? He'll be on French soil, doing a man's job! Showing what he's made of!*

And Berthe nodded, weeping in defeat, but assuaged. Yes, he'll be leaving home but not leaving France, not in the army, that's something, at least. Luc's sudden buoyant spirits cheered her, too, made the whole house a happy one, his joy and excitement at the important responsibility he'd waited so long for, *Don't worry, Maman, I'll make you and Papa so proud!*

And he'd be gone, far away and for a long time, Marie-Jeanne couldn't help but feel pleased about that, like a prayer had been answered. But no, Jesus wouldn't answer a selfish little prayer like that—this was really a blessing for everyone, a gift, an answer to Luc's prayers, and everyone's, as well as her own.

And now, the *Milice Francaise* as well! A chance for tonton Claude himself to serve again, yes, our people need us for protection, a true French Militia, we're needed to help keep peace and order, keep those Maquis in line. She asked Tonton what "maquis" really meant, the strange word was everywhere now, and he mumbled, unsure, until Luc offered it was Corsican, a kind of dense, bushy scrub. Ah yes, a *weed,* Tonton said, the kind of ruinous thing that must be cleared from the field, ripped out or burned down before it takes over your healthy crop. Yes, we'll destroy those miserable weeds! She and Tante and Luc watched Tonton take his oath of allegiance in Monsieur Druot's mairie, swearing his loyalty to Marshal Petain and the French State, condemning *democracy, individualism, international capitalism, Bolshevism, Freemasonry, Jewish leprosy, black marketers,* vowing to *defend Christian civilization, seek out resistants, criminals, black marketers, all enemies of the state, and report them to the higher authorities*. Luc saluted him afterward, so proud of his papa, she saw the tears in Tonton's eyes, and it made her want to weep too, to see how happy he was. He will attend weekly meetings with *miliciens* from other villages and towns, go on surveillance patrols in the region to sniff out black market dealings, track down young men seeking to evade their STO duty, submit reports. And in exchange, an increased ration, a small salary to make up for time away from the farm and mill—although there's less grain to farm or process now anyway, so many fields lying fallow for lack of equipment and seed, so few men to do that hard work. And the uniform, the fresh official clothes supplied by Vichy, no guns for those holsters, however, the Germans still not allowing us to have weapons, but once they see the good work we're doing, the increase in peace, *then* we'll be given guns. After all, we are *the vanguard in maintaining order* now, as Petain himself says!

Yes, things were turning around, looking brighter!

"You look very handsome, Tonton," she tells him.

"Oh . . ." He waves away her words, embarrassed but pleased.

"You do, dear," Tante says. "We're very proud of you."

He clears his throat. "Just clearing out weeds, that's all. It's Luc we should be proud of."

"Monsieur Druot said my commission'll come through in a few weeks." Luc nods at his father. "And I'll have a uniform, too."

"Thanks to Marie-Jeanne," Tante says.

"Well, yeah," he says. "I did thank her, Maman." He avoids her eyes, as usual, but nods in her general direction.

"That Monsieur Bonnard, what a good, kind man," Tante says.

"Always remember, Luc, the uniform honors the office, not the man. A uniform might command respect from your men, at the beginning, but you still have to earn it." Tonton adjusts the medal on his chest, frowns at tarnish.

"Of course, Papa. I will. You'll see."

"A shame it's come to this. Having to protect my family against my own countrymen. But a good opportunity for Luc, at least. And for you too, Marie-Jeanne."

"Tonton?"

He rubs a medal with the end of his tie. "I'll be submitting my first report soon, about suspicious activity in our area. And you're good at that, writing those stories for school, so . . ."

"Perhaps Marie-Jeanne could work with you on that, dear?" Tante pats Marie-Jeanne's shoulder. "It would be educational for her. And she has such nice handwriting."

"Of course, Tonton, I want to do anything I can to help."

"Very good. We'll destroy the weed at the root!" His face brightens at the unfamiliar sound of an engine outside, a truck rumbling up the gravel road. "Fellow miliciens, from Ambazac," he tells them. "I'm off!"

"Where are you patrolling tonight, Papa?"

"There's reports of theft in Lauriere. Petty thieves, those maquis. Lock up, Luc. I'll be back in the morning!" He tightens his empty holster and leaves, giving them a jaunty wave.

Luc fidgets a moment, watching Tante prepare to cut rutabagas for the evening meal. "Are you hungry, dear? We might have some stew left. Marie, would you—"

"Some of the Chantiers guys are waiting for me, Maman," Luc says. "I said I'd meet up with them tonight. So we can do drills and stuff. Really important work. I should go, too . . . ?"

"I know, all right, go. Try not to get back too late. I'll leave your supper on the table." She waves him out the door, smiles at Marie-Jeanne. "How lucky we are, to have such men."

~

**April, 1943**

A terrible, terrible thing! A whole month's worth of ration tickets, for the entire village! And all the stamps the tabac had on hand, all the cash, the medicines and foodstuffs from Madame Gaillard's grocery, all the supplies recently delivered from Limoges, the tea and sugar and baking soda and salt, the canned goods. And the last of the dry goods from Madame Richie. The mill, too, they'd smashed the lock on the door, taken most of the oil and sacks of grain, the precious food to get the village through the last of this hard enduring winter. Tonton, in his Milice uniform, stood with Monsieur Druot before the villagers, assembled in the schoolhouse, not waiting until Sunday, they'd called an emergency meeting to keep everyone informed, forestall false rumors, keep everyone calm. Now now, everyone, stay calm! Our own Monsieur Leroux, Monsieur Druot explained, awakened in the middle of the night by suspicious noise and hurrying downstairs to investigate, the poor man ambushed, left bound and gagged on the floor of the tabac, his wooden leg flung across the room.

"A hero, our very own hero!"

Everyone applauded Monsieur Leroux, who sat visibly shaken, a blackening bruise to the side of his face and a still-oozing split lip. Simone was teary-eyed, and Hortense was crying, too, clutching her mother's hand. Marie-Jeanne gave them both a supportive smile, her poor friends, they never meant any harm, they or their parents, of course not. There were tears, fear, shock, how could this happen *here*? What should we do, how do we protect ourselves?

"Yes, the dangerous seditious element has unfortunately struck here, in La Perrine," Tonton said. "But they won't come again, now they know what kind of brave citizens live in our village. A good man,

Monsieur Leroux, defending his family, his property. Defending all of us! We owe him our thanks!"

Everyone applauded again, and Tonton shook Monsieur Leroux's hand, respectfully.

"I'll be requesting relief from our leaders in Vichy regarding our quotas," Monsieur

Druot added. "They'll help us through this, I'm sure."

She wondered if she should write again to Monsieur Bonnard, ask for more help . . . no, that would be asking too much, perhaps. He's helped her and her family so much already. Lucien.

"And I'll report this attack to the authorities, of course," Tonton said. "Tell them about our brave village. Our unity in the face of the enemy. No, we aren't going to give in to fear!"

~

"Marie-Jeanne?"

"Mmm?"

She looks up from the pail of frothy white milk, her rhythmic tugging at the cow. She can hear the cluckings from the chickens pecking at their withered vegetables, only two hens left now, the old rooster eaten long ago. She loves the peace of these early mornings, the sleepy smell of warm animals and cool fresh earth, the large brown eyes greeting her, her nudge of the taut udder and the cow's answering *moo*, the teats warming her chilly fingers when they begin their rhythmic tug-pull-squeeze, the scratch of the animal's bony warm flank against her cheek, listening in the quiet dark to the tinny swish of milk hitting the pail then the rich thick sound of milk hitting milk. Everywhere else, things happen so fast. Didn't time used to pass more slowly? It's like a churning river now, rushing her along. Maybe time stays slower when you're a child, she thinks, so you can hold on better to things, take small steps. And being older means you're supposed to go faster, too, be able to quicken your pace and keep up, without feeling swept along and lost. But here, everything slows to this small perfect task she has in hand, the prayerful repeat, day after day, exactly the same. Interrupted, though—"Yes, Luc?"—with him here, at the door, a tall silhouette against a milk-blue rectangle of sky, knapsack slung over one shoulder, his bicycle propped in the frame. His breath makes small puffs in the chilly air. He wears his knitted scarf dashed across his shoulders, waves his new black beret at her in greeting.

"I just wanted to say . . ." His voice wanders down into the straw-flecked mud.

"Are you ready?" she asks.

"Yeah." He gestures behind him, to a small leather valise strapped to the back of his bicycle, that old suitcase, didn't that once belong to her . . . ? "Maman was up all night, packing. Trying to cram more sweaters in. You know how she is."

"Mm hm." She can feel the change in the cow's teats, the shifting of her feet. She looks in the pail—is that all? And she was going to take some milk to Father Tournel, so he might share it with the villagers. She squeezes the final drops, a belly rub to the cow, lifts the pail out, sets it by her stool. She rubs her hands together, lifts the pitchfork from its nail on the wall.

"Want me to do that?" Luc asks.

"No, I'm okay." She pitches the cow's dirty old hay into a pile. "Thank you, though." He nods, watching her.

She doesn't know what else to say. When have they ever been alone, had a conversation, really? "Tonton and Tante are very proud of you, you know," she tells him. "We all are."

He nods at her again.

"Will you be able to write to us, do you think?"

"Maybe. I'll try." He sets his knapsack down, puts his beret on.

"Come on, here . . ." He takes the pitchfork from her, and she sees, for the first time, the armband he is wearing on his new khaki shirt, the red band, white circle, crawling black scar. She steps back, a little. He pitches fresh hay for the cow, careful not to waste a single strand.

"You'll be busy. It's going to be very exciting for you. Traveling. Contributing."

"Uh huh."

"And it's very patriotic, what you're doing."

"Yeah. Patriotic." He pauses studies the pile of hay. "Marie-Jeanne . . . I'm not going."

"You're not going to Normandy?"

"Well, yeah. But I'm not really going to build coastal fortifications, I mean."

"Are you, you're not going into the army? Oh no, Luc!"

He laughs. "Sort of. In a way . . ." He shakes the pitchfork free of its last straws, faces her. "Look, what they tell us, what they've been saying . . . that a German victory's good for France. Our glorious new era, returning to honor . . ." He shakes his head. "It's all a lie. You know that, don't you?"

"But the Germans can't lose, it would mean we—"

"They *are* losing, Marie. And thank God they're losing. Thank God *we're* losing!"

"But the Marshal says we—"

"The Marshal!" He punches the pitchfork into the pile of dirty hay. "Petain's no *marshal* anymore. He's just some old guy they drag out and prop up for parades. Laval's running the show now. And what he's done, what they're all doing, it's evil."

"Evil?" She smiles at that, one of Luc's crazy rants, that's all.

"Yeah, it *is* evil, what's been happening. What we've let happen. Don't you get what we've all gone along with?"

"But we haven't done anything."

"Yeah, exactly. We haven't done *anything*. Everyone's just pretended not to see or hear any of it, just acted stupid. Or like we've been asleep or hiding in bed. Or like we haven't had a choice. That's what I mean. That's what makes us evil, too. All of us."

"But everyone's doing their best. Look at your father, and the Milice—"

"The Milice . . ." He chuckles, but it's in disgust, not humor. "The Nazis just want us doing their dirty work for them. Spying and denouncing on each other."

"Tonton's not doing that! He's keeping law and order, so we'll all be safe and—"

"Papa has no idea what's going on. Maybe he thinks what he's doing is honorable, but he doesn't really see. Maman doesn't see, either, she's too frightened."

"Of course she's frightened. For *you*. She's worried about you leaving and getting—"

"Oh, but I'm doing my *duty*!" He stands up very straight, tall as the pitchfork, but it's a mocking kind of straight, as if he's about to salute her. "She should be *proud*!"

"She *is* proud," she says, confused. "Of course she is."

"She's asleep. Like everyone. But this STO, it's the best thing Laval could've done, making us go serve in Germany. It's finally waking people up. They want us to go fight and kill? Yeah, okay. But not for the Nazis. We're not going to build their airplanes and tanks. Be their cannon fodder. We're not going to be dutiful soldiers for them anymore, or for Vichy. We've been like little kids, doing what we're told so we'll get patted on the head, get our supper and a glass of milk. But *we're* taking care of things now! We're organized, we've been training—"

"Who's 'we'?"

"—we have *real* leaders, men like de Gaulle and Moulin and—"

"Luc, wait, stop." She's still confused. "Are you, are you going with the *Maquis*?"

"I've been working with them for months, Marie."

"What?"

"I fooled you, huh? Good, that's good." He nods, pleased. "That's what we wanted."

"But they're criminals! And . . ." And what? It's terrible, what he's doing, but how to make him understand? She thinks of the *Principles of the Community*, the poster on the school wall, what was that one, number ten? ". . . and *no group can be tolerated that discredits the authority of the state*," she tells him.

He laughs. "Look at you, reciting their slogans! You're supposed to be so smart. Vichy doesn't have any authority. The Nazis don't, either, not in the eyes of God. Or anyone who cares about justice and humanity. Freedom. And not just our country, for everyone! *To live defeated is to die every day*'!"

"That's a slogan, too, you know. You should hear yourself, you're crazy, you sound like de Gaulle. You should *see* yourself, all puffed up."

"De Gaulle's telling the truth."

She remembers him huddled in the kitchen, listening to the radio. Oh, Luc. "If you're with the Maquis that just makes you a criminal."

"Criminal. Patriot." He shrugs. "Fine. Call me whatever you want."

"A common thief, then. A thief who steals from his own people."

"That's true, too. You're right." He stands tall and straight, for real. "Okay."

She stares. "You broke into the mill? You stole from the village? From your friends, your own family?"

"I had to—"

"You beat up Monsieur Leroux?"

"That was *his* idea—"

"What?"

"Leroux's been helping us, the whole time, Marie. Madame Gaillard, too. Papa was right about them, at least. They've been fixing their books, getting extra food and clothing for us. Breaking into the mill and tabac was even Leroux's idea, he planned it with me and some of the Chantiers guys. To keep Papa and Druot from getting in the way, with their stupid reports and patrols. And take the heat off La Perrine. Vichy and the Nazis'll target any place they suspect's got Resistance activity, or helping maquisards. Leroux said it was the best way to show we're all innocent, here, like the Resistance hit us and moved on, he kept telling me to hit him harder—"

"You—"

"I didn't *want* to, Marie! It was awful, he was already bleeding, but I had to, he said it would keep all of us from suspicion. And Father Tournel, too, he's been printing pamphlets for us, hiding our supplies in the rectory—"

"Father Tournel?"

"Of course." He shrugs. "He's a Christian. It's what any real Christian would do." Father Tournel, pasting that terrible star on Baby Jesus, defiling our Savior, the Holy Family, a true priest wouldn't do that, no, not the living symbol of God's presence among us . . .

"Good Christians follow the law," she tells him. "They submit to secular authority. It's a moral obligation!"

"Secular authorities have a moral obligation, too."

"And Christians don't steal and lie and beat people up, they don't kill—"

"Well, God hasn't stopped it, has He? All the killing? Divine intervention isn't going to save anyone. Sitting back and waiting, keeping the faith, talking about repentance." He sneers. "Father Tournel doesn't even believe that anymore, he says. He says it's up to us, now."

"But God trusts *us* to turn away from evil. To show our faith through our actions."

"That's what we're doing. Taking action. Taking responsibility. And no more kid stuff, hiding out in the woods. Scribbling graffiti, passing pamphlets around. We have networks now, all over the country, the Allies are dropping supplies, we have radio transmitters and electrical equipment and real dynamite. Look . . ." He crosses eagerly to his bicycle, tosses his scarf ends over his shoulders, wrenches the seat loose. "I've been smuggling plastic explosives for months, see? Fooling everybody. I hide the stuff in the seat and the tubing, carry it into Limoges. I ride right past German troops! And we're getting guns now, they drop in the parts and ammunition, we assemble them. We're target practicing. We'll be ready for real military action soon, not just pretend. We'll kill if we have to, we will!"

Little boys being soldiers, she thinks, sadly. Oh, Luc . . .

"And I can do something really important now. Thanks to you."

"To me?"

"They would've sent me off to some German factory, I'd be stuck on some assembly line. Making tires or tea pots. What could I do there, throw sand in machine parts? But like this, don't you see? I can wear their stupid uniform and report for duty like a good law-abiding Frenchmen. I'll get there and pretend to build their wall, but I'll really be doing surveillance. I can scout around, survey stuff, get information on munitions or strategy, anything the English and the Americans can use. And pass it along. It's the perfect cover for a spy."

"Oh, Luc, a *spy*!" It is almost funny, his play-acting, his little fantasy of espionage, like in the movies.

"You're not listening." He looks indignant, snugs his scarf. "Or you don't want to understand."

"I do understand." She tries to stop smiling, act like she takes him seriously. "I'm just worried about you. Being a big spy is dangerous as fighting, isn't it?"

"I know what I'm doing. Like getting information from Papa, what the Milice were always doing. So I could tip off the Maquis guys and—"

"You were spying on Tonton?"

"I *had* to. You have to do stuff like that sometimes. To save lives. He'll understand someday. So will you. You have to stay focused on what's important. Like Jean Moulin does"—Yes, just like Moulin, she thinks, that silly scarf!—"the way he takes risks. It's worth sacrificing anything for, to do what's right. It's how he gets everyone working together. We've got Communists and royalists, Spanish guys who hate Franco. Italians against Mussolini. And there's refugees, thousands of them. British airmen that got shot down. And Gaullists and democrats, Catholics, Protestants, we don't agree on almost anything except the one single most important thing to believe in, and that's what holds us together, makes us strong. And there's Jews fighting with us, too—"

"Jews?" It slaps at her, a poster flapping against a wall.

"Yeah. The lucky ones, who've escaped the roundups and the trains." He turns away from her, reattaches his bicycle seat. "The camps . . ."

"But you always said those people . . ." She blinks, confused, *The Jewish Peril*, that's what Luc says, *The Jews are corrupt, unclean* . . . "You always said they—"

"Yeah, I know." He steadies his bicycle, still not looking at her. "I know what I said. I was . . . it's like you hear stuff when you're a kid. They tell you what to think, about right and wrong. And about people. Who's okay, who's not okay. And you're just a kid, so you don't know. The words seem important, so you say them back, you think you're talking like a grownup. And they nod, they get all happy with you, and proud. So that means it's the truth, right? Even if . . ." he kicks at straw, "even if maybe you see someone just sitting in school one day, or playing a game, some regular thing, just like anybody else. But they're *not* like anybody else, it's true, you can *see* they're different. Because they're an even *better* person than just okay. They're more beautiful and good than anyone . . ."

He tightens the strap hard on his valise, and she wonders if it's hidden away in there, his secret treasure, or kept buried and safe deep in his knapsack, a little scrap of pink cloth, a long dark strand of hair.

"But you can't think that," he says. "You can't feel that, right? You can't care that way. So you hold on tighter to that other stuff that's supposed to be true. You're scared not to, like Father Tournel says. You keep saying those other words back at everyone, even if they're ugly and making you feel sick inside. And then one day . . . one day it's like a bomb goes off right in front of you, like the only thing you ever cared about explodes and is gone forever. And it's the worst thing ever." He looks up, looks at her. "But it makes you finally see and think what those words mean. What they can make happen. You see *yourself*, and you hear yourself, finally. And that's the most horrible, because you were yelling those words louder and uglier than anyone the whole time, and it's all your fault, and it's too late. And you just want to be dead now, too."

"You're being ridiculous." She grabs the pitchfork, grips it with shaky hands.

"But you're still here. Everything's blown up dead and your whole world's gone and you don't care about anything anymore. But you're still alive, so now what? You get one more chance, maybe. And what are you going to do about it, now?"

He is glaring at her, and she turns away, hangs the pitchfork back on the wall. "There *is* right and wrong, Luc," she mumbles. "Some people *are* different. That is true. Different from us. They were foreigners."

"What does that word really mean? 'Foreigners'?"

"Stop it, you know what it means. From somewhere else." She picks up her milk pail, clutches the wooden handle. "They didn't belong here."

"So, it's where someone was born? Or what they look like, if they talk funny, maybe?"

"I have to go, Luc, Tante's waiting for milk—"

"How they pray, is that it? The whole thing?"

"It's a bigger difference. Anyone can pray and just, just go through the motions and make it look and sound right. It's what's inside you, for real."

"Inside where?"

"All over, inside."

"Oh."

"It's in their blood."

"Their blood?"

"Yes, their blood. Their blood is different. You said so yourself!" *And good blood doesn't lie.* "They're racially different, in their blood."

He gives another disgusted chuckle. "Maybe you're right. I mean, *you're* different."

*I am different,* a girl's voice tells her. *And there's something different about you, too.*

"No, I'm not!"

"Yeah, you are, Marie—"

"I am *not,* don't say that!"

"—because you're lucky, you're one of the *luckiest* ones, and you don't even know it. You don't want to know."

"Know what? There's nothing to know."

"Oh come on, Marie . . ." He studies her face. "Everyone they're rounding up, all the Jews they're sending to Drancy? To be *relocated*? All the men and women and little kids they held at Vel-d'Hiv? Thousands of them, and they've barely started, they have *quotas* for how many Jews they have to pack up and turn over. Like potatoes."

"Well, that's the spirit of collaboration." She tries to move past him with her pail, but he steps in front of her, blocking the door.

"Yeah, *collaboration*. We're doing a really great job of that. It isn't the Nazis rounding up the Jews, it's *us*. We're hunting them down, like rabbits, or deer, we're the ones stuffing them in cattle cars—"

"You should go, Luc. Go on, go start your big fancy spy mission—"

"—and they're crammed in there for days, *weeks*, sometimes, like garbage, without food, maybe a bucket of water, no place to lie down, they have to shit on themselves—"

"You're so disgusting—"

"—and when they get there, finally, to those *camps*, they make them take off all their clothes and they shove them in rooms and lock the doors, they spray all of them with gas, and they choke to death, all the men and women and old people and babies, little girls—"

"That's a lie, just shut up!"

"—and then they burn the bodies. So they all disappear. Just get rid of all that different blood, like you say, that's what they're doing, what we're doing, to *your* people—"

"Those aren't my people!"

"Well, that means you're killing them, too, then. If you're one of *us*!"

"Stop it, just stop—" and she is screaming, *stop*, shoving and scratching at him and feeling him flinch away, she's grabbing his wrist, feels the bones shift, is twisting with both hands, she'll make him go snap and everything will be peaceful, it will all stop. Twisting harder, her own hands aching, until it's ended, stopped, there's just quiet, now. She sees his wrist in her red hands, red crescents under her fingernails, his wrist skin wrenched a dull white and the milk pail lying on the ground, white foam settling into the straw and mud, and she lets go, steps back and away, hears in the quiet the sudden choke of air escaping from her chest.

"That's the spirit of collaboration, Marie-Jeanne," his voice says. "You need to understand."

"Why?" She stares at the foamy straw on the ground between them. So wasteful, a sin. "I haven't done anything wrong, I *haven't.* It's got *nothing* to do with me. I'm just some stupid kid, like you always say. So please, Luc, please stop . . ." She closes her eyes, tries to steady her breaths, measure them out, and when she opens them he's looking at her, his face sad. Pitying, almost. A thin welt on his cheek, swelling red. She looks down again, at the chickens, the cow, the foamy mud, anywhere but at those wide smudged eyes, sad face, the new raw pain there.

"Okay. I just figured you'd understand. That you'd want to, you'd want to know. I'm sorry." She sees his hands pick up her pail, set it right. "I'm really sorry," he says again, and she nods, nods at the ground. "Look, I can't tell Papa what I'm doing. Or Maman. Not now. They're too worried about me. But if anything happens . . . you'll tell them later on, okay? What I was doing, and why. The truth."

"If you want."

"Promise you'll make them understand. So they can, you know . . . be proud of me."

She nods again. "I promise."

His feet step toward the door, then stop. "Marie-Jeanne . . . I haven't always been very nice to you, I guess. I'm sorry."

"No, you were right about me. When I was first here." She tries to laugh, a little. "I was so spoiled. And ungrateful. I was such a brat."

"Well, you were just a little girl, you know? Really scared, like kids get. But you're okay. And you've been really good to Maman and Papa. They love you a lot. It's good you're here. It's good they have you."

His feet approach her suddenly, tripping slightly in the straw, and she is startled to feel his arms around her, startled by how strong they feel, no delicate skinny boy bones, no, he's a grown-up man, his familiar boy smell is even stronger male now, too. She presses her face into his khaki shirt, feels the edge of his swastika armband against her chin. She feels him shaking, a tremble in those strong, grown-up arms.

"You'll take care of them, right?"

"Of course I will." She looks up, and his face is suddenly a little boy's again, hopeful and frightened, the red white scratch on his face from tree-climbing or rough horseplay, and she tiptoes up, kisses first one cheek, and he lets her, then the other, and she feels the sudden warm blush to his skin.

"Please be careful, Luc."

He releases her, ducks his flushed face, steps back. "Yeah, sure. Don't worry."

"I'll light a candle for you every Sunday. And ask Jesus and Mary to watch over you."

He smiles, nods. "Okay. Thanks." He picks up his knapsack, shrugs. "Well, see you."

She nods one last time, and a moment later she hears gravel crunch under the wheels of his bicycle. She picks up her pail, goes inside, Tante is waiting, yes, the pail is shaking, she grips the wooden handle hard to stop it, her arm around the pail to steady it, but it doesn't matter, anyway, there is no milk, nothing left to spill. She will have to explain that somehow to Tante, her carelessness. She puts the pail down and heads back to the house.

~

When the radio voices began telling of miliciens ambushed or kidnapped or shot to death by Maquis fighters, tante Berthe insisted tonton Claude resign, turn in his emblem and empty holster, stay in La Perrine where it was safe. It was just too dangerous to be out roaming the woods, confronting desperate criminals, and *unarmed, how do they expect you to fight without weapons? And at your age, I'm sorry, dear, but that's the truth, you're too old for that kind of work, Marie-Jeanne, help me talk sense into Tonton!*

She'd try to soothe, make peace, *Oh, Tante, I don't think—*

*No, you tell your aunt, Marie-Jeanne, you tell her I'm not shirking my duty! You tell her it isn't her place to tell me what to do!*

And she'd clap her hands over her ears, *Please, Tonton, don't fight, Tante, please!*

Until finally Tonton forbade Tante to read the papers anymore, or listen to the radio, even for music, or watch the newsreels, in the future he'd inform her of anything important she needed to know, and they all did their chores and ate their brief meals in a careful hush, the taut silence like a sick person in the house no one wanted to disturb.

"You never know when news might break in," he explained to Marie-Jeanne, "it's just too upsetting for her. But you, well, you understand these things, child."

She nodded, agreeing. They were working together on his Milice report, in Marie- Jeanne's attic room so Tante wouldn't have to hear, Marie-Jeanne propped on her bed with Vichy-supplied paper and pencil stub, Tonton pacing around the hanging braids of onion and garlic as he dictated about *excessive stores of grain in a Lauriere mill, possible black market dealings,* about the *absence of a portrait of our glorious leader in the schoolroom at La Jonchere St. Maurice,* about a *dark-skinned "citizen" in Razes, whose papers seem in order, but further investigation is warranted.* At first she'd assumed he would write out those reports and she'd just recopy them in her nice handwriting, but from the beginning he merely dictated facts to her, then asked her to write it all up and read him her official version afterward.

It was so boring, his rounds of storerooms and schoolrooms and churches, listening for accents, counting sacks of grain. No storming the woods, certainly nothing dangerous or dishonorable or glorious, maybe the Milice leaders were being mindful of Tonton's age and giving him the easy, clerical kind of assignments. And Luc was exaggerating, of course, all these boring reports were probably just going to end up in a drawer somewhere. Just stupid paperwork. But she wanted to help Tonton, was warmed by how he relied on her, trusted her enough to confide. So she tried to make the reports a bit more exciting, sometimes, spice up his words—the *scheming dark face of the tabac clerk is an obvious indicator of speculative practices;* the *impenetrable accent of the swarthy baker reveals he is likely of Hebraic origin and should thus be stripped of his business ownership, and the bakery assigned a provisional administrator of French blood*—to make it all more interesting, and make Tonton appear even more discerning and alert.

Although she heard the bigger, more real and dangerous things anyway, you couldn't cover your ears all the time, couldn't not listen to the voices everywhere talking of more assassinations, train derailments, bridges blown up, the increasingly violent skirmishes between Maquis and Milice. And the Germans, increasingly frustrated by those messy French-on-French brawlings—Petain and Laval won't even stop squabbling!—at the French's inability to properly police themselves, at having to bring in more of their own precious troops to get things done, those special elite SS units, stepping up their own attacks on the Maquis.

Thank God Luc isn't involved with that anymore, Marie-Jeanne thought, grateful he was safely away in Normandy, busy building a wall. Who would take him seriously, a puffed-up, wild-eyed boy like that, playing espionage games, whispering self-important secrets to other boys running from shadow to shadow? Better he keep busy with bunkers and concrete, surveying and scouting, instead of running around here with his plastic explosives and makeshift guns.

But they say there are more bombings in Normandy now, white-hot hailstorms falling on Le Havre and Amiens and Rennes, and they say Paris is next. They say Allied air raids on German installations have intensified, destroying shipyards and foundries and oil refineries along the western and northern coasts. They say the Allies don't care how many civilians and noncombatants are killed in their rain of death and destruction, they're prepared to destroy us all in the name of saving us. Maybe Luc was safe from the dangers of the Maquis, she thought, but he isn't safe from all those bombs. Or from himself, all his ridiculous dreams of glory. And wouldn't that be her fault, if he were blasted to bits?

*I can do something really important now, thanks to you.*

She said nothing of her fears to tante Berthe and tonton Claude, only smiled when the first postcard from Luc arrived and they took turns reading it aloud, over and over, his childish scrawls describing the rise of those concrete bunkers and gun emplacements, assuring he was fine and well-fed, *How proud we can be of Luc, how wonderful to know he's safe!* At least it got Tante and Tonton talking to each other other, and happy. But wasn't she lying to them, in a way, colluding in their fantasy of his well-being? Didn't they realize he was still in a danger zone, even closer to the perilous enemy now, an easy target for Allied invasion or attack? She'd slip away when she could and hurry to the church, light candles at the feet of the Blessed Virgin, kneel in the soothing dark and pray the bombs might fall elsewhere, on anyone, just not on Luc. Father Tournel, passing to pray the Liturgy of the Hours, would nod at her and smile, but she could barely meet his eyes now, after the sharp points of a bright yellow star and the vision of him stashing smuggled gun parts and mimeographing those seditious pamphlets, after seeing his disapproving look when Tonton attended Mass in his Milice uniform. She would give him only a brief nod back and bow her head lower, clutch her beads to steady herself, mea culpa, although she could sense him watching, waiting for something from her. She even went less often to Confession now, because couldn't she examine her own conscience and send her heartfelt Acts of Contrition directly to our Father and the Holy Ghost, *IfirmlyresolvewiththehelpofThygrace, tosinnomore*? God and Jesus and the saints were with her, she could feel their love in the jewels of light they sent through the window and the candles she lit, the very scent of their sweet affection in the smoky incense. They would speak directly to her if only she prayed hard enough, was virtuous like Jeanne or Saint Bernadette. She thought about nuns, Brides of Christ, sacrificing their lives to Jesus. What a lovely idea, cloistered away with the roses and sweet smoke, always breathing the safe soft air of church. Eating just bread and water, and dry bread at that, hunger is purifying, there's no need for anything more when one is sustained by God's nourishing love. She began dabbing bits of her meal onto Tante's plate when she wasn't looking, an offering, a penance. She pictured herself forever on her knees or lying prostrate on the ground, the cold stone bruising her bones, mortifying her frail flesh, helping her share Christ's agony. A life dedicated to prayer—how wonderful to be silent all the time, it means you can never say anything wrong! Holy vows of poverty, chastity, obedience—well, they're already poor, she's used to that. Chastity would be easy, none of that grubby business with boys—marriage to Jesus would be sinless, fleshless and pure. And obedience—hasn't she been trying so hard to obey the word and will of God? So her bravery and blessedness would keep everyone safe? Yes, God and Jesus and Mary would look upon her with even more love, if she made a sacrifice like that, became so holy.

She thought of asking Father Tournel about all of it, but no. He wasn't to be trusted, not anymore. So she prayed, listening, waiting. For mellifluous voices to awaken her in the middle of night, or angels to appear in heavenly beams of light, or speak to her through golden sunflowers. They would speak to her, tell her what to do, if she did everything right. Of course they would.

~

**July, 1943**

That traitor Jean Moulin was captured by SS forces in the Rhone, they said at Monsieur Druot's café.

(*No, betrayed by fellow Resistance leaders,* they mumbled at Madame Richie's dry goods shop . . .)

Moulin was personally interrogated by Lyon Gestapo Chief Klaus Barbie himself, they said at the tabac.

(*No, personally tortured by Barbie,* they whispered at the butcher shop in Limoges . . .)

Moulin slit his own throat to escape justice, the coward, they said on the tram to Oradour-sur-Glane.

(*No, he was beaten to death, they say,* Juliette murmured over Gabrielle's sleepy head, weeping, *because he wouldn't confess, wouldn't betray anyone, he wouldn't speak a word . . .*)

A hero, a coward, traitor, patriot, spy. Which were the real and true Jean Moulin words? Which was the real Jean Moulin face, the handsome newspaper newsreel face or the other one, flashing across her mind now, intruding upon her prayers, her schoolwork, her chores, all her earthly tasks, no matter how she tries to shrug or sweep it away, the image of Luc's face swelling purple and black, sliced by bayonets, his eyes—huge, smudged, pleading—blinded by pounding, practiced fists?

She tries to stay focused on the rosary in her hands, the clutched stub of pencil or the cow's warm teats, even digs her nails into her own palms to make a pain that's all her own, but why is his face there all the time, pleading? His face is crying for her to help, and she doesn't know how. His face beaten, pounded like raw meat, bits of wet red flesh flying at her, and she ducks from the flash of metal, from his screams.

*Help me, save me!* she hears. A fedora falling to the floor, stained with blood, crumpled by boots, and a dashing scarf twisted tight around a neck, a slow twist twisting strangulation, the sound of a slow choking rattle gasp . . .

And suddenly she realizes, her hands stilled in mid-onion slice, she *sees* the true message that has been sent to her in that pleading, bloodied face. Only a child would expect the prettiness of musical angels or talking sunflowers, a storybook message undemanding of decision, of real responsibility or sacrifice or painful, real action. Yes, finally, the gifts of wisdom and judgment have come upon her—*Time to take action. No more kid stuff*—and the true ecstasy of understanding His word. And the path she must follow, so clearly laid out for her, marked like a map on the schoolhouse wall.

~

It hadn't looked so far on Monsieur Monzie's map, the distance from here to there. A hundred kilometers, well, that's only a few hours by bus. Plenty of time to pilgrimage there and back in a day. Saint Jeanne traveled all the way from Domremy to Chinon to see the young Dauphin Charles, hadn't she? And on foot, across valleys and over mountains, and through hostile territory. But she's been jouncing on the hot bus for three hours now, and feeling very unholy, her cheeks smudged with road dust blowing through the open window. She's already sweated through her pretty dress, chewed away the lipstick Juliette had given her, that she'd been saving for a special occasion. She'll have to reapply some later. She'll have to fix herself up when she gets there, comb her hair, maybe find a place to wash her hands and face. She mustn't look ragged, like a poor little beggar girl. And thank goodness for that pair of high heels Juliette had given her, she'll change into those from her wooden shoes when she arrives. It helps to look right, to be properly dressed. Like wearing a uniform. Because even if you carry yourself well, a uniform will command respect. She'll still have to earn it, though, say and do exactly the right thing. She needn't worry, she tells herself, just trust in Him. He has led you here, to this task. He is with you, always.

Vichy looks exactly like the newsreels. A thousand hotels, there must be, the beautiful promenade surrounding the *Parc des Sources*, the lacy white ironwork eaves and well-groomed oak trees, the little gazebos, the Grand Casino, the colorful carousel, its gay music. And yet there's something gloomy, too, even in the hot sunshine, the tinny music trying to sparkle up the air. People's faces are dark, with shadows and lines on them. And Germans everywhere, in the cafes, driving along in trucks, hurrying in and out of all those stately, official-looking buildings. Her breath catches at the first sight of those black uniforms, so many of them, and leather coats, how can they wear all that in this heat? The city is bruised with all the shiny black. No, they aren't our *occupiers*, she reminds herself, they're not here to conquer us, they're our friends, here in our country to protect a good young Frenchwoman like you. She feels for her identity papers in her basket, in the event they ask *Your papers, please?* And what place could be safer than Vichy, home of our own French government? Where else could she be so protected? Wouldn't it be something if she saw the Marshal himself? Strolling the park, taking the waters? She looks for the white hair, the twinkling blue eyes, the little cap. But a shame, really, if she were to spot him—she couldn't tell tonton Claude about it, after all.

No, tante Berthe and tonton Claude think she is visiting Juliette in Oradour-sur-Glane, despite their reluctance for her to leave La Perrine, but she'd pleaded how much she missed Juliette and Gabrielle, she should go into Limoges, they needed meat, salt, tea, there was nothing for purchase at Madame Gaillard's, and perhaps there would be some piecework for her at the milliner's, they needed the money, and wouldn't Tonton like some real tobacco, she might be able to find some in Limoges, surely he's earned a treat after all his hard work? She'll have to tell them there was simply nothing for sale when she gets back, and no piecework to be had. The kind of lie that's easily forgiven, one of the tiny sins she doesn't have to mention to God because He already knows and understands it's for the right reasons. Although she wishes now she'd actually gone to Oradour, that she and Juliette and Gabrielle were having a peaceful picnic bythe Glane, even a picnic of bread and water would be lovely. And her feet hurt, the high heels fit her now but she can feel a blister forming from their unfamiliar tilt and shape, it would be good to sit down for a while. She's being cowardly again. And she must hurry, mustn't miss the bus back to Limoges. But she feels weak, and thirsty, it's so hot, she should gather her strength, first.

She looks around for a church, a quiet moment of prayer, the reassuring hand on her face, the humbling press of cold stone beneath her knees. Maybe she could hear Mass, be strengthened and affirmed by the sustenance of a single drop of His precious blood . . .

But there is no church in sight. Where are all the churches, in this important city? Well, some water, maybe. A drink of mineral water, the famous Vichy springs, yes. She enters the large glass-enclosed *Halle des Sources* at the edge of the park, blinks at the sudden humidity, the smell of sulfur and wet metal. There are bubbling blue-tiled fountains, water trickling from chipped nickel faucets, old and unhealthy-looking people perched on white metal chairs or traveling from fountain to fountain, in wheelchairs or leaning on the arms of young nurses in harsh-starched white, everyone clutching at or sipping from a small glass cup. A high arched ceiling with black iron chandeliers, the walls and trim painted a sickly green, and there is a quietude here, like at church, everyone sipping from their cups as if drinking a blessed holy water. But it's a damp, desperate quiet, the quiet of ill health or uneasiness of body and soul that seeks in vain for cleansing and healing, not the cool soothing peace of church, and there is no sweet incense or rose or breath of saints, just the waves of sulfury, wet old egg. If the waters are so healing, shouldn't all these people be well? She pays a few precious centimes, accepts a glass cup from a shriveled attendant, holds it a moment beneath a fountain, the sign above explaining the water's therapeutic effects on the pancreas, colon, diseases of the heart and lungs. It *will* be healing, like the waters Bernadette was guided to . . . She sips, grateful, and the sulfur fills her nose, warm and salty, thick, it's dreadful, but a penance, perhaps, and she forces herself to hold the penance in her mouth a moment as the sign advises, then swallow it all down. But the humidity is dizzying, making her feel stupid and dull. She hands the cup back, hastily exits the hall to the shaky click of her heels on the tile floor.

It's time. She must do this. The *CGQJ*, it's over by the park, the man at the bus depot had told her, where all the government offices are. But which building? There are so many of them. Must she go door to door, searching? Why hadn't she written ahead, asked for a formal appointment? Perhaps he would have met her at the depot, even. Why didn't she prepare better, plan this out? She stiffens her spine, looks a black-leather German officer straight in the eye as he strides down the promenade. She will ask him for directions, he will know which building is the *CGQJ*. He is smiling at her and she suddenly sees another smiling German, holding out a piece of chocolate to a little girl, so long ago, where was that, when? But this German's smile is different—he is looking at and she is suddenly aware of the low sweetheart neckline of the dress, the tug of brassiere straps and the lifted curve of her breasts, her bare calves aching from the wobbly high heels, the waxy lipstick on her lips, and she smiles back, confused, flushed, remembering the creamy luring sweet of chocolate in her mouth, its illicit warmth. She feels faint again, no wonder, she's eaten nothing, she remembers, since early that morning, a bite of dry bread, a sip of acorn coffee. She can't do this, she can't help it if she's too weak for this, she's still just a child, this is impossible, get away from here, just go home.

She turns quickly down a side street, away from the smiling German, then another street, but which way to the depot? How to find her way? She walks on, turns left, then right. How long must she wander the streets and alleys of Vichy? She hears footsteps, are those boots, *crack cracking* hard on cobblestones? She stumbles along, turns again, how can she even find the park, now, after all this wandering? Is she lost forever? Are they—

"Mademoiselle?"

—coming for her, are they after her? Do they suspect her, will she be questioned, found out? She quickens her steps, *hurry run*, but the bootsteps are louder, behind her as she hurries, *run hide*, has she been forsaken?

"Mademoiselle! Marie-Jeanne?"

She is thrown off-balance, tottering on her heels, falling. But there's a sudden firm grip on her arm, catching her, steadying her,

"It *is*, Marie-Jeanne, isn't it?" He removes his cap, holds her hand—

"Monsieur Bonnard!" Oh Lord, *your smooth arm on my own was laid*, thank you for sending him, forgive my moment of doubt! She struggles to catch her breath, "Yes, it's me . . ."

"Dear girl, how are you? What are you doing here?"

"I came to see you, for a visit, but I couldn't find . . ."

"All this way by yourself . . . ?"

They babble over each other, then stop at the same instant, shake hands formally, and laugh to fill the silence. He observes her, and she stands straight, balances to keep her line graceful.

"Well," he says. "It seems we are destined to always meet this way."

"Yes," she says. She fumbles for her handkerchief, dabs her sweaty face.

"How wonderful to see you. Look at you, how grown up you are, how pretty! But are you . . . excuse me for asking, but have you been unwell? You're so—"

"No, I'm fine, thank you." She tucks her handkerchief away. "I'm very well."

"I'm glad to hear. Well, you must be quite fatigued. May we sit somewhere?" His bright clean smile. "My office is just over here, but . . . would you like to take the waters, perhaps?"

"Oh no, I don't think so."

"Could I offer you some other refreshment, some tea?" A little laugh, a nervous one. He swipes at his blond hair, his boyish face eager. And yet there are creases across his forehead she doesn't remember, and crinkles around his eyes, like an old, crushed piece of linen you'll never be quite able to iron smooth. "I was just about to, myself."

"That would be very nice. Yes, thank you." She hopes she is saying it elegantly, as if granting him the favor of escorting her, not out of hunger or thirst or fatigue.

"Excellent, there's a place nearby, real coffee and tea they had last time. It's this way . . ."

He extends his arm, the way gentlemen do, and she takes it, the way ladies do, and he leads her down the street, speaking rapidly all the way. What a fortunate surprise to see her, she has often been in his thoughts, he has sent his prayers for her and her family and all of La Perrine, how fondly he remembers her beautiful village, that wonderful visit! No, not 'Monsieur Bonnard,' please, she is to call him Lucien, remember, aren't they dear old friends? And her letters are so delightful, much appreciated. And look at her, here, now! He *is* nervous of her, she realizes. She remembers that long-ago time in La Perrine, the stone wall against her spine and her babbling fear he would discover some secret thing about her. And now he seems like a fidgety, nervous little boy, and she feels suddenly serene, regal, assured.

They approach a café full of chewing, black-uniformed Germans, no French in sight, and she hesitates, fumbles for her papers, but he escorts her right in, and they are seated immediately by a bowing maître d'. The sudden relief in her feet, how lovely. The Germans nod respectfully at Monsieur Bonnard, and she feels an easing pride at such welcome. She sits, elegantly drapes a napkin across her lap, insists she just wants tea, but no, he hasn't had luncheon yet and she must eat something, he insists, he orders a full meal for two from the black-vested waiter, No entrecôte today? Too bad, it's excellent here, well, the roast chicken, potatoes, a green salad. And yes, wine, of course! Just the words of food make her dizzy, and the scent of it from other tables, the smells and sounds of cheeses and meats and bread chewed by all those German officers. She feels the raw throbs in her toes, slips her feet partway from their shoes. There is still sulfur in her mouth, and she swallows.

He smiles at her across the table. "Well!"

"Yes," she says. How to begin? How did Jeanne know what to say, when she approached the Dauphin? Perhaps she simply trusted God or the saints to speak through her, that's what makes it a divine mission, after all.

A bottle of red wine is brought, examined, poured, and he raises his glass.

*"Let us ride away on wine, to heavens magic and divine!"*

Baudelaire, that must be. She hopes the Germans aren't listening. She smiles, sips carefully, how delicious. Her first all-her-own glass of wine, she realizes, not a taste from an adult's glass, or that purple-sweet silver cup sip, when was that, drinking from a passed-around goblet of wine? But here is a crystal glassful to drink all by herself like a grown-up woman. So much tastier than that old fruity wine, better than that terrible sulfur water, too, definitely a blessing and not a penance. Another good sign. She takes another sip, holds the dusty warm velvet on her tongue.

"And your dear uncle and aunt, are they well?"

"Mmm, yes, very, thank you." She swallows, feels a glow in her chest, her belly, the fruit of the vine, no wonder you always thank God for the blessing of it. "Tonton Claude is with the Milice now—"

"How wonderful!"

"—yes, he's very proud. Although some people don't approve of the Milice, of course."

"Not approve?" Monsieur Bonnard raises a polite blond eyebrow.

"Well, they say Frenchmen shouldn't . . . I don't know, spy on each other that way . . ."

Don't babble, she chides herself.

"Spy?" He chuckles. "That's a foolish way to look at it. Who is saying that?" He smiles pleasantly at her. "Your priest, I'm sure he doesn't understand. Father . . . ?"

"Father Tournel. Yes, perhaps, but he—"

"Well, we need such men of peace and faith, of course, that's a source of our strength. But the rest of us have to do the hard work of that. Do what has to be done. There's probably others in La Perrine, though, who agree with Father Tournel . . . ?"

No, this isn't going right. She sips more wine, for another dusty-red blessing pause, but thinks, for some reason, of the velvet curtains in a movie theatre, the heavy shivering burgundy, and that excitement, the anticipation of what beautiful things you might soon escape into.

"People are just scared these days, that's all. Being foolish, like you said."

"I see." He sighs, heavily. "It's unfortunate the Maquis have created such mistrust among us. And that we're forced to respond to their treachery. Their violence."

"That's what my tante Berthe is afraid of, that's really why I—"

"We've had a few obstacles we didn't expect. A few setbacks." The waiter hurries to pour more wine but Monsieur Bonnard waves him away, touches the bottle to their glasses himself. "But so much of that is just rumor. That *Comite Francais de la Liberation Nationale,* for example, that's meaningless. De Gaulle's just a figurehead. Thinking he can condemn Petain and Laval as traitors, spread rumors the Marshal is senile! That just shows how crazy he is."

He continues to speak about de Gaulle moving his headquarters from London to Algeria, and Roosevelt's distrust of him, the power wrangling between Roosevelt and Churchill, Petain's astonishing vigor for a man his age, as she sips her wine again, rubs her bare feet together. They're getting away from the point, she thinks, what difference does it make who calls himself President, which leader is getting along with which?

"Tante Berthe isn't very interested in politics," she interrupts. "She's more worried about our own family. Like tonton Claude being in the Milice, she's worried about him fighting the Maquis. And my cousin Luc—"

"That's very dangerous work, fighting those terrorists. I can understand her being concerned . . . Ah, here we are!"

Heavy plates of food are set before them, golden chicken and potato platefuls, glossy with butter, and a basket of white bread, soft with fresh slicing, and she can feel the twist deep inside her stomach, how hungry she is, suddenly, hungrier than the petty gnaw she's gotten so used to she doesn't feel it anymore, but now, so much food, for her, her belly, her mouth, no, don't rush, don't gobble, pick up your fork, your knife, eat like a lady . . . He is watching her, over his own food, and she forces herself to take another sip of wine, first, to show her elegance, then which to start with, a bite of chicken or a bite of potato? A small, ladylike bite.

"But perhaps I could help with that," Monsieur Bonnard is saying, chewing. "Some of the miliciens will be serving in a different capacity soon. More specialized."

"Doing what?" Chicken, a mouthful of rich chicken, of salt and crisp fat and herbs, she hopes his answer is a long one.

"The Germans are taking over certain operations our own French police have been responsible for, this whole time. They seem to feel . . ." He becomes aware of a trio of German officers behind him, puffing on cigarettes and speaking urgently with harsh *Ich Ich Ichs*.

Monsieur Bonnard lowers his voice, leans toward her. "They seem to feel we aren't doing our jobs. Meeting our quotas, for example."

"Quotas?" She should listen more carefully, be sure she is asking the right questions, but the salt, the meat, a full mouthful . . . She forces herself to swallow. "Yes, of course, I'm sure that's so difficult now. Is it about grain, or vegetables, or . . . ?"

"Oh, no. No, no . . ." He pauses himself to finishing chewing, then a full swallow of wine. "Jews."

"Oh." *Packed up and turned over like potatoes*, she looks down, busies herself slicing a potato. *Jews*, she doesn't want to hear about those people, why does everyone keep talking about all that?

"It's ridiculous. Our own police forces have done magnificent work."

"I'm sure . . ." She puts potato in her mouth, chews carefully to steady her jaw.

"We've done everything the Germans have asked. Above and *beyond* what they've wanted. They haven't had to lift a finger! It's been entirely in French hands until now. I don't mean to brag, but that's been a big part of my job, in my own small way. But it's outrageous, what they expect. Why, we were rounding up Jews in the Unoccupied Zone before they even *asked* us to! We were doing an outstanding job before they came last November. And now they've taken over the management of Drancy . . ."

"That's, it's a camp near Paris, isn't it? Like a hotel?"

"The best in France, yes. A holding center, to load the deportees onto trains. We've been very successful there. Last year we were able to send away over forty thousand Jews."

"Forty thousand . . ." No, that number can't be right, how many trains would that even take? She pictures one of Monsieur Monzie's equations on the board, *X* bushels of grain being carried to market or *Y* goats in a flock, how many *X* Jews in a flock, rounded up, loaded on each *Y* train, crammed into trains, penned like rabbits, like cattle, how many cattle cars would you need . . . ? She squints, calculating. The wine, it's making her thick in the head. She touches her lips with her napkin, realizes she's been squinting at a German captain seated behind Monsieur Bonnard, and she looks hastily away from his sparked eyes, the sudden amused tilt to his mouth and eyes beneath his hard-brimmed black cap. That German phrase Monsieur Monzie taught them, what was it? *Ihre Papiere, bitte!* Her face flushes hot, the wine, all this rich food, such gluttony, she's not used to it.

"Forty thousand," she repeats. "My goodness. Such a big job."

"Well, it helped when Switzerland refused to take any more of them," he says, modest. "And we lowered and raised the age limit, we could round up a lot more after that. You should see the lists and lists of names we have! But the SS act like we're not up to the job anymore." He smiles respectfully at the neighboring officers, lowers his voice again. "It's never enough for the Germans, you can't satisfy them. No, they want every single Jew found out, every last one rounded up for deportation. Resettlement, that is. It's an insult, really."

"Yes . . ." Resettlement, that's all. Monsieur Bonnard would know, it's his job, such an important man. Luc and his horrible stories, his crazy lies . . . She drinks from her wineglass.

"It's Laval's fault, in a way, promising them the moon and stars, but he really has no idea what goes into this kind of work. I don't mean to sound disloyal, you understand—"

"Of course not . . ."

"—and it's true, our numbers are down a bit this year. We've only been able to round up, oh, fourteen, fifteen thousand of them so far. The SS expected at least twenty thousand from this area by now. Personally, I think they inflated estimates of their presence from the start, just to make us look bad. The truth is, we've done such a good job, we're simply running out of Jews."

"That makes it easier, then, less work, doesn't it? If they're all gone?"

"In a way. It makes for a different kind of effort, now. A different kind of peril. The ones still around, they've gotten very slippery, very clever at evading the law. Their true nature, that kind of cunning. Anyway, the SS will take over most of that now. And use the Milice. Older men like your uncle. Veterans, men who have proven themselves in defense of our country. So, perhaps I could help your uncle be reassigned?"

"That would be wonderful," she murmurs.

"Yes, he could be tracking down Jews who haven't registered for resettlement. Or the ones who've been hiding. And exposing those who've been helping them, too, colluding with the enemy. It's still extremely important work, of course. Very well-compensated."

"That would be so helpful, thank you."

"And so many still left are women and children, at this point. How dangerous can that be, rounding up children? Looking in hospitals, orphanages, schools. I've heard stories some of them hiding in barns, in haystacks. In sewers. Like animals." He smiles at her. "But we'll ferret them all out. And they'll be allowing the Milice guns, I hear, very soon."

She smiles back, looks at the remains of the chicken on her plate, the gristle and bone. Bits of skin. She sets her knife and fork to rest.

When she glances up again the German captain is still looking at her, boldly this time, an admiring nod of his head. She feels the flush on her face, it's so warm, *Ich bin Marie-Jeanne,* she thinks, the *Ich bin* words in her mouth, and the slickness of butter and oil and chicken skin, another gulp of wine to clear the grease, rinse it all away, thank goodness for the wine, thank you, Blessed Lord, blessed are you, Creator of the universe, *Baruch atah Adonai eloheynu melech ha-olam.*

Black insect letters, vermin crawling across a page. She coughs, shakes her head. She feels her short hair swing, her golden red hair. Scottish, I look Scottish. "I'm sorry, Monsieur, you were saying?"

"That I could look into that, for you? If you like."

"Thank you." She clears her throat, swallows again, "You're so kind to us. So helpful."

"I still have a little influence, in my position. For the time being, anyway. Are you ready for your salad?" He lifts his finger for the waiter.

"Oh no, I've had enough. It was delicious, though."

"Something sweet, then? Please, you seem so, well, so delicate."

"No, thank you. I couldn't eat anything more." She dabs her sweating forehead with her napkin.

"We'll have our coffee, then. And you must finish your wine." He pours more wine, makes a red jewel of her glass. "The truth is, I'm not sure how all these changes will affect my job," he continues, with his nervous laugh. "They say the Germans might be 'reorganizing,' as they call it. I've been promoted twice, that should count for something, I shouldn't have to keep proving myself." He shrugs. "But enough of this unfortunate business. For now, today, let's enjoy! This fortuitous event!" He raises his glass to her again. "How does that other one go, let's see . . . *Wine conceals the most sordid rooms, in rich, miraculous costumes . . .*" He swallows wine. "'*Le Poison,*' I think is the title."

She nods, swallows. "I'm sure they appreciate how hard you work, the Germans. All the good you've done. What you did for my cousin

Luc, for example, that was so good of you. To keep him safe."

"Ah yes, your cousin. How is he getting along? Is he enjoying his position?"

"Very much, he—"

"So many young men are avoiding their duty these days. But an honorable young man like your cousin, he knows there's something bigger than self. Something more noble."

"Yes, he's just like that. He wants very much to be honorable and noble. But I'm worried, that what he's up to could still be, well, dangerous . . ." Monsieur Bonnard gazes at her, expressionless, dear Lord, Blessed Mother, please be with me, help me, where are you? ". . . and I was thinking, maybe he'd be safer if he could do his duty somewhere else? Maybe there's a different assignment for him you could arrange? Away from what's happening up north?"

"You're worried about the bombings, aren't you?" He smiles, gently.

"Yes, that's it." She nods. "Yes."

"Those reports are so exaggerated, Marie-Jeanne, I assure you." He narrows his eyebrows at her, mock serious. "You haven't been listening to the BBC, have you?"

"No, of course not!"

"Thank goodness! I'd hate to have to turn you in!"

He laughs his easy, assured laugh, and she laughs too, gaily, along with him, as the waiter clears their plates and the German captain's eyes dart her way. His eyebrows seem to shrug, he says something to his friends, and she hears a hearty male laughter from their table, a schoolyard kind of laughter, *Settle down, young gentlemen!* she can almost hear Monsieur Monzie say. She thrusts her naked feet back into their shoes and feels the protest of her tender flesh, her sore heels and toes.

"But think about it, Marie-Jeanne, he's up there building air raid shelters. Underground refineries. It's probably the safest place for him to be. Safer than being in Germany, even."

"Yes, but . . ." She mustn't seem so hesitant, so afraid. She thinks of rabbits in their pen, how you must reach in for them steadily, surely, until you can grab one close and tight. "It's just I'm also concerned he maybe isn't seeing things the right way . . ."

"What do you mean?"

She grips the stem of her wineglass. "He's such a fine young man, like you said."

"I'm sure." He looks at her, intently. Those eyes, she'd forgotten how sapphire-rich they were. "I'm sure he is, but . . . ?"

"He's still so young. Like a little boy. Dreaming of adventure."

"Mmm, yes. Sometimes a young boy wants so much to be a man. Do a man's work. Seek a man's glory."

"That's just what I mean! I'm so glad you understand!"

He nods. "I was a young boy once, myself." And there's his pretty smile on his boyish hot chocolate face.

"And I think my cousin has maybe allowed those . . ."

"Dreams of glory?"

"Exactly, those dreams. Those voices in his head, or the voices of other people, the wrong people he's been listening to . . ." She pushes her feet hard and deep into the harsh shoes, worrying the little raw pains there. Mortification of the Flesh. "Oh, Monsieur Bonnard—"

"Lucien, please."

"Lucien, I'm so worried about him. You have to help me!"

"Marie-Jeanne, of course." He pours the last of the wine into her glass. "You know I'll do anything I can for you."

"If he were off in a factory somewhere, on an assembly line, maybe. Far away. Soup cans and machine parts. Where he wouldn't get into any trouble. Or get anyone else in trouble. Or . . . put anyone at risk."

Monsieur Bonnard nods, listening.

"I know it's not your job, Lucien, but you have important contacts, maybe you could speak to someone? Make that happen? Lucien? Because I want to do the right thing for Luc. And for tante Berthe and tonton Claude. And La Perrine. For everybody. Sometimes I feel like it's all up to me, I have to do the exactly right thing, to keep everyone safe."

"A young girl like you?"

"I know it isn't, really, Lucien, that's crazy, to think I could save everyone. Like Luc, and his crazy ideas. His silly dreams."

"Your dream isn't silly, Marie-Jeanne. Just impractical. The dream, the aspiration, is wonderful."

"But it should be more than a dream, shouldn't it? It's not enough to just hope or pray for things to be better, or say we want them to be, we're supposed to . . . like you said, before, we have to do the hard work of it. Don't we?"

"That's true. Each of us must do our part, even a young woman like you." He takes her hand, squeezes it, and she remembers its steadying strength and warmth. Although it's cool now, his hand, how nice that cool smooth palm feels in all this heat. "It might seem difficult in the moment, that's true. Or seem like such a small little thing, how could it possibly make a difference in the world?"

She nods.

"Or . . . it seems like you're breaking a promise, perhaps?"

She nods again, "Yes . . ."

"Like . . . a betrayal?"

"Yes." She swallows the last of the wine in her glass, the last thick and precious drop.

"But it isn't, really. Because sometimes there has to be a sacrifice. To do what's right. For the greater good."

"And that makes it worth it?" she murmurs. "It's worth sacrificing anything for?"

"To keep everyone safe, yes." He nods, solemn. "And God doesn't trust just anyone to do that. He only chooses someone special to play that role. Someone very strong and brave."

She licks her lips, feels the wine blush in her blood, the delicious warm kiss of it in her cheeks. "Yes. Yes, Lucien."

"It isn't easy to be so selfless. To do what needs to be done. Of course I'll do whatever I can to help. Whatever it takes."

He releases her hand, gently slides his own unfinished wine before her on the table, to where a beam of light strikes it ruby-bright. She smiles in thanks, raises the glass, sips, watches as the SS Germans get to their feet, adjust their black jackets, their caps, toss bills to the table. The officer catches her eye briefly, touches his cap in acknowledgment. She lowers her eyes, sees the bright buckle of his uniform, *Unsere Ehre ist unsere Loyalitat. Our Honor* something. *Our Honor Is Our Loyalty*, that's right, so true, and how wonderful he understands her so completely.

Lucien leans toward her again.

"So, about your cousin, you were telling me . . . ? What is he up to, really?"

~

**October, 1943**

"Marie-Jeanne? There's a letter here for your uncle . . . ?"

Monsieur Leroux, stacking newspapers—copies of *Je suis partout*, she'd noticed he'd begun selling that again, after the phony attack, he thinks he can fool everybody—stops to pull an envelope from a slim pile of mail, hands it to her with a smile, a crooked smile, his split lip healed and twisted now in a shiny pink scar, but she gives him only a brief nod in return, a polite "Thank you, Monsieur."

Although her heart is beating, the old heart-skip of an anonymous envelope arriving, the tiny hope at the sight of it, unopened and promising . . . But this one has a return address, and is thin formal stationery, and *Lucien?* she thinks. But why would he write to Tonton and not her? No, it isn't from the *CGQJ*, she sees. It's from the *Ministry of* something, typewritten in the corner, blurred but inky, official.

"Not bad news, I hope . . . ?" Monsiseur Leroux murmurs. Like an invitation, a prompting. He has often looked at her that way recently.

But she simply shakes her head, hands him her letter to Juliette, hurries outside. That terrible summer heat, thank Heaven that's over. La Perrine is taking on its wintry gray, the street empty of villagers, cafes and shops closed, a hesitant whirling snowflake or two, everyone home preparing supper, it will be good to get home, out of this cold. Hurry home. She can smell the burning wood, Advent coming soon, the most wonderful time of year, readying for the birth of Jesus, preparing the Advent wreath with tante Berthe for their family devotions. Something special, she'd like to do this year, something extra meaningful, maybe a crèche? She could make the little Joseph and Mary and Baby Jesus and manger animals all by herself out of clay or flour paste, if there's old weevilly flour to be had. She can piece together the robes from scraps in Tante's sewing basket, fill the manger with straw from their own barn, maybe use strands of her own golden red hair from her hairbrush, make a real crèche for their home, honest and holy and pure. What a wonderful idea, how pleased tante Berthe and tonton Claude will be! How nice it will be on these icy evenings, the three of them kneeling before the warmth of their very own Holy Family, her and Tante and Tonton, that's right, the letter for tonton Claude, she should get home, give him his letter, the *Ministry* of something, official, important . . .

She tucks herself against the wall of the tabac, out of reach of questioning sight or icy wind, tugs off her mittens, slits open the tissue envelope, unfolds the translucent sheet of paper,

*We regret to inform you,* she reads, and then more words, *traitor, arrest, dishonorable,* and *freely confessed under questioning,* and *attempting to escape during transport to military tribunal, shot, killed, a lesson to all involved in seditious activity . . .*

She stops reading. She blinks. She refolds the thin sheet, replaces it carefully in its envelope.

*Sometimes there has to be a sacrifice.*

The paper tears easily as fresh bread in her hands, tears down to the tiniest of pieces, rolls like crumbs between her fingers and scatters under her shoes as she walks, hurries, runs, white tissue bits dancing along the gray stones and hard dirt of the road, fluttering away like flakes of wheat chaff, of ash, of snow.

It is tonton Claude whose cries fill the house, whose face is broken, shoulders and chest jolting, who is clutching at tante Berthe, head pressed against her breast. And it is tante Berthe whose eyes are bone dry, whose face is heavy and blank. Marie-Jeanne reaches out to take her swollen hand, grips it hard to stop her own shaking.

*Promise you'll make them understand. So they'll be proud of me.*

"He died so honorably, tante Berthe. He was such a hero, that's what Monsieur Bonnard's letter to me said. Doing noble, honorable work for his country,"

*You'll take care of them, right? Promise me.*

"I just, I just couldn't bear to show the letter to you, to make you have to see it. I was upset, I had to destroy it, please understand!"

"Yes, of course. Thank you, dear . . ." Tante Berthe says, almost absent mindedly, as if it's a fact of no importance. She is gazing over tonton Claude's head, at the portraits of Marshal Petain and the Virgin Mary, at a pallet bed on the floor. Kept waiting, linens smoothed, pillow propped straight. She lets go of Marie-Jeanne's hand, pats tonton Claude.

"And . . . he . . ." she doesn't know what else to offer. *He died for us. He is with God in Heaven now, at peace, watching over us,* she could say. But she knows tante Berthe already knows that. *Blessed are they who mourn, for they will be comforted,* she thinks, but that sounds in her head like empty words, a mere slogan.

*I'm sorry,* she thinks, the hot rock words sealing up her throat, keeping her own eyes burning and dry.

But tante Berthe's face suddenly flickers alive; she seizes Marie-Jeanne's hand again, so hard it hurts, but just a little hurt, not quite enough.

"You'll never leave us?"

"Oh, tante Berthe . . ."

"You won't! You're our child. You're our Marie-Jeanne!"

"Of course I am." She squeezes tante Berthe's hand gently in return, leans to put her arm around tonton Claude's shoulder. "We'll always be together."

"Promise us. Promise me!"

"I promise, of course. I'll never leave you, not ever!"

And tante Berthe nods, comforted, the three of them sitting and rocking together in the dimming afternoon light, as the kitchen shadows flatten to gray stones and the trees to a black lace against the window's darkening, then dark at last, sky.

## *MY HOME*

*by Marie-Jeanne Chantier*

*10 April, 1944*
*La Perrine, France*

*When I was a little girl, I thought about being an actress when I grew up, how I'd travel the world that way being famous. I also contemplated becoming a nun, so I could devote myself to faith and good works and austerity and live in a lovely stone convent, where it is always peaceful except for soft organ music and mellifluous voices lifting in prayer.*

*Tante Berthe says I could be a teacher or a governess, because I've done so well at my studies, and tonton Claude agrees, after we worked together on his Milice reports. Of course, a woman's most important way to contribute to our homeland is to get married, have many children, and create a happy, healthy home for her family. Now that I'm fifteen it's time to think seriously about this, and reflect on who I am, and who I wish to become.*

*But I can't imagine leaving my home, here in La Perrine. Tante Berthe and tonton Claude devoted themselves to taking care of me when I was a child, and I feel blessed that now it's my turn to care for them.*

*So perhaps one day I'll become a teacher, or maybe get married and have children—who knows what might happen, with all the possibilities in this world! But what you can always know for sure and depend on, even when times are hard or the future seems uncertain, is that your family and your home will always be there for you, and with you forever in your heart.*

*2 May, 1944*

*Mme. Juliette Arnaux*
*Oradour-sur-Glane, Limousin*

*Dear Juliette,*

*How are you and Gabrielle? I miss you both so much! Writing letters back and forth just isn't the same. But tante Berthe gets so anxious if I'm out of her sight now, and even Tonton says No, your aunt is right, Marie-Jeanne, you don't realize what's going on out there these days! I try to reassure them there's nothing to worry about if I visit you, there's no Maquis or Milice or Resistance activity at all in Oradour, how you've never even seen a German soldier there. But they just keep saying No, you're to stay home with us!*

*I understand how they feel, or at least I try to. Tonton Claude even retired from the Milice and signed trusteeship of the mill over to Monsieur Druot, he says he's not up to that hard work anymore. And tante Berthe spends so much time in bed or sitting by the fire in her nightdress. She used to stare a lot at Luc's bed still on the floor, and that upset Tonton, so one night I put away all his bedding, and packed up his clothes to send to the soldiers, because I thought it would be easier that way. But they didn't even notice, I don't think—Tante still sits and stares, I have to remind her to pray the Rosary with me. Even then, I'm not sure her heart is in it. And Tonton wanders the house mumbling about chores he needs to do, but nothing ever really gets done. Sometimes even I forget and set a place for Luc at the table, or I expect a pile of kindling to just appear by the stove. But more and more now it's hard to remember there was ever an actual real boy named Luc, his tall skinny bones and dark eyes. I hope that doesn't sound terrible of me, does it? To forget to remember him? But there's so much else to do now, and maybe it's good to forget and just be here with Tonton and Tante.*

*I can only pray they'll stop getting so much older so fast. And that the war will be finally all over with, and everything can go back to the normal way it was before. And I can come visit you again!*

*Gabrielle will be three years old soon, won't she? I wonder what and who she'll be when she grows up? Please give her a hug from me, and to you, too,*

*Much love, to both of you, Marie-Jeanne*

~

**Friday, 9 June, 1944**

"Don't get up, tante Berthe, I'll see who it is!" Marie-Jeanne calls, and the tired voice wisps from upstairs, the thin "Thank you, dear . . ." She wipes flour from her hands, dusts every precious speck back onto the loaf she is kneading, such a small loaf, no more extra flour from the mill anymore, only official rations for three that look more like a meal for one. Some dried beans left, she thinks, they should try bean flour, they say that works fine . . . She goes to the door, probably Madame Richie for a gossipy visit, a cup of carrot-tops tea, she always comes here now it's so hard for Tante to walk to the village . . .

But standing there is a stranger, a woman in a ragged sweater, a faded scarf wrapped tight and close to her skull, a sun-blistered face, soiled socks visible through cracks in the sun-bleached leather boots. Shaking hands, wizened hands. The whiff of a long-unwashed body enters the house, following the breeze of the opened door.

"Can I help you?" Polite, but not too welcoming, a firm stand in the doorway. She can see grime buried under the fingernails, ringing the cuticles black. A refugee, it must be, wandering and lost. They pass through the village sometimes, fleeing a burning town or ravaging troops, or traveling on foot to find scattered relatives. Father Tournel collects scraps to offer them a meal, but Monsieur Druot says to turn them away, they could be Maquis or foreign agents, or even if they're real refugees we mustn't encourage their coming here. But she agrees with Father Tournel about that—it's their Christian duty to feed the hungry, and she sometimes gives them the least withered of the old vegetables they keep for the rabbits and chickens. And how desperate they must be, to have walked all that way up the mountain to La Perrine . . .

Like this lady, poor thing, looking too exhausted to even speak.

"Are you hungry, Madame? Would you like something to eat?"

But the woman shakes her head, gazing at her with brightening eyes.

*"Mein oitser . . ."* she whispers.

Oh, a foreigner. Probably doesn't even speak French, this one, sounds almost like German, whatever she's mumbling, a good thing Tonton is in the village.

"Hungry?" she says to the woman. She makes exaggerated eating motions, rubs her stomach. "Food? Are you—"

"Danielle." The woman says, like a sentence all on its own. "Danielle." She exhales a deep breath, and Marie-Jeanne takes a step back from the smell that emanates with the word.

"I'm sorry, there's no—"

"Danielle, it's me."

*Me*, but who is me, she knows all the *me*'s who might knock on their door—

"It's *me*, cherie, it's me,"

—except this woman, that isn't a *me*, it's a *her*, it's

"Maman."

*Maman*, standing there, flesh and blood. But this is not her mother's flesh and blood, no. There is no satiny fair skin, no gleaming red crown of hair. No roses in the sun. It's some other woman's flesh and blood, dirty, old, it must be, *her* mother is in Heaven, her Blessed Mother, the perfumed golden glow and sweet smile, *that's* her real

"Marie-Jeanne?" The voice from upstairs, calling, "Who is it, dear?"

mother, not this

"Nothing, Tante, it's no one!"

filthy old woman,

"Don't get up, Tante, I'll be right back!"

and she sweeps at it, the *her*, pushes her away, then jerks her hands back, horrified to have touched. The woman stumbles backward, and Marie-Jeanne steps through the door, closes it fast behind them, resists the urge to wipe her hands on her skirt.

"Danielle?" The woman holds out her arms, but—

"No, don't!" She steps away. She peers up the road, blinking in the harsh sun, there's no one around, thank God. "Please, you can't, we can't . . ." They can't stay here, out in the open where they could be seen, found out, "just come with me," and she turns, "come on, *hurry*," hurries toward the barn, that woman is following, good. She pushes open the barn door, stands to one side, allows the woman to enter, she's limping a bit, a stagger to her walk, and that smell again, foul, unclean. She closes the barn door after them, grateful for the loomy shadows and rich healthy odor of animal and manure and hay.

"Danielle." The woman reaches her hand out again, but stops, sways a little. "I need . . . I think I need to sit down?"

She reaches for her milking stool, sets it before the woman, steps back. The woman sits, thankfully. A slim shaft of light through a crack in the wall rests on her face, shows the damp in her still-gazing eyes, the tremble of her mouth, lips dry, white, thin as garlic skins, but an eagerness, too, like a meal has been laid out before her she can't wait to consume, a hunger that makes Marie-Jeanne step back again, away.

"I've startled you. I'm sorry. I didn't think it would be safe to write or . . . this must be very . . ." The woman pauses. "Surprising."

"Yes." She doesn't know what to say, where to look. Her eyes roam the barn, so quiet, soothing, the low of the cow and the cluck of the chickens, a scramble from the rabbits, a fat horsefly buzz, but no human sounds. Except, "Look at you," the woman is saying. "Just look at you."

She glances at the woman, sees the damp eyes shine more damp, shine up and swell into tears. One falls, then another.

"You're so beautiful. You're such a big girl."

*You have to be a big brave girl now.*

She looks away again, pitchfork on the wall, rafters, the pile of clean straw. Eggs, she thinks, I should see if they've laid recently, if there are any eggs to be had . . .

"I've thought about you all the time. Every day, every minute."

"That's nice," Marie-Jeanne says.

"I was so frightened. So worried. Are you all right? You're so thin.

Have you been all right?"

"Yes, I'm perfectly fine. Thank you."

"And Berthe, and Claude? Are they well? Have they," the woman wipes her dripping nose on her sleeve, "have they been kind?"

"Of course they are." She's embarrassed for the woman, making such a fuss. "They're very good to me."

"I knew you'd be safe here. That you'd be. . . " The woman seems to run out of words, ". . . warm."

"They've sacrificed a lot for me."

"I knew they would. And I told you I'd be back, when it was over. That I'd come back for you."

But you left, she thinks. You left me.

"Where have . . . where have you been?" she asks.

"Oh, everywhere, I suppose." The woman laughs, a laugh that's tired and shows stained teeth, and makes Marie-Jeanne avert her eyes again. "You have to move a lot, keep moving. At first the cities were dangerous, the woods were safe. Now it's the other way, it's easier to hide in plain view in a city. They figure we're all gone. The woods, they're more crowded now. Milice, Maquis. German troops out to shoot one last Jew." She clutches the neck of her sweater, rubs at her arms, as if cold. "Sometimes you recognize someone you know. You come upon a friend, someone who's hidden you or gave you a piece of bread, maybe just a day or hour before, and then you find them again. Lying there. They're still bleeding, or naked, the SS strip them for clothing or shoes. To die there that way, like an animal. Or sometimes you need the clothes yourself, you see? You find yourself taking from a body, unbuttoning off a blouse, it's so cold at night, or you're grabbing a sweater, you're pulling it off a stiff body, you need a sweater, it gets icy, you go through pockets, you're looking for anything, feeling in hidden places, the body, you're scavenging for—" The woman stops, abrupt. "No." She shakes her head. "No. I'm here now. With you."

The woman wipes at her eyes, her cheeks. "And it's warm, here. It's so warm now. It's June, isn't it?"

"Yes."

"June . . . We should be buying you a new swimsuit, shouldn't we? You grow so fast! And a new summer dress. Something fancy, for parties. With lace. Blue, a pastel blue. Summer sky blue."

"I don't think—"

"And some play clothes. So you can run around, get all smudged or wrinkled." Her stained smile, again. "Don't worry, I won't scold. I promise."

"I'm not—"

"Oh, I know. I know. That was before. I'm just remembering. I do that all the time. Those crocheted gloves, the lace, you always wanted a pair. With little roses, the ones we saw that day, remember? That pale blue thread, almost like milk. Such a pretty color on you. I've thought a lot about those gloves. That's so silly, isn't it? And I said no, they're too delicate, too fine, you'll just lose them. I said maybe when you were older, remember? If you were a good girl."

"No, I don't." She looks at the woman, keeps her face unmoving, her eyes clear. Gloves, little roses, what is she talking about, this woman? "I don't remember any of that."

"And now look at you. You're so tall. And your hair . . . why didn't I buy you those gloves, when I could?" The woman abruptly leans forward. "They landed in Normandy a few days ago. Allied troops, they came. The fighting's terrible. But it's happening, finally."

"Oh. That's nice."

"I have a place we can go. I have friends in Toulouse, their church has a refuge for Jews. We'll be safer there, they'll keep us hidden until it's all over. Think about it, Danielle."

*No.*

"We can stay in Toulouse, if you like it there, I'll find work, or we can go back to Paris, even, we can go *home* . . ."

*No.*

". . . pretend this never happened and—"

"No," Marie-Jeanne tells her. "Wait, please."

But the woman is nodding, "I know, I'm rambling, I'm just so—"

"No, *stop*." she says. "Stop."

And the woman stops, smiling, waiting.

"I can't go," she tells her. "I can't leave."

"Oh, not this minute. But soon, we'll talk with Berthe and Claude about—"

"No, you can't do that."

"What?"

"You can't talk to them. It isn't safe."

"Not safe for who?"

"For anyone! It's too dangerous. It's perilous!"

"But it's different now, chèrie!" The woman leans forward again, coming at her, hungry. "It'll be hard for a while, I'm sure, but we don't have to be afraid, anymore. It's all right, it's safe now! We can have our real lives again, you and I, together, we can—"

"You don't understand."

The woman shakes her head, smiles again. "What do you mean?"

"You can't just come here and . . ." her throat closing up, she swallows, "just do whatever you want. Like you always do."

Still smiling, "What?"

"Well, yes, *you* can. Do whatever you want. That's fine, leave again. Go! I don't care. It doesn't have anything to do with me!"

The woman's smile drops away. She leans back.

"And they can't know you're here. You can't be here."

"Oh," the woman says. "Oh. I didn't think . . ." The woman presses her papery lips together. "Yes. I think I understand, Danielle—"

"No!" That's a, a *quota* name, a name on a list, she thinks. A cattle car name. There is no Danielle here. "Stop it, stop calling me that!"

"All right," the woman says carefully. "Yes. I know, I know this is so sudden. But in a few days, maybe, we can—"

"You're not listening. This is my home. My family. My life. Mine. You, *you* have to go!"

There is a moment of breathlessness, of pain in her chest, she has stopped breathing, she realizes. But it is too late, now, to gulp a deep loud breath, the woman will see, so she tries to take a slow and quiet one, as if everything is normal and fine.

"I see." The woman presses her dirty hands to her face a moment, then drops them to her lap. She nods, slowly. "All right. I understand. Yes. Well, what if I stay for just a little while, just to rest? Before I go? Can I do that? Out here," she adds, hurriedly, "I'll hide out here in the barn?"

"Well . . ." Be charitable, at least, and you're the only one who comes in here, after all, ". . . yes, all right. But just for a day or two. That's all. And then you'll leave."

The woman nods again at her, still slow, careful. "Yes. I understand." She wearily pulls her scarf from her head and Marie-Jeanne startles, blinks, waiting for the crown, the shining jewel braid, but no, it's just a head of regular red hair now, cut very short and so dirty, shiny with grease. She must be covered with vermin. And that face, her cheek, her hands, once so creamy and fine, a faint dusting of powder on her nose, the sweet fragrance from her wrists and throat, the folds of a satin gown, all of it gone now, her skin gray as dust, freckled, coarsened by sunburn and wind and grime. A ragged sweater, a dead woman's sweater. She closes her eyes.

*Pale girl, with auburn hair, whose tattered dress reveals your poverty and your beauty . . .*

"And could I have something to eat, perhaps?"

"Yes, of course." She opens her eyes, nods. "You must be hungry.

I'm sorry. Here . . ."

She grabs her milking pail, there won't be much milk right now, but . . . She places her pail, kneels in the straw before the cow, grateful for the task. It will be good for the woman, those vitamins. She seizes the warm teats, and the cow moos again at this surprise attack. She squeezes, tugs, her fingers working their smooth rhythm and she closes her eyes again, presses her face against the animal's scratchy warmth. She listens for the soothing prayer of it, to hush and slow the world and hold her in just this moment, this one steadying and exact place. Just stay here doing this, forever. A fat fly buzzes, circles the pail. A few drops, that's all. She feels the cow shift. Her hands grow still, and she pauses, still waiting, hoping. No, that's all.

She lets go of the cow, gets to her feet, brushes straw from her skirt. "Here." She holds the pail out and the woman reaches, abrupt and inelegant, although it doesn't seem like hunger for the milk itself. But she grabs at the pail, clutches it, gulps.

"I'll get you some food, too. There isn't much, though." She sees the rabbit nibbling a piece of brown lettuce, the stump of a hoary carrot, no, she can't give this woman such scraps, she must treat her with dignity and respect, like any fellow human being. Even one of those people. It's your duty. That is how you show your love for God, that's what He wants from you. Your share of the bread, you'll give her all of that. You can fast for the rest of the day. Sacrifice. Austerity of the flesh, God will be pleased, will forgive.

"Anything. Thank you." The woman raises her chin, swallows.

"And I'll bring some water, for you to wash with. And a blanket."

"Thank you." The woman wipes her mouth with a grimy hand. She straightens her spine, lifts her chin again. Elegant, almost, a glimpse of it. "And could I maybe have a candle?"

A candle? "It's still light out, it won't be dark for hours."

"I'm sorry to ask. But it's Friday."

Marie-Jeanne looks at her, bewildered. "I *can't*. If anybody saw the light—"

"Oh yes, you're right—"

"—they'd *see*! They'd suspect. Don't you understand? They'll come get everyone, all of us, they'll take all of us! We'll all be killed!"

*Baruch atah Adonai, blessed are you,*

"I understand, really, Danielle, I—"

"Don't call me that!"

*who has created the fruit of the vine . . .*

"Oh God, I forgot. I'm so sorry. Marie-Jeanne, yes." The woman shakes her head, swallows. "Marie-Jeanne, I'm so very sorry."

"It doesn't matter. I don't care." She backs away, feeling for the barn door behind her, stumbles in the straw, steadies herself by putting her hand on the latch. "Just stay away from the window. It's very dangerous. You have to understand that. I don't even know you, you aren't really here, you have to remember that!"

"I will, Marie-Jeanne, of course," the woman says. "Thank you. Marie-Jeanne."

Yes, it's Marie-Jeanne. Named for saints.

She unlatches the door, peers out. It's safe. She hurries back to the house.

*Dear Saint Jeanne, but she left, that woman, she was gone forever, help me, dear Jeanne please instill in me the desire to serve God first and perform my earthly tasks with that ever in my mind . . .*

She drops to her knees before her bed, breathing hard, presses her hands in prayer, looks desperately up at the card pinned to her wall, *please, Jeanne, what do I do, please help me!*

But Jeanne is gazing up at Heaven's golden beams, busy with her own divine mission, her duty to save all of France, too busy to bother with some girl's silly problems, or even look down upon her, or maybe she can't look, because maybe what if it isn't really Jeanne, not actually her presence in the room, just a fake piece of painted gilded cardboard . . . ?

*Hail Mary, full of grace, the Lord is with thee, blessed art thou among women,* and she grabs her rosary, fumbles for the first bead, the tiny dry rose, presses it to her mumbling lips, *Hail Mary, what does that woman want from me, you must guide me, Mother, you have never left me, please . . .*

Yes, Mary *is* blessed, to conceive a child so immaculately, so holy and chosen and smiled upon, how could she understand such a thing, an unclean mother gulping milk from a pail, give your sweet, always-there Blessed Mother a rose, so she'll look upon you with love, help you, but maybe maybe it's just a handful of dried old rosebuds on a string . . . She grips them tighter, feels a dusty crumble in her fist, no, there's no rose there, just a handful of brownish dust, flakes of dead flower . . .

*Our Father who art in Heaven, hallowed be Thy name,* and she crosses herself, implores the crucifix hanging on the wall, *why couldn't she have stayed dead, Father, in Heaven with You, disappeared here on earth, people don't come back from the dead, give you their body and blood, that's so crazy, oh, forgive me, Blessed Father,* she crosses herself, crosses herself, *sweet Jesus, You came back from the dead, of course, to save all of us, I believe that, I swear I do, so save me now, please, Thy will be done . . .*

But there is only silence. No soft answering voice, or gentle caress or illuminating light. And all of this must be His will, too, mustn't it? If He is Maker of all that is seen and unseen, and you mustn't question His will, just give yourself over to the faith of it, so He'll shield you under His wings, be your Savior and Redeemer, keep you and everyone protected and safe . . .

But what if it *is* His will to punish you, this time,

*Danielle,*

because

*God is my judge*

of your unworthiness, your mistakes, all of your sins?

What if it really has come again, the *end*, is here at last, the marching, the peril, the punishment, final judgment, the end of everything, the bayonets, guns, burning blood, howling dogs, you must run, escape, get away from here, get somewhere safe, you must

*hurry, hide, flee.*

~

**Saturday, 10 June, 1944**

Limoges is a panicked churn, not the happy-busy it used to be, now there are stricken faces, worry packed stiff inside rushing bodies, even the Germans look frantic, and they're mostly the shiny black leather SS Germans now, like in Vichy, not the ordinary Wermacht soldiers she used to see here, all the city sounds now drummed out by German voices and boots, everything swollen dark by those gleaming uniforms and coats and truncheons slapping into hands. Even the bus from La Perrine was full of boiling-up whispers, hissing over the engine's drone, They say there's bloody fighting to liberate Argenton-sur-Creuse, that an SS captain was kidnapped in Gueret by Maquis and the SS are butchering French citizens in reprisal, eighty-six civilians slaughtered in Lille, yesterday they hung ninety-nine men from lampposts in Tulle, they say it would have been more except the SS ran out of rope! They say Allied troops are spreading thru northwest France, liberating villages and towns, the Resistance is trying to delay German troops getting there, they say de Gaulle's returning in victory, the SS are announcing *a brutal crackdown in the zones of resistance*, look, there, posted to the depot wall, a new *avis*:

**TO THE POPULATION OF LIMOGE, 10 JUNE, 1944: The Waffen SS Das Reich will take full administrative and executive control of the area, in order to protect our troops and maintain order against bands of terrorists. Any act of violence or sabotage, disturbance of business, or failure to follow orders will be cause for immediate arrest and trial by a German military tribunal.**

But who is coming to *end* it all, the Germans, the English, the Americans, the Soviets? No one seems to know, but it doesn't matter, it's coming. Don't think about bombs and blood, about people lying in ditches, living in sewers, hiding in barns, just hurry, get away. She pushes her way through streaming, steaming crowds to the tram stop, people gripping suitcases and boxes, the smell of sharp fear in the air. She pictures dogs, their gone-wild, bloodied jaws. She can't get onto the first tram, already crammed with people, *Tobacco day in Oradour,* a yellowed old man tells her, shrugging, *Germans or no, everyone's going for their rations,* and she must wait for the next one, sweating, *And vaccines for the schoolchildren, too,* adds a harried woman about Juliette's age, clutching a smear-faced toddler in her arms, *It'll be overrun with kids there today,* and she nods at the woman, tries to smile, be polite, but what does she care about tobacco and vaccines? What's taking so long, the sun is baking the air white, making a glare of the buildings, the streets. She imagines tante Berthe and tonton Claude finding her scrawled note that morning:

*I just had to see Juliette, I'll spend the night in Oradour, be home tomorrow, I milked the cow, please don't worry!*
*I love you, always,*
*your Marie-Jeanne.*

They're probably so worried about her, missing her, don't think about that right now . . .

Finally, the next tram. She grips her basket and pushes her way on board, shoving rudely past all the women and children and old people, *Excuse me, Excuse me,* and into a seat, no time for good manners. The tram lurches off, its electrical *clicking* audible, thank goodness, she'll be there soon. She takes a deep breath of the hot air. She'll see Juliette in the window seat with Gabrielle, their blonde hair gleaming in the sun, the sweet whiff of lavender, flowered wallpaper, music on the phonograph, lace curtains dancing in a breeze, and Juliette will be there, smiling, will hold her in fragrant, warm, clean, flesh-and-blood arms. The tram rolls along the hills, away from the truck engines and leather boots and frightened people. She takes another deep breath. Music and dancing, happy dress-up, a picnic, pretty colors, everything peaceful and normal and safe. Free of care.

There it is, the tall church spire up ahead, its tower and tile roof a welcoming silhouette against the hot blue sky. The Glane will appear soon, alive with fish and fisherman, they'll ride along the green river bank and across the little bridge to enter the village, its shining white stone, Juliette and Gabrielle so surprised to see her, so happy.

But the "*Achtung!*" is a sudden cough, the shiny black SS German discoloring the bright blue and green and white by his sudden leap onto the tram, holding tight to the door against the jolting stop.

"Achtung, *attention*! Halt the tram!"

People frown, confused. *Just an identity check,* begin the whispers, the rustling for papers, faces struggling to rearrange in placid lines, *Not to worry, don't upset the children*. The SS officer eyes them all, then steps down from the tram, confers with a cluster of other SS seated in trucks, turns to speak to a helmeted soldier nearby. The soldier nods, salutes, pedals off on a bicycle. The SS officer leans with the others at the trucks, looking bored. She sees a few French Milice with them, recognizes their black berets and brown shirts. Their holsters stuffed with real guns, now. Everyone on the tram remains still, hands touching papers in pockets, frozen inside baskets and pocketbooks. A mother hushes a fussing little yellow-haired boy with blueberry eyes, gives a sharp reprimand; he looks at Marie-Jeanne, as if pleading for an ally, and she looks away. An engine rumbles up behind them; she glances, trying not to alter a muscle in her face, sees this truck has a machine gun perched in its bed, with soldiers in soup-bowl helmets and multi-beige uniforms, ammunition belts around their necks, yelling cheerily to each other in perfect French. *Alsatians*, the old tobacco man side-mumbles to her, *our own men, they seem to be having a pretty damn good time for conscripts, don't they?* The Alsatians are welcomed with casual accented shouts from the SS. There is a collegial swapping of cigarettes, exhalations of smoke. Heat beats inside the tram; the church spire ahead appears to ripple, waver in the hot white air. Is it ten minutes? Fifteen, twenty? A bark of laughter from the trucks. She wipes sweat from her forehead, the back of her neck with her handkerchief, wishes she could wipe away the sharp odor of everyone's sweat, agitation, the fear creeping from inside blouses and coats. A fly whirs, no, that's a thin tire against concrete, the soldier returning on his bicycle. He pedals up to the SS officer, whispers urgently, retreats, and the officer nods, crushes his cigarette beneath his boot, steps up again to the tram.

"Residents of Oradour-sur-Glane! You will descend the tram! Residents only! Now!"

An even deader stillness—which is right, better, should one be a resident of Oradour, or should one not be?—before the flustered surge, older people clutching for canes or each other's arms as they rise from seats, push through the aisle and climb down the steps, mothers balancing their baskets and children. The little boy with yellow hair is jerked to the pavement by his mother, stumbles after her.

Marie-Jeanne's eyes meet those of a spindly old woman she recognizes from the group of praying ladies in the Oradour church; they look at each other, as if waiting for the other to speak, to affirm or deny. Which is right? The spindly woman crosses herself, firms her hat to her head, slowly gets to her feet and exits; the SS officer extends his hand to support her down the final step. Marie-Jeanne sees a rosary wound tight around the woman's veiny hand. She wants to cross herself, too, *Hail Mary, Holy Mother, please,* but instead clutches the seat frame in front of her. She'll get off the tram, yes, just like normal, follow the line of people trudging up the glaring road, she'll stroll into the village, to Juliette's lavender and lace, Gabrielle's jam-sticky hug, *Yes, it's me, your Marie-Jeanne,* she'll say, and the day will cool to a soft happy evening . . .

Or she'll get off the tram, this is not normal, dash past the glinting machine-gun truck, something is wrong, very wrong, she'll run ahead of them all, run boldly and bravely, find Juliette and Gabrielle and warn them an end is coming, she'll save them, save everybody, the whole village, and they will all escape to safety together, they'll flee, run, hide . . .

Do something.

But they'll stop her, the Germans. *Your papers, please,* they'll ask, *Ihre Papiere, bitte.* Everyone is showing the SS officer their cartes d'identite, and it's right there in her basket, undeniable, *Chantier, Marie-Jeanne; address: La Perrine,* her home, and the *MJ* embroidered on her blouse, and what story can she come up with not to be who she is? She can't lie; she is Marie-Jeanne, there's no escaping that.

"That is only who we want, residents of Oradour. There is no one else?" The SS officer queries those still seated in the tram. "That is all, then?" He is looking at her, a smile flicker-carved on a stony face, studying her, her face is burning, her hand is crawling, she starts to raise her hand, get to her feet, It is all up to you, she thinks, you must take action, she'll stand up to him, insist she be allowed to go into the village, he isn't here to conquer her, tell her what to do, a patriotic Frenchwoman, but she stops. She mustn't stand out or make trouble, *arrest, military tribunal,* she mustn't make a mistake. *Captured, interrogated, tortured. Shot* and *killed.*

She blinks, drops her shaking hand back to her lap.

"Then you will now return to Limoges, the remaining of you," the SS officer announces, descending. "Immediately!"

A mechanical lurch as the tram retreats, clicking, advancing backward, but she keeps her gaze forward, her face still, as the villagers continue away on their way, accompanied by the SS and Milice and trucks and Alsatian soldiers and machine guns, as the church spire grows smaller, blurrier, more wavery against a white sky that's rippling now, and thickening with billows of dark air that float upward, into gray curls, hover and finally thin to soaring black wisps.

The sky is a bowl of ink, pinpricking stars, brief blinks of a high cream moon through heavy branches and she climbs, is climbing, must climb forever beneath their nightshade, up a mountain of coal-gray shadows and dark blue rock and onyx trees, only the sound of her wooden shoes hitting pavement or crunching gravel when she crosses loose roads, or the licking swish of grasses against her legs as she pushes through fields, *I know you're tired, just keep walking,* she remembers hearing, tells herself now.

But there's another voice in her ears, the sound of the weeping mumbling man:

*All of them, in Oradour, they killed them, they're all dead!*

Back in Limoges she'd exited the tram, stood there, stupid, blinking, where to go now, what to do? She'd wandered, lost, and then there was the butcher out in the street, crying and hands gripping his bloody butcher's apron, and he told her of the end of the pretty little village of Oradour-sur-Glane, choked off by SS trucks, encircled by SS guns, the village men marched into garages and barns, all women and children ordered into the church, the babies and old people, everyone locked in, hundreds, and—

*Oh my God, I am heartily sorry for having offended Thee,* she'd thought, crossing herself.

—hundreds of them, the butcher said. A friend of his, he hid in a cabbage patch, heard machine guns and the men screaming, he'd never heard men scream like that, they'd been shot to suffer and bleed and burn to death, as if just killing them wasn't enough,

*And I detest all my sins because of thy just punishments,* she'd thought, but why did God punish them for *her* sins, make them suffer, all those innocent people?

—and there was an explosion in the church, the butcher told her, the women were screaming, my friend saw the roof of the church crack and fall,

*But most of all because they offend Thee, my God,* she'd thought, but she's been so well taken care of, warm clothing, warm bed and family and home, rose-scented soap, *You're lucky, you're one of the luckiest ones,* but why did He choose to save *her*?

—and there were fires and smoke everywhere, the butcher said, my friend waited for people to flee the barns and garages and the church but no one came out, they couldn't escape, just the screams and exploding fires and how can this happen, why?

But she had no answer for the weeping man, just shook her head, patted his shoulder,

*And I firmly resolve, with the help of Thy grace, to sin no more and to avoid the near occasion of sin,* she thought, told God, tells herself, now, stumbling in the dark as she climbs.

All of them killed, gone, dead. So why was she still alive?

Don't think about that, just climb, keep climbing, keep praying . . .

But they had probably prayed too, they would have thought they were safe in the church, the Father and Son and Holy Ghost would watch over them, forgive and save them but it was too late for them, too late for anybody. Because of her sins, her unworthiness. *Mea culpa,* my fault, but it won't wash away, can't sweep this away. They were probably crossing themselves too, lighting candles and kneeling before the Virgin and Saint Bernadette, kneeling in contrition while smoke blackened the marble, streaked the altar, choked the candles, the very moment the iron scrollwork crucifix fell, Jesus searing into their flesh, all of them burning, a little girl with white-blond curls, a young woman in a flower-ruffled dress, their reaching arms and hands and hair wicking upward to flame, their bodies' oil bubbling and fueling the blaze, the babies' fat rendered to soap, all of them melding at last to hot smoky ash and it could have been her, should have been her. Why was it not her?

And somewhere else, too, a pretty young girl in a pink dress and long dark hair, handed over, packed away like trash, sent away like an animal to die, to burn,

*God loves me exactly for who I am, I don't need to pretend anything,*

and a black-eyed delicate-boned, almost-man boy,

*I'm not getting shot, just because of her,*

served up to be beaten and torn apart with hands, rope, knives.

All of them sacrificed, instead of her, because of her. Her mistakes, her fears, cowardice, her sins.

No, not sacrificed. Betrayed.

*That means you're killing them too, then!*

And that last bullet, shower spray of gas, final skull-crushing crash of iron and stone, were probably what all those innocent people were praying *for,* at the end, to end it all, how can that be anyone's last hope, a child's last prayer?

But how could a child pray anything to the God who handed to someone that gun, that bayonet, that match, the God who—Maker of all that is seen and unseen, so that means He made those guns, the bayonets, matches, gas—a God who led them into His very own sacred holy Church, and Himself set it on fire?

No, it can't be. God couldn't have closed His ears to those innocent prayers, those screams.

He must not have heard them. He must not have been there to hear. He was absent, disappeared, abandoning and forsaking them all, and she is falling in the darkness, foot twisted at a root, a piercing stone, a sudden pain in her palms, a knee,

*Help me, Heavenly Father, please . . . !*

but maybe God isn't here with her, either. Maybe He never has been here, or Mary or Jesus, or Jeanne and Bernadette and Jerome, just painted cardboard, dead roses, pressed metal, dead statues of dead people, maybe there is nothing here on earth or there in heaven but this forever blackness, this endless mountain you have to climb alone, that must be climbed . . .

*Hurry up, just keep walking.*

But where? To whom? Who is there left to listen, to understand, to forgive?

"Father?"

She pounds again at the rectory door with her chilled numb fists, her cold-brittle bones will shatter if he doesn't answer, he isn't asleep, she can see candlelight, "Father! Father Tournel! Let me in, please!"

"Who is it, who's there?"

But she hesitates, there is no answer for that, and the door cracks ajar, she blinks at the light, at the sight of Father Tournel in the doorway. No priestly vestments, no soot-black soutane or white linen collar, and no sleepy priest in pajamas or long nightgown and robe, either—"Father Tournel?"—just an ordinary man in a lumpy sweater unraveling at collar and cuffs, a pair of saggy flannel pants, peering.

"Marie-Jeanne? Come in, what are you doing here?"

"I'm sorry, I know how late it is, Father, but please . . ." babbling as he pulls her inside, pushes her into a chair, fumbles for a blanket from his cot, wraps it around her shoulders. A candle flickers violently with his movements. There are papers lying across his table, a sheet half-filled with writing, a pen set to rest, he must have been composing a letter, she can smell the ink still fresh on paper, and the warm human smell of a boiled onion, toasted bread, the old blanket, a worn sweater, unwashed hair, an unshaven face.

"I needed to see you, Father."

He has seized her hands, is rubbing them between his own, they flash from burn to numb and back again, but it's lovely, the feel of his hands, his touch, the pain, and she bites her lip, stays very still with it. But he stops, is looking down at her hands, smeary with thin blood, in his.

"What's happened?" he asks. "Is it your uncle, your aunt? Are you all right?"

"Yes, I'm sorry to disturb you, but I need to tell you something . . ." She reaches for her basket, to find her handkerchief, but it's gone: the basket, her identity card, all left behind somewhere, on the tram, at the butcher shop in Limoges, in the black mountain dark.

"Where have you been?" He motions. "Your feet."

She looks; the wooden sole of one shoe is gone, the other sole flapping loose, the leather split across the arch of the foot. Blood stains one of her socks, seeping up to an ankle.

"I was in Limoges, I missed the last bus—"

"You walked from *Limoges*? All that way, in the dark?" He bends, removes what's left of her shoes, her bloodied socks.

"A man gave me a ride to St. Sylvestre, but he couldn't bring me further, he didn't have enough gasoline, and I had to come to you. I need you, Father. I need your help."

But he is busy, fussing, not listening, rising to pour water from a pitcher into a basin, gathering a towel. He kneels before her, sets the basin at her feet, settles the blanket across her lap, looks up at her, finally, sees her face, and is still.

"Marie-Jeanne, what is it? What's wrong?"

She breathes, deep. "I have to confess, Father. About me, about everything."

"At this hour?"

"Right now. Could you, could we go into the Confessional?"

"Yes, of course." He hesitates. "Or, it's warmer here. Couldn't you just tell me what's worrying you? I'll try to help. If I can."

She nods, "All right," whatever he wants, bows her head.

"Wait, first let me . . ." He gently lowers her raw feet into the basin. The water blushes pink, then sears, then grows dull. He brings a pair of worn but sturdy boots, a roll of heavy socks. "You can wear these home."

*Home,* she thinks, "Thank you," but what is that, where is that?

He pulls a second chair close, looks at her with his red-rimmed eyes. "It's good to see you, Marie-Jeanne," he says. "I've missed you."

"Yes." Time to confess. Repent. And then he will absolve her, make her clean again, tell her what to do, how to make everything right again. "I'm sorry, Father. I know I haven't been very . . . I need to explain . . ." But it's too late, she thinks, helpless. She turns her face away from him, studies her hands.

"It's all right, Marie-Jeanne. You needn't try to explain any of that," he says, as if he's hearing inside her head. Didn't she used to think he could do that, all those years ago, see and hear inside her? She longs for him to do that now, just see inside her heart and soul so she won't have to tell him the truth. Maybe that's the real reason for Confession, she thinks. Not for God, or priest, or anyone, to bless or forgive you, wash away your sins. Maybe they don't ever wash away or disappear. But having to put yourself into words means you have to hear yourself. Look at yourself. Make yourself and who you are real. There is no *explain.* There is only what is true.

"But I have to," she insists. "Please. I have to tell you about what I've done. Or haven't done. I have to tell you the truth. About all of it. I have to try, at least."

"Of course, yes." He lowers his head to her in profile, eyes on his clasped hands, waits. "Bless me Father, for I have sinned," raising her hand to make the sign of the cross, then stops, her hand paused at *In the name of...* She tightens her fingers over her face and she can sense him nod, waiting.

"It's been, oh, I don't know how long it's been since my last Confession." She lowers her hand. "I mean, my last Confession to you, Father. I've been confessing on my own, talking to God and examining my conscience, all the time. I've tried, really. But I don't know anymore..."

"What don't you know?"

"I don't know if God has been listening."

"Why would you feel that way, Marie-Jeanne? That God isn't listening to you?"

"Maybe because I wasn't *really* confessing, before. I don't mean God wasn't listening. It was me, my fault. I wasn't confessing anything real. Anything true."

"That's difficult to do sometimes, acknowledge the truth. Even to God." She can see a half-smile on his profiled face. "Let alone to yourself. Or a fellow human being. A priest, a friend—"

"But why should it be so hard? If God already knows and understands everything?" He doesn't answer, and she rushes on. "Maybe He's angry with me. Maybe I've been asking for too much. And that isn't what God is for, is it, to ask for things all the time?"

"That depends. What have you been asking Him for?"

"Not *thing* things, like dresses or shoes. Just for Him to . . . if He'll . . . understand. If He'll forgive me."

"Forgive you?"

"He will, won't He, Father? Even if I don't deserve it? He'll let me start over, even if I've done *horrible* things, ugly sinful things. But I was just so scared. And I thought I was doing right. Or I told myself so, I wanted to believe that, so I would be safe, everyone would be safe, and He'll understand and forgive me if I see now how wrong I was, how guilty I am. How selfish I've been. Won't He forgive? No matter what I've done? Or *haven't* done, I don't know which is worse. Or who I've hurt? Or . . . who I've become?"

He raises his head, and she expects his serious face, pondering, the way a father might consider a child's silly question and in doing so be reassuring and kind. And he'll take and warm her hands in his own once more, let her feel them, or the ash-stroke of his finger on her forehead, the blessing of his palms against her hair, all atonement and repentance and no more pain. But he is gazing past her, at nothing.

"Father? Please, is it true? God will forgive anyone, anything?"

His eyes, so empty.

"That's what they say," he replies.

"Unless," she swallows, "unless maybe He isn't really listening? Because," wishing he would stop her, "because maybe He isn't really there?"

His face, so resigned.

"Father? Is that what you . . ."

He shakes his head, his eyes and face back with her. "Oh, Marie-Jeanne. I'm the one who's sorry."

"But it's *my* fault, all of it—"

"No, no it isn't—"

"It *is!* And I don't know what to do, how to change anything, start all over, tell me how."

"None of this is your fault. I swear to you. It's mine. I've failed you."

"I don't understand."

He reaches, touches her face, a reassuring caress, and she closes her eyes, *thank you, Father.*

But then his touch is gone. "It's been how many years, now? Since you came to La Perrine?"

She opens her eyes; he has stood up, is pacing.

"I don't know," she says. "It seems like always." My home.

"It was like a gift, when you arrived. To me, I mean. I'd been here so long, like always, yes," a brief smile at her, "and I wanted everyone to feel they weren't alone. God was with us, but we all had each other, too. And I was here, to help. As a friend. That I could be a friend, not just a priest. But people are busy with their farms, their families and homes . . . But that first day you came, you were sitting there, trying to smile, I remember. You were wearing a white coat. And I watched you. I could see you were struggling, inside. There was something about you . . ."

"I was trying so hard," she murmurs. "To look . . . real."

"I could see that. How lost you were. Everyone was listening along as always, but your face was different. As if the words were hurting you. Frightening you, somehow. And I wanted to ease that pain, offer you not just God's comfort, but a human comfort, too. During Mass you'd look at me, your eyes were pleading, like you needed someone to listen, truly hear you. I don't mean at Confession, beyond that. And you'd come see me, you'd ask questions and share with me your thoughts and feelings, and we'd just talk. After a while you seemed less lonely. More peaceful. More yourself, maybe. And *I* felt less alone. Thinking I could help. That I was doing good, for someone. Something real."

"You did," she tells him. "You do."

"No. The truth is, I was thinking of myself the whole time, Marie-Jeanne, not you. This child had been sent to me, this desperate soul in need of help, and I was being so selfish, I—"

"Oh no! It's like you said, Father. You're still a human being, too. Not just a priest."

"But still a priest. Maybe . . ." His eyes wander to the table, the pen, the paper with the many lines of writing. "But then, time went on, you looked at me differently. You drew away. I missed you. I missed that feeling. You didn't need me the same way, and I told myself well, she isn't a little girl anymore, she's growing up, of course she doesn't need you so much."

"I just didn't," she lowers her eyes, "I didn't trust you anymore."

"I know. Because you'd come to see I *couldn't* help. That I had nothing to offer you. Or anyone."

"But you do! You're always there for us, and your sermons are so helpful and—"

"My sermons. Of course. We should all love one another."

"Yes. Like that. You're God's presence among us, Father. Reminding us."

"How we must all follow the path toward His grace. We must all sacrifice. We're all His children, we must accept His will."

"Yes . . ."

He shakes his head. "You were right not to trust me. All that preaching. The little stories, the rituals to keep us all so busy. I've stood there for years reciting those words, talking about God's mission for us, how we all have a role to play—"

"You don't believe in . . . ?"

"Oh, of course I do! I believe the *heart* of it. The possibility inside each of us for redemption, what Christ wanted us to understand and embrace. That hope for goodness in the world, and within ourselves.

The feeling of love. That's very real to me. That is why we're here."

"And that's who you are, Father, to all of us. To me."

"What have I been doing besides *announcing* all of that, offering homily? Nothing. Because surely the *Church* will take action, that's not my job. The Holy Father himself will lead the way," glancing at the portrait on the wall, "but what has *he* been doing? I've been reading his lectures," waving at the table, "and on the radio, all his fine words about our salvation through faith, about poor suffering people everywhere and the flood of tears we must shed, we must beg the Holy Ghost to come liberate the world from violence and terror. Speeches that seem like they're truth, but he's said *nothing*, really. It's all pretty words, how the Star of Peace will shine out again someday. As long as we're faithful, just wait, if we believe and pray hard enough. But where are the ugly words? The true ones? Nazi, or Hitler? Gas chamber? Extermination? Is he so terrified of political retribution? Bombs falling on Rome, on the Vatican?" A harsh laugh. "Is he so frightened of making things *worse* with those words? Worse for *whom*? And I've been sitting and waiting, I told myself I'm being obedient and keeping the faith, and that's my role, but that's all been an excuse, too, to just sit here and be crippled by fear. And *talk*. Say pretty words. And do nothing. All I've been is afraid. I'm the one who's been sinful."

"But what else could you have done, Father? You're just one person, and, and it *is* frightening, you've said that. We all do things out of fear sometimes, don't we? Or we do nothing, and, and then people get hurt, or maybe we even do terrible things by mistake, even if we're trying our best, but you—"

"Marie-Jeanne, other people are frightened too! We're *all* frightened. And they've fought anyway, they've been tortured and destroyed, helping people for real, and now, in *this* life, not for some *theory* about souls or faith. Not some dangling promise of Heaven or fantasy peace coming some day. While I printed a few pamphlets?

Hid a box of meat, a bag of salt? How do I make up for any of that? For my selfishness, my cowardice? How do I start over? How do I even begin to repent?"

"I don't know," she says. "I don't know how anyone can."

"I've wasted hours on my knees, lighting candles, moralizing," he waves at the crucifix on the wall, "being a symbol of God's presence. A *symbol.* A lie." His hand drops.

*A lie of a girl . . .*

"Oh, Father . . ."

"Please, don't!" He turns his back to her.

"Everybody here needs you. Everyone loves you. So much."

"They love an idea of me. They love believing who they think I am, the role I play for them," he says. "That I can offer hope or forgiveness. But I can't. I don't deserve that love. I'm not that person. I'm not any real person, am I? I'm not anything, anymore."

She reaches out, touches his sleeve. He leans away, and she closes her hand around the hem of his sweater. He pulls away, but she holds fast, and he suddenly turns, is on his knees again before her, is gripping at her chair.

"Marie-Jeanne, please forgive me!"

She places her palm against his cheek, sees the candle flame flickering in his wide wet eyes. He drops his head to her knees, and she feels the dampness of tears through her skirt.

"It's all right," she says. "You can start over. You will. You have to. Even if you don't know how." She strokes his back. "Really. God understands."

"And if He doesn't?" His voice, choking. "And what if He isn't listening? Or if He isn't really there?"

His arms tighten around her, holding on.

"Maybe that doesn't even matter so much," she says, slowly, and she leans, puts her arms around his thin shoulders, hoping he'll absorb her warmth. "Either way, you're still going to be a good man."

She feels the protest trembling in his bones, holds him closer.

"You are. All that goodness, and hope and love are still inside you, Father. Whatever, or whoever you're going to be now. That's the faith you have to keep. It's the heart of everything, in all of us, like you said. Maybe that part of us just gets . . . lost sometimes. Or hidden away."

She rests her cheek against his hair, feels his trembling soften then fade, his breathing grow steadier, calm.

"And then somehow we have to find it again," she tells him. "We have to try. Maybe that's where all of us have to begin."

The woman is almost invisible in the shadows, a slight blanketed figure half burrowed like a baby animal into the straw. The girl peers, makes out the weave of a sweater sleeve, a pale, sleep-loose hand, a lock of hair escaped from the scarf, gray in the dimness but slowly, slowly, warming to red, as she stands there, looking, looking, and then there is a stirring, a murmur . . .

"Marie-Jeanne? Is that you?"

The girl steps forward, then stops.

The woman lifts herself up on one arm, rubs at her face, her eyes. "It's very early, isn't it? It's still dark."

The girl nods.

The woman searches her face in the gloom. "Are you all right?"

No answer for that, either, but the woman doesn't seem to need one, the way she is looking at her, studying her face, the way she reaches out a hand, slowly, then stops herself.

"Are you . . ." The woman clears her throat. "Are you ready to go, then? Maybe . . . ?"

The girl hesitates, then nods again, yes.

"Well," the woman says, "why don't we wait until—"

"No!" the girl says. "Please, we can't wait."

"But when there's more light we can—"

"We have to go now," she insists to the woman's confused face. "We just have to begin," she tells her. "Please?"

"All right," the woman says carefully. "Why don't you just get some of your things, first? And maybe some food?"

The girl nods, turns to go, then stops. Perhaps when she returns there will be nothing but the blanket, abandoned. A shallow absence in the straw. A few strands of red hair. The memory-sound of her voice.

*I will come back for you,* she hears. Yes, she thinks. Yes.

"But I'll be back," the girl tells her. "Don't worry, I'm coming right back. I promise."

"I know," the woman says. "And I'll be here. I promise."

"And then we'll start?"

The woman smiles. "Yes, chérie. Then we'll start."

The girl walks to the door.

"Oh, and maybe the jewelry?"

She looks back. "What?"

"The jewelry." The woman brushes straw and blanket away, tucks at her scarf. "My jewelry. I gave it to Berthe, so she could sell it, or trade. If things got too bad."

"Oh," the girl says. "I didn't know."

"It could help. If there's any left."

She nods a last time, steps to the barn door, but looks back again. She can see the woman's body taking shape in the creeping light against the whitewashed wall of the barn, the bed of straw. She could trace the woman's shoulders with a finger if she wanted to, the line of her jaw against her throat. She could burrow into the bed of thick straw with her, next to her, curl in her arms, feel her chest rise and fall with her steadying breath. She almost reaches out to draw her, touch her, breathe and hide with her there forever, but stops. If she touches, then the woman is real. And that means she can disappear again, vanish, leave.

Better to trust the woman will still be there. Better to just believe a little, for now, keep that tiny new seed of faith alive.

The house is still dim, but she is familiar with the dimness, knows her way around by the subtle shifts of air and smell and the wood-creaks under her feet, even in the unfamiliar, thick-soled boots. She climbs the stairs carefully, pauses at the slightly open bedroom door on the first landing. She can hear a man's slumbering grunt, a woman's sleepy throat cluck. She pauses. You must, she thinks, you must tell them thank you. For their sacrifices. For everything. You must say goodbye. So many things to say, things, yes, get your things together, first. Let them sleep. She continues to climb.

The moon is passing across the attic window and in the faint milk of its light she sees, on a shelf, a white leather book that glows blue, a small booklet holding a family's blood. On the wall above the bed is a small wooden cross, a dying man. A picture of a girl soldier, kneeling. She tugs at the string around her neck until it breaks, rests the silver medal upon the shelf, next to a necklace of little brown beads. There is a linen dress of pink and violet flowers hanging on a nail, and one of heavy yellow wool, a white dress serrated with lace. A patched white coat, aged to a lifeless gray. She is wearing a thin summer skirt, a blouse with *MJ* over the heart, and she moves quickly, takes off that skirt, that blouse, hangs them with the other clothes. She fumbles to find an old, shapeless gray dress, worn to threads, and pulls the dress on over her head. That's all, then. There is nothing else here that belongs to her. There is nothing here that is hers.

In the kitchen's slipping shadows she kneels before the small oak trunk, opens it slowly, quietly, remembering how the hinge whines at half-way. She lifts out a little boy's knee pants and sweater, folded with care. An old man's old medals. A bible heavy with old dust, and a cracking book of saints, a children's catechism. Beneath that, wrapped in sepia tissue, a pair of long golden red little girl's braids, their ends tied with worn yellow ribbons. And beneath everything, something hard, a bundle of cloth, swollen and lumped, familiar. She lifts it out, remembering. But now on this cloth is a painstaking embroidery, she must squint to see in the dimness, see the green floss letters, a word, a name—

*Danielle,* it reads.

She unwraps the cloth and a starscape of greens and blues and reds spills into her lap, onto the floor, silver and gold, brilliant, tinkling jewels. Bracelets, necklaces, combs. A small treasure. For *Danielle,* it has all been kept hidden for her, saved for her. It all belongs to a girl who once had that name. Who once was.

She feels the choke in her chest, her throat, and she hurries, on her knees, reaching, grasping, she gathers up the scattered jewels, wraps the cloth tight around them, pushes the bundle back deep in the trunk, replaces everything exactly as it was, before. Where it belongs. She clutches at the trunk's open lid to steady herself, sees, on the table, a left-behind note—*I love you, always, your Marie-Jeanne*—scrawled in a young girl's hand. Another girl who is gone.

She did tell them, she thinks. That girl did tell them goodbye. Told them she loves them, always. At least they know that. And they will know she went to Oradour-sur-Glane, that girl, they will know what happened there, the fire, the smoke, all the death, they will know that girl is disappeared and vanished forever, too.

The choke rises inside her again, a gasp, and she covers her face with her hands. Cry, she can do that at least, it's safe now. She'll cry like a child, a little girl, sob all those hopeless baby tears. She takes a deep breath, tries to breathe the sob all the way through her body and out into a cry, aloud, she'll cry so loud her lungs will crack and she will smash into a hundred pieces, spill all over the floor. She leans over, wraps her arms around herself tight, waiting to break, for the spill, the tears, for then maybe someone will hear her, someone will come gather up all those broken apart pieces and sort them through, find that one most hidden and real piece of her once more.

She waits, eyes shut, listening, hearing only the quiet gray air with her in the room. There's no cry building, no baby howl rising inside her. Because who is left, anymore, to cry? To think or feel or move, to stand up, to do anything?

Who is even here, in this room, right now?

No one, she realizes. I am not any real person, anymore. That's what has ended, now, is over.

She will sit here, then, alone in the dark forever, eyes closed. Escape back into an endless night, a nowhere dream where a nobody girl can be lost and hidden away for good. It doesn't matter what frightening thing awaits her there. There is nowhere else to go.

She feels a warmth pass across her face, a delicate shift in the air. She raises her head, opens her eyes, blinks. No, no one is there. But, still. She turns.

Berthe is standing at the foot of the stairs, in her nightgown, eyes swollen and weary with grief. She is looking at the girl's stricken face, the body curled tight into itself, at the gray dress. At the open trunk, at the note on the table. Berthe's eyes cross to the window and look out, and the girl looks, too, sees the other woman standing there at the barn, half hidden in the shadows of the open door. Berthe turns her gaze back to the girl, and she sees the tears shine in Berthe's eyes, then a faint smile, the slight nod. Berthe steps closer, and the girl closes her eyes again. She feels a touch on her cheek. She feels a steadying, assuring hand on her shoulder, its warmth, its soft pressure, then its release. She hears the long quiet moment, then hears the heavy footsteps slowly climb the stairs. She feels tears come to her eyes, now, the hot real dampness of them on her face.

When she opens her eyes a fresh brightness is glinting off the hanging copper pots, the halo of the blue-robed woman on the wall, reflecting gold off the mirror above the sink. She can see the ghostly seams of her old dress, the fine grain of the sturdy leather boots on her feet. The windows are new paintings of a lemon-white dawn, and she wonders when that happened, the exact moment when the night's long darkness shifted back once more to illuminated sky. But maybe it doesn't matter exactly when it changed, she thinks, only that it did. It always will. Like sleepy garden roots, or a secret treasured thing, hidden away for you to find again. She can see the outline of awaiting sun around the heavy wooden door, the sudden keyhole peep of light.

She wipes her face dry with her hands, gets to her feet. She walks quietly, opens the door, looks out. The last of the midnight ink is slipping far behind the mountains, the sky shifting a brighter and brighter blue, to where it becomes silver, over there, becomes a crystal day. The path to the woods, the road to the village are empty. But the woman is there, still there, standing at the barn door, watching for her, waiting.

The girl steps through the door, and closes it behind her, gently.

## ACKNOWLEDGMENTS

I'd like to thank the National Endowment for the Arts, the City of Los Angeles Department of Cultural Affairs, the Corporation of Yaddo, *Women's Studies Quarterly*, and Hawthornden Castle Writers Retreat in Scotland for their generous and much-appreciated support.

My heartfelt and humble thanks to the friends, family, and colleagues who not just supported but actively encouraged my obsession with this project for so many years, who read draft after draft and gave me insightful notes, offered counsel and advice, traveled with me throughout France, brought me back to reality, let me dream.

Deep gratitude to my agent, Jessica Felleman, for her warm wisdom, and her steadfast, unflappable commitment to this book.

And to Robert Lasner and Elizabeth Clementson at Ig Publishing—you are every writer's dream. Thank you for your vision and tender care for this challenging child of mine; I cannot imagine a better home for her.